AFRICAN SURVIVOR

Dear Veronica

It's so good to find another South African friend and I trust the Lord blesses you as you read these lines.

With love

Denyse

7/6/2022

AFRICAN SURVIVOR

Love, *Apartheid*, Flight

Denyse Wild

Published by Halse Publishing

A catalogue record for this book is available from the British Library

ISBN 978-0-9576184-1-1

Photographs from family albums

Cover design by Robert Cobey.

Acknowledgement and thanks to P John, the owner of the photograph on pages 68-69 of 'Touring in South Africa' by Maxwell Leigh and published by Struik, South Africa in 1986.

Printed and Bound in Great Britain by
CPI Group (UK) Croydon CR0 4YY

For my children,
Chandrè, Anton, Brent, Alyson Byron and Liesel
and grandchildren,
Jaime, Adrienne, Jordyn, Peter and Matthew.

I never intended to offend anyone when I recorded events as I perceived them at the time.

Denyse Wild

ACKNOWLEDGMENTS

My children prompted me to write my extraordinary life-story to keep alive the country of my birth South Africa, and the way of life I experienced when I lived there. The eyes of the world have followed the country's transition from Union of SA to Republic of SA to its present-day government of National Unity, remembering on the way the struggles against *apartheid*. Writing my story has been cathartic. It has made me realise how relationships, both good and bad, have impacted on my life.

I would like to thank each and everyone who has touched my life, both family and friends. My thanks go to those whose names are not mentioned in my book, but who played just as an important a role in my life. I am deeply indebted to Rose Blakeway who was instrumental in changing my life forever and to the many people who picked me up when I fell down.

I thank Brendan McCusker, my tutor at the autobiography class, for encouraging and guiding me week by week for two years. *'Baie dankie'*, thanks, to my friends in this class – Adele, Tony, Jo, Christine, Flo, Renee, Lorna, Lynn, Isobel, Caryl and Chris – for their positive criticism and friendship.

I extend my sincere gratitude to Barbara Large, Director of the Winchester Writers' Conference, for her inspiration and sound advice.

"How's your book getting on Denyse?" was my weekly encouragement from Alan Pearce, a short mat bowling friend who never ceased to spur me on. I thank my friends at Ashley Baptist Church, the Hordle Short Mat Bowling Club and the Lymington Bowling Club for believing in me and giving me confidence to reach my goal.

My heartfelt thankfulness is owed to my two honest friends, Janet Skirton and Jill Havelock-Stevens, who painstakingly and diligently proof-read my manuscript.

Thank you Robert Cobey, for designing the cover of my book, which took patience and perseverance. I thank Geoff Fisher and the staff of CPI for their guidance in the publication.

For the loyal support and wisdom of George, my husband, on whom I depended, I thank you from the bottom of my heart.

With a good part of my life spent, I have so little time left to emulate the words which Albert Einstein wrote: *"Only a life lived for others is a life worthwhile."*

CONTENTS

Part Three
IN HIS LOVE

Part One

1945 - 1966

BY HIS GRACE

2 Thessalonians 2:16
May the Lord Jesus Christ himself and God the Father who loved us and by his grace gave us eternal encouragement and good hope, encourage your hearts and strengthen you in every good deed and word.

My wedding day 20 November 1965

Back row left to right: Granny, Mom and Mrs Smith
Middle row left to right: David Pohl, Hugh Johnson, Donald Smith, Denyse, Topsy, Margy
Front row left to right: Donnaleen Johnstone, Ann Johnstone, Patrick Leary

Above: Eileen and Donald Brown, my grandparents.

Right: Eric and Peggy Lloyd, my parents.

Left: I watch Pop piggy-back Patrick

Left: Denyse with her cousins Neville, Jeanette and Vivian

Right: With my siblings, Topsy and Margy at 'Kildare'

1

NEYSE AND DAFOO

In 1950 the Population Registration Act classified all citizens by race and the Group Areas Act was passed to segregate Blacks and Whites.

WORLD War II ended, President Roosevelt died, Adolf Hitler and Eva Braun committed suicide, Winston Churchill was rejected at the polls and South Africa became a charter member of the United Nations, but refused to sign the Universal Declaration of Human Rights – all these major world events took place in 1945.

This was the year I was born on 20 March in Kokstad, then part of East Griqualand in South Africa. I was named Denyse Estelle and lived with my parents, Eric and Peggy Lloyd in Durban, situated about 201 kilometres from Kokstad.

My tall handsome, father, who had served in the SA Irish regiment in North Africa between 1940 and 1943, now worked as a store manager on the docks. My musical mother was a book-keeper in Kokstad, before she married. My parents were poor and rented a small flat, 1 City Court. We spent weekends on the white sandy Addington Beach. This became my childhood playground where I met Nigel, my very first friend. Without a care in the world, we splashed in the shallow waves and built castles in the sand together.

As a chubby toddler with blonde hair combed into a quiff on top of my head, my mother told me how she wheeled me in a pushchair when she went shopping. I wore a smocked dress which my mother had sewn by hand, white crochet socks with black patent leather shoes. My engaging smile attracted passers-by, who smiled, bent over me and asked, "What's your name?"

"Neyse," I smiled, staring back at them. (From an early age, my grandfather called me *Neyse*, which has become my life-long nickname.)

"Where do you live, Neyse?"

I feigned coyness momentarily before answering, "One *Titty Tourt.*"

My answer, for reasons unknown to me then, caused the strangers to shriek with laughter. My mother's apology ensued, "I'm sorry, but my little girl can't pronounce *City* and *Court* correctly." I laughed. They left. Looking around, I used my beguiling smile to attract my next victim. Somehow I never grew tired of this amusing game.

On 11 April 1947 my mother gave birth to a second baby, Jennifer Ann, nicknamed *Topsy* and called by that name today. When we moved from Durban to Mount Ayliff, Topsy was two and I was four. This small village, renowned for trout fishing, agriculture and forestry and situated 1000 metres above sea level, once had a productive sawmill. Today Mount Ayliff is in the *Alfred Nzo District.*

I remember playing with Topsy in an overgrown garden. On hot days we cooled down in either a little zinc bath, half-filled with water, or splashed each other with a trickle of water from the hosepipe we dragged around. We had few toys. We played happily outdoors supervised by our black nanny, Violet. Amongst other chores, she cleaned the house, hung the washing on the line, prepared the meals and kept an eye on us. From 8 am until 5 pm, my parents worked in a general dealer store which my grandfather had bought. They came home for lunch at 1 pm.

Margaret Carol, my youngest sister called Margy, was born on 12 February 1949 in Kokstad. She was too small to play with Topsy and me, but I do remember how proud I was when my mother permitted me, with difficulty, to put Margy on my lap. Margy was my real live doll. From an early age, I played 'mother' to my younger sisters.

One day I innocently annoyed my father. He returned to the house mid-morning, to settle his hangover. Little did I realise what I was letting myself in for as I ran up and down the passage making a rumpus on the wooden floors. Despite several warnings from my dad, I continued to clatter around in the house...

"Play outside, Neyse," my father said. I did not listen. Very soon my run down the passage ended abruptly. Grabbing my arm, my father marched me off to the outside toilet.

"You stay here until you learn to listen to me."

The door slammed shut. My father locked me in the toilet. I heard his footsteps fade as he walked away to the house. Here I was in this small, smelly place, with a shaft of light filtering under the door. I was imprisoned for several hours...

Meanwhile Violet put Margy in her pram, held Topsy's hand as she toddled along beside her. She took my sisters for a walk in the dusty village.

I screamed, "Help, help! Open the door, *please*!" but nobody heard me. I shouted and banged my hands on the door. The noise would save me. Surely my nanny would hear. She would let me out. In between my sobs, I listened. Nobody came. I yelled louder and banged harder...

Hours later, hearing my screams, my mother opened the toilet door. She found me, red-eyed and hoarse from shouting. Her brown eyes revealed her deep concern.

"What happened Neyse?" she asked, drawing me into her arms trying to mend my broken heart and fretful spirit. Her kisses comforted me, "There, there, Neyse."

I tried to speak. The words would not come. Much later I told my mother the story. Claiming that this incident had caused a squint in both eyes, my mother said, "Your eyes were perfectly normal until then."

My father continued to drink excessively making it extremely difficult for my mother to cope. I was unaware of their marital problems. Life dished up more 'downs' than 'ups' for my mother. She since told me:

"In November 1949, I could take no more. I telephoned my dad to fetch us. The few clothes we had, I packed into one suitcase. My dad drove to Mount Ayliff in his *Dodge*. We moved into their home, 107 Hawthorn Street, Kokstad."

The house was already crowded because my mother's sister, Joan, her husband, Slabs and their four children, Vivian, eight, Jeanette, six, Neville, four and Diana, eight months old, lived there with my grandparents.

At the age of four, a life of love and security, devoid of parental fights and arguments, began for me when three generations, comprising twelve family members, lived together under one roof... Vivian, Jeanette and Neville became my playmates. Diana was still a baby.

When Uncle Keith and Aunty Ruth, whom we called Aunty Buzzy, visited Kokstad, I got to know my cousins, Myrna aged three and one-year old Norman. My uncle and aunt lived and ran *K N Rock General Dealer,* their own store in Flagstaff. We were a close-knit family.

At 107 Hawthorn Street each day started with, "Goodbye mommy."

"Be a good girl. Look after your sisters."

I waved until I could no longer see my mother as she drove off to work at *D M Brown General Dealer Store* coming home at our bedtime. Granny, Aunty Joan and Evilina, our new black maid, cared for us.

This house and garden were different from what we had left behind in Mount Ayliff. On opposite sides of the front of the property, two pairs of cast iron gates hung from tall concrete pillars and were separated by a fence with climbing roses. Bordering a semi-circular lawn, a driveway led up to the verandah steps. *Broekie lace* spanned the verandah. The huge front door boasting a decorative brass knocker and letter-box was flanked by two bay windows. Flower beds spilled off the verandah.

Inside the gleaming polished wooden floors of the hall, a door opened into a long passage leading to three bedrooms and a second door opened into the lounge, with a fireplace and a mirrored mantelpiece. Glass doors opened into a study on the far wall. Filling this room were a radiogram, a two-seater sofa, a rocking chair, an armchair, a glass cabinet safe-guarded the family heirlooms, a piano and a bulging bookshelf. The drawn heavy curtains made the room dark even on sunny days.

"Children should be seen and not heard," granny reminded her grandchildren. The dining room – with an oak table and eight chairs, sideboard, refrigerator and two palm stands with lush ferns falling over the edges – was used on high days and holidays only.

"Shush!" I warned my sisters hearing the hum of the *Singer* treadle machine coming from the bedroom-cum-sewing room. We tiptoed not wanting to disturb granny, who made skirts and aprons to sell in the store.

The small bathroom with an enamel bath and hand basin seldom had hot water. The outside toilet, with a dangling chain which had to be pulled to flush, had newspaper squares hanging on a hook and sometimes *Jeyes* squares in a box.

An *Esse* stove, fuelled by anthracite, stood in the kitchen. Children sat on a bench against the wall. On the opposite side of the table adults sat on odd chairs.

"Close your eyes," my grandmother said, checking to see if each grandchild had obeyed before she said grace. "Bless us O Lord and these Thy gifts…" We all said, "Amen," before tucking into our food finishing everything on our plates.

Outside a tall hedge bordered the driveway leading to the garage where dahlias grew alongside the wall. Aunty Joan picked and arranged flowers which stood in a vase on the hall table. I loved these sweet-scented arrangements.

In the back garden, a straight pathway cut through the lawn to the orchard. Every year the pomegranate, red and yellow plum, peach, apple, quince and pear trees were laden with fruit. Sometimes hailstones battered and bruised the fruit. The *fowl run*, chicken coop, behind the garage, was home to many egg-laying hens and several haughty cockerels. *Mielies* grew at the very back. There were trees to climb and lawns to do cartwheels and headstands on. Anthracite and coal were stored in bags in a dark cellar, directly under the pantry. Outside the cellar door, hydrangeas bloomed.

107 Hawthorn Street, with my cousins as playmates and my grandpa to protect me, was my new-found paradise. I laughed, ran free and forgot everything that had *once* made me feel sad. With this security, I knew when grandpa returned from work.

"Vivian! Jeanette! I hear grandpa's car," I shouted to my cousins. He stopped at the driveway gate. We ran towards the *Dodge* for our ride. Grandpa opened the boot. We jumped in, legs dangling over the edge. He drove slowly down the driveway and into the garage as we shrieked with joy.

"Out you get children!" grandpa called, banging the car door closed. We bounced off, waiting excitedly for the next treat. Grandpa slammed the boot shut.

"Who wants to be first?" he challenged.

"Me! Me! Me!" we answered together, jumping up and down. Picking us up one by one, grandpa threw us into the air and caught us again. Our excitement intensified.

"Higher, *dafoo*," I begged. Sometimes he tossed me into the air and I landed on top of the hedge. I looked down at grandpa. His kind eyes looked up at me. He smiled.

"Jump, Neyse." He stretched out his arms to catch me. Fearlessly, I flung myself forwards into the air. I fell downwards and was scooped into my grandfather's arms. Grandpa loved his grandchildren. He *always* had time to make us laugh even after a busy day.

Evilina, our maid, who lived in a small room alongside the garage, stood no nonsense from us. Using our hands, she allowed us to taste her lunch, *'umngqusho,'* comprising boiled *samp,* dried and crushed maize kernels, and beans or *'imfino,'* a *Xhosa,* black tribal dish of *mealie,* maize, meal and vegetables.

She looked ever so smart on Thursday afternoons when she donned a black skirt, white blouse, red jacket and red beret, the uniform of the church she attended. I can still see her. Her head held high. Her black legs shining from the *Vaseline* she rubbed on them. Her white teeth gleamed beneath her smile as she marched off to join her friends.

Too young to understand the meaning of Lent, but keen to emulate the adults, I gave up sweets. I remember Easter Sunday when I was given an Easter egg. A photo taken of Vivian, Jeanette, Neville and me sitting on the front steps, holding our Easter eggs, showed how happy we were to have *one* chocolate egg each.

My sisters and I loved our new life. My father and Mount Ayliff faded into oblivion. I suppose, for my part, my grandfather was the father figure I needed. My grandfather gave me the love of a father I longed for. He enabled me to laugh again and to be a child once more. He took away the premature responsibility I had previously borne, of looking after my two little sisters when our nanny was busy. I loved grandpa so much. He was kind, never raised his voice, laughed and played with me. He listened. He was strong and never shouted at me. Grandpa was my hero, but would this last?

***

My mother and sisters slept in the inner bedroom with my cousin, Jeanette. My bed, covered with a multi-coloured crochet blanket granny had made, stood in the corner of my grandparents' room. They slept in a large brass double bed. Granny's dressing table and stool stood to the left of the bay window. Brocade curtains were drawn at night making the room very dark. Every morning granny opened them allowing the sunlight to stream in and light up the room.

My grandfather slept on the side of the bed nearest to my bed. I affectionately called him '*dafoo*. My mother told me: "You heard Uncle Slabs frequently saying, 'Dam fool' when he spoke to grandpa. You insisted 'dam fool' pronounced *dafoo*, was his name."

To me, grandpa was my *dafoo*. My grandmother, the first to rise, went off to Mass daily at 6.30 am no matter what the weather. When granny combed her hair and put on her hairnet, my *dafoo* would wake me. Sitting on my bed, he told me a story. The stories were never long, but captivated me. I looked into his brown eyes and watched his mouth as he spoke. Grandpa was the best storyteller in the whole world.

One morning as usual, granny was combing her hair when grandpa climbed out of bed. Kissing me on the forehead he called, "Neyse." I woke and sat up in bed, anticipating my story. However, grandpa did not sit down... He just stood looking at me...

"*Dafoo*, story time please!" I pleaded. When grandpa looked down at me with his kind eyes and said, "Not today, Neyse," I could not understand and begged him, "Please *dafoo*, please." The words were hardly spoken, when I saw, with horror, my grandfather falling and sliding under my bed.

"Granny, granny, come!" I yelled. She was at his side in seconds. I sensed there was something wrong, but I could not understand what was happening. Granny was bending over *dafoo*. Granny was crying. Grandpa was not moving. Granny screamed, "Joan, Slabs, Peggy, help! Come quickly!" I started to cry.

Why had grandpa fallen under my bed?

Uncle Slabs and Aunty Joan rushed into the bedroom. Aunty Joan picked me up and took me to my mother. I then heard Uncle Slabs talking on the telephone in the hallway. I wanted my *dafoo*. My mother said, "Look after your sisters, Denyse." She, too, disappeared into my grandparent's bedroom. I listened and overheard the adult voices saying, "The doctor's on his way." This sounded bad. Something was wrong. Grandpa must be very sick.

The whole household was awake. Uncle Slabs took charge of the children. Warning us to be quiet and to behave, he said, "Grandpa's ill." (I am sure he meant *dafoo*.) Margy, my baby sister started crying so I put her on my lap and rocked her. It seemed such a long time waiting, listening and growing more afraid. *Hurry doctor; please come quickly to make my dafoo better again.*

I heard a car then footsteps down the passage. Aunty Joan said, "This way doctor. My father's in here." The bedroom door closed. Silence followed. The bedroom door opened again. I heard the footsteps go down the passage. My mother's voice sounded strange when she said, "Thank you doctor. Goodbye."

The front door closed. We listened. We heard sobs and whispering. Our bedroom door opened. My cousin, Vivian entered, looking frightened. We followed Vivian down the passage to the exterior door. He thought we should be outside. Margy was heavy to carry. Topsy tugged at my pyjamas as I struggled along.

Outside I heard a vehicle approaching the house. I looked down the driveway. A strange-looking vehicle drove through the gates. "Viv, what's that?" I asked.

"It's an ambulance. Takes sick people to the hospital."

Oh please don't let them take my *dafoo* away. I will go with you *dafoo*! I was so confused.

Uncle Slabs took us to the kitchen, the furthest room from the side entrance of the house. We waited, still in our pyjamas, sleepy-eyed and upset. With tears streaming down their faces, my mother and aunt came in. Between sobs, they told us the ambulance had taken grandpa away.

"The doctor couldn't help," my mother explained between sobs, "Grandpa's dead," to which Aunty Joan added, "Grandpa's in heaven with the angels." I hugged my mom and we cried together. The realisation of what had happened slowly sank in. I would never see my *dafoo* again. He would never tell me another story. I would never call him *dafoo* ever again. Tears welled up in my eyes. I sobbed and sobbed and sobbed.

My grandfather was 54 years of age, when he passed away on 1 May 1950. He'd had a heart attack. He had never been ill in his life. This tragic event left me feeling lonely and sad. Could it really be true I would never enjoy any fun times and laughter with my grandfather *ever* again? Will grandpa tell stories to another little girl in heaven now? What was I to do?

I will miss you so much, my *dafoo*.

2

A RICKSHAW RIDE

In 1950 the Communist Party was banned and Springbok Radio, SABC's first commercial service, was augmented.

ALTHOUGH I cannot remember standing at my grandfather's graveside, I do remember how different life was without him. Our sleeping arrangements changed. I moved into the bedroom with my mother and sisters. Uncle Slabs and Aunty Joan slept in the room I once shared with my grandparents and my grandmother and Jeanette moved into the room her parents had slept in. Gran wore black. The house felt sad.

My mother took over from my grandfather at the store. Her duties included ordering the supplies from the travellers, who called in; unlocking and locking up; paying the wages and keeping the books. All this additional responsibility and work meant she returned home late and exhausted every day. Aunty Joan and granny shared the domestic duties in the home, meals, bath, story and bedtime, for seven children, ranging in age from the youngest, Margy and Diana both aged one, to Vivian the eldest, who was nine.

"Something must be done about your squint eyes," my mother said.

"What are squint eyes?"

When I started school in January 1950, pupils stared at me. To avoid their glares, I bowed my head shyly. After a consultation with an eye specialist in Durban, my mother learnt my squint eyes could be rectified. Three separate eye operations performed in Durban. A slow process depending on how my eyes responded after each operation. I am truly indebted to my mother today, because she could ill afford one operation, let alone three.

We journeyed to Addington Hospital in Durban where these eye operations were performed. My left eye was operated on first then the right eye two months later. After each operation, I wore a pink eye-shield, which covered a small bandage and protected my eye. In the final operation, adjustments were made to both eyes, which were then heavily bandaged. The surgeon ordered my hands to be tied loosely to the bed to stop me removing the bandages. His intricate surgery depended on this precaution, which for me was difficult.

I was pinned to the hospital bed, unable to see. The more I struggled to free my wrists the worse they became, until my wrists bled. A warm trickle of blood tickled my arms but I could not wrench my hands free. I shared a ward with seven other children. In my dark world I put a name to each voice. John aged eight, in the bed directly opposite me, was cruel. He teased and taunted me. A nurse fed me at meal-times. I enjoyed the smell and taste of the food, but John spoilt my one small pleasure whenever he could.

"Baby! Baby! She can't even feed herself," he goaded the minute the nurse was out of earshot. More cruelly, he continued, "Look out, Denyse! There's a big, black spider on your bed! Oooooh! It's near your chin now!"

My *already* raw wrists were succumbed to more pain when I pulled and twisted.

"The huge, hairy legs are ..." produced an ear-deafening scream from me. The nurses rushed to my bed. When I explained some nurses sympathised with me, but others reprimanded me. John, the culprit, never owned up. The six children in the ward remained silent. Presumably they, too, were scared of this bully.

On one of my mother's visits she warned me, "Just look what you've done. Both your wrists are bleeding, Neyse. You *must* control yourself. Stop tugging to free your hands. You *know* what the doctor said." I *could not see* my bleeding wrists but I felt the pain. I accepted the blame. My mother only learnt the true story much later.

I was pleased to have the bandages removed, but I could barely open my eyes. It was like looking directly at the bright sun. I wore dark glasses but was also fitted with my first pair of tiny, gold-rimmed spectacles with long arms curling around my ears. Today I still have these teeny spectacles.

After we left the hospital, I realised I was bald! My mother had no explanation for me. She consoled me, "Your hair will grow back again." It did. My hair sprouted tufts of tight curls. Shirley Temple's curls did not outmatch my curly head!

When I was in the car with my eyes closed, I smelt my mother's perfume and imagined what she looked like: shiny dark hair parted to the one side; pink lipstick; bright beads adorning her neck; wearing a floral sun dress and sandals. Beautiful as always, I thought.

"Are we going home now?" I asked, longing to see granny and my sisters. Sadly, leaving hospital did not mean I was going home.

"No, Neyse. You're staying with Mrs Tudor-Jones until your eyes are stronger."

"But you promised me, mommy. Please..."

"It's only a short stay. You'll love it there. You'll make friends with her son."

With me whining, my mother drove to Mrs Tudor-Jones's home in Vause Road. A kind widow, with two grown-up daughters and a *laat lammetjie*, Watkin, a year older than me, would take me for my daily eye checks.

All too soon it was time to say goodbye.

"But I *want* to see Topsy and Margy."

"It won't be for long. You'll survive," were the words which were to become my survival kit. I was taken to the eye specialist by the matronly Mrs Tudor-Jones, her hair scraped into a bun on top of her head, wearing a *crimplene* dress and sandals. During the muscle-strengthening eye exercises, he tested my eye co-ordination moving a pencil slowly from right to left in front of me. My eyes followed the moving pencil with difficulty.

During my stay with Mrs Tudor-Jones my father visited me in Durban where he lived with his brother. Wearing grey flannels, a white shirt and a dark tie, my father looked smart when he took me out for the day. His shoes shone. He lived with his brother, where I met my 'Lloyd' cousins, mostly boys, who were all very musical. One cousin played the violin and another, the piano. I loved our sing-a-longs, humming when I did not know the words.

Daddy spoilt me on these outings. "Choose a sweet," he'd say, when we stopped at the corner shop. "*Please* may I have a lucky packet?" I loved lucky packets, because not only did they contain a few sweets, but more importantly, each held a silver-plated charm. Handing me the lucky packet, he watched me tear it open.

"*Thanks* daddy. Look, a silver kitten!" Granny, Aunty Joan and my mother had trained me to say *please* and *thank you*. Without these important words, I got nowhere. Daddy bought me a silver bracelet soon weighed down heavily with my collection of charms.

On one of these outings, daddy and I went to the beachfront where we rode in a *rickshaw*. The *Zulu* 'driver,' who pulled the decorative cart, wore many jangling bracelets around both his ankles, feathers in his beaded head-dress, beads and sea-shells around his neck and wrists and an animal hide around his waist, leaving his torso naked.

The cart tilted forwards pushing us high above his head as he jogged along, dragging us behind him. When he jumped into the air, we were flung against the backrest which seemed only inches off the tarmac. The cart levelled when his feet hit the road, making a crashing sound. His bracelets clanked on this melodious uncomfortable exhilarating ride.

The sun burnt hot on our heads. Our driver sweated. The strong smell of perspiration wafted towards us as he pulled and jumped higher and higher on this rigorous ride. Every jump was unpredictable and *always* took us by surprise as we listened to the rhythmic sound, 'smash-crash-clang-a-lang...dash-dash' of his be-jewelled feet as he ran along. His weird shouting sounds to clear his path, sounded like an 'African beat' yodel.

On the way we passed an ice-cream cart, the huge paddling pools with slides and fountains, the merry-go-rounds, a toffee-apple stall and a candyfloss kiosk. We even caught glimpses of bathers splashing in the breakers and surfers, riding the warm waves of the Indian Ocean and life-savers sitting on raised chairs and monitoring the scene.

At the end of the ride, our 'driver' extended his hand to help me dismount. He beamed at us, his broad smile revealing his white teeth. My dad dug into his pocket for his wallet. We thanked him for the ride. Our *rickshaw* 'driver' was happy. We waved goodbye. I looked over my shoulder and saw our 'driver' attracting his next customer.

"Would you like some candyfloss?"

"Yes, please daddy."

We walked hand in hand. Daddy handed me a large plastic bag of pink candyfloss. We sat on a bench together watching the passers-by. Contentedly, I swung my legs backwards and forwards while pulling off little pieces of candyfloss and popping them into my mouth. There was no need to chew or suck. It simply disappeared!

These were *such* happy times. Daddy made me feel very special. I loathed going back to Mrs Tudor-Jones and Watkin, but I knew it was for my own good.

"Goodbye, Neyse. I'll come again."

"Bye daddy."

My father picked me up and hugged me. He put me down. I felt all alone. My heart ached, as I watched him walk away...

When I came home from Durban after three eye operations and a stay with Mrs Tudor–Jones, I was packed off to the Holy Cross Convent boarding school in January 1950. This was my first year at school and I was five. I did not understand why. Maybe the nuns could supervise my muscle-strengthening exercises more efficiently...

Inserting a picture into the apparatus, the mirrored image reflected. I positioned my eyes over the spectacled section and I traced the outline onto transparent paper with a pencil. Sister measured the accuracy of my drawing by placing it over the picture, before she inserted the next picture, which was an introduction to art, which I grew to enjoy...

At boarding school I could no longer play with my cousins nor could I daydream. My life was controlled by regimental rules, beckoning bells and deathly silence. My fun-loving family was whipped away from me like a rug pulled from under my feet. The grown-ups I saw were nuns. Faces peered at me from under a stiff white coif, black veil and habit; rosary beads swished at their waists and a crucifix glistened against their black bodices. If the nuns had hair, I could not see any, not even a stray strand!

Remembering my mother's words, "You'll survive!" I bit my bottom lip as I faced up to new challenges which would fashion my life... With only a small suitcase of belongings I was installed as a boarder and the routine began.

We followed a stooped nun, Sister Benvanuta up a polished staircase, in crocodile formation to the dressing room. This room comprised two large, low tables housing rows of small enamel basins, where we washed, brushed our hair and put on our pyjamas. I missed squirting Topsy and Margy with water from my mouth when I brushed my teeth. Afterwards we filed into a line and waited. "To your beds, no talking on the way!"

The beds were covered with white quilts and bordered both walls of the immaculately clean dormitory. A white curtain sectioned off a cubicle where Sister Benvanuta slept. A statue of the Virgin Mary with a candle on each side stood on a table at the far end of the room. As I knelt down I thought Mary was watching me.

Sister Benvanuta prompted our evening prayer, *"Gentle Jesus…"* Kneeling with eyes tightly closed and hands pressed together, we prayed aloud, *"Gentle Jesus, meek and mild look upon a little child. Suffer me to come to Thee and if I die before I wake, I pray to God by soul to take."*

My version, a little different, ended: *"I'll meet you at the garden gate."*

Sister Benvanuta watched as we put our slippers neatly together before we jumped under the bedcovers. When she switched off the light, the room plunged into darkness. No bedtime story... No kiss or cuddle... No tucking up into bed…

Every morning a small shrill bell woke me. Half-asleep, I stumbled out of bed and fell onto my knees. Sister Benvanuta recited a morning prayer. Back in the dressing room we completed our toiletries and dressed. A bell summonsed us into a line. She inspected us, straightening a tie, tightening a girdle, pulling down a gym dress hooked in a pair of knickers or pulling up sagging socks. Satisfied, she said, "Lead off to the dining room. *No* running!"

No morning hugs and kisses or lovely stories my grandfather once told me…

Every meal, including breakfast, was structured around more bells! A bell rang for us to say grace and another to sit down in silence. On birthdays and feast days *only,* a bell rang allowing us to talk awhile and another to be silent. Three more bells rang; to stand, to say grace and the last one, to leave the dining-room.

I ran to the playground but the older girls already occupied the four swings and the seesaw. My friends and I skipped with our hand-held skipping ropes or played hopscotch. I watched the day scholars arrive, carrying either a small school suitcase or wearing a leather satchel on their backs.

Sister John Thomas, a tall beautiful nun, the principal, was a strict disciplinarian. She walked holding her head high, her habit swishing as she passed. Promptly at 8.30 am she swung a hand bell vigorously. Pupils assembled in the hall in seven lines, one for each class from kindergarten to Standard Five.

"Come along children, form a line!" she said.

Shoving, nudging and whispering stopped for morning prayers and a hymn. After which, we were dismissed to our classrooms, trooping in time to the piano, played by a nun. I swung my arms from side to side saying, "Left... right..." Like little toy soldiers, we marched to our classroom. On the first day our class teacher, Sister Agnes clapped her hands and said, "I'm going to show you where to sit."

She took each child by the hand to a desk. Boys at the back. Girls in the front. I sat in the front row next to a dark-haired girl, Ann Mundell. Her parents farmed at Karg's Post. Ann promptly sat down. Sister disapproved and reprimanded her immediately.

"Stand up child. Sit only when *I* tell you to sit."

Sister gave the command, after our greeting, "Good morning Sister."

I admired the alphabetical pictures on the walls. On the front wall a crucifix on which Jesus hung wearing a crown of thorns caught my attention. Religious Instruction, our first lesson began. We learnt the questions and answers parrot-fashion from a catechism.

"Who made you?

God made me.

Why did God make you?

God made me to know Him and love Him and serve Him in this world and to be happy with Him forever in the next."

Eventually I was able to recite my catechism off by heart.

Arithmetic, known as 'sums,' followed. We were taught to count. Picking up one book Sister asked, "How many books am I holding?"

Our hands shot into the air. Desperate to answer, I waved my hand vigorously. Sometimes she chose me. John, at the back of the class, was very enthusiastic. He jumped up and down on his seat like a Jack-in-a-box. If that did not get Sister's attention, he flicked his fingers and hands in the air, making a clicking sound. He invariably answered incorrectly and his bad behaviour was admonished.

Writing with white chalk on our slates, we copied the sums from the blackboard: 1 + 1 = 2; 1 + 2 = 3; 2 + 1 = 3. The screeching, scratching sound of chalk squeaking on small slates was spine-chilling. We read the sums aloud before cleaning our slates with a wet cloth, but I noticed John spitting on his slate and using his shirt sleeves to wipe it clean.

A thirty-minute tea break ended when the bell rang. Reading followed. From a card with ten words, we had turns sounding each word phonetically. When it was my turn, I stood up and began, "m-a-t, mat; b-a-t, bat; h-a-t, hat." At the end of the day, we tidied the room; put our heads on our desks. We listened to a story read to us by Sister Agnes. This was the routine of my *kindergarten* years. Over the years the sound of bells would enforce more rules which were ingrained in me for life...

After lunch we wore little black aprons to keep our gym dresses clean, whilst playing. I befriended Yvonne van Heerden, who lived on a farm. Her family were Afrikaans-speaking and so her English was not very good. Unable to speak Afrikaans, I soon learnt a few basics: "*Asseblief, kom saam met my,*" Please, come with me; "*Baie dankie,*" Thank you and "*Hoe gaan dit?*" How are you? We spoke *Xhosa* when we had a communication breakdown.

At 3.30 pm a shrill-sounding bell motioned us to line up for a warm mug of tea in winter or mug of juice in summer. We were given one slice of bread, no butter, with a scraping of grape-jam, mixed fruit jam or dripping, but on Wednesdays we had peanut butter.

When a bell signalled older children into the classroom for homework, black maids took us to the bathroom and washed and dried our feet. We put on our slippers. When the maids polished our shoes, I greeted Violet saying, "*Molo,* Hello. *Ninjani,* How are you?"

"*Ndiphilile*, I'm well."

"*Ngubani igama lakho?* What's your name?" Violet asked.

"N-Den-ee-see."

Violet popped my shoes into the locker before the bell rang.

My life revolved around a cacophony of bells. The church bells in the belfry pealed five times daily. The never-ending tinkling and clanging of bells dictated *exactly* what I should do – wake, line up, eat, sit, stand, play and sleep. Bells, bells, bells! The best bell of all was the one which freed me from the classroom at the end of the year for six weeks' summer holiday.

Hooray... Home... Happiness...

3

107 HAWTHORN STREET, KOKSTAD

In 1952 the Pass Laws, restricting black movement were introduced. Prisons were overcrowded after the implementation of the Defiance Campaign of 1952. The Government introduced severe penalties against offenders, making protest virtually illegal.

HOLIDAYS at last and back to 107 Hawthorn Street. I was so happy. No more bells. No more don'ts. No more silence. "Don't slouch. Sit up straight. Elbows off the table! No talking! Don't talk with your mouth full. Who burped? Don't slurp."

For six weeks, I was back with my mother, two sisters and cousins. Living in granny's home, home to the Slabbert family too, was home to me. Granny was a devout Catholic and we lived by her rules. We knew when she was going out. Her hair, covered with a net, would be adorned with a hat in summer or beret in winter, a brooch held the scarf around her neck in place and over her lower left arm, she draped a handbag, which matched her shoes. Popping her head around the door, the scent of *Eau de Cologne 4711* wafted towards us.

"Now, children, behave while I'm out. Goodbye."

"Yes Granny," we chorused. She was gone.

The huge property was our playground. Barefoot, we climbed trees, built 'pretend' houses in the hedge or made roads in the dusty pathways. I drove my car, which was a stone, making the appropriate noises. When we played 'Hide-and-seek,' I hid between the rows of *mealie* plants.

Some days, Vivian, Jeanette and I were each given a basket. We picked plums, figs, apricots, apples, peaches and pears and, of course, ate a few too! The over-laden baskets free of any *vrot* fruit were returned to the kitchen. "Thank you children," Aunty Joan said as she set about washing the fruit.

Using a special peeler fixed to the wooden table, she plunged the fruit on to the sharp spikes and turned the wooden handle. The peels fell into a bucket on the floor. The peeled and cored fruit was stewed in two enormous pots on the *Esse* stove. The delicious smell of fruit enveloped the kitchen. One pot was for jam and the other for stewed fruit. The preserving bottles were heated in the oven, before the jam and stewed fruit were ladled into them. When cool, all the bottles were appropriately labelled and dated, *Apricot Jam, 1952*. The jam was sealed with melted *Holsum* before the lids were screwed down. These preserving bottles stood on the pantry shelves like soldiers on parade.

We took turns feeding the chickens and filling the water troughs. My aunt collected the eggs. I loved the little bantams. The bantam rooster made a raucous noise for its size, strutting in and out of flowerbeds. By day the bantams roamed freely but they were locked up in a coop at night.

On summer afternoons we lay on our backs on the grass in the shade of the tall hedge. We watched the storm clouds gathering. The shape-changing 'nimbus' clouds instigated a game we called, *'Clouds in the sky.'* With imaginations running wild, we concentrated on the ever-changing shapes of wind-chased clouds. When I saw a discernible shape, I shouted, "I've got one. Who can find my rabbit cloud in the sky?" Fingers pointed heavenwards with calls, "There it is! There it is!" until I decided who had found my cloud.

This game often ended abruptly with the onset of a summer thunderstorm. Loud claps of thunder preceded streaks of lightning. The fluffy white clouds darkened from grey to black. Before the storm clouds bulged with rain, we were summonsed indoors.

"Come along, now," Aunty Joan wearing her fruit-stained apron, beckoned to us from the *stoep*. "Hurry inside!" When this warning came, we knew our game was over. We scurried into the kitchen. Sometimes the storms brought more than a heavy downpour. Hail clattered on the corrugated roof and covered the grass in millions of tiny hailstones. The church bells of St Patrick's cathedral rang out warning the townspeople of a severe hailstorm. During these storms the wind got up. Doors banged. Curtains were sucked out of the open windows. At 2 pm the house grew strangely dark. There was no sign of the fluffy, white clouds we had enjoyed only a few minutes before.

"Close the windows and stay in the lounge," commanded Aunty Joan. This sent us running from room to room, slamming the sash windows closed. I was frightened... The sheets of lightning leapt through the window-panes, lit the room up in a silver whiteness and then disappeared into the heavens again. *Crash, bang, boom, bedash-adash-adash,* the thunder clapped on and on...

"Whew! I'm scared," Topsy said as Margy clung to me. But nobody heard her as the storm raged on. The heavens opened. Rain bucketed down with relentless force. We could not hear each other talk.

"Get away from the window, Jeanette!" Vivian screamed.

We huddled together on the carpet in the middle of the lounge trying to escape our fear. Bunched together and afraid, we waited for the storm to pass...

After a severe hailstorm, the ground was covered in hailstones, fruit was damaged, cars were dented and windows were broken. These hailstones were freezing cold and we were forbidden to put them in our mouths.

When we heard, "You can go out to play again," we were relieved. Trying to see who could make the biggest splash, we darted barefoot from one puddle to the next. The sun shone. The clouds were gone. Everything was rain washed. I loved the fresh smell of wet grass and damp soil after the storm. This was a chance for us to play *'boat races'* with acorns. The gutters separating the oak-lined streets from the pavements carried the rainwater away. We collected a handful of acorn cups, our 'boats'. Vivian shouted, "Go!" Dropping our boats into the gushing water in the gutter and keeping our eyes on them, we ran along the edge of the gutter to the bridge, the finishing line. We waited, bending over for the best view. The acorns bobbed, dived, disappeared and surfaced in the fast-flowing stream.

"Mine's coming first."

"Neville your boat's stuck!"

"Our boats are tie, Jeanette."

We repeated this game with glee oblivious of the mud oozing

between our toes and covering our legs and feet as we trailed up and down. When it was 'game over', we abandoned our boats. We washed our feet in puddles before scampering inside for supper.

And so the long lazy days of summer passed. One day seemed endless. A week felt like a month. The simple Christmas decorations were strung from the central light fitting and fastened with drawing pins to the picture-rails around the lounge. We made paper-chains by folding two coloured strips of crepe paper. Paper Christmas bells, stars and trees dangled from the ceiling. We had no Christmas tree.

Instead the nativity scene captivated young and old. Granny arranged her prized nativity figures, positioning the shepherds with their sheep, right of the crib. To the left, three kings rode on camels, bearing gifts. In the middle was the stable. Joseph stood behind the manger and Mary knelt with bowed head. A star above completed the scene. Straw was strewn around sheep and cattle. These beautiful life-like figures brought Christmas alive. Granny always put baby Jesus into the manger on Christmas morning.

The cloudless blue skies intensified the sun's heat, but in our *cozzies,* we ran in and out the sprinkler on the lawn to keep cool. We counted the days to Christmas until one night we were told, "Only one more sleep!" intensifying our excitement. Weeks before Christmas our dolls disappeared. Our presents were slipped into pillow-cases on the foot of our beds. On Christmas day our dolls appeared. Not only had granny made a complete new set of clothes – dress, bonnet, petticoat and frilly knickers, but she had made a mattress, a pillow and blanket, turning a shoe-box into a doll's cot.

After Mass the family gathered for Christmas dinner. Aunty Molly and Uncle Stewey, Aunty Buzzy and Uncle Keith joined us. We pulled Christmas crackers, snatched up the novelties and wore coloured paper hats. We searched for a *tickey* in the Christmas pudding. It was a happy time for the whole family.

I hated leaving home when the summer holiday was over. Back into school routine and playing new games, made me forget my cousins and 107 Hawthorn Street. Yvonne and I added Pat Harwood from Kitwe as a friend. Pat was spoilt and spoke with a hoity-toity accent. In class my teacher asked me to teach Agnes Botha and Muriel Bucholtz to read. They were slow. Muriel held the book close to her eyes. I was bored and hated missing drawing and writing.

Preparations got underway to receive two sacraments. Penance was a confession of sins to a priest, who sat on one side of the dark confessional box separated from the confessor by a wooden partition and small grid window. On the day of my first confession, I knelt inside the confessional box. The priest said: "Yes, my child."

"Bless me father, for I have sinned. This is my first confession. I fought with Neville. I bullied Margy. I told a fib. I forgot to say my prayers…" I rattled off my sins and waited.

"For your penance child, say three Hail Marys."

I went out with a sigh of relief, said my penance, genuflected, dipped my finger in the holy water font and made the sign of the cross before I stepped outside the church. This became a regular Saturday afternoon event until I left school.

When I received my first Holy Communion the next day, I wore a new white dress and a short veil. The church was packed. I knelt down at the altar rails. The priest, carrying a chalice, held up a round wafer saying, "Body of Christ." He put the wafer on my outstretched tongue. All communicants had to fast from midnight. Granny and our family members were proud of Neville and me on our First Holy Communion day. Neville a day scholar was in my class at the convent.

***

That year I developed a sore throat. Our family doctor, Doctor Bosman examined me. "Open your mouth wide and say, Aaaah!"

He tilted my head back gently and shone a torch down my throat, using a wooden spatula to hold my tongue down. "I'm afraid, Peggy, I'll have to remove her tonsils."

"Would it be possible to remove Topsy and Margy's tonsils, too, doctor?"

"What are their ages?"

"Five and three."

"Well, I could remove Topsy's tonsils, but not Margy's. She's still too young."

My mother prepared us. It was agreed to remove our adenoids as well. "You won't feel a thing. You'll sleep in a hospital bed and eat jelly and ice-cream until your throat's better," my mother comforted me. At the hospital we were put into two separate beds in the children's ward. As soon as mom left, Topsy scrambled into my bed.

"I'm scared," she said.

"It won't hurt."

A nurse put the bedsides up and we cuddled together and slept. In the morning Topsy started again, "I'm scared Neyse."

Our tonsils and adenoids were removed and we went home. Our cousins envied us as we ate jelly and ice-cream, but not for long... This experience was soon forgotten.

***

I was the only pupil who wore glasses. This and the fact I had a mop of unruly curls, freckles, gangly arms and legs, made me feel like an ugly duckling. Three friends moved up with me from kindergarten into primary school. Yvonne van Heerden, with dimples in her cheeks, shiny black hair and brown eyes, was good at games. She shared her tuck with me.

Ann Mundell, with big teeth and straight mousy hair, was old-fashioned and shy. She was a bookworm and allowed me to read her books. She made me a small Christmas card which I have kept all these years. Blonde blue-eyed Lianne Bastard, with an infectious laugh was a tomboy and lived on a farm. When I had sleep-overs the servants picked up our dirty clothes from the floor and at mealtimes I could leave food on my plate. Lianne replaced Pat who found new friends.

We had two teachers in primary school who were not nuns, Miss Monnim and Mrs Nourse. My Standard One teacher was Miss Monnim. She wore glasses, was short and had a loud voice. I sat in the front row, probably to see the board better.

"Good morning Miss Monnim," we greeted her.

Monitors handed out pencils, collected books and cleaned the blackboard dusters outside. Books were covered in brown paper. Religious Instruction, Grammar, Composition, Arithmetic, Nature Study, Writing, Art and Needlework were some of our subjects.

We played on the playground during break time. I never walked on week days, but skipped along, happy to have my friends. Week-ends were different. The weekly boarders, including my friends, went home on Friday afternoon and only returned on Monday morning. Wearing casual clothes on Saturday, I waited for the tuck shop to open at 2 pm. Clutching my *tickey* (three *tickeys* bought an Eskimo Pie) I lined up, waiting for my turn.

"Next!"

"One penny *nigger-balls*, one penny toffees, one penny *Nestle* chocolate, please."

Carrying my brown paper bag with seven sweets, I sat on the grass and popped a toffee into my mouth. Sucking and swirling it in my mouth, I watched the queue deplete. The shutters crashed down until next week when I would buy my favourite sweet. *Sherbet,* a lollipop sucked and dipped in sherbet inside a triangular paper packet. With saliva, this made a little explosion in my mouth.

On Sunday morning my second *tickey* went into the collection at Mass. I ran out of *tickeys* by the end of each term. My mouth watered when I watched others eating sweets and I had none.

It was in the convent swimming pool that I learnt to swim. Gripping a rail, I kicked my legs. Before long I jumped off the edge of the pool and doggie-paddled, spitting and spluttering to the side. With practice, I was like a fish in water. Easter came and went. The oak trees put on their autumn shades and dropped their leaves. The bare trees and frosty mornings ushered in the start of winter, chilblains and malt and cod-liver oil before we set off on our midyear three-week holiday.

***

With my suitcase packed, I joined my sisters and cousins, whom I had missed, at 107 Haw-thorn Street. The strangest thing happened...We were playing at the bottom of the garden. Skipping along heading for the toilet, I heard a voice calling, "Help, somebody, help!"

Who was this? Where was the voice coming from? Who needed help?

I listened carefully. It sounded like granny. The calls came from the cellar. I ran to the tiny cellar door and crept through. It took a while for my eyes to adjust from the bright sunlight outside to the darkness of the cellar. The coolness and dankness of this stuffy space enveloped me. I spotted granny spread-eagled and *motionless* on a pile of hessian bags with sooty coal spilling out of an open bag. One of her shoes was missing.

Her face was covered in a white powder. My poor grandmother!

"I'm here, gran. I'll help you up. "

"My child, fetch somebody to help you. Be quick. My body aches."

Reluctant to leave her alone in pain, I knew I could do nothing on my own. I crept out into the daylight. What should I do?

"Evilina! Help!"

Evilina hearing my shouts dropped the peg-bag where she was hanging washing on the line and hurried towards the cellar. "What's wrong?"

I babbled so fast Evilina could not understand me. Shaking me by the arm, she asked, "What's matter, missy Neyse?"

"Granny."

She followed me. Evilina, with great difficulty being a large woman, crouched down and squeezed through the small door. "Oh, my *medem*! Granny! It's Evilin, come help you."

Evilina reached out and held granny's hand. Gran said, "Telephone for help."

"Yes gran."

I ran to the phone. Evelina stayed with granny. Children were not allowed to use the phone. I cranked the handle and picked up the earpiece. "Number please."

"265."

In those days, all telephones were connected to an Exchange, from where the calls were connected on request. At that moment, Jeanette walked into the hallway and saw me on the phone. "Using the phone eh... Wait until I tell my mother and father on you!"

I ignored her. My mother answered, "265. *DM Brown General Dealer*."

"Mom, it's Neyse. Granny fell. She's in the cellar. She needs help. "

"Who's with her?"

"Evilina."

"Is granny hurt?"

"I don't know. She's crying, mom."

"I'll get help straight away. Give granny sugar water and cover her with a blanket."

"Yes mom. Goodbye."

I hung the earpiece on the brass hook. Jeanette, who had been eavesdropping, confronted me as I fetched a blanket from my bed.

"Where's granny?"

"She's in the cellar Jeanette."

Not believing a word I'd said, she marched off to the pantry. Jeanette was shocked to see the open trapdoor. She bent down and called to granny, "Granny help's on the way."

Jeanette made the sugar water and I returned to cover gran with my blanket.

"Have a sip gran."

She refused saying, "I hurt all over!"

Time seemed to stand still. At last we heard voices. Evilina had the sense to walk to the gate and she showed the doctor the way. He crept through the door with a stretcher. Outside Jeanette and I listened. We heard gran's shouts as she was transferred on to the stretcher with Evilina's help. She was carried and placed on her bed. The doctor examined her. I was very concerned. I wondered, would she too like grandpa, die and go to heaven. Please granny *not* now, I thought. Eventually the doctor told us that granny had been lucky. The bag of coal had broken her fall.

"Nothing's broken, but plenty of bruises. Your granny's had a shock. Her ankle's swollen. Her body will ache, but I've given her something for pain. I recommend a few days bedrest. Then she'll be fine!"

What a relief. Granny had given us such a fright. Now it was our turn to help her. We took turns playing 'nurse'; bringing granny her post or breakfast tray; puffing up her pillows and sometimes I just sat with her. We chatted. I made granny laugh.

4

DM BROWN GENERAL DEALER STORE

The Separate Amenities Act of 1953 introduced "petty apartheid" segregation, for example, on buses and in post offices. Malan retired and JG Strijdom became prime minister.

SOME weeks after this fall granny told us, "I wanted to bake a cake. I walked into the pantry never thinking the trapdoor was open. My eyes were focused on the shelf where I reached for the flour and baking powder. It all happened so quickly. One minute I was holding the packet of flour and the next, I was dropping through the floor. I landed in the cellar. I could not get up. Thank you Evilina, Neyse and Jeanette, for coming to my rescue." Gran was truly grateful for the kindness everyone had shown her.

Grandpa's store in Kokstad known as *D M Brown's*, named after himself, Donald Moses Brown, was frequented by Whites, Blacks and *Coloureds*. It reminds me a little of "*Open All Hours*", a British television programme about a corner store featuring Arkwright and Granville. The entrance was on a corner of Main Road and Dower Street. The display windows, facing the street, were jam-packed with goods. What fun it was to creep in the windows and see the expression of surprised passers-by!

Coming into the shop from the bright sunlight outside, it felt dark. The shop oozed with different smells from the merchandise stacked high on shelves behind wooden counters, which separated the customers from the shop attendants. How very different this shop was when compared to shopping in a supermarket *today*!

My nose picked up the smells of fresh bread, leather, paraffin, snuff, rolls of material and blankets, tobacco and much more. There were four main sections – food, materials, blankets, clothes and shoes. Buckets, saddles, ploughs, three-legged pots, billycans and small trunks were hung and secured from a pole reaching up to the rafters in the centre of the dusty wooden floor. In the clothes section, a glass cabinet displayed jewellery, radios, bracelets, beads and watches. It was kept locked. Strung from the rafters of the roof were bicycles, bridles, more saddles, stirrups, forks, picks, spades, sickles, rope, wooden window frames and stable doors. Directly opposite the front door entrance was a full-length mirror. This intrigued the customers who had never seen their reflections in a mirror before.

"What is *this*? *She* is like me and copies me."

"Where did *she* come from?"

"Come and see this. A man like *me!*"

"Is *this* me? Let us look behind *this* thing!"

When *Xhosa* men and women unexpectedly saw their reflections, they moved, exclaimed and touched the mirror in sheer wonderment. Some pointed, laughed and looked behind the mirror. Others examined themselves. Noses were picked, mouths opened wide and teeth scrutinised, soles of the feet were examined, headgear was adjusted and noses pressed up against the mirror. Totally uninhibited, others sang and danced. These *apparent* shadow-imaged people of kindred likeness mesmerised them.

Clouds of dust rose from the floor as their rhythmic, bare feet danced in time to their harmonious song. Bystanders clapped. Timid participants were nudged out of the way by those who wanted the prime position. Women, with babies strapped in blankets on their backs, joined in the jamboree. This mirror was a constant source of live entertainment.

Tinned foods, *Reckett's blue* and *Sunlight soap*, matches, snuff, tobacco, candles, bread (white and brown, either a full or half a loaf), *mealie meal, samp*, beans, sugar and tea were replenished on the shelves daily. The bread was wrapped in newspaper. Brown paper bags, placed on scales, were filled using scoops from the appropriate hessian bags. Each bag was weighed accurately. Sweets were displayed in glass jars.

Paper cones made from old newspaper were used for smaller amounts. Grandpa had taught me how to make paper cones. The shop 'boys' as they were called, worked in the storeroom. Customers brought their own cans which were filled with paraffin from a fifty-gallon drum. The shop 'boys' also filled the customers' bottles with methylated spirits from a large container. They offloaded the merchandise from delivery trucks through the back door of the storeroom. Here, too, the shop truck was loaded by them for daily deliveries to the *location*. Rather a fire hazard by today's standards!

From the storeroom at the back I could hear customers in the shop playing a penny whistle. From floor to rafters, huge hessian bags of samp, beans, sugar, flour, mealie meal, bales of blankets and rolls of materials, boxes of shoes arranged in shoe size, stood, leaving a narrow passage to pass through. A huge scale was used to weigh items exceeding five pounds. The weight in pounds was inscribed on one side of the T- bar, which balanced when the correct weight was added on the opposite side. I learnt to weigh myself on this scale.

Customers rubbed material between their fingers like tobacco before it was measured and cut using a metal tape-measure fixed to the counter and scissors tied securely with string dangling from the counter. Brightly coloured scarves hung on the cross-beams of the material shelves. These were bought and used by *Xhosa* women as turbans. Others looked, touched and admired berets, heaped in bundles of red, black and navy, below the scarves. I learnt the value of money and the basics of business here. For safe-keeping, the *Xhosa* women tied their money in handkerchiefs, which were buried deep in their bosoms. They delved down and pulled out the hidden handkerchief. *Only* one coin was exchanged with each purchase. The sequence went something like this:

"Sixpence mealie meal" followed by "Thank you." The change was examined.

"*Tickey* flour. Thank you." Again the tickey change was examined before deciding on the next purchase, "*Tickey*, bread. Thank you."

When one shilling was spent, two pennies still remained, tied up in the handkerchief.

"Penny matches," and "Penny snuff," concluded the sale. Snuff was placed directly into the customer's hand, which in turn, was put into their own snuffbox.

D M Brown's taught me, when *buying,* to prioritise my basic needs first and to indulge in a small luxury with any left-over money and when *selling*, to exert patience. Correct decisions, I learnt, were time-consuming. I learnt to show respect and gratitude after each sale and to bid the customer farewell, saying, "Goodbye and travel home safely."

The more I learnt to understand the *Xhosa* people, the more aware I became of huge differences between myself and them. I was starting to experience how little they had and the awful division of different races in my country called '*apartheid…*'

***

Back at boarding school it was that dreadful time, Friday afternoon, letter-writing. "Come along now," Sister Peter called, "Have you washed your hands?"

We were dragged away from the playground, stood in a line, before we marched into the classroom. The youngest sat in the front rows whilst the older girls handed out the writing pads and envelopes. Sister Peter insisted, "No talking at the back."

She picked up the chalk and wrote on the blackboard. "Put your hand up if you have something to say."

The room fell deathly silent. I covered my ears to avoid the scratching sound of the chalk on the blackboard. The screechy sound sent shivers down my spine. Sister, it seemed, was oblivious to this. Without warning, she whipped her head around, checking on us. She wrote 'Dear daddy and mommy,' on the left of the board, returned the chalk to its place, before patrolling and scrutinising our letters.

"You'll never finish in time if you day-dream," she told me making my pencil hit the paper. I wrote: *Dear Mommy, How are you? I am fine* and finished with a drawing at the bottom of the page. I have these letters today.

***

Moving up into Standard Three in 1954, Sister Mary Bernadette, a short smiling happy Irish nun was my favourite teacher. She gave me good marks for my 'compositions' and told me how much she liked my illustrative drawings.

We swam in a primitive pool, with three diving-boards at the deep-end. There were single changing booths on each side. Without chlorine or a filter, the water turned pea-green and became home to hundreds of tadpoles and enormous frogs. We were forced to swim with them. I felt the slithery soft-bellied frogs rubbing up against me. The pool sides and bottom were slimy making it slippery to get out.

"Don't swallow the water!" the nun warned us.

Eventually four black men scrubbed the drained pool with brushes and brooms. When the slime was hosed off, it was re-filled. Crystal clear water was sheer bliss.

In one letter I wrote: *I got a nice Rainbow pencil because I had a neat book'* hoping to please my mother, adding, *I have played my first music lesson to-day*. My mother hoped I would follow in her footsteps. Deviously I enrolled for ballet and wrote: *I am taking up dancing*. We stuck drawing pins into the soles of our school shoes, which produced a good tapping noise. I imagined I could dance like Fred Astaire, which was my escape from the rigidity of convent life.

I am sorry I didn't give you a birthday present I wrote and begged, *Do come and see us'* with drawings of Margy, a bow in her hair; granny reading a book and my mother, working in *D M Brown's*. On 16 July 1954 I wrote: *The first school week is over. I work hard to get high marks. We have a new music teacher, Sister Mary Joseph. She gave me a sweet,* and ended, *we are having Sister Benvanuta's feast day on Monday.*

Sister Mary Joseph paraded up and down, staring through the window panes as we practised the piano in one of eight small practice rooms with glass windows.

Addressed to my mother, *Mrs P E Lloyd, 107 Hawthorn Street, Kokstad,* my letters were stamped and posted by the nuns. Letter-writing always made me sad...

***

My composition, titled *When I grow up,* which I illustrated oozed happiness. From under a short skirt my spindly long legs and high heels emerged and in my arms I held a baby, with a second baby hidden in a pram alongside me; two children were on a swing and two were on a see-saw. A smiling husband stood at my side not forgetting a cat and a dog looking on. The sun shone in a blue sky. Even the flowers wore smiles. If I'd only known how difficult it was to create this idyllic situation in real life. If only I had known how cruel life could be. If only I had known that life brings out the best and the worst in people...

Whenever my temper flared, my mother said, "You've got your

father's temper." At the convent where I went to school, Mary refused to give me a turn on the swing even after I asked her politely. She smirked, swinging to and fro, intensifying my frustration. The bell rang. I had not had a turn. Anger welled up inside me. The minute the bell rang, Mary jumped off triumphantly and I exploded like an atomic bomb. I grabbed her by the shoulders. I shook her and eye-balled her with contempt.

Sister Peter wrenched us apart, saying, "You come with me, Denyse," comforting Mary, who was blubbing her eyes out. I felt bad. The whole school had witnessed my temper tantrum. "This will not be tolerated! You may not swing for one week. Do this again and you'll be marched off to Mother Superior's office."

"Yes, Sister," I stammered. "You've got your father's temper," drummed in my head. This was the start of learning how unfair life was...

One day at 107 Hawthorn Street Neville, six months younger than me, lured me into the study. This was forbidden territory. "I'll surprise you, Neyse," he fibbed and I fell into the trap. He locked the glass doors. He pulled faces at me saying, "I got you!"

"Let me out Neville," but my pleas only increased his victory. Neville pulled even uglier faces at me. Then he scarpered. I was angry. I hated to be defeated and I was. In a fit of rage I pushed both my fists through the small panes of two glass doors. Shards of glass crashed to the floor. Looking at the blood pouring from my hands shocked me. I could not believe what I had done.

The window panes in the door were broken. I panicked. I needed to get away. The only window which opened was six foot above the ground, my only escape. Stepping onto the window seat and opening the window as wide as possible, I balanced on the ledge before I dropped down, landing on top of the hydrangeas. I scrambled to my feet and headed towards the bathroom.

Just as I stepped inside, granny appeared and said, "What's wrong my child?"

Silently I held up my bleeding hands hoping she would feel sorry for me. My grandmother was very sympathetic, thinking I had fallen outside. In the kitchen she bathed my hands in a solution of *Dettol* water, which stung. It was game over when gran removed a piece of glass from my knuckles. Looking at me over the rim of her glasses, she asked, "What happened? Did you break something?"

I answered between a staccato of sobs, "Neville... sob...locked me...sob...in the study...sob...and I was...sob... scared and poked my fists through the study doors."

We were both reprimanded. I was learning the hard way.

"You've a good guardian angel," granny said. My guardian angel had a busy time.

***

Playing a game involving dodging stones, I was caught off-guard. Neville threw a stone at Margy and it caught me on the back of my head. Blood spurted out. He was petrified.

"They'll *donner* me," he shouted as he ran away.

Aunty Joan put a cold compress on my wound and made me lie down. My head ached. When mommy came home, she cut my hair, cleaned the congealed blood and bandaged my head with a crepe bandage. "You're my little wounded soldier."

Her love healed my wounds but Neville and I had many more squabbles...

***

The New Year brought surprises. My new cousin Michael, born on 12 July 1953 was adopted at eighteen months by Uncle Stewey and Aunty Molly. David, who had also been adopted at the age of four, now had a brother. David, with red hair and freckles, was cute.

My mother, sisters and I rented house in Coulter Street which bordered on the convent grounds. I was no longer a boarder but this meant caring for my younger sisters. We had a stupid maid, Beauty and a dog, called Winkie. He chased us down the passage. We jumped onto the beds. The dog barked. Standing on his hind legs, he tried to jump onto the bed. Success! We clambered on top of the wardrobe. The more he barked the louder we shrieked. Beauty ignored the mayhem. When Mom returned, we welcomed her and weary Winkie waited to be fed.

I missed my cousins and my friends. I plaited Margy's hair. Because she was the baby of the family, she had everything done for her. Topsy, eight, and Margy aged six, took ballet lessons held in the Kokstad Town Hall. On Wednesdays it was my responsibility to take them to ballet at 3 o'clock. "Put your ballet dress and pumps in your bag, Topsy."

"Where's my bag?"

Struggling to put Margy's hair into a ponytail, I ignored her.

"I can't find my bag." Topsy responded.

"I'll get it."

Carrying their bags and holding hands, we set off. A lesson was in progress when we arrived, Mrs Rose played the piano and Mrs Dillon, her back to the pupils, demonstrated saying, *"Pliè! Pliè!"* and *"Point those toes."* Green with envy, I helped my sisters into their ballet dresses and pumps. I was left watching. The pupils took their positions at the bar. Mrs Dillon marched towards me with my sisters trailing behind her.

"Denyse, do you realise that Jennifer and Margaret have measles?" she blurted out. "Look, they're covered in spots."

"No, I don't know anything about measles," I whimpered.

"Well," she continued, "take them home immediately."

Off we trudged, not a happy trio. Feeling mortified and somewhat confused, I walked ahead of my sisters. Without looking right, then left and then right again, as had been drilled into me, I stepped off the pavement. The next moment there was an almighty crash! I went sprawling onto the road. A bicycle lay partially on top of me. A black man on his bicycle swerved, but collided into me. He fell off his bike. All over and around us were the broken contents of his delivery – flour, eggs, tea leaves, *mealie* meal, and cooking-oil – which were flung out on impact.

"Shoo!" I said, dusting flour and raw egg from my face. I sat up. Goodwin staggered towards me, his hands grazed and his trousers torn. With his newly-acquired white complexion, he apologised, *"Iss memmy oh righ*? Are you alright?" in his best English. To his utter relief, I stood up. But then his face changed...

He recognised me... I was one of the *D M Brown's*... Fear gripped him... Goodwin rattled on. He would lose his job! He had a family to feed! Look at the broken bicycle!

"No, no, Goodwin," I urged, "It was all ***my*** fault."

By now a few anxious bystanders had gathered around us as I searched the faces for my sisters. Oh, dear me! Things were going from bad to worse. In my shocked confusion I had to get home with my sisters. Goodwin and I must have looked a sorry sight because an elderly lady, Mrs Wilmot, took one look at us and burst out laughing. I accepted her kind offer to walk us home. Before leaving I held out my hand to Goodwin, saying, "*Ndiyagoduka ngoku*, I am going home now," as a token of apology, friendship and re-assurance.

I looked back where Goodwin was tidying up the mess and salvaging what he could before he pushed his bike back to the store. It seemed a long walk home. My poor sisters had measles. I had grazes and bruises. What would my mother say?

Mrs Wilmot telephoned my mother and told her the story in detail and ended, "Don't be too hard on Denyse, Peggy."

When Goodwin reached the store, the news was out. He was pleasantly surprised to learn he would not lose his job neither would he pay for the bicycle repairs or the damaged groceries. Instead my mother said, "What size are your trousers? I'll buy you a new pair, Goodwin and I'll arrange to have the bike repaired. Are you sure you're not hurt?"

My mother returned from work. The back door closed. Her footsteps came closer. I dreaded this moment. I was to blame. "Well, well, well," she said, looking at us, "What happened this afternoon?"

My mother answered her question. "So, Topsy and Margy, you were sent home from ballet with *measles.*" Turning to me, "Neyse, you could've been seriously injured had it not been *just* a bicycle that hit you!"

There, it was all out. Mom knew both stories. I stood motionless and silent before I ran into my mother's arms. "I'm sorry mom," I sobbed.

5

ONE NIGHT OF HORROR

In 1955 the government changed the composition of the Senate by increasing its size and House of Assembly in order to gain the two-thirds majority required by the 1910 constitution. On 6 June at the Congress of the People the Freedom Charter –based on the principles of human rights and non-racism –was signed. In 1957 South Africa's first computer is installed.

ONCE we were over measles, my sisters and I climbed through the fence, satchels strapped to our backs, on our way to school. We came home the same way and Beauty stayed with us until mom came back from work. Most evenings my mother rushed off to the Royal Hotel, where she played the piano accordion in a small band, with Dorothy Rose on piano and Jack Sutherland on drums. This job, 'Happy Hour,' between 7 and 8 pm, supplemented her income. Beauty stayed on until she returned.

When we lived at Coulter Street, mom took me to Durban for my eye check-ups every two months. When granny joined us, I accompanied her to have her corns treated or her hair done. We stayed in *the* Royal Hotel. After dinner, dressed in my Sunday best, we walked to the Playhouse Theatre. I marvelled at the ceiling, which looked like a myriad of tiny twinkling stars shining down on me and also the red velvet curtains, which swished open automatically revealing the cinema screen.

On one visit I was sad when mom told me I would not be accompanying her to the cinema. It was very lonely and scary to be left in the hotel bedroom alone at night. A few years later, I discovered my mother had met up with Jack, the drummer from the band. *What was wrong with me that I could not join them?*

Awake and trying to be brave, I heard a loud knock on the door. My heart raced. Who could this be? Mom would not knock. She had a key. It must be the hotel staff. I leapt out of bed and opened the door… But, I was wrong!

Unable to utter a word, I stared up at a face I knew so well. Standing, looking down at me was my father. "Daddy," is all I managed to say. I wanted so much to hug him, but held back, never guessing he was not only drunk, but very angry, too.

"Denyse, I want you to give your mother a message from me. Remind her of this date, 22 December. Do you think you can do that?" he said trying not to slur his words.

"Y…y… yes," I stuttered, "I'll remember." With that he turned, and was gone…

The following day we packed our bags. After breakfast the porter took our suitcases to the car. Another long but very familiar journey home lay ahead of us. From Durban the road climbed from sea-level, through twists and turns, which took us through Pinetown and Westville to a shortcut by-passing Pietermaritzburg. We drove through the Valley of a Thousand Hills before the road snaked precariously through the cuttings over the steep mountain. At the peak the road widened slightly making a sharp hairpin bend, where a small brick wall separated the road from a sheer drop to the river valley below. I dreaded this treacherous Umkomaas pass and welcomed a toilet stop at the next town, Ixopo.

This was the halfway mark from where the terrain transformed into rolling countryside. A one-way bridge across the Umzimkulu River separated Natal from East Griqualand, giving access to Umzimkulu, a farming village.

On our homeward journey I sensed something had upset my mother, but try as I did, her mood remained sombre. Without warning I blurted out, verbatim, the message from the night before, "Daddy visited me when you were out last night and he asked me to give you a message. *'Remind her of this date, 22 December.'*" I was glad I had remembered… Mom never replied. Holding the steering wheel more tightly she focused on the road. To make sure she had heard me, I questioned, "What's happening on the 22 December?"

"Never you mind, Neyse," was her way of dismissing the subject.

It was good to be home. My sisters were delighted to receive the pink and white rock candy in a paper bag, which I bought them.

"Tell us about your candyfloss," Margy begged. "What happens when you bite it?"

Margy asked me the same question every time I returned from a trip to Durban and each time I explained as best I could. To every answer, she would hammer me with a never-ending string of one-syllable questions, "Why?" Topsy, on the other hand, was more interested in opening her bag of candy and getting her teeth into it.

***

Dating my schoolwork in December triggered off what my dad had said to me in Durban. What did he mean? Remember 22 December… mom was unperturbed, or so she pretended. I dismissed my concern. Six glorious weeks of holidays with Christmas cards and carols made me happy. Long hot summer days stretched out ahead. Sandals, sunshine and swimming! After scary lightning storms the sun shone brightly and scented flowers lifted their heads in gratification. My excitement mounted. "How many more sleeps?" I asked.

On the 22 December, mom kissed us goodnight before dashing off to 'Happy Hour,' saying, "Only two more sleeps."

Beauty waited in the kitchen. We went to sleep. Soon after my mother's departure, a loud knock on the front door woke me. I was in charge. I instructed my sisters to stay in bed and called Beauty. We walked to the front door… She cautioned me, carefully peering through a slit in the parted curtains. She shut them quickly, saying, "It's a man."

The banging on the door sounded like drumbeats, so loud and urgent.

"Stay with me Beauty, while I see who it is."

Before opening, I called out, "Who is it?"

There was no reply… Plucking up all the courage I could muster I turned the key. I opened the door. Daddy? My fears floated away. Beauty's fear increased because she had detected danger. This time there was no hug or smile as we faced each other, but instead, "Where is she?" my father frantically shouted at me. Not too sure what to say I remained silent. This angered him. He turned and locked the door behind him before yelling at me, "Where's your mother?"

"Mommy's at the Royal Hotel."

Why do I feel alone? Where was Beauty? Fearing for her life, she tiptoed stealthily from the room when my father's back was turned.

Suspicious silence kept me in suspense in the following seconds, like something sinister was about to happen. The sound of my sisters sobbing released more anger in my father.

"Tell them to shut up," he shouted so loudly that I think even the walls of the house trembled. I dashed off to comfort my sisters, who had crept into one bed.

"Nothing will happen if you're quiet."

Neither of my sisters knew daddy. To them there was a strange man in the house threatening us. When their crying stopped, I returned to the lounge. Where is he? I had an idea – telephone mom. I know the number. His footsteps came from the kitchen. With no time to lose I turned the telephone handle and picked up the receiver. To my horror the telephone wires had been cut. *Just* in time I put the receiver back and moved away.

My father entered the room. He came towards me. I backed away from him, my heart thumping so loud I thought he could hear the *doof... doof... doof* and see my hands trembling and my knees knocking. Never in my life have I felt so frightened. He was in front of me, staring at me. In a more controlled voice, he asked, "When will your mother come home?" I glanced at the wall clock. It was 7.45 pm. "At 8 pm."

"Be a good girl. Go back to bed with your sisters," he urged. A horrid smell went up my nostrils when he breathed on me.

"Yes daddy."

I turned and ran. I climbed into bed with my sisters. They clung to each other. Then, without warning, the back door slammed. Silence. No footsteps. I heard the clock ticking. Every shadow threatened me as I scanned the room, searching for any signs of danger in the darkness. I hoped mom would come home soon. Did I do the right thing by opening the door to my father? My teeth chattered. My knees shook like clanging cymbals. 'Oh, please God help us' I prayed in my head. Next, the back door opened... mom was home...

Pandemonium broke out in the kitchen with shouting and banging. My mother's blood-curdling yell filled the whole house and sent shivers down my spine. Her awful scream echoed in my head when I heard a loud thud. Something fell on the wooden floor.

Frozen with fear, I could hardly breathe. Stampeding footsteps came down the passage towards me.

My father switched on the light. His hands and white shirt were covered in blood. "Where's she?"

"I don't know."

"*You* know where she is. You'd better tell me where she's hiding. Where's the key to this room?" he bellowed, pointing to the small room outside our bedroom.

With my father following, I fetched the key, which was hidden in the piano stool. I unlocked mom's private room, which was locked to safe-guard her cocktail dresses, piano accordion, sheets of music and important shop papers. I hoped my mother was *not* hiding in there. I did not want to betray her. My father pushed past me and rummaged in the room, sending her expensive dresses flying off coat-hangers and sheets of music fluttering into the air and onto the floor. I ran back to my petrified sisters...

"You can't escape now. I've got you..."

His blind rage intensified when he *still* could not find my mother. *This* was not my daddy... Where was my mother hiding? My father continued his search rushing from room to room. When there was another knock on the front door, he disconnected the electricity mains, before opening the door. The entire house plunged into utter darkness! When would this nightmare end?

Was somebody coming to rescue us? A further rumpus erupted outside. My body and mind were numb. We clung to each other in a huddle, too frightened to cry. This is how my mother's sister, Aunt Molly, found us. "You're coming home with me tonight," she said putting her protective arms around us. I remember nothing more of that evening, except that was our last night at Coulter Street.

The next day my grandmother told me what had happened. My father had attacked mom in the kitchen, lashing out at her face, breaking her nose and breaking her jaw in three places. Blood gushed from her face. My mother screamed as my father, brandishing a carving knife, came for her. Somehow she managed to trip my father with a stool. He dropped the knife when he fell to the floor. In that instant, she escaped through the back door, running for her life. My mother took *our* shortcut through the fence to the convent, where she rang the doorbell and collapsed. Because it was late, the nuns were reluctant to open the door. Was this another tramp or drunk?

"There's a white woman lying in a pool of blood at the door," Sister Mary Bernadette announced. She bent down to check if the woman was still alive. "It's Peggy, *Eileen Brown's* daughter. Call the doctor and an ambulance. Fetch a blanket...Telephone Joan and Slabs!" she screamed. Sister Mary Bernadette stayed with my mother and recited prayer after prayer for her. She covered my mom's shivering body with warm blankets.

By the time my grandmother received the telephone call from the nuns, my mother had been rushed to the hospital. Gran telephoned her daughter, Molly. With Uncle Stewey driving, they hurried to rescue us at Coulter Street. On their arrival, my dad gave Uncle Stewey a black eye; he pushed granny down the stairs, before the police took him away.

On 24 December, Aunt Molly took us to see mom. I was shocked to see the figure in the hospital bed, hardly recognising my mother. Her whole face was bandaged up, with only slits revealing her sad eyes. There were drips on each side of her bed. The doctor operating on my mom, wired her jaw, re-set her nose and stitched up her gashes. The tears ran down my cheeks like a river in flood. mom reached out and squeezed my hand. She could not talk. She longed to know we were alright. I was not prepared for what I saw neither will I ever forget that moment.

This was the saddest Christmas day. We moved back to 107 Hawthorn Street, where granny, Uncle Slabs and Aunt Joan cared for us. Granny took us to visit mom after Mass. We picked a few flowers for her. We could not see if she was happy. We could not kiss her. We could not cuddle her. My mother lay there, her eyes moving from child to child.

"When are you coming home?" Margy asked, repeatedly. This agitated my gran, who answered with a big sigh, "It'll take time for mommy to be well enough to come home, Margy." It was time to leave and we followed granny out of the ward.

Life seemed *so* unfair. My cousins had a daddy and a mommy on Christmas Day. This Christmas I didn't *even* have a mommy. I tried hard to be a mother to my sisters. To make me feel worse, Neville innocently said, "Your father beat your mother..." Little did I know then, this would be the last time I would ever see my father. I would have to wait a long time, before the full story of this tragedy unfolded, revealing the full significance of 22 December 1955...

6

KILDARE

In 1956 the government arrested 156 activists, including all the senior ANC leaders and white radicals, and charged them with high treason 'for the overthrow of the State by revolutionary methods'.

THE farming village of Kokstad, was a self-contained town where everybody knew everybody else and what was not known was published in the local press, '*The Kokstad Advertiser*'. Businesses of note included, among others, EG Meat Supplies, *Moir's* Stationers, *Thorn's* Jewellers, Daddy Bros & *Johnstone, Mundell's* Bakery, the Royal and Balmoral Hotels, Elliot & Walker Attorneys and *Rolyat's,* the Greek corner shop. In the early hours of the morning a night cart pumped sewerage from manholes in the road making a horrid stench.

Today, the twin-steeples of St Patrick's Cathedral are a well-known landmark. Tennis, bowls, croquet, golf, polo, swimming, hockey, cricket and rugby were popular among sports enthusiasts in my day. The town was named after Adam Kok, a Griqua chief. He left Griqualand West and travelled east to this new land, which became known as the 'District of East Griqualand' for many years.

After vacating Coulter Street, we lived at 107 Hawthorn Street where my mother revealed her secret, saying, "Granny and I've bought a plot of land. An architect is drawing up plans." She took us to the corner of Hope Street and the Avenue, a sloping plot. Pointing at the weeds and rocks my mother said, "The house will be on three levels with a spectacular view of Mount Currie. It's north-facing so the house will be bright and sunny."

"How many bedrooms?" I asked.

"Four. Granny's coming to live with us."

We watched the building progress each week. The house looked small when the walls went up. Halfway through the build there was a water seepage problem. Mom agreed to pay the extra to waterproof a south-facing embankment.

The day we moved in I remember running up the stairs and down the long passage to the bedrooms, shouting, "Whoopee! Whoopee!" I surveyed the bedroom which I would share with Topsy. I had never slept in a double-storey house. Looking through the window the ground seemed a long way down. Gazing over the treetops, I watched the fluffy clouds cast shadows over Mount Currie, drifting across the blue sky. Our home became affectionately known as *Kildare* in 123 Hope Street, with an indoor toilet and shower in the bathroom. An *Esse* stove beamed out heat like a steam train warming the whole house. In the dining room we enjoyed granny's cooking of *frikkadels* and pumpkin fritters, my favourites.

Every day granny left through the turn-style gate on her way to morning Mass or rosary and benediction in the evening. She played bridge in the dining room and on these days, the smells of banana bread, scones, biscuits or *melktert* from the kitchen made my mouth water. We were forbidden to disturb this game played behind closed doors.

My mother worked at *D M Brown's* and she continued to play the piano for *'Happy Hour'* at the Royal Hotel. She also played the piano or piano accordion at weddings in Kokstad, Franklin, Cedarville, Matatiele and Swartberg to swell the coffers. We lived in our new home. We learnt new rules. We loved every minute, but would this last?

On one particular evening with both mom and granny out, Elsie, our maid, looked after us. The graze on my knee, I decided, needed a dab of *Gentian Violet* which was kept in the bathroom cabinet. Being the eldest, I took advantage and sometimes bossed my younger sisters. I switched on the light.

"What's wrong?" Topsy asked. Soon Margy tiptoed into the room. My knee was on display. My face expressed feigned pain as my pleading began, "My knee hurts. Look! *Gentian Violet* that's what I need." Topsy was unsympathetic, but I had won Margy over. "You'll find it in the cupboard above the hand basin."

Off she went. I waited. Breaking glass shattered the silence. Margy screamed. When I reached the bathroom Margy was standing stock still in the white bath, covered in splashes of violet with broken glass near her feet. "Elsie! Elsie! Come!" I yelled.

"Yo! Yo! Yo!" Elsie exclaimed. Picking Margy up and putting her down on the bathroom floor, she removed the broken glass before she scrubbed the bath and tiles with *Vim*. Satisfied, she started on Margy's legs and feet using *Vim*. Margy's skin was red and she begged, "Stop! You're hurting me."

"Your mommy *velly* closs!" Elsie warned in her broken English.

Elsie was right. Mom would be furious. I was worried. I woke early on Saturday morning and crept into the bathroom hoping for a miracle, but the once new white bath was still splotched with purple stains.

My mother broke the uncomfortable silence at breakfast, "What happened last night?"

When we did not reply, granny said, "Have all three of you lost your tongues?"

"Mmmmm...Mom...my," Topsy muttered.

"It was *all* my fault. I'm very sorry. I promise I'll scrub it clean," I butted in.

"What *happened*?" mom snapped.

"I asked Margy to fetch the *Gentian Violet* from the bathroom and she dropped the bottle in the bath. It broke and splashed everywhere. It was an acci...."

"Do you mean you sent your little sister? You know you're not allowed to touch anything in the medicine cabinet."

I knew. I had broken a house rule. I had ruined the expensive new bathroom.

"Yes, I know mommy, but..."

"No buts... It was *your* fault, Denyse. Margy could've cut herself badly."

How I wished I had just gone to sleep the night before. Should I have fetched the *Gentian Violet* myself? It was too late for deliberation. My bottom lip quivered.

"Topsy and Margy you may play in the garden."

They ran like cheetahs hunting prey. I looked at granny and mom expecting the worst. My mother addressed me in her serious voice,

"Denyse you disobeyed us. Margy's guardian angel protected her last night. Because you owned up, you will *not* be punished."

"By the way, the stains will eventually wash off," granny added.

I apologised but I would soon forget this lesson on obedience.

***

My mother wore beautiful cocktail dresses to play in the band. We sat on her bed watching her dress. She stepped into a strapless powder-blue dress with a taffeta petticoat, which gave fullness to her calf-length skirt. She handed Topsy the powder puff, saying, "Just a little." Topsy dusted my mother's back with a smattering of talcum powder. She slipped her stockinged feet into silver high-heels; secured a string of pearls around her neck and dabbed perfume behind her ears and on her inner wrists. Mom applied red lipstick, pressing her lips between a tissue afterwards. She looked beautiful. Checking her reflection in the mirror, mom spun round, kissed us lightly and said, "Good night children. God bless."

She exited elegantly. We were safe. Gran was with us.

We emulated these observations. *'Dressing-up'* on Thursday afternoons when gran played bridge at her friend's house, became our favourite game. Topsy and I squabbled over the powder-blue dress. She won. Margy tinier, wore evening blouses only. Adorned in mom's evening wear, necklaces and high heels, we paraded in single file up and down the long passage. Wearing over-sized high-heel shoes, we clip-clopped clumsily on the parquet floors. Very awkwardly we kept up this imaginary grandeur. When the game was over, *everything* was packed away exactly as we had found it.

One afternoon we strolled *outside* playing *'dressing-up'*. Negotiating the stairs without falling, with dresses dragging in the dirt, we paraded down the driveway into Hope Street. This was far too adventurous. Unbeknown to us *then*, Mrs Rose, my mother's friend, walked by. She could hardly believe her eyes. When granny came home we were the three well-behaved little girls she had left behind. Then mom returned from work. Mrs Rose had spilt the beans. "Show me which cocktail dress you wore today, girls!"

My face turned blood red. How *did* my mother know? She stepped closer. "Right I'll do the talking for you..." She emphasised our misdeeds saying, "You wore *my expensive* clothes, dragged them in the *dirt* traipsing about in Hope Street this afternoon."

My eyes grew bigger. My mother knew about our secret *'dressing-up'* game. Putting more guilt on me she said, "I worked *very* hard to buy those expensive clothes which I need when I play in the band. This is to earn extra money to make a better life for us. Now you're ruining my best clothes?"

It was meant to be a game. Things looked different through the eyes of an adult. We felt awful. "I'll give you some old clothes and shoes you can dress up in."

My mother examined the state of her dresses and scuffed shoes. Her face showed how disappointed she was. We apologised but after this *'dressing-up'* lost its appeal and the box of old clothes and shoes remained untouched.

***

Blood-curdling screams woke my mother in the middle of the night. The pains in my stomach were excruciating. Delirious and sweating, my mother carried me to her bed. Granny in her nightdress and hairnet bent over me saying, "Peggy, we must get her temperature down." Returning with a bowl of cold water and a flannel, my mother swabbed my forehead, arms and legs. Granny held my hand in hers. Her lips moved in prayer.

"Get into the bed with me, mommy."

My mother sat closer.

"Granny, come into my bed."

My grandmother stood closer. I hallucinated: A man stood over me, counting. He warned me, "When I reach one hundred, you will *die* Denyse." I did not want to die. Frightened, I remembered how bad I had been. What would happen when I was dead? Where would I go? I wanted my mother and grandmother to come with me when I died. I clung to them more tightly, hardly breathing…

"96… 97… 98… 9…"

I screamed with all my might, "No...oo!"

The counting stopped. I was alive. Exhausted, I slept.

After my examination, the doctor performed an emergency appendectomy on me. Nurses fussed over me during my ten-day stay in hospital. My revolting appendix floating in a bottle of clear liquid, my trophy, was shown to visitors. On the seventh day a nursing sister removed the bandages and left the room to fetch a tray of sterile instruments. I lifted my head and peered at the yellow-striped worm on my tummy. I flicked it. That hurt.

"What are you doing, Denyse?" the returning nursing sister asked. She explained, "The worm's your wound, painted with iodine and pinched at intervals with black clips."

I gritted my teeth and she gently removed the clips. She covered my wound with a fresh dressing and told me, "Your stitches will come out next."

True to her word, the stitches were removed and with my bandaged stomach, I went home. A week later we holidayed in a boarding house at Southbroom on the Natal coast, surrounded by sugar-cane fields. I remember evenings of bingo, table tennis and cards. After our holiday, my tummy had healed. Once again I could skip, jump and play sport.

***

Films were screened at the Kokstad Town Hall on Wednesday and Saturday evenings at 8 pm. We called this bioscope. Saturday matinees started at 2 pm. As a special treat my sisters and I attended a matinee. In our Sunday best, clutching the money, we joined the queue. With jostling and pushing, we snaked our way to the ticket office.

"Next!"

"Three tickets, please."

"That'll be three shillings."

Pushing the coins under the grid, I retrieved three tickets. At the entrance the usher took our tickets and showed us to our seats. Margy sat on one side of me and Topsy on the other. The lights dimmed. The velvet curtains parted. *Metro-Goldwyn-Mayer* announced the trailers. *The Wizard of Oz* began.

At the interval the lights came on. I could not stand. My legs were dead. Topsy took charge. Holding Margy's hand, they went out to buy sweets. I looked around. A few elderly people were seated. I tried to stand up, but my legs were numb. Not wanting to spoil our treat, I hoped my legs had gone to sleep and would recover during the main film. When the film ended, patrons stood up to go home. I could not stand. To avoid drawing attention to myself, I said, "Let's wait for everybody to leave."

"Everybody's gone now, Neyse," Topsy chirped.

"Okay, let's go!"

How would I get home? My legs refused to work! Using my arms, I heaved and dragged myself from chair to chair. Difficult. No more chairs... What was I to do now?

Putting my arms over Topsy and Margy's shoulders, they supported me to the fence outside. I dragged myself using the fence. My hands hurt. It would be dark before we reached *Kildare*. Mrs Wilmot peeped through her net curtains. She realised something was wrong. Still in her pinafore and slippers, she called, "What's up? Did you fall?"

"No. I can't walk."

"Wait. I'm coming."

She crossed the road and carried me into her lounge where she put me down on a chair. Topsy and Margy, on either side of me, looked worried. Mrs Wilmot was on the phone, "It's Denyse... She can't walk... Yes..."

Old enough to be my grandmother, she was concerned. "Do your legs hurt?"

"A little. They're dead. I can't move them." She covered me with a rug. Uncle Slabs and Aunty Joan arrived and took us to 107 Hawthorn Street, where Doctor Bosman asked, "Can you touch your chest with your chin?"

My uncle and aunt told my mother the story when she arrived to take us home. I remained in bed for two weeks. Twice a day granny massaged my legs. Two hot water-bottles kept my legs warm. Slowly I regained the feeling in my legs. Afterwards my mother said, "You've had a mild attack of polio. You're lucky to have pulled through, Neyse."

Polio, you woke up and you had it. It was a plague entering the Central Nervous System of the body through the bloodstream causing limbs to become crooked or de-formed. Breathing became impossible. In severe cases the polio victims were put into an iron lung, a breathing coffin, but many died. Granny and the nuns prayed for my recovery. Sadly several boarders at the convent died suddenly from polio.

Soon after this, Diana my cousin was struck more severely by polio, joining hundreds of polio victims in a special school in Natal. Although she received specialised treatment and everything possible was done to help her, Diana never regained the full use of her left arm and hand completely. Her handicap did not prevent her from playing tennis and living a normal life overshadowing her deformity. I am grateful to Mrs Wilmot, who helped me survive polio. Another dilemma was about to challenge me yet again…

***

Mom and granny played tennis at the Kokstad Tennis Club and we accompanied them on condition we were seen and not heard. I hit a tennis ball against the practice wall as Topsy and Margy played with their dolls in the shade. They helped me to find my ball when it bounced into the long kikuyu grass. My mother met Major Philip Hughen Leary at the club.

"This is Uncle Phil,' my mother introduced us to this handsome divorcee. Both his moustache and his English accent intrigued me, but I shied away from his twenty-year old son, Anthony Hughen Leary. Tony, as he was known, studied at Cedara Agricultural College in Natal to take over the dairy and sheep farm, *Strathneva*, from his dad when he retired.

Because my mother's previous romances with Van, divorced with two children, Vanessa and William; and with bachelor Lionel, a musician, younger than my mother, had fizzled out, I was sure this would too, but I was wrong…

My mother blossomed like a spring flower. She disclosed her plans. My sisters were thrilled. I listened in disbelief. Her words repeated in my head: "Divorce… Granny's written to the Pope… Divorce… Marry Uncle Phil!"

The word 'divorce' made my stomach curl. I reasoned. Would my *own* father no longer be my father? Why write to the Pope? The Catholic Church forbad divorce? Society frowned upon divorce. My friends deserted me. Worried thoughts pounded my brain. I released my fears, screaming for the *whole* of Kokstad to hear, "I hate *him!* I hate *you!* No, mommy, no...oo...oo!"

"Stop that at once, Denyse!" had no effect. Hitting me where it hurt most, my mother tossed her trump card at me, "You have your *father's* temper. If you're not careful, it'll be your ruin!" Slamming the door in her face gave me some satisfaction. My sisters had temper tantrums, but she never threw hurtful words at *them*. Why is it always *me*?

I became an introvert carrying this heavy burden alone. My concentration crumbled and my school marks plummeted. The whole school knew of my mother's pending divorce. Friends pitied me. Anger boiled up inside me. I blamed my mother for my unhappiness and worried she was a sinner. The Catholic Church would excommunicate her. *My* whole world seemed upside down. Things were to get even worse...

On 25 March 1957, five days after my twelfth birthday, my parents were divorced in the Supreme Court, Durban. My mother was given custody of her three daughters. Her fourteen-year-old marriage of 19 July 1943 was dissolved.

The leaves dropped from the trees. The days shortened. It grew colder. I became increasingly withdrawn. My mother said, "We've been invited to holiday in Jack and Dorothy Miller's cottage in Port Edward." The news lifted my spirits, but the next turn of events saddened me more than ever.

We arrived and explored the cottage and garden. We spent the first two days on the beach. On the third day mom's friends, Archie and Daphne Gerardy and their two children, Desiree and Gavin, joined us. I still did not smell a rat. On returning to the cottage a strange car was parked in the driveway.

"Hello Peggy. Hello girls," Uncle Phil greeted us.

When my mother kissed and hugged him I withdrew. The adults went into the lounge for drinks and the children scampered outside. Desiree, a year my senior, befriended me saying, "You must be glad because your mom's marrying Uncle Phil tomorrow."

"What? When?"

"Tomorrow. At the Magistrate's Office in Port Shepstone."

I could not sleep that night. The following day 9 July 1957, my mother was elegantly dressed in a suit, hat and gloves and Uncle Phil wore his suit. Jack and Dorothy Miller, Archie and Daphne Gerardy accompanied them. The six adults drove off in two cars. Two hours later they returned. We were officially told, "A toast to Major and Mrs Leary!" Glasses were raised and clinked in the air amidst smiling faces.

"Children, Uncle Phil's your stepfather. He'd like you to call him Pop," my mother said beaming at him. "Pop! Pop!" Topsy and Margy chorused, hugging him. I watched, aching with pain and shame. It was another night of crying silent tears into my pillow, until I fell asleep. This event was about to usher in *more* pain.

***

After holidaying in Port Edward, we never returned to *Kildare,* but drove to the farm, *Strathneva*, which was to be our new home. It was twenty miles from Kokstad.

I slept alone in a small bedroom at the end of the passage. Margy and Topsy shared the bedroom next to mine. Once the electricity-providing generator was turned off at night, the house was dark and quiet. After supper we sat in front of a log-fire in the lounge, reading books, before being sent to bed. Meal-times were different. A maid, Annie, responded to a bell which my mother rang. Annie removed the dirty crockery to the kitchen and returned, carrying the next course on a large tray. During the day we played in the garden, but this did not feel like home.

My mother had booked us into the convent in Pietermaritzburg, which meant being away from home for six months. I helped her sew the specially-printed nametags onto our new school clothes, an endless task. Before long our suitcases were loaded into the boot and the three-hour journey to Pietermaritzburg began.

Margy sat between Topsy and me in the back. My stepfather, wearing his hat, drove his maroon *Ford Zephyr* with my mother in the passenger seat. I peered out the window. The dust spun into the air and left a brown trail behind the car. We bumped along the rough farm road, splashing through the cause-way and passing the farm labourers' thatched huts. After leaving Kokstad we crossed the railway-line and headed towards Umzimkulu. My sisters sniffled. Would I cope with new subjects halfway through Standard Five? Would I make friends? Would Margy cope separated from mom?

We drove through Ixopo amidst rolling green mountains and valleys where Alan Paton's novel, '*Cry the beloved county*' was set. Then we drove through Richmond before we reached Pietermaritzburg sunk in a valley. Tension mounted.

"Let's stop for a milkshake or ice-cream, Phil," my mother suggested.

"Good idea Peggy."

Feeling nervous and uncomfortable in my strange uniform, I gulped down my milkshake. Nobody spoke on the last lap to the convent. Mother Superior had been expecting the Lloyd girls from Kokstad. We completed the necessary preliminaries. Sister Magdalene showed us round. It was time to say goodbye. Margy held on to mom's skirts. We all cried. My stepfather took control, "Come on Peggy. It's time for us to leave."

After wrenching Margy from her skirts, mom climbed into the car. We clung together like three lost sheep, waving feverishly. The car disappeared. Now I had to find our way back to the dormitory.

The following days were a nightmare. Topsy and Margy were homesick. I felt hopeless as I did my best to mend their broken spirits. It was difficult to make new friends and more difficult to know where to go and what to do. I had never taken Mathematics or English History and so I dreaded writing a *College of Careers* examination in November. The examiner, unaware of my personal problems, would not be lenient. My academic pendulum swung from topmost achiever to lowest loser. Spare moments were spent consoling my sisters. I had no time to catch up with my studies. If only my mother knew what was happening to us.

After three weeks we were each assigned to different families for an outing weekend.

I climbed trees, rode a bicycle, went to bioscope, but worried about my sisters. How relieved I was to be re-united with them again.

Swimming brought some relief. With *cozzies* wrapped in towels, we boarded a school bus to the Municipal Pool. This was the biggest pool I had ever seen. In contrast to the convent pool, the water sparkled and smelt of chlorine. A swimming instructor coached us.

Our ten-day Michaelmas holidays were spent with families who were willing to take us in. I do not know where my sisters were, but I joined Myrtle. She wore glasses. We had little in common. I played outdoors even when there was a *monkey's wedding*. She cooked and baked indoors with her mother. This made me forlorn.

The nuns advised my mother we were homesick. She arranged for an aunt and uncle to take us out for a day. They arrived in an old-fashioned car with a *dickey*.

"Hop in," my uncle held my hand. Embarrassed I hoped nobody saw me climbing up. Margy was squashed between Topsy and me. Clutching our panama hats, we drove off. With the wind in our faces and our hair blowing about, we felt exhilarated. We laughed for the first time in weeks! They promised to take us out again and they did.

In November the dreaded external examinations began. I could only do my best. My sisters cheered up when I said, "Only four days left." They jumped about excitedly when I said, "We're going home today!"

"I'll see mommy," Margy said.

"Hooray, home, home, home!" Topsy shrieked.

Before leaving I gave my class teacher a stamped postcard, addressed to my mother: *Mrs P E Leary, P O Box 155, Kokstad*. This would be forwarded with 'Passed' or 'Failed' written on the postcard when the examination results were known...

7

STRATHNEVA

In 1958 Hans Strijdom died. Hendrik Verwoerd, a Dutch-born ideological fanatic, became prime minister ambitious to put apartheid on a scale as never previously envisaged. Hendrik Verwoerd removed representatives of black Africans from both Houses of Parliament and the Cape provincial council.

HOW good it was to be going home but odd to pass our former home, *Kildare*, on the way to the farm, *Strathneva*. The rambling old farmhouse had gauze doors which I learnt kept the flies out. The house was filled with heavy old-fashioned furniture. Numerous book-shelves bulged with books. Mom's piano was in the lounge. With our personal possessions around I felt happier.

Pop kept a *sjambok* in a *rondavel*, his office, at the far end of the garden. He gave us our own toy room, a *rondavel* in the garden which looked like a park. A variety of vegetables grew in raised beds in the vegetable garden alongside a huge strawberry patch and an orchard laden with ripening fruit. We explored *Strathneva* learning about the twenty dams, irrigation schemes, jackal-proof fencing and milking sheds. The NCD (Natal Co-operative Dairies) truck collected the milk cans daily. The cheese made there is still in demand nationwide.

We experienced farming activities. I watched the sheep being shorn when the thick dirty wool peeled off to the sound of clicking shears, leaving the sheep looking thinner and whiter. The wool was baled in barns. After jumping on the wool in these bales which oiled my legs with lanoline, I bathed to remove the ticks.

Packs of specially-trained dogs were hired for a fortnight during the annual jackal hunt. The dog handlers culled the jackal which killed the sheep. The livestock were dipped regularly. Sheep and cattle were driven into pens then filed down a narrow fenced-in path into the dipping-tank. The animals swam across, scrambled up a ramp and were herded in a holding camp.

Seasonal guinea-fowl shoots were sociable events. Our red Irish setters, excellent hunting dogs, were trained to retrieve the birds. During the afternoon shoot, each farmer was allowed to shoot three birds. At sunset the adults assembled inside for drinks and a hearty meal, sharing their experiences. Our three guinea-fowl hung upside down in the pantry with blood dripping into an enamel basin beneath. A gruesome sight!

Lambing season was a busy time when I fed lambs and calves with a bottle of milk. They sucked and slobbered greedily. Milking was done in the mornings and evenings by hand. A large steel gong, strung on a willow tree outside the kitchen, was struck to summon the black workers to the milking sheds. My attempt to milk a cow failed. The black labourers made it look so easy, as they sat on low stools, rhythmically pulling the cow's udders. Soon the bucket was filled with frothy warm milk.

My mother learnt to trout fish in the river. On these relaxing family afternoons the adults fished and we paddled. The hooked trout, splashing and struggling to escape, eventually gave up and floated on the water. The fish was scooped into the net and landed on the grassy river bank. We soon forgot the trout's demise when we tucked into a delicious supper that evening.

My mother had incubators and the day-old chicks were kept warm in cardboard boxes in front of the *Esse* stove. We helped my mother smear fat over eggs to preserve them. We drank *maas* made in a *calabash* on the sideboard and ate warm *mealie* bread with melted butter and *Lyle's* golden syrup.

One day I became a photographer at my first *Xhosa* wedding using my *Box Brownie* camera. "Where's Denyse?" Pop enquired.

"At a wedding at the huts. She'll be fine," my mother answered.

Being the *only* white person amongst black people I had been warned not to drink their home-made beer. Young and old, men and women, mingled happily. Mothers strapped babies on their backs. Women scooped beer from a large drum. Taking a swig of beer, the tin can was passed around, men first. A spit-roast sheep was suspended over open coals. Green flies hummed and buzzed. Scantily-clad, bare-footed children flicked flies off their faces.

The sun beat down on this windless day. Two wooden chairs looked out of place in the dust outside one hut. The smiling bridal couple in Western wedding attire emerged from the open doorway to the sound of clapping hands. I stepped forward with my camera as the wedding party squashed closer to me. Inquisitive faces wanted to be photographed or to see the peculiar object I operated.

Drumbeats introduced dancing. Children, even naked toddlers, danced with natural African rhythm. The tangible excitement was enhanced by harmonious song. Some women stirred beer in drums; others turned the meat or chased off uninvited chickens. I do not remember the wedding ceremony. I slipped away unnoticed when the merriment picked up momentum and the beer flowed freely. I was proud to see my snapshots a week later when they were developed at *Dyson's* chemist.

My stepfather built two tall silos to store silage over winter. Climbing to the top of the steel-rung ladder, I leapt into space. With screams echoing in the cylindrical concrete silos, I gravitated twenty feet to the bottom, where I lay laughing on soft damp fodder. Eventually this game sapped all my energy. I was horrified to learn in later years, that poisonous snakes inhabited the silage.

Summer on the farm reminded me of the movie, *'Out of Africa.'* The days were hot and dusty. A permanent heat haze hung over the hills. We cooled off in the top dam, which was a short walk from the farmhouse. Welding two halves of a drum together, putting rowlocks on the sides and inserting sturdy planks for seats, my stepfather created a boat. Clad in a bathing costume and barefoot, I carried the oars. We spent summer evenings at the dam. Rowing the boat with my sisters aboard, we explored the dam amidst lurking dangers.

At the far end of the dam was an island, home to *legavaans* (monitor lizard: *Varanus Abigularis*). Some were bigger than others. They dozed in the sun on the banks of the dam seemingly asleep. A sudden splash alerted me to imminent danger when a legavaan lunged into the water. Avoiding danger, I distanced the boat from this predator. Their strong tails whip back and forth unexpectedly, attacking prey. One smack from the legavaan's tail would break both my legs. With my eyes glued on the legavaans, I rowed away unobtrusively.

"There's another one in the water."

"Shush Topsy!"

My sisters were scared. I lifted the oars from the water and let the boat drift silently. Scary as this was, we met the challenge of sneaking away from these seemingly-innocent predators unscathed.

My stepfather built a diving-board on the bank of the dam. We were warned *not* to dive too deep because of the thick reeds and mud at the bottom. We jumped off this board splashing as we tried out a string of fancy jumps.

"Scissors! Soldier! Star!" we shouted jumping off the board.

My sisters cleared a patch for my feet because I hated the mud oozing between my toes. We never felt cold but as the golden sun sank slowly behind the steep slopes of the silhouetted horizon my mother called, "Time to get out!" Wrapped up in our towels we headed home, listening to the unique sounds of Africa, coming alive at dusk.

On some summer evenings the sounds of crickets competed with the conversation of the adults, who sat on raffia chairs on the red polished verandah, enjoying *sundowners*.

"Topsy and Margy will return to the convent in Kokstad," I overheard my mother say, "…and Denyse will return to Pietermaritzburg."

This was unfair. Would I *ever* pass Standard Five? Storm clouds gathered in my world once more. Waiting for the arrival of the postcard week by week was stressful. One day my mother, sorting through the post collected from the post-box in town asked, "What's this postcard about?"

I snatched it from her, turned it over and read…. The single word, 'Passed,' leapt off the page. Yelling, "I've passed!" released my pent-up tension if only by the skin of my teeth.

"No need to get so excited," my mother said, not understanding the relief I felt at that moment. I had not failed. My mood improved. I was polite to Pop. Now I had to persuade my mother to change her mind…

"Mom, could I go back to the Kokstad convent?"

"Why? *All* the girls your age go to boarding schools in Pietermaritzburg."

"But mom," I cut in.

"Be *grateful* for this opportunity."

"You don't understand. Mom, *please*. I miss *you*, Topsy and Margy."

My mother softened, replying, "I'll see what I can do."

"Thanks a lot mom."

The next day I entered a competition on *Springbok* radio. I jotted down the numerical value of the alphabet. The letter 'Y' was valued at 26, the highest. On a postcard I wrote my name 'Denyse Lloyd' with the tally of 183 alongside. I posted it off in Kokstad.

***

Never before was I so happy to be back at the Kokstad convent boarding school. Now in Standard Six, I was a senior, but a pipsqueak really. My friends were young ladies; they wore bras and teased their hair. Some shaved their legs. They were boy crazy. I examined myself, becoming self-conscious of my flat chest and bald armpits. Boys bored me. My gangly long legs, unruly curly hair and spectacled face made me an ugly duckling. Would I ever turn into a swan?

The government segregated English and Afrikaans-speaking pupils. New schools sprang up everywhere. Yvonne, my friend attended the *Afrikaans Hoërskool* and was now an arch-enemy. It was difficult to understand these changes...

A joyful distraction in February 1958 lifted our spirits. Granny flew to England to adopt an Irish baby for her daughter, Molly. Whilst overseas, the Catholic adoption agency offered her a second baby. Aunty Molly was delighted to be adopting two babies. Granny flew back to South Africa with three-month-old Ann, born on 14 March and Donnaleen, born on 10 March. She was named after my grandparents, *Dona*ld and Ei*leen*.

"A kind gentleman sitting opposite me bottle-fed and burped one baby and I fed the other," granny announced stepping off the plane with one baby on each arm. She was met by Uncle Stewey and Aunty Molly in the terminal building. We met our new Irish cousins, known as 'the twins'. They were beautiful. I held Donnaleen briefly. Baby paraphernalia dominated their house. Everybody adored them. Ann was outgoing and in contrast, Donnaleen was reserved and shy.

This pastime helped me settle into class with a short rotund German nun, Sister Dionysius, my teacher. She walked slowly and had a strange accent. It was silkworm season. Boarders were forbidden to have silkworms. The temptation was too great for me. All I needed was a shoebox. The mulberry tree behind the swimming pool was a ready food supply. My unauthorised shoebox held hundreds of minute black silkworms crawling on mulberry leaves. I stashed the box under Sister's platform, which gave her an elevated view. I visualised the slow-creeping, soft-bodied worms munching on the leaves inside the shoeboxes while she, oblivious to this, said, "Put away *ze* books and pay attenzion."

The worms grew fat quickly. I put them in two additional shoeboxes. They devoured more leaves. I allowed these cold white worms to crawl on my hands. After twenty-five to twenty-eight days they began to cocoon. These silkworms would change into pupae attached to the box by fine lustrous fibres of the cocoon. When I cleaned the boxes, my friend, Jenny, kept guard. If a nun approached, she asked: "Denyse are you in there?" One day the warning came too late…

"What have you got zere?"

"S…S…S…silk…..silkworms, Sister."

"Show me."

Lifting the lid, I stepped forward. Jenny scarpered.

"Hmm…and who do *dese* silkworms belong to?"

To escape trouble, I lied, "I'm feeding Pam's silkworms. She left them at school." Riddled with guilt my face turned scarlet. On Saturday I'd confess my lie and be forgiven.

"*Vell*, put *de* boxes under Pam's desk and go."

"Yes, Sister Dionysius."

That was a let-off. I consoled myself because originally the silkworms had belonged to Pam. I would warn her in the morning, but I forgot.

"Stand up Pam," Sister Dionysius said.

She stood. Sister held up the silkworm boxes, "Are *dese* yours, Pam?"

I faced Pam. My lips mouthed the word 'yes,' which she understood.

"Yes Sister."

"I do not *vant* silkworms in *ze* classroom. Ja! See *dat* you take *dese* home *wiz* you today. I *vill* put *dese* two boxes on *ze* top of my platform until *ze* school is over. Do you understand, Pam?"

"Yes Sister. I'm sorry, Sister."

"Sit down child. Now *ve* can begin *vith ze* lesson."

I apologised to Pam and our friendship lasted until Matric. Academically I improved and came third in class. I was a strong contender on the sports field, netball and hockey in winter; tennis and swimming in summer.

Thirty-yard petticoats, broad, elasticised belts and puffed sleeves, high fashion, were worn on Saturdays. We adhered to a strict dress code. Sleeveless blouses and stiletto heels were prohibited. On Sundays we wore white dresses, fluffed out with thirty-yard petticoats. In winter we wore mid-calf pleated navy skirts and black stockings held up by a suspender belt. The nuns regimented every activity. On Friday afternoon I filled an enamel basin with cold water and shampooed my hair. A refill rinsed my hair. I rubbed my hair dry with a towel. There were no hair-dryers, hot curlers or even a mirror.

On Saturday mornings we starched our thirty-yard petticoats, spread them in a circle on the lawn and waited for them to dry in the sun. My starched petticoat pricked my legs, but my skirt billowed out like a circular balloon. I loved it.

I took comfort seeing granny in the same pew in church morning and evening. I missed the good times with her at *Kildare*. Was she coping with two boarders?

One day my mother told me a parcel had arrived for me. It was a hamper of groceries valued at R100 (£50 in those days). I remembered the *Springbok* Radio competition I had entered on a postcard. I gave mom my prize.

Her life had changed. She was a farmer's wife. Mr and Mrs Mundell managed *D M Brown General Dealer Store,* but mom kept the books.

Our next summer holiday would be spent at a remote fishing spot, Umsikaba, where Pop co-owned a cottage with Colonel Felix Colvin and his wife, Constance. We set off in the *International* truck, all five of us on the front seat...

8

UMSIKABA

Unveiling his master plan in 1959, Verwoerd announced that South Africa would become a 'multi-national' state with separate homelands for eight black 'nations'. In 1959 the Pan-African Congress (PAC), founded by Robert Sobukwe – demanding 'government of the Africans, by the Africans' and promising militant action to achieve it – broke away from the Congress Alliance.

WITH the *International* truck packed and Craig Adam managing the farm for three weeks, we drove through Kokstad to Umsikaba. After Brook's Nek we left the tarred road taking the Flagstaff turnoff. The truck trundled along the dusty, pot-holed roads through *Pondoland,* in the Transkei. The countryside was rugged. Soil-erosion exacerbated by overgrazing. The hillsides dotted with thatched huts their mud walls painted white. Women hoed *mealie* lands and *piccanninies* herded cattle, sheep and goats. Livestock roamed freely on the roads.

"Hold on." Pop said before he slammed on his brakes. The tyres skidded on the gravel road. He blew the hooter. The cattle stood in the road unperturbed by the commotion. Slowly the herd moved off in single file. We settled back into our seats.

"I'm sorry about that. There's nothing I could do."

We journeyed on passing *Pondo* women balancing buckets of water on their heads. Unhurriedly they waved to us. We waved back.

"How far do they walk to fetch water?"

"Mmm...several miles, Pegs. To the river in the valley. They do this several times daily. It's a social outing, shouting back and forth to friends from a distance."

I decided to try this out on the beach. If the bucket of water fell off my head, it would cool me. The road worsened. We bounced about in the cab. The luggage, covered in dust in the back, slid everywhere. We swerved missing squawking chickens as they flapped furiously to safety. "Look!" Topsy said pointing, "Blankets and clothes on the grass and bushes."

"They're drying their washing. They don't have washing-lines like us." This journey was too interesting to play *'I Spy.'*

I watched a man thatching his newly-built hut, single-handedly. Flagstaff, home to my mom's sister, Ruth, came into view. With her husband, Keith, they worked in their own trading store similar to *D M Brown's*. Pop parked and locked the truck. We all traipsed into the store.

"Hello Peggy, Phil and girls." Aunty Buzzy greeted us.

"Can we..."

"Certainly, off you go. Ask Regina to make you a cup of tea, Pegs."

"Thanks Buzzy."

Uncle Keith served customers. We waved to him and retreated to the house, next door to the shop. Shyly, my cousins Myrna aged ten, Norman seven and June six, greeted us. Regina entered the lounge carrying a tray saying, "*Molweni*. Hello. *Ninjani?* How are you?"

"*Siphilile Enkosi,* We are well thank you, Regina," Pop acknowledged.

Tea over, we said our goodbyes and returned to the shop. Above the din, Uncle Keith said, "Have a good holiday. I hope the fish are on the bite, Phil."

We never stopped in Lusikisiki, which derived its name from the sound of the wind rustling in the reeds, *'siki...siki...siki...'*

"Who'll be the first to see the sea?" Pop challenged.

I scanned the distant horizon.

"The sea!" Topsy yelled.

"That's not the sea."

The road wound downhill through cuttings, with sharp bends. Ahead there was a small, unoccupied, broken-down house. Pop pulled the truck off the road and switched off the engine. "Well, Peggy, here we are," he announced.

"Is *this* the cottage Phil?"

"Yes, as I said, it's a *small* cottage and isolated."

Trying to sound enthusiastic, my mother replied, "This is our cottage girls."

Nobody spoke. I looked at this dilapidated building in disbelief wondering how we would fit in. My mother reached for the door handle. Then Pop relieved our worst fears, saying, "No, Peggy, I was pulling your leg, but the cottage is *small.*"

Back in the truck we travelled on. My mother caught a glimpse of the sea but twists in the road obliterated the view. The road levelled out clearly revealing a distinct horizon separating the dark-blue sea from the cloudless sky.

"The sea! *I* saw the sea *first,*" Topsy insisted.

"No, *I* saw the sea *before* you, Topsy."

"No. *I* did." Topsy always wanted to be *first*, to be the *best* and to have the *most*...

My mother ended our argument by asking, "Who can see the lighthouse?"

I was confused. It was not yet dark. Topsy sulked. Margy asked, "Where?"

"It's the tall white building on the cliff edge."

Pop stopped the truck. We soaked up the panoramic view. He pointed out some landmarks, "The cottage is directly at the bottom of this hill. Do you see the island offshore? We'll cross over there at low tide tomorrow. To the left of the island the river runs into the sea in front of those sand-dunes. Sharks frequent the river mouth and the currents are dangerous. Across the river is Mkambati, a leper station. I must warn you, leopards roam on the *krantzes*. I was flabbergasted. A whole new world opened up in front of my eyes. I decided to avoid the river. In low gear we drove down the last steep hill, heading towards the cottage. After passing the long-drop Pop parked the truck.

"Welcome to Umsikaba," he said, climbing out. We were covered in dust. The waves thundered beyond the bush, which ran the length of the sandy shore.

Two water tanks on each side of the cottage were kept locked. Pop removed a wooden gate to keep livestock off the verandah. A bedroom off there belonged to Colonel Colvin and his wife, who were co-owners. Once the three locks on the front door were unlocked we entered the living room, housing an oak dining room table and chairs and an old-fashioned sideboard. In the far side of the room cushioned easy chairs were arranged in a semi-circle, interspersed with side tables and cozied up with a carpet over the cement floor. The curtains were drawn. The cottage was dark and smelt musty.

From the living room two more doors opened into two bedrooms and a third door led into the primitive sparse kitchen. A wooden work table stood under the window, a gas stove alongside, a bucket nearby on the cement floor and a primus stove on a shelf, from which cups dangled from cup-hooks. One door off the kitchen, always kept under lock and key, opened into the pantry. Our provisions were locked away. The closest shop was in Lusikisiki.

"Pegs, can you open the curtains and windows? I'll fill the fridge and lamps with paraffin. It'll be dark soon. Girls, how about offloading some of the luggage?"

"Mom, I can't carry the heavy things," Margy whimpered.

"Girls come inside now. I'll show you your bedroom."

"A bunk! *Please* may I sleep on the top bunk?" I begged.

My wish was granted. Margy slept in the small single bed and Topsy on the bottom bunk. The window in our bedroom had a view of the sea. My stepfather had built the bunk but he had not yet made a ladder. I climbed on Margy's bed and walked over the chest of drawers, to get into bed. It was very high. The room had no ceilings.

Each bedroom had a soap-dish, jug and basin on a washstand. Alongside was an enamel basin with a lid to dispose of the dirty water. A porcelain chamber pot was hidden under the bed.

My mother unpacked the food onto shelves in the pantry. Pop lit the paraffin lamps. He entrusted us with matches and a candle in an old-fashioned candlestick-holder in our bedroom. Inside the lamps hissed and outside the sea roared. Tucked up on the top bunk I soon fell asleep. At sunrise, Pop called, "Wake up sleepyheads. It's time for a swim before breakfast."

We slipped into our bathing costumes and drove towards Fawcett's cottage where Pop parked. We raced ahead of Mom and Pop, down a steep sandy path through indigenous bush to the golden sands of a remote beach. Skinny-dipping followed but not me.

Afterwards I climbed into the back of the truck in my wet *cozzie*. In order to turn, Pop reversed towards the bushes. The tyres spun in the loose sand and the vehicle edged nearer and nearer the edge of the sheer drop. "Stop! Let me out" I yelled louder and louder. I walked home rather than go through that again.

We spent every day on the beach. At low tide we crossed to the island where we explored rock pools. *Pondo* women in tribal orange blankets and beads used *pangas* to scrape mussels off the rocks. Hopeful fishermen stood at the water's edge holding upraised rods. A herd of cattle meandered across the white sands. We never tired of swimming, paddling and sliding down the sand-dunes. Despite my previous resolution, we walked to the river mouth one day and watched the incoming waves compete with the outgoing swift-flowing river. I saw the leper station on the other side.

We obeyed the rules governing the long-drop buzzing with green flies – we closed the lid, used toilet paper sparingly and never threw rubbish into the cesspit. A *Heath Robinson* shower, protected by hessian bags strung around four creosoted poles, held a paraffin drum of water. Standing on a cement slab, I pulled the rope attached to the drum. Cold water tipped over me. Quick and economical!

Mrs Colvin was lucky to find a valuable ring said to have come off the wreck of the *Grosvenor*. All we ever found were worthless pieces of china and red beads.

This had been one of my happiest holidays ever. When we returned at Easter we transformed a cave with shells and wild flowers we had collected for a visit from the Easter Bunny. Happily we collected Easter eggs in the cave on Sunday morning.

Pop gave us each a rod and reel enabling us to fish in gullies. He taught us the names of the fish we caught. Some were used as bait and others were thrown back into the sea. When we dragged the net up the river with the help of adults, we were warned:

"Keep your mouth shut. A ten year-old boy died when a mullet stuck in his throat."

Two incidents dissolved the Colvin and Leary partnership. We played 'hair-dressing' pretending the lime-green seaweed on the rocks was hair and the shampoo was the froth off the waves. Mrs Milton from Kokstad dyed her hair blue.

"We're washing Mrs Milton's hair! Washing her hair!"

Constance Colvin overheard us, tut-tutted and walked off. She reported this to mom. Diplomatically my mother gave us a lesson on respecting our elders, saying, "You made fun of Mrs Milton. She is an adult and you must respect her."

One evening we eaves-dropped on the adults' conversation. They moved from pre-dinner 'spots' to the supper table. Constance said, "Please pass me the butter, Peggy."

Opening the butter dish with the butter knife poised, she turned to Felix, "Look at the butter. This is *revolting*!"

We suppressed our laughter in our pillows before we fell asleep. At breakfast the next day Topsy remembered, "Mom, what does '*revolting*' mean?"

You could cut the atmosphere with a knife. Breaking the silence, mom wisely replied, "We'll talk about that word after breakfast, Topsy." Because we had not used the butter knife, traces of strawberry jam had been left on the butter. Mrs Colvin found it revolting!

On windy days we climbed to the top of the *Big Rock,* where we tanned, read and surveyed the view. In the afternoons we swung like Tarzan quite fearlessly from monkey-ropes in the indigenous forest unafraid of the thirty-foot drop. Pop sought inspiration for our bedtime story. He lit a cigarette and began his story of a train, the *State Express,* his cigarette brand, which fascinated me.

Once a week, water heated on the gas stove was poured into a zinc bath in the bedroom. We took turns in the same water. The last one had dirty, soapy luke-warm water.

When we were not at the cottage, my stepbrother Tony's wife, Rhoda, made an unforgettable entry into Umsikaba. While she was seated in the long drop a snake slithered towards her bare legs.

"Snake! Snake!" she screamed arriving in the lounge minus her bikini bottom. The mamba was killed and her bikini bottom retrieved!

His Master's Voice gramophone player, in a wooden case, had to be cranked. Then the needle was placed carefully on either a 45 or 33 long- playing record. We rock-and-rolled to Elvis's *'Jailhouse Rock'* and did the twist to Bill Hayley's *'Let's twist again'*.

There was no television only a battery-operated radio to listen to the weather report and the news each morning; no telephone, mobiles, laptops, electricity or running hot and cold water. The tranquillity of those holidays, food for the soul, will always remain one of my most cherished memories.

***

Strathneva was home to me and I warmed to my stepfather. He was strict kind and went out of his way to make us happy. We understood his habits, but Eileen, my cousin had to learn.

"If you'll excuse me, I'll check if it's raining," Pop said after supper as usual.

"I'll come with you Uncle Phil!"

Eileen followed him. This prevented Pop from piddling in the garden as Eileen learnt much later, the underlying meaning of his remark.

Mom planted a new orchard. I like nothing better than eating fruit freshly-picked off a tree. Barefoot and in shorts, I wandered into the new orchard examining the red plums which shone like Christmas baubles in the sunlight. My mouth watered. I stared at the yellow plums on the next tree when I felt somebody was staring at me.

I glanced over my shoulder. Nobody was about. Hearing a hissing sound, I looked down. I disturbed a metre-long yellow-brown puff-adder. This highly venomous snake, head high, was about to strike and push its sharp fangs into my leg at lightning speed. I fled the scene and like an Olympic hurdler, cleared the rose bushes. I jumped up six steps landing on the verandah. I caught my breath and screamed. My stepfather and my twenty-one year-old stepbrother, Tony, tall tanned with blue eyes, every girl's dream, were at my side.

"What's all this about?"

In shock, I stammered. "Sss...Sss... Snake."

Tony ran to fetch his gun. He loaded it with several rounds of ammunition.

"Where did you see the snake, Denyse?"

"In... in...the new... orch... orchard, Pop."

Carrying their guns, they headed for the new orchard. Two shots later and Tony held up the 6 kg (13.2 lbs) puff-adder proudly for me to see. Blood spewed from its patterned body. Coming close to being a victim of the second most venomous snake in South Africa after the black mamba, I learnt its life-threatening bite required a blood-transfusion to avoid necrosis, known as tissue death. Despite Tony reminding me of Rhoda's encounter with a snake in the long drop, which made us laugh, my narrow escape haunted me for days.

***

"You'll soon have a baby brother or sister," mom told me. I was fourteen and found this embarrassing. My sisters were thrilled. There would be a ten-year gap between Margy and the new baby. We teased her, "You'll be the ex-baby soon."

Mom, proud of her ever-enlarging tummy said, "Feel the baby kick."

Taking their hands she placed them on her bump, but I refused. Over the winter holiday baby preparations got underway. Mom's sewing room off the main bedroom was converted into a nursery. Pop bought a new pram. The blue enamel baby bath in wicker basket stood in readiness. Baby clothes, nappies, creams and lotions dominated the room.

Before returning to boarding school, we enjoyed the winter evenings reading books in the lounge. Before bedtime, we peeled oranges and tossed the skins into the log-fire. This gave the room a citrus aroma.

On 11 September 1959 Pop announced the birth of his son, Patrick Hughen Leary, our baby brother. He drove us to the Kokstad Memorial Hospital, where we stood outside my mother's ward. At the window for us to see, a nurse held up a tiny baby, red-faced and crying. Margy and I stared at his wrinkled little face. Topsy unthinkingly blurted out, "What an ugly baby. He looks like a pink rat!" My mother was told this much later.

It was strange being in Standard Seven, a teenager and having a baby brother. My subjects included English, Afrikaans, German, Arithmetic, Botany, Geography, Shorthand and Typing, Domestic Science and Religious Instruction. Sister Therese Martin, an Irish nun with a vile temper, was class teacher for combined Sevens and Eights. Red-faced, thin lipped, with dark-rimmed glasses partly hiding her cruel eyes, she sneaked around the corridors, hoping to pick on some undeserving pupil. During a poetry lesson my friends and I giggled every time we reached the third stanza of the poem we recited aloud.

"Stop that and start again."

"Yes, Sister Therese Martin."

Our giggling persisted. Coming up behind us, she hit Pat, Jean and me on the head with a hard-covered book. She dismissed us in a rage, "Get out of my class this minute!"

We closed our books and left the room, heading for the pool, where we stripped off our shoes and socks. Dangling our feet in the cool water, Jean, Pat and I agreed, "Thanks Sister Therese Martin. This is much better than reading."

"Feel here," Pat said, "A lump on my head where she hit me."

"It's no use reporting her," I decided even though things got worse.

By the time we came home for the Christmas holidays Patrick was a three month-old chubby smiling gurgling baby. We watched him being bathed. We took turns pushing him in his net-covered pram on the verandah.

Patrick soon grew up playing with his own black playmate and tinkering in the workshop with Pop. Just as mom taught us to make home-made ice-cream and bake, Pop taught Patrick how to maintain engines and repair irrigation schemes... I had driving lessons with my mother on the farm roads. The days I practised a hill start, six-year old Patrick chirped from the back seat, "Stalled!" before I had even attempted to take off. He had heard my mother say, "Stalled again!" so often during my many failed attempts. When Patrick was older, he jumped out the car, unhooked the wire loop and pushed the gate open, before swinging back on the gate, hooking it closed and jumping into the car.

On 6 March 1960 Aunty Buzzy gave birth to a daughter, Patricia. There was a seven-year gap between June and Patty, as she was called. Today I wonder why the last two grandchildren were called Patricia and Patrick, shortened to Patti and Pat. I will never know!

9

TEENAGER TO TEACHER

From 1910 to 1961 the Union of South Africa maintained international respect with British Dominion status. In the 1960's international pressure against the government began. South Africa was excluded from Olympic Games and in 1961 was declared a republic, leaving the Commonwealth. Nelson Mandela headed the ANC's new military wing. In 1961 'Rands and cents' replaced pounds, shillings and pence. Nelson Mandela was arrested in August 1962 and received a three-year sentence for incitement.

HOCKEY. I played centre-forward and clicked my stick three times determined to get the ball. Practising late on winter afternoons, we trudged back to the convent in the fading light and dropping temperature. One evening I limped back. My toe ached. I went to the infirmary. Sister cleaned the dirt and coagulated blood. She applied a dressing saying, "Hockey's a rough game. Wear your slipper. Return tomorrow."

"Could I see the doctor?" I asked the next day. "I can't sleep at night."

Sister was shocked that I *dared* to doubt her nursing skills. That afternoon the severe pain forced me to bunk out to see granny. Hobbling along Hope Street, I looked over my shoulder to make certain nobody had seen me. Reaching *Kildare,* safe in those days to leave doors unlocked, I went inside.

"Hi Gran."

"Is that you Neyse?"

Granny appeared on the landing asking, "Is something wrong?"

"My toe, gran."

"Sit down my child and tell me what happened."

"I've been to the infirmary twice. My toe's *very* painful."

"Let me have a look. Take off your sock. "

I cringed when I removed the dressing. With her spectacles teetering on the tip of her nose, granny examined my toe. Her face depicted bad news. "Eddie Dyson had better look at your toe. I'll fetch my handbag and car keys..."

What had I let myself in for? Gran, at age sixty-six, decided to buy a car and get her Driver's Licence having *never* driven before. Her driving skills were bad. This was my *first* and my *last* ride in gran's new car.

Gran revved up the engine before reversing out the garage narrowly missing the garden wall on the passenger side. We just made it over the bridge to the road. She drove to *Dyson's* chemist in first gear, parking badly. Holding granny's arm, we entered the chemist.

"Hello Eddie. I was wondering if you'd have a look at Denyse's toe."

"Certainly Eileen. Would you both like to come this way?"

Seated on a chair with granny at my side, Mr Dyson asked, "Now young lady, what've you been up to?" I re-told my story nervously knowing I risked being expelled if I was caught bunking out. "The damage to your nail has caused an infection."

Turning to my grandmother, he continued, "Denyse *must* see a doctor. I suggest you take her to the surgery."

Things were going from bad to worse. My quick-fix plan took on a different turn. Fear engulfed me in a situation out of my control. We arrived at the surgery where I recognised the receptionist. Her daughter attended the convent. She knew boarders had to be accompanied by a nun. In a bid to save the situation, I said, "Gran, my toe will be okay. May we go home?"

"You heard what Mr Dyson said."

Waiting to see the doctor I listened to the clock ticking on the wall. 4.30 pm. Homework began at 5 pm. Sister Therese Martin, the nun in charge, would notice my empty desk. I could hear her saying, "Where's Denyse. Late *again!* She'll be *punished* for this."

Dr Veel examined my toe. He gave his verdict, which shocked me..."Denyse, I'm afraid I'll have to remove your toenail. There's a nasty infection in the root of your toenail. Eileen, could you take her to the hospital? I'll make the necessary arrangements."

Nail removed? Hospital? Straight away?

Back in the car granny said, "I'll go via St John's Street to miss the rush hour traffic."

"Good idea, Granny."

Our trip into town had been nerve-racking. Gran grated the gears; made too wide a berth around every corner and swerved to the left to miss an oncoming car; she over-corrected and almost hit a parked car. She applied brakes and I smelt rubber burning. I admired her courage. She was proud to drive after all her years of walking everywhere.

There was no traffic until... Gran pulled off from a stop-street in the wrong gear. The car chugged. To the right, an overloaded taxi sped towards us. In a split second, with a deafening crash of metal on metal, the taxi hit the rear bumper of gran's car. The collision pushed her car sharp left. It jumped a gutter, broke through a hedge, hurtled across a rose garden and stopped with the bonnet resting on the verandah of somebody's house. Gran switched off the engine. Deathly silence.

The occupants of the house rushed out. No... This can't be... But it was... Pamela, a day scholar in my class, lived here. I could not stop crying. Everybody told me to stop, but my sobs were uncontrollable. Much later, I learnt my mother had been told, "Your mother and daughter were involved in a car accident. They're both in hospital."

Next I remembered seeing my mother at the side of my hospital bed. She said, "It's all over now, Neyse. I'm here with you."

"Granny?"

"Granny's cracked her ribs."

I felt bad. In helping me, granny was injured.

"Will I be expelled?"

"Sister Superior concerned about your disappearance, was very understanding. You won't be expelled. The Sisters visited gran and apologised to her for not taking you to see the doctor. I saw the narrow gap between the oak tree and the telephone pole, which gran drove through. Even an experienced driver would have found this difficult. Gran's car's written off. You've had a narrow escape!"

It was a lot to take in. Gran had broken her ribs. Her car was a total wreck. Even though I had bunked out I would not be expelled. My toenail had triggered off all these catastrophic events. Most importantly, God had spared ten lives, ours and eight unknown black people in the taxi, a miracle.

I retained my *'Prefects'* badge. Many pupils dropped out of school after JC (Junior Certificate). Jean McMillan fell pregnant; Felicity Reed worked in the bank; Pat Gwalter modelled in Durban. Denise Byrne, Pamela Webb and I were the only *matriculants* in 1962. Pamela was captain of *Botha House* and I was elected Head girl and captain of *Rhodes House*. Being the only matric at boarding school, I was allowed to board with Uncle Slabs and Aunty Joan at 107 Hawthorn Street.

Neville attended the Kokstad High School, my rival school. He argued with me, "The standard of education at *my* school is far superior. My dad told me."

"We'll see about that," I retorted.

"The nuns are so old-fashioned," he added, having the last word.

Living with my cousins meant sharing a bedroom with Jeanette, nineteen, who worked in Kokstad. She had boyfriends and came home late. I studied in the room off our shared bedroom. At 9 pm Uncle Slabs, cigarette in hand, asked, "Have you finished your homework Neyse?" my cue to go to bed.

Every day Diana aged thirteen, and her sister Eileen, aged ten, and I walked to school. Whenever I returned with a few sweets from the Tuck shop, they were waiting for me, "Give us a sweet, Neyse!" I always did, but they *never* shared their sweets with me.

Vivian obtained a Teacher's Diploma and taught in Pietermaritzburg. He had a steady girlfriend, Denise Albers. Educated at Marist Brothers, gran earmarked him to be the priest and me to be the nun in the family, which was what was done in those days.

I excelled in netball, hockey and tennis, won trophies for diving and swimming. Sport came naturally to me and Rhodes House was victorious that year. My twelve-year school career was coming to an end. I had strived to please my mother. Her words, "You'll survive," had enabled me to overcome hardships and succeed in difficult situations.

One thing I would not miss was Sister Therese Martin's sarcasm and spite. She ridiculed me at assembly for shortening my red First Team hockey dress, shouting, "All that flesh showing! You sinful girl!" If I had not shortened it, I would have tripped over it.

On another occasion I ran from the toilet to the infirmary and nearly knocked her over in a doorway. She stopped me in my tracks. I crossed my legs awkwardly because my monthlies had started for the first time.

"Denyse, where are your manners?" she screamed. "You almost knocked me over. You should let me pass through the doorway first!"

"Sorry Sister Therese Martin," enabled me to escape. I never explained to her the predicament I was in. I laugh remembering another incident in the classroom. Our class tricked her. We inked our tongues. When Sister Therese Martin arrived late for the lesson, we articulated the words as we recited a poem. We made our tongues as visible as possible. Ignoring what the nun saw, she picked on Mildred Schoeman, "Who do you think you are? Queen Elizabeth?" Mildred opened her mouth wider, ignoring the question.

"Come to the front and show the class."

Mildred aggravated Sister Therese Martin even more. Mildred, haughty by nature, held her head even higher. Facing the nun, she looked down her nose and said, "You may pour the tea if you please. Milk first."

We could not contain our laughter. For once Mildred did what Sister had commanded her to do and was one up on her. Soon my school years would become a memory. The question arose, "What would I do when I left school?"

"I want to be a vet," was not accepted, after all girls either became teachers, nurses or secretaries. I applied, with a second-class Joint Matriculation pass, to study at a Teachers' Training College, but I was refused because I was too young. Neville with five A's had a scholarship to study at Rhodes University. He later became a professor. He had won!

Deflated, I wondered what lay ahead for me after twelve years of schooling...

***

My application to take up teaching at the Grahamstown Training College was refused in December. Following this my stepfather secured a secretarial job for me. I would start at *Eagle & Barnes* on 15 January 1963. The week before this a vacancy at the training college meant my application had been accepted. I notified my employer, Mr Eagle who said, "If it were not for the fact you're pursuing a career, I'd force you to work in your notice. Every success with your studies Denyse."

Not fully understanding what he meant, I escaped this dreary world sitting at a desk behind a *Remington* typewriter in a dimly lit office. The next ten days were hectic getting clothes sewn and marked. My basic requirements obtained from *D M Brown's*, were put on the slate (my mother's account). Granny gave me a brand new red portable FM radio.

Leaving the farm at 3 am, my mother and I drove to college passing through Umtata. I drove on the national road for the first time to give mom a break. The year President Kennedy was assassinated would be a year of many 'firsts' in my life.

On arrival the principal Sister Virginia interviewed us. Then a second-year student escorted us to my residence, Lincoln House. Sister Gloria in charge welcomed us before we climbed the stairs to the dormitory comprising seven wooden cubicles. In the two bathrooms a red line inside the bath denoted how much water we were permitted to use due to a severe drought. Looking at the tiny cubicle I exclaimed, "Wow! A matchbox!"

At the foot of the iron bed was a curtained space with a rail to hang my dresses and opposite the bed an old chest of drawers. I unpacked and pushed my case under the bed. My mother hid her disappointment. Gaynor Meyer with short brown hair, laughing green eyes, arrived with her parents asking, "Do they expect me to sleep in this mouse-hole?"

"Ssh, Gaynor," her mother cautioned, "other people can hear you."

"But, it's true."

I popped my head out of my cubicle. We introduced ourselves. Gaynor Meyer from Uitenhage became my first friend. I called myself Denyse hoping to be rid of my childhood nickname Neyse.

"Gaynor," her dad interrupted, "Help me with your luggage."

"I'm coming dad. See you later Denyse."

I heard the strong Afrikaans accent with the next arrival.

"Ag Pa. do they rrr…really *expecked* me to move into this?"

I saw a beautiful girl with shiny black hair, black arched eyebrows, dark eyes and long lashes. She was immaculately dressed with an air of sophistication about her. Behind her was an elderly grey-haired man. Before they saw me, I snuck away.

"*Ag* Pappa *werr* will I put *all* my clothes? This place is so class…trrro…vobic! (Claustrophobic!) I can't sleep on that drrr…eadful bed. Asseblief, Pa, ek wil huis toe gaan." (Please, Dad, I want to go home.)

Her dad's reply was inaudible except. "Finished and *klaar!*" a South African saying which meant subject closed.

My mother and I walked to the car. She gave me some last-minute advice, "Settle down and study hard, my girl." Noticing a tear in my eye she added, "Whatever happens, you'll survive!" With those words we parted. I watched her car filter into the traffic and disappear. Sue Mulder, the pretty girl, spotted me when I returned.

"My sisters are both older than me. One lives in America. I'll go there one day. I want to sing and act." Exuding confidence she sang, *The Young Ones,* which lifted our spirits.

Joy Puttergill and Pam Whitfield, our last two dormitory mates, arrived from the *Transkei* where, when the sun dipped low in the sky, the fires burnt. Joy, with short blonde hair, blue eyes and a baby face, was taller than me. Pam, wearing her long blonde hair in a chignon, was old-fashioned.

Although the college was run by Anglican nuns, Miss Marzo and Mr Hairbottom were two lecturers in P1A (Primary First year, A). I befriended Jennifer Hairbottle, June Marcus and Sandy Malcomess. Lectures, initiation, meetings and sport dominated my life. Two of my favourite places were the library, the biggest I had ever seen, and an Olympic-sized swimming pool.

During initiation Gaynor and I were asked to light a cigarette for a second-year student. Never having held a cigarette before, I did not know which end to light. I held the burning match at the end of the cigarette. Nothing happened. With the wrong end between my lips, I tried again. I sucked foul-tasting tobacco bits into my mouth. The soggy cigarette broke. My splattering and spitting entertained the second-years. Gaynor lit the cigarette eventually, but we were humiliated. I disliked being the laughing stock of these students...

"Denyse, let's buy a packet of ten and practise secretly," Gaynor suggested.

"Okay."

We shared the cost of the cigarettes. Gaynor paid one penny for the *Lion* matches. In a secluded spot we practised lighting a cigarette, an awful experience. With Gaynor's help, I succeeded. My head felt dizzy and light. Not wanting to waste hers, Gaynor drew on it, puffing out a mouthful of smoke. She coughed. "You try."

"No thanks."

We put the blackened remains into the *Dunhill* box.

"We'll show these second years," she enthused.

Soon we were put to the test. I managed, to their amazement, to light my cigarette with my first attempt. Triumphantly, I handed the lit cigarette to Ann, a second-year. Pushing the cigarette into my hand she said, "Take a puff."

"I'd rather not."

"Did you *hear* that? This nincompoop said, 'she'd rather *not'."*

"What a cheek!"

"Who does she think she is?"

"This upstart has the nerve to disobey orders from a second-year!"

"You *heard* me, smarty-pants, have a puff."

The curling smoke from the cigarette in my hand wafted into my nostrils. I felt nauseous, but to avoid further ridicule, I took a draw. The filthy smoke sank into my mouth and into my throat, travelling deep into my lungs. I blew out, expelling the horrid fumes. I spluttered and felt dizzy.

Sadly that was the start of a habit which neither Gaynor nor I wished upon each other. Neither were we aware of the hazards of smoking in those days. We became the prized trophies of second-year students. The dirty and costly habit was born... I was hooked on something, I was to learn, would be hard to break...

***

Initiation, supposedly an ice-breaker, was established to uphold the hierarchy among students and to eliminate pre-conceived ideas of grandeur or self-importance. This practice included barbaric rituals causing serious injury and, at times, even death. The governing body instituted strict regulations but these were ignored. I was relieved the fortnight's initiation was over. No more skivvying for second-year students, gyrating to Elvis Presley's *Love Me Tender,* or swallowing foul-tasting potions! I could settle down to college life.

Sport had always dominated my life. I was selected to play in the first tennis team. We competed against Rhodes University and several

Grahamstown tennis clubs. I took part in the swimming gala and was awarded a silver medallion. My friend Gaynor invited me to her home in Uitenhage for the Easter holidays. We slept in a caravan on the property. Her three elder brothers teased me. I blushed easily. Gaynor's family smoked and accepted that we smoked too.

I never applied my full academic ability. Sport and a new social life distracted me.

On my first date, John Priestley, tall blonde and blue-eyed, walked holding my hand through the Botanical Gardens. Was the ugly duckling turning into a swan?

Boarding the train for the mid-year holidays some Rhodes students on the platform gave us a send-off, singing *When the saints go marching in*. The train whistled and chugged out of the station as girls hung out the windows, waving.

During this two-night journey, black soot flew into open windows. I shared a compartment with five others and slept on the middle bunk. A second engine at the rear powered the train up steep mountain passes. The panoramic views seen in slow motion included herds of buck springing through thick bush, goats climbing steep rock faces and birds taking off from treetops into azure blue skies.

The train stopped in Umtata where I boarded the local bus transporting mostly Blacks to Kokstad. Surplus luggage, including chickens in a coop and wheelbarrows, were strapped to the roof of the bus. I was tired, dirty and hungry when my mother met me at the bus stop.

My sisters, my captive audience, listened to me describing college life. Did I inspire them? Both of them trained as teachers.

One day I lit a cigarette in the lounge.

"Denyse. Are you smoking?"

"Yes, I started during initiation. It's quite the rage at college."

Disappointment was written all over her face. I knew I had let her down. My mother never smoked or drank alcohol because of my alcoholic father.

I spent the next short holiday with Joy Puttergill on her parent's trading station, *Sabalele* near Cofimvaba in the Transkei. Her dad, short and stocky with bushy eyebrows, limped due to a spinal abnormality. Her auburn-haired, blue-eyed mother, a homemaker had a beautiful garden. We played tennis at Cofimvaba. Joy had a married sister, Erica and an elder brother, Lyle, a student at Rhodes University. Pam Whitfield fancied Lyle.

Before the year ended Joy, Pam and I spent a weekend without adults in a cottage on the riverbanks of Kenton-on-Sea, close to Grahamstown. Every evening our boyfriends cooked *boerewors, sosaties* and chops on a *braaivleis*. We laughed, chatted and canoodled under the stars.

Back on the farm with my family, I waited for my year-end examination results. I had changed from naïve schoolgirl into a young lady... I had adjusted from my sheltered upbringing to the harsh outside world. There was still so much for me to learn...

10

YOUNG LOVE

Nelson Mandela, Walter Sisulu and other senior ANC colleagues stood trial from October 1963 to June 1964 during the Rivonia Trial. They were charged with sabotage which carried the death penalty. On 12 June 1964 Nelson Mandela then forty-five years old, was sentenced to life imprisonment on Robben Island. He endured years of hard labour working in the island's quarry and collecting seaweed.

MY protective plea, "Don't even ask me," was uttered when we returned home from a tennis tournament dance at the Kokstad Town Hall. My mother waited up for us and asked how we had enjoyed ourselves. *Both* my younger sisters were asked to dance. Try as I did to smile and to make myself attractive, I was a wallflower all night. Were my glasses and round-shoulders a turnoff?

"I danced with Nigel, but Ricky's my favourite," Topsy said adding fuel to my woes. But this was soon to change...

No longer antagonised by Topsy calling me *Donsie* at every opportunity I made the most of my looks. I wore my hair in a modern beehive, applied make-up and used my perfume sparingly. I modernised my home-made dresses with a belt, which nipped in my small waist and with a brooch on a white collar.

Social life at the college was controlled by rigid rules permitting two dance passes until midnight and eight evening passes until 10.30 pm but every day we had to be in the college grounds by 5.30 pm. When we left and returned to the college grounds we signed in and out in a special book.

On Sunday nights we enjoyed a social in the Anglican Church hall. Rhodes University students and army boys, stationed in Grahamstown for compulsory one-year training, attended these socials. They had the same 'boy meets girl' intention. I danced all evening, which boosted my self-confidence. I agreed to walk home with a young Rhodes student. Holding hands, we chatted as we walked but I avoided his kiss. "May I see you again?"

This was my second date. Dates, in my day, progressed from a walk in the Botanical Gardens; to a milkshake with the juke-box playing in the local café; to holding hands at the movies and the big one, an invitation to a ball. Previously I dated John Priestley, but chose to go steady with Tony. I had used up all my evening passes but I wanted to see a movie with Tony. I bunked out without signing the book. My mother telephoned and I could not be found. Sister Gloria was told and waited for my return. I tried to sneak in unnoticed, but…

"You have no evening passes left Denyse. You bunked out."

"Yes, I'm sorry, Sister."

"Go to Sister Virginia's office tomorrow before lectures."

Nothing more was said. I would not be expelled but what would happen? After a sleepless night I entered the office and the principal grounded me for the rest of the term.

"Sorry Sister Virginia."

Guilt-ridden, I left her office.

In our second year Sue, Joy, Gaynor, Pam and I had lovely big rooms on the third floor. I saw my steady good-looking boy-friend Tony again. He was studying to become a pharmacist but this friendship would not last long…

"May I have this dance?"

I swung round expecting to see Tony but a tall dark young man stared back at me.

"Why yes."

Tony was not at the social that evening. I danced with my new acquaintance, Donald Smith, who worked at the Eastern Province Building Society in town. He drove me back to college in his red *Triumph* sports car. Charming and well-mannered, I was drawn to him. I accepted his invitation knowing I had a date with Tony that week. I was two-timing. Tony and I went to movies as arranged. Walking me back to college I told him the truth, breaking the news gently. "Thanks Tony for a lovely evening. I have a confession…"

I squeezed his hand feeling guilty.

"What Denyse?"

"I can't go out with you anymore."

"Have I upset you?"

"No."

"Well, what's the trouble?"

My words would damage his ego. "Tony I've met somebody else."

"You've met somebody else?"

I nodded. I saw how this hurt him. He let go of my hand, his eyes pierced my entire being. He turned and stalked off. "Goodbye, Tony. You'll meet somebody else…"

I do not think he heard me. I ran to my friends for support.

"You did the right thing."

"Shame, poor Tony!"

"But he was so handsome… a good catch!"

I was more confused. What had I done? My name would be mud amongst the Rhodes students. I was not certain Don would ask me out again. I could only wait and see…

The days dragged. One evening I heard a first-year calling, "Telephone for Denyse Lloyd." I rushed down the stairs two at a time, breathless, I heard, "Is that you Denyse?"

"Yes. Hello Don."

That was the start of a very steady friendship. Don spoilt me. We ate strawberries and cream in his sports car. He brought me gifts. I was smitten. For my birthday he gave me a gold signet ring with my name engraved on it. He took me to movies; we drank milkshakes at the café; he played the jukebox and we listened, holding hands. We teamed up with Sandra Malcomess and Neville Wiblin. I was in love. He partnered me at the Lincoln House Ball at the end of the year. I wore silver shoes and a shimmery white evening dress with a red rose clipped to my belt.

"When I saw you coming down the stairs," Don told me much later, "you looked like a princess. I fell in love with you."

One weekend we travelled to Komga for the engagement of Neville Wiblin to Sandy. Her diamond ring sparkled. Don and I listened as they discussed their wedding plans.

I had completed my course and returned home with all my worldly possessions. I had a teaching post at *Riebeek* College in Uitenhage. Would this affect our young romance?

Riebeek College, a girl's school in Uitenhage was my first teaching post. I had a class of twenty bright Standard four pupils and twelve slow Standard Five pupils. My first payslip revealed: R95 (£47.50) with deductions – Pension R7.13; PAYE (pay as you earn) R5.94; student loan R15 totalling R28.07 leaving me with R66.93 for board, clothing and toiletries.

I had a forty-minute walk to school from my boarding house, where I shared a room with Marie, who worked in the Post Office. The owners had three school-going daughters, all of whom only spoke Afrikaans. I either joined in or was left out. As a *rooinek,* I was odd-man-out amongst the *hairy backs,* as we called them. There was a division between English and Afrikaans-speaking South Africans.

My board included an evening meal and a weekly change of bedlinen. I laundered and ironed my own clothes, prepared and marked books on my bed, whilst Marie's portable radio blared out *boeremusiek, 'Sarie Marais'.* This was too much for me. I was *gatvol,* a guttural Afrikaans word meaning *I had had enough.*

My pupils brought me sweets, bunches of flowers and cake. I was touched by their kindness. Twice weekly I coached tennis. I met Carol, the PE teacher who owned a *VW Beetle.* We travelled to Grahamstown on Friday afternoons to see our respective boyfriends. I stayed with Don's friend Stinker's parents. Mr and Mrs Johnson made up the sleeper couch for me in their lounge. My friendship with Don grew more serious. The weeks flew by. I struggled with an armful of books and my briefcase daily. Whenever I felt down, I popped coins into the slot of the public telephone booth and dialled Don at work.

"Hi my love. You okay?"

Just hearing his voice made me feel better. Our exchange of words ended abruptly when my money ran out. Before term end I broke my ribs playing hockey. Unable to teach, I went home to recuperate. On my return to the boarding house, the owners had vanished. I spent a week with the neighbour before moving into a room at a seedy hotel in town.

Don and I drove to Kokstad for the mid-year holiday. After a few uncomfortable days, Don mustered the courage to approach my stepfather. They spoke behind closed doors before I was called in. "Well, well, well Denyse! Don has asked me for your hand in marriage."

The mention of the word *marriage* made me blush. I retreated into my shell. Sex in those days was brushed under the carpet. I clung to a childhood concept of marriage, confetti, wedding bells, a home, children and happily ever after… My mother was already planning the wedding stating, "You'll be married in St Patrick's Cathedral and the reception will be at the Balmoral Hotel."

"When's the big day?" Pop asked.

"Not until June next year."

"That gives me plenty of time," my mother said.

"This calls for an engagement party," Pop decided.

"We're happy to have a drink with you," Don replied.

In front of a roaring fire, Don wore a smart blazer and tie and I wore a charcoal tunic dress over a white jumper, we celebrated our engagement with mom and Pop. Don knelt down and proposed, "Will you marry me Denyse?"

"I will," I answered shyly. He slipped a solitaire diamond ring onto my finger. A tear rolled down my cheek.

"To the engaged couple!"

"May you both be very happy together!"

Champagne glasses clinked. I wanted the whole world to know we were engaged.

Back in Uitenhage I moved from the seedy hotel. As a special favour Mrs Marsh took me in. I shared a large bedroom, divided by wardrobes, with three schoolgirls. The room was far from private. The house was nearer the school. I was grateful for the evening meal. Don bought me a mahogany *kist* with brass handles, for my trousseau. This was the first piece of furniture I ever owned and I was truly grateful.

My pupils admired my ring and asked questions. As the year drew to a close, a string of inspectors called on the school among them the needle-work inspector, a short fat woman full of her own importance. Strutting around the classroom in her high heels, brimmed hat and two-piece suit, she cast a critical eye on the needlework and knitted items which were displayed on a trestle table. "Miss Lloyd, hand out the knitting."

"Certainly, Miss Jones."

Two pupils distributed the knitting. My pupils knitted not daring to look up.

"What are you doing? Keep your hands on the needles. By now you should know how to knit. I can see Miss Lloyd hasn't taught you a thing!"

Before leaving, Miss Jones threw her weight around and reminded me, "You've failed to teach your class. This will appear in my report."

My class and I were in tears when the headmistress entered the room.

"Do not upset yourselves. I am aware of the position."

The headmistress knew I had not been prepared to take Needlework but had agreed to help knowing I had no training. The subject was closed. I was forced to resign from my post after three terms, because Don could not get leave in May 1966. We moved our wedding forward to 20 November 1965. My resignation was accepted. I was very sad to leave. A pupil, Sharon Gillmer, wrote to me on 4 October 1965. I kept her letter all these years and wonder where she is today.

78 van der Stel Avenue,
Uitenhage.

Dear Miss Lloyd

I am writing this short letter to thank you for teaching me. Those days were the happiest days of all my school days. I shall miss you very much and I am sure the class will also miss you. I could never understand Grammar, but I understand it now. You might have taught us different to other teachers, but I still think that you taught us the best.

It has been very miserable weather. It kept on raining and raining and raining. At least it did not rain today. I hope the weather is more pleasant up there in Kokstad. May God bless you and keep you, to live happily with your husband in the years to come. Good luck.

Best wishes.

Sharon Gillmer

With so much excitement in my life and so much to look forward to, I never dreamt it could all end so swiftly...

11

WILL I WALK AGAIN?

In September 1966 Hendrik Verwoerd, the driving force of apartheid, was assassinated in the National Assembly by a deranged parliamentary messenger. He was succeeded by John Vorster, the then Minister of Justice who declared, 'My role is to walk further along the road set by Hendrik Verwoerd.'

PATRICK, stirring his porridge at the breakfast, asked "Is the wedding today?"

"Today is the 20 November 1965. It's my big day!"

I could not eat. My mother spoke aloud, checking her *"To do"* list. Hardly noticing Annie, our servant, put the tea tray on the table, she rattled on.

"The corsages will be delivered to Molly's. Yes, Phil your suit's there, and your shoes. Our hair appointments start at 9.30 am. What else? Patrick, don't tease Donnaleen and Ann. Neyse, pour the tea, will you? I've arranged for Vivian to collect all the wedding presents at the reception."

My mother thought of everything. I chose a classic Empire-line frock in plain white satin. The bodice was edged with drop pearls, and the sleeves were covered with white Chantilly lace. The long train hung from the shoulders and my veil was offset with a diamante coronet. I would carry moth orchids.

There had been weeks of careful preparation. My beautiful wedding dress was my mother's labour of love. Her sewing machine had hummed late into the night until my frock and the peacock-green bridesmaids' dresses for my two sisters were complete. For the last time I was squashed on the backseat with Patrick, Topsy and Margy, as a *single* sibling. I comforted myself, thinking they would *always* be my sisters and my brother.

As we bumped along on the dusty farm roads towards Kokstad, Patrick announced, "I'll catch the garter," He never understood why his remark was met with peals of laughter.

As time ticked by my excitement intensified. Aunty Molly snapped photographs of me looking in the mirror, standing on the staircase until I climbed into the ribbon-clad *Chevrolet*. Uncle Stewey drove Pop and me to the church. Was this really happening?

"Look at them singing and dancing!" Pop commented.

I watched as our servants, dressed in their Sunday best, expressed their happiness despite restrictions imposed on them by *apartheid* laws, with '*Slegs vir Blankes*' signs everywhere. I waved to show them my appreciation, before I walked arm in arm with Pop to the big wooden door of St Patrick's Cathedral. Topsy adjusted my train before we entered the crowded church. Hat-covered heads turned when the organist played the wedding march and I walked down the aisle to my awaiting bridegroom.

Father Manion conducted the marriage service and Father Baptist performed the Nuptial Mass, during which we exchanged wedding vows and rings and received God's blessing on our marriage *'til death us do part.'* My grandmother was happy Don had agreed to bring up our children as Catholics. Had I let her down by not joining the convent as she had planned for me or had I pleased her by being her first grandchild to marry? I never knew, but she agreed to make our three-tier wedding cake and was very fond of Don.

After signing the register we emerged from the church into the sunlight, bombarded by handfuls of confetti and cheers, as husband and wife. The local photographers, from the Kokstad Studio, took professional photos. Hugh Johnson, best man and David Pohl, grooms-man, Don's friends from Grahamstown, accompanied my sisters who were the bridesmaids. My flower girls Donnaleen and Ann wore long white dresses. Patrick was a shy page-boy.

A reception for over 300 guests followed at the Balmoral Hotel, where Vivian, my eldest cousin, officiated as Master of Ceremonies and Mrs Malan sang *I Believe* and *This Is My Prayer,* our theme songs. We took to the floor for the first waltz. Dancing and drinking accelerated and heightened the noise and party mood. I slipped away to change into my 'going away outfit', a pink lace ensemble with matching accessories and hat.

On my return I stood on a chair to throw the garter, which Patrick failed to catch. Jeanette caught my bouquet. We crept under an arch of raised arms, kissing our guests goodbye, until we reached Don's *Cortina,* parked at the hotel entrance. With *'Just Married'* written across the back window and a trail of cans bouncing on the tarmac behind us, we waved goodbye.

The long wait for us was over. Don stopped the car at a filling station. After cleaning the car windows and untying the noisy contraptions, he kissed me. "I love you Mrs Smith!"

A sudden fear gripped me. I knew nothing of the facts of life. My previous concerns seemed unimportant now that I faced new challenges. *What lay ahead? Was I ready? Would I be all Don expected as his wife?*

We spent our first night at the Richmond Hotel, honeymooning at the Plaza Hotel in Durban and a cottage belonging to Aunty Molly and Uncle Stewey at Umtumvuna. Newly-weds making plans for our future. On the way back to Grahamstown we collected our wedding presents in Kokstad. On arrival at the flat, Don parked. I rushed up the stairs with Don following. "What are you doing?"

Don scooped me up and carried me over the threshold of our first home.

"It's tradition," he said putting me down. I surveyed my new surroundings.

"What do you think?"

"You've done a great job. I love it."

Don had furnished our first home. As a child I had dreamt of this day…

We settled down as newly-weds do. Don went to work at the building society. I applied and secured a job working for Professor Gledhill in the Physics Department at Rhodes University. (In November 1965 Rhodes University became the first university to install a computer). Before I started work in January, we spent Christmas in Kokstad.

Soon after we returned, Don arrived at the flat one day carrying a wriggling puppy.

"Where'd you get him? He's so cute."

"He's yours, my love, a wedding present."

Holding the puppy in both hands, I tucked him under my chin

enjoying the puppy smell and little snorting noises. His soft warm body nestled against me.

"With the white markings on his front legs, I suggest we call him Spatts?"

"Spatts. Thanks Don. I adore him."

I had only once had a puppy of my own, Winkie. Because he bit me badly, Pop shot him when I was at boarding school. This nearly broke my heart. "I'll love and care for you always," I promised Spatts. I found it hard to leave my new puppy when I went to work.

On my first day Professor Gledhill introduced himself and showed me the ropes. As I uncovered the typewriter, the professor called me, "Denyse, come to my office with your shorthand notepad. I need to dictate a few letters."

"Yes Professor."

I listened filling the pages with shorthand squiggles. I hoped to transcribe these accurately. I put carbon paper between the pages to make copies when typing letters. Once typed, I put these with relevant envelopes on his desk for signature. I also typed reports received from scientists on a ship on an expedition in the Antarctica.

Our friends David a car-salesman and his wife Lorraine had two children. Their four-year old son, Grant visited me in our flat. Holding Kim, born on 20 August 1965, made me broody. I wondered when we would become parents...

***

Life was exciting and full of surprises. In mid-January Don announced, "We're the proud owners of a plot of land."

"Where?"

"Let's go. I can't wait to show you."

This corner plot with a fantastic view over Grahamstown in a good residential area was ours. Don's brother Anthony and his wife, Lucy owned the adjoining plot. Their house was already roof high. "I've arranged to meet Anthony's architect and builder."

We wandered over our plot before exploring Anthony's building site. I had barely come to terms with living in a flat. We were about to take the next step, to build a house.

"Do you have any ideas?" Don asked me.

Flummoxed, we met the architect and builder. They listened,

suggested, scribbled and sketched ideas on paper. Jotting down facts and figures, they kept within our budget. We agreed to meet them two weeks later.

Picking up the post one day, I recognised Sue's handwriting. Sue my college friend is getting married, I thought. My excitement crashed like a tree falling to the ground. I read in disbelief, *my mother, after a long illness, passed away on Sunday*. She had been a mother to me in Uitenhage. I ached with sadness. Suffering from cancer, she never complained.

I remembered when I stayed with the Mulders during my teaching practice. Sue's mother woke us at 5 am and prepared a hearty breakfast. She waved goodbye when we caught the bus to the station, where we journeyed to Port Elizabeth. The wind howled. Port Elizabeth is aptly known as *the windy city*.

Sue, Joy and I went our different ways and met again for a tedious journey back to Uitenhage. Conversations faded fast with the rocking train motion lulling us to sleep. Sue's smiling mother opened the door to three worn-out budding teachers. She bubbled, reviving our weary spirits. "Tonight we're having roast chicken," she announced. "Now put your dirty washing in the laundry and I'll see to it."

Those were happy days. I appreciated all she did for me. I mumbled, believing she could hear me, "*Ma* Mulder, I'll miss you. You were a second mother to me." I thought of Sue. I could not imagine what it must feel like to lose your mother… When Don dried my tears and hugged me, I had a desire to attend Mass for her. Mass was said every Wednesday at 5.30 pm in the Catholic Church. "Could I go to church tomorrow evening?"

"Of course, my love, you'll be out by 6.30 pm."

"The car rally," I remembered, "we're giving Dave and Lorraine a lift. Perhaps you could pick me up at the church?"

"That's fine," he said. His comforting arms around me eased my sorrow. I hoped my prayers for Mrs Mulder would help her family. On Wednesday I fed Spatts. Drawing comfort from my puppy, I cuddled him on my lap before parting. "Sorry Spatts, I'll be back."

I placed him in his little basket. Pulling on a pair of cotton slacks and a white blouse, I slipped into my sandals and hurried off. My grief sucked my joy like a blood-sucking leech. How I wished we were not going out. Don, Dave and Lorraine waited in the car. I kissed Don. Jumping into the car, I sat beside Lorraine in the back. She looked gorgeous. Fingernails painted. Hair perfect. "Hi Dave. Hi Lorraine. Sorry to keep you waiting," I said.

We drove off. This was my first car rally and by all accounts, it promised to be fun. Our destination was a farm on the Beaufort West road, where, after a *braaivleis*, prizes would be awarded. We were spurred on by Don and Dave's competitive spirit:

"This is the shortest route to the ..."

"You turn the car around Don and I'll hop out and count the steps!"

Lorraine and I read and ticked off the list.

"We've found a fig leaf. We need a live flea." Lorraine announced.

"I'll drive to our flat. Spatts'll be pleased to part with a flea!" Don enthused.

Returning to the car, he handed me a transparent plastic bag. Inside a live flea hopped about. "Was Spatts asleep, Don?"

"Yes. His tail wagged when he saw me. I felt guilty leaving him. He'll be fine until we get home again..."

We arrived at the venue, parked the car and walked towards the combined smell of smoke and meat coming from the *braaivleis*. We mingled with friends, exchanged stories and enjoyed mouth-watering mutton chops, *boerewors* and garlic bread, and a variety of salads and my favourite *pap en sous*. After prize-giving, we snuck away to the snooker-room, where Lorraine and I watched our husbands, Dave and Don, play pool with friends.

It grew late and cold. The game was nearly over. Lorraine and I waited for our husbands in the car. I sat behind the driver's seat...

"I'm freezing cold, Lorraine."

"I'll grab Dave's *jersey* for you."

Before I could stop her, she made her way through the darkness towards the distant light of the snooker-room. Lorraine returned to the door of the car where I sat. I slid over which meant Lorraine now sat *behind* the driver's seat...

"Thanks Lorraine. This'll warm me up."

I buttoned up Dave's jersey. Within minutes, our hubbies climbed into the car. We drove off at 10.45 pm on a very dark night. There was no traffic on this lonely farm road. The men discussed their game, whilst we made plans for coffee.

"Have coffee at our flat," Lorraine suggested.

"You come to us? We *always* have coffee with you."

"Mom's looking after Grant and Kim. I'm sure she won't mind. Okay?"

"I'll tell Don."

I faced the front of the car to tell Don our plans, but before I uttered the first word, horrifying, almost Dracula-like screams pierced the air and intensified around me. I heard, felt and saw nothing after those screams, which I later learnt, were from Lorraine. Next, I remember being alone, engulfed in an eerie silence and darkness. I had no idea how long I lay on the front seat of the car, before my confused mind scrambled into survival mode. I needed Don. "Don! Where are you? Don! Don!" I screamed desperately hoping Don or *somebody* would hear me... Somehow stomach-down on the ground, unable to stand, I pulled on tufts of grass worming my way over the rough boulder-strewn *veld,* towards a voice calling out.

"Lorraine! Lorraine!" Dave was calling. He reached out in the dark, grabbed hold of my leg, thinking I was Lorraine. Just as quickly he withdrew his blood-smeared hand from a deep gash in my calf. Unbeknown to me then, a carload of people returning from the same *braaivleis* arrived on the scene shortly after the accident. There were no mobile phones in those days so they raced into Grahamstown and notified the police and the hospital.

The distant screeching sirens of ambulances and police vans grew louder and louder, the nearer they got to where I lay. Swirling lights illuminated the roadside. Torchlights streaked across the *veld*. Footsteps tramped through the long grass. Activities accelerated. I felt no pain when paramedics slid me onto a stretcher, transferring me into an ambulance and strapping me down. It felt like a nightmare. The awful sirens screamed and flashed as the ambulance sped to the hospital in Grahamstown. Today, ambulance and police sirens rekindle the memory of that fateful night...

A doctor was at my bedside in the hospital. His calmly-spoken words have remained embedded in my brain forever: "Denyse, I'm sorry to break the bad news to you. You've been in a car accident. Lorraine, your best friend, died of internal injuries on the way to the hospital… David suffered minor injuries. Your husband died instantly!" He paused before adding, "I'll stitch your leg up now."

When I looked up, the doctor was gone. Topsy, my sister, a student at the Grahamstown Training College, was at my bedside. She repeated, "I'm sorry. The Catholic priest's on his way."

I had no conception of time or of my condition. The same Catholic priest who earlier on had said the 5.30 pm Mass I attended, now administered the Last Sacraments to me, thinking my death was imminent. I slipped into a coma. A frightening experience! I could hear doctors, nurses and strangers talking at my bedside, but though I tried, I could not utter a single word.

"Poor girl. Paralysed for life.

Shame, she'll be in a wheelchair for the rest of her life.

Her spine's broken in two places.

Siestog, sy sal nooit weer loop nie, shame, she'll never walk again.

Two funerals! Such young lives lost.

A paraplegic! Little ones, left without a mother. The baby's only six months old!

It's too dangerous to move her now.

Will she survive? It's still touch and go…"

In the twinkling of an eye, my marriage of two months, emerging with dreams of young marrieds – plans to build a home, plans to train a puppy, plans to design a garden, plans to start a family and plans to grow old together – had crumpled in a heap like buildings demolished by a tsunami. It was only by the grace of God I had survived.

Whilst in a coma my mind fought the negative words I could not respond to, willing my broken body to survive and to prove them wrong. I argued back but nobody heard me, "I'm not going to be in a wheelchair for the rest of my life. Please, God, help me make it. I *will* walk again…"

I was in a hospital bed with my mother beside me when I opened my eyes after being comatose for three days. I stared at her. Words, I formed in my mind, were now audible.

"What's happened, mom?"

"You've been in a car accident."

My mother, gripping my hand as tears rolled down her cheeks, continued, "Don died instantly. Lorraine died on the way to the hospital. The cause of the accident's unknown. An autopsy ruled out a heart attack. The car rolled several times, bonnet to bumper, and was extensively damaged. A general consensus leant towards a burst tyre. If excessive speed, as some had speculated, was the cause, the car would not have finished up where it did."

She went on, "We'll never really know what happened, my girl. The phone rang and woke us at midnight. When we heard we drove through the night to get to you, leaving Patrick with Aunty Molly and Uncle Stewey. I've not stopped praying for you, my child."

The doctor, uncertain of my injuries, told my family I was on the critical list and could die from internal injuries. My spine broken in the thorax and lower lumbar regions had left me paralysed from the waist down. Sobbing, she ended, "Both funerals are over."

I had numerous lacerations on my body; the worst was on my lower right leg.

"Will I walk again?"

"There's a chance you'll walk again."

To give me hope, she added, "They'll move you to East London when your condition has stabilised."

A few days later I was transferred to the Frere Hospital in East London. My mother accompanied the ambulance driver. The siren was silent on this sixty-kilometre journey but my body ached feeling every bump of the tarred road. On my arrival, nurses wheeled me on a trolley. I was put in a bed in the corner of the orthopaedic ward. After numerous X-rays of my back, three orthopaedic surgeons discussed what should be done. Two suggested surgery, but Mr Smit disagreed.

"Surgery's too risky. A minute error could increase the risk of permanent paralysis."

"She might not regain the use of her legs."

"There's a good chance she'll walk again. It'll take time," Mr Smit argued.

"Her parents will be the ones to make the final decision."

My parents took Mr Smit's advice. My spine would be left to knit on its own, which meant lying flat on my back in hospital for three months. Mr Smit allowed the nurses to wash my hair lying horizontally. I looked bad. Dried blood, grass and mud congealed in my long, matted hair. Turning my head from side to side, I listened to the hairdresser's scissors snipping off my hair. I looked like a shorn sheep.

Pushing thoughts of my appearance aside, I faced more important issues. Not yet twenty-one years of age, my mother was given Power of Attorney to handle my affairs. I needed answers to many questions:

"Where's my puppy?"

"Pop's caring for him on the farm."

"Does Professor Gledhill know I'm in hospital?"

"He's been told."

I faced difficult decisions. Don nominated me the beneficiary of his life cover, but his written request had not yet been finalised in Pretoria, making his mother the legal heir. My lawyer asked her to waive her right. She refused. She was paid the money and I have never heard from her again. Dave claimed compensation and he was paid out a large sum of money from Don's Third Party insurance cover. This upset me because Don was blamed and money could never replace a mother. My mother planned and paid for Don's funeral; had the tombstone erected which I designed from my hospital bed; arranged for a removal company to pack and move the contents of our Grahamstown flat when I left hospital.

"What's to become of our plot of land?"

"Had the building commenced, the insurance company would have paid for the house to be built. The plot will be sold, Neyse."

"Be strong, my girl. You'll survive these knocks and overcome this tragedy," she encouraged me. My mother never missed a hospital visit.

Lying on my back, I had time to think: Earlier that night *I* sat *behind* the driver's seat...Lorraine's kindness had killed her. Don and I almost died together... God was merciful to me... My life had been spared...

Driven by my mother's words, 'you'll survive' and my faith, I regained more feeling in my feet and my legs day by day. There *was hope.* Will I walk again? I believed I would, but only time would tell. My hospital bed was wheeled onto the verandah on fine days where I escaped the humdrum clatter of hospital life and medicinal smells. I glimpsed treetops, blue sky and clouds drifting by. I felt the sun on my legs and arms and I smelt the scent of flowers and mown lawns. In the fresh air, mom and I worked things out privately. On 1 March I wrote to my mother lying flat on my back.

Really words cannot express my gratitude... you are a wonderful mother...you sat at my bedside day after day, gave me courage and always came with a cheery smile and left me feeling so much better. I lived for 10am, 3pm and 7pm...

I still cannot comprehend the full significance of the words, 'Don is at rest'. To pacify my perturbed mind I find consolation in expecting a hearty greeting from Don when I return to Grahamstown. However, this is my imagination running away with me and how hard the reality will be when at length I am discharged... Sister Smith wanted to know the date of my birthday. She ***thought*** *I would be out by then.*

With my 21st birthday pending, Mr Smit allowed me to go out warning me, "You may, Denyse, but I must tell you, you're not ready to take such a big step."

"Thanks Mr Smit."

Determined to please both my family and my friends and to prove to myself I could do it, I arrived at the hotel in an ambulance on 20 March, 1966. I was wheeled into the dining room on a stretcher. Hotel guests glared at me and tut-tutted as I passed by. With difficulty, I lay across cushioned chairs, on my back. My body was engulfed in excruciating pain. I could not bear the agony. When the first course arrived, I begged, "Please take me back!" My body was not ready. I had let my family down. What a way to turn twenty-one!

One of many letters of condolence I received in hospital dated 1 March from the General Manager of the EPBS, Eastern Province Building Society, inspired me to continue my fight.

Dear Mrs Smith

The members of my Board directed me to extend to you their sincere sympathy in the passing of your late husband whose service to the Society had been so much appreciated.

I know that words might seem meaningless on an occasion such as this, but I want you to know how shocked I was to hear that Don had passed away and how very sorry I feel for you in having lost a devoted husband.

Although I feel that the sympathy which I offer in this hour of sorrow cannot lighten the burden which you have been called upon to bear, I sincerely hope that it will strengthen and encourage you in the sad loss you have sustained in the unfortunate passing of Don, and I mourn his loss with you.

I realise that there is no greater loss than to lose a dear one, and I pray God will give you strength in your hour of need and the courage and faith to face up to this tragedy…

In mid-March, aqua-therapy began. Every day at 10 am, lying on my back I was wheeled to the hospital pool. My legs strengthened in the buoyancy of water.

"Today I'd like you to stand at the side of your bed with the physiotherapist for a minute," Mr Smit instructed.

"Only *one* minute?"

"You'll understand Denyse."

After lying horizontally for seven weeks, I was delighted to be helped off the bed. Barely lasting the allocated one minute, my world spun around me. My legs, limp and wobbly, could not support me. Each day I stood for a longer period until I learnt to walk again little realising what was happening in my country. Before my accident I had taken so much for granted. Walking, sitting, standing, running, dressing, dancing… Elderly patients in my ward encouraged me.

"Well done!

You're walking on your own!

Take two more steps today, Denyse."

With their support I increased the distance I walked in the ward each day. Though difficult, my unrelenting determination drove me on. I believe the God-given wisdom of my orthopaedic surgeon made it possible for me to walk again. I left the hospital feeling optimistic, but not for long.

Since that fateful night, I had been sheltered in the confines of a hospital. I looked at the world through the car window as we drove off. An emptiness and a longing overwhelmed me. People went about their everyday lives. Nothing had changed in *their* lives, but mine would never be the same. I was a widow. I was alone. I had not said goodbye to Don.

I had a panic attack. I wanted to shout for everybody to hear. "Can't you understand? I've lost my husband. We were *only* married for two months!"

Instead, I said, "Mom, please stop the car and buy me a packet of cigarettes."

My mind flashed back to that catastrophic night. It happened without warning, in the twinkling of an eye. Previously when I had read newspaper reports of car accidents, I pitied the families involved, but I thought something like that would *never* happen to *me*...

Would a cigarette calm my nerves? My mother gave me the packet of *Rothmans* and a box of *Lion* matches. It seemed she understood. I lit up, but soon stubbed it out. We continued the journey in silence with the lingering smell of stale cigarette smoke clinging to the inside of the car.

I longed to be in Grahamstown, but when we arrived my emotions were in turmoil. The familiar landmarks in Grahamstown were shrouded in gloom. A cloud of sadness hung over the town like mist rolling off a mountain top. I expected to see Don walking towards me, drawing me into his arms, saying, "Hi Neyse, my love, I've missed you!" I imagined his warm arms around me... I swallowed the lump in my throat, not trusting my voice to speak.

Where do I begin? Will my life ever be normal again? How could I separate my joyful memories of the past with the solitary grief of the present?

We accepted Dave's invitation and visited him where he lived with Lorraine's parents. Mr and Mrs Tasmer cared for Grant and Kim. What was his motive? I remembered his claim against Don's Estate. He had only visited me once when I was in hospital.

I soon found out. When we were alone, Dave proposed to me, adding, "Grant's very fond of you, Denyse. Kim will grow up knowing you as her mom..."

Flabbergasted, I snapped, "I've only come out of hospital today, Dave. I'm grieving for Don."

My mother saw the panic on my face when we joined them. "We must get back to the hotel now. Denyse's exhausted after the journey."

I never saw Grant and Kim or Lorraine's parents again, but I met up with Dave years later. He was happy, had re-married and had a new family...

The next day I faced another hurdle... Attending neither Don nor Lorraine's funeral, I went to their graves. Armed with an enormous bunch of roses, we drove to the cemetery. My mother parked. I got out gingerly. It was eerily quiet. There was no life here. The tombstones named the dead of so many forgotten souls. Hearing my footsteps on gravel, I followed my mother between the rows of graves. She stopped. I stared at his tombstone.

This was not a dream…

In loving memory of my beloved husband,
DONALD DANVERS
Born:16 October 1942 Died: 9 February 1966
Not only today, but every day, remembered by your loving wife
For it is in dying that we are born to eternal life.
God will link the broken chain
Forever when we meet again.

I tried to imagine Don's body lying in a coffin, six foot under the ground where I stood. Still…Cold…Lifeless…

I erased this image. Instead I saw his warm smile and his brown, laughing eyes; I smelt the *Old Spice* aftershave he wore; I heard his deep voice, *'Neyse, my love …'* as he held my hand in his. I had exhausted my tears. Kneeling down at the graveside, I prayed silently, ending, "I love you. Don. You're waiting for me..."

We left. Grief-stricken, I could not visit Lorraine's grave that day. We drove to the flat. Everything remained exactly as it was on 9 February. Don's discarded newspaper lay on the coffee table; his clothes hung in the wardrobe. He had found a flea the last time he was here. Every trace of a puppy was gone.

Overcome with grief, my mother helped me pack a suitcase of clothing. I looked away from our framed wedding photograph on the bookshelf. Locking the door, I shut out the memories of a short-lived marriage. I had been Don's wife for eighty days!

We journeyed to Kokstad to face an adjustment. No longer a child, yet dependent on my folks, a once radiant bride, I was returning to Kokstad, a wounded widow… I moved into the new wing of the farmhouse, built for my stepbrother, Tony. I had my own bathroom.

Alone, the nights were long and difficult. I cried myself to sleep.

Spatts wagged his tail and cheered me every morning. Friends wanted to visit. Whenever I saw a car spewing dust on the gravel road heading for the farmhouse, I withdrew.

"I don't want visitors. They're curious to see what's become of me. I'm a misfit... You do understand, mom..."

"But Denyse, that's not so."

"*Please* mom."

I locked myself in my room, safe from prying eyes. I had to move on from all that had happened in the past: resigning a teaching post, announcing my engagement, marrying my first love and becoming Mrs Smith. Why did I think the whole town was watching to see, what next? How could my parents transform me from recluse to the fun-loving person that I had once been?

"We're going into town. Mom's made an appointment for you with Dr Veel on Mr Smit's recommendation," Pop said to me one day. I could not argue. Against my will, I accompanied him. On arrival Pop said, "I want a quick word with Peter. I won't be long."

I waited in the car. I watched Peter Horsley driving a brand new four-door saloon car, the latest *Ford* out of the show-room. He parked it in front of Pop's car. Peter was at the car window. I wound it down.

"Hi Neyse. It's good to see you," he said extending his hand to me.

"What's this all about?"

He handed me a set of car keys. Pop smiled and said, "It's yours."

"No! I can't."

"You can. I'll leave you. Peter will take you for a test drive. I'll be off then."

Before I knew it, I was behind the steering wheel smelling the newness of an off-the-show-room-floor car, admiring the polished dashboard with a fitted radio. Peter took me through the motions of driving.

"Put the keys in the ignition and start the engine. You'll be fine, Neyse," he said.

I did as I was told. I drove. I put the wipers on instead of the indicator. When I dropped Peter at the show-room, he winked, saying, "Enjoy your new car. We're all behind you, Neyse."

Don had always driven me everywhere. Now I was in the driver's seat. A turning point in my life which prepared me for future challenges. I overcame my fear of being in a car and I became independent. Unappreciative at the time, I realised later the importance of driving a car after my accident. I had taken a leap forward in starting a new life.

The nuns offered me a Standard Three teaching post commencing in July 1966. I accepted. I boarded with Aunty Joan and Uncle Slabs. I taught at my old school. With twenty-two pupils, we shared a happy six months. My mother coaxed me back to tennis. We practised alone until I was able to play social tennis at the Kokstad Tennis Club on Saturday afternoons, another milestone. I am indebted to her for so much. Wearing a tennis dress, I could not hide the hideous scar on my right leg resembling a nine-inch purple worm.

Before leaving Training College, Joy, Sue and I had planned an overseas holiday. I had dropped out to get married. Joy extended the same invitation to me. I accepted. We would sail on the *Africa,* a *Lloyd Triestino* liner, from Durban to Venice, in early January 1967. I had something to live for. I had a goal. I would travel and see the world.

Part Two

1966 - 1985

THROUGH HIS MERCY

Psalm 57:1
*Have **mercy** on me, O God, have **mercy** on me, for in you my soul takes refuge.*
I will take refuge in the shadow of your wings until the disaster has passed.

Nolyn and I marry on 23 August 1969

Left to right: Ruth Wild, Hugh Preston, Nolyn, Denyse, Margy, Peggy Leary, Phil Leary and Eileen Brown

Above: A camel ride in Cairo with Joy Puttergill

Above: Chandrè watches Nolyn play golf at Coffee Bay

Right: Brent, Chandrè and Byron taken at Brechanby

Left: Denyse with Brent, Chandrè and Byron

Below: Nolyn and Denyse holiday in the Algarve

12

SETTING SAIL

A government circular in 1967 stated, 'No stone is to be left unturned to achieve the settlement in the homelands of non-productive Bantu at present residing in the European areas.' This implied that 4 million Africans would be deported to black homelands.

CHRIS Barnard performed the first heart transplant at Groote Schuur Hospital in Cape Town. Abortion became legal in the UK and the pound devalued. Flower power was the new way of protesting for peace in the USA. In that year 1967 my friends and I set sail for Europe on the *Africa*. Many carefully planned preparations included: clothes, money and medication. My suitcase, bulging with luggage, had no wheels to drag it along in those days. My handbag held my passport, traveller's cheques, camera and cine-camera, *Kodak* spools, a journal, ball-point pens, make-up and perfume. The long-awaited day had finally arrived.

Leaving Kokstad meant leaving Spatts. My puppy was a living reminder of a world slipping further away from me. Before boarding the ship, Joy, Sue and I said our goodbyes. Standing on the upper deck holding tightly on to the rails, we waved to our parents, who stood on the wharf. The '*Africa*' hooted and sailed into the Indian Ocean.

We had never sailed before and neither had we left South Africa. This once-in-a-lifetime adventure began. Rushing down flights of stairs to our cabin in the bowels of the boat, I chose the bottom bunk in our cramped cabin, which was just adequate for sleeping and showering. To overcome seasickness on the rough seas, I floated in the pool. In the dining room, Joy and shared a table with two strangers. Sue sat elsewhere. We joined in the evening entertainment and by day we played deck quoits and table tennis if we were not swimming. In the library I wrote postcards and updated my journal.

After crossing the Tropic of Capricorn the ship docked and Joy and I went into Beira with Bruno, a German friend. Patrol cars were on the alert for terrorist attacks. I recorded: *I watched natives building dug-out boats and mending nets*. We sailed out of Beira at 5 pm.

Today Beira, a sprawling city at the mouth of the Punge River, owes its existence to the Beira Corridor, a road and railway line providing Zimbabwe with an outlet to the sea.At the next port of call Dar-es-Salaam inaccessible to South African passport-holders Joy and I accompanied by John, a fellow passenger, went ashore in a broken-down boat. *We escaped customs easily; swam amidst seaweed; wore costumes and beach-wraps*.

Today Dar-es-Salaam is the third fastest-growing city in Africa. During World War I the British captured German East Africa. It became Tanganyika attaining its independence in December 1961. Tanganyika and Zanzibar merged to form Tanzania in 1964.

In Mombasa, Kenya, we disembarked with cameras. I photographed the Tusk Archway erected for Princess Margaret's visit to Mombasa in 1955; the *Uhuru* Fountain, a continent-of-Africa shaped pond with two dragon fountains and the *Nyali* Pontoon Bridge. *I watched two Arabs de-flea-ing each other's heads*.

Today Mombasa is frequented by cruise ships, navy ships and the famous QEII. After Mombasa and before reaching Mogadiscio, we crossed the Equator with extraordinary celebrations. After eating spaghetti from a plate on the floor on bended knees, Karl, my friend and I, covered in raw egg, were thrown into the pool. The ship called at Mogadiscio, Somaliland. *Somalis boarded the ship in baskets*.

We rounded the Horn of Africa sailing into the Gulf of Aden where the *Africa* anchored offshore.

"Tomorrow's an early start into Aden."

"*Ja*."

"It's a tax-free port."

"We'll have to be careful!"

It was dark. With water lapping against the side of the boat, the golden ball peeped over the horizon, enlarged and sent golden rays across the shimmering water. Day broke. Ashore Joy and I wandered through 'Happy Stores'. We met up with two British soldiers who said: "There are 4000 British soldiers stationed in Aden.

The port's due to get its independence in 1968.

Let's hope we make it. Another soldier was shot earlier today."

Passengers boarded the *'Africa'* laden with duty-free purchases. Sailing into the Red Sea, we were bound for Suez, where tourist buses collected us. The *'Africa'* sailed through the 102 mile-long Suez Canal, 38 feet deep and 200 yards wide, taking 15 hours to reach Port Said. We drove into Cairo, the largest city in Africa, and shopped with piastres. *Dilapidated 1947 flats; street children wore pyjama-dress: saw horse-drawn carts with bells.*

Between sightseeing we had tea at the Shepherd's Hotel and lunch at Elborg Hotel, before visiting the pyramids. The largest comprising 2,500,000 stones took 30 years to build and stood 471 feet high. We climbed the uneven 320 steps to the top. The Great Sphinx is made from one piece of stone. Pieces of the beard are in the British Museum in London.

Joy and I rode a camel. She was astride upfront and me behind her. The camel on bended knees lurched and rocked upright, its back legs rising high, sending us forward. Then her forelegs straightened and I thought I would be tipped off backwards. We were sitting high off the ground, when the camel swivelled its head around and eyeballed us.

"Hang on for dear life, Joy!"

"We're off!"

The lead camel plodded off towards the pyramids on padded feet the size of dinner plates. All the camels followed in a line, moving with the same jerky gait and emanating a stench only fitting that of a camel.

"So much for our first camel ride," Joy concluded when we dismounted. I stared back at the Sphinx, large and sombre. With the thoughts, those stony eyes had seen empires rise and fall; we boarded the bus for afternoon tea at *Omar Khayyam Hotel* and dinner at the Italian Club, before driving on to Port Said.

Our bus driver hooted at the *'Africa'*. It hooted back. Weary, hot and dusty, we waited in the stuffy bus. Windows were closed to prevent unrelenting Arabs plying their wares at us. In the dark and cold we were ferried across the harbour to the *'Africa'*, which sailed at 2.30 am. The *'Africa'* sailed through the Strait of Otranto docking in Brindisi. *We had difficulty crossing roads as traffic approached from the opposite side.* We disembarked in Venice, which was our destination port. Braving the cold, we visited the famous landmarks. We took a train to Innsbruck, Austria. Joy had coconut poisoning, but recovered before we journeyed to Westerndorf to ski. *Westerndorf, near Kitzbuhl, is a small country town where folk wear traditional costume. 36 Austrian Shillings is equivalent to one Rand.*

I was fearless despite my recent spinal injury. After ski-ing instructions, I took the ski-lift to higher slopes zigzagging down the slippery slopes at speed. In the quaint village with gingerbread-like houses, the air so fresh it almost felt mint-flavoured, we tobogganed, drank mugs of hot spicy *glühwein* or *schnapps,* wolfed down *apfelstrüdel. We ate beef goulash, crispy schnitzel and Käsespatzle, Austria's macaroni cheese, before we danced until 2.30 am.* Following this a courageous hitchhiking adventure began. Our first ride was in a *Citroen* from Zurich through the St Gothard's Pass. I wrote: *We travelled through heavy snowfalls. We crossed from Switzerland to Italy. At 2 am in Bergamo we hoped to board a train.* In Genoa an old man, who spoke English showed us *where Christopher Columbus lived, leading up to Fort Soprano, and a tall archway dating back to the Middle Ages.* Hitchhiking in a transport van carrying apples, we travelled along the Riviera. *Overlooking bays and coves, the sea was a deep-blue, dotted with small vessels. We wound along twisting roads edged with pines, vineyards, hothouses and vegetable fields on terraced slopes. Chateaux, perched on cliffs, reminded me of the Garden Route. We hitched from Nice to St Raphael. The Sirocco blew gales.*

Jean-Claude, whom I met at Westerndorf, lived in Toulon. Joy and I spent two nights at the Hotel Strasbourg. When we danced Jean-Claude said, "Cheri, you look so beautiful!"

"Thanks," I pulled away from his advances.

The next day he took us to the main highway. *We hitched through Aix-en-Provence to Grenoble. We drank pastis in Annecy and felt light-headed. We hitched from Geneva, to Bern, to Biel, to Zurich, where we caught a train and arrived in Paris at 10.30 pm.*

We loved romantic Paris and the famous sights but we were pleased to be on a train to Calais, and from there ferried to Dover.

"We'll have post waiting for us in London." I said.

"I can't wait to hear from John," Joy said, missing her boyfriend at home.

"I've had enough of hitchhiking and sight-seeing."

"I wonder what the *Underground* will be like Neyse."

"At least the people talk English."

Hitching through Europe, we had one nasty experience. The trucker who drove the apple van had ulterior motives when he pulled into an overnight stop for truckers. He locked our luggage in the cab. We ate spaghetti with him in the cafeteria, feeling out of place. Danger loomed. We planned our escape in Afrikaans. Joy asked for truck keys to fetch her pills and I excused myself to go the toilet. I met Joy at the van. We grabbed our luggage, left the keys in the door, and ran.

Cold wet and penniless we met an elderly gentleman at the railway station. He realised our plight and bought us a train ticket saying, "If my daughter were in trouble, I hope somebody would help her."

Thanking him, we boarded the train with Joy crying uncontrollably. On the journey I thought of all our firsts: cruise, camel ride, ski-ing and tobogganing, hitchhiking, hearing foreign languages, tunnel journey, ferry crossing and seeing the white cliffs of Dover. We were about to catch a tube for the first time in London...

Because we were far too polite, passengers disembarked and boarded ahead of us. The doors slammed shut. The tube disappeared in a flash, leaving Joy and me standing on the platform. We finally boarded and grabbed a strap as we stood in the over-crowded carriage. With relief we sank onto vacant seats and giggled. Our fellow passengers were hidden behind newspapers. Nobody spoke but, oblivious to that, our naïve chatter continued.

"What unfriendly people!" Joy remarked. I kept my opinion to myself. We climbed off at Earl's Court and went to the Overseas Visitor's Club, where we read our post from home. We booked into dormitory-type accommodation and sought employment. Joy worked as a waitress and Sue as an *au pair* in London.

I joined three South Africans in a *Microbus*, on a two–week tour of Ireland. Dave, the only male, drove the vehicle and Miralee Cooper and I became friends. Crossing from Holyhead to Dublin, we explored Ireland. I remember singing to a honky-tonk piano in an Irish pub. Inebriated, we collapsed in our *Microbus* for the night. A tapping on the window woke us…

"Is there anyone in there? Please move your vehicle? We're digging up the road."

Embarrassed we moved on. Although we spoke English with

different accents, I learnt subtle differences in the use of words: *tackies,* trainers; *circle,* roundabout; *cubbyhole,* glove compartment and many more…Richer for these experiences, I longed to tell Joy and Sue.

***

Without mobile phones in 1967, Joy, Sue and I met up at Earl's Court. Sue pursued her ambition to become an actress/singer, but now sang at a London nightclub. She was not happy. Joy shared her waitressing experiences telling us, "Sometimes I confused the order, but a wink and a smile sorted it out!" She was about to tour with nine South Africans in a *Microbus, Zulu*. She suggested I do the same. Needing money, I secured a job in Newick, Sussex as a live-in *au pair* for a lovely family, Mr and Mrs Lamdin. On my free weekends I caught the train to London.

Before Joy toured and before Sue flew to America, we met at a dance hall in Earl's Court. That evening, a tall dark Irishman asked me to dance. We danced all night. Up until then I had kept all men at arm's length. He invited me for coffee. Before we slipped away I introduced Donal to my friends.

Six-foot six inches tall, this Irishman in a dark suit, swept me off my feet. I loved his accent and his humorous story-telling. Oozing charm, he made me feel safe and secure. We went to his flat in Bayswater. My new friend, Donal Clarke, made coffee. We talked as though we had known each other for years.

"It's too late to catch a tube, Denyse. Will you stay the night?"

I did. But nature surprised me. I stood up aware I could not conceal my misery. My face flushed red. This would surely end our friendship. My monthlies had stained the back of my brand new lilac dress. "Don't worry, Denyse. I'll nip out and buy you some sanitary towels at the emergency chemist. I've put clean towels and a pair of my pyjamas in the bathroom for you." He kissed me lovingly on my forehead and left.

When he returned, he gave me the sanitary towels. I wore his over-sized pyjamas. Don gave me directions to Newick before we fell asleep. Early the next morning he left for work on the tube. Returning to Newick by bus with a skip in my step I wondered: Was I in love? Was this love destined to last forever?

Don, fifteen years my senior, a chartered accountant worked for Cooper Brothers. He had been educated at Taunton College and Paris

University. Three letters from him arrived in rapid succession. The first was dated 17 April 1967.

My darling Denyse

Thank you for the two wonderful surprises on my return home – your note and our tidy flat. You must have worked very hard. This must be a very short note if it is to catch the post this evening. Thank you for a marvellous weekend. I cannot recall a time when I have ever been so happy for so long. I am missing you desperately – I need you so much.

I hope the journey back was not too unpleasant and that your reception by the Lamdins was not hostile. Roll on Friday, it can't come too soon. I love you my dearest, with all my heart. You have been in my thoughts all day. Look after yourself.

Your loving, Don.

The second dated 20 April 1967 read:

My darling Denyse.

Thank you for your letter. It was most welcome. I've been watching the post like a hawk – hoping – I can't describe the pang of relief and excitement when I saw your writing. I am missing you terribly. It is so strange; to miss someone whom I didn't know a week ago and yet, to feel their absence as though vital pieces have been ripped from my body and from my mind. I want and need you here, with me.

I'm sorry that my directions to the bus were so unclear. I wondered, later at work, whether you would catch the right one. Each evening since you left, I have sat in my room and thought of you and of how much I love you. I want to do things for you. Above all I want to make you happy. Even now it all seems like a wondrous dream and then I read your note, touch your coat and suit, and now I read your letter and know at least, it all really happened.

I love you my dearest Denyse. I do hope you can come to me on Friday and bring my happiness back to me.

All my love to you – always

Your, Don.

I want to make you happy broke down my protective barriers and awakened in me a trust and a longing to love again. I needed to be loved. A third letter read:

My dearest

Thank you for your telephone call, although your news was not very welcome, it was good to hear your voice again. I'm sorry if I sounded off-hand but you caught me by surprise.

I was disappointed with the news and I was in the middle of a conference.

Darling, the prospect of not seeing you has cut the ground from under me. I slept so well last night, safe in the knowledge that there was only one more night without you. Now the appalling prospect of eight nights without you, towers before me.

This letter seems to be full of I's and me's which is very egotistical, but it would be presumptuous of me, at this stage, to try to discuss your emotions. I hope you are disappointed but then again I want you to be happy. For a supposedly mature man, my emotional mix-up is very calf-like.

I can only apologise and offer as my excuse the fact that I love you very dearly and that I have never felt such overwhelming emotions towards anybody in my life as I feel towards you. For once in my life I am frightened – frightened of losing you.

Just a thought, the end of the month is Sunday after next. Since you are entitled to every other fortnight off, you are within your rights to leave on Friday. I must close now if I am to catch the evening post. I wanted to write to you to explain my behaviour on the telephone.

I love you Denyse, with everything that is in me, I love you. I need and want you beside me – always. Since you left I've done nothing but sit and moon, I think tonight you will forgive me if I go and get good and drunk. I ache for you and long to have the chance to make you happy. All my love to you.

Your, Don.

He was honest about his feelings for me. My tragedy had matured me for my age. Life held a deeper meaning for me. Then his letter dated 23 April 1967 arrived.

My dearest

Thank you so much for your letter. I have read it and re-read it. I cannot begin to describe the comfort and pleasure your letters give me.

At the moment I am sitting in my room amidst a shambles of newspapers and general untidiness. You made the bed so well on Monday that for reasons of sentiment and practicality I have not re-made it until today. I had intended to re-inforce your grand clean-up with another on Thursday evening – prior to your arrival on Friday – but your news took the heart out of me and a gradual accumulation of rubbish has been the result.

However I have a friend coming to stay for two nights tomorrow and Friday - so I'm having a grand clean-up this evening. He is going to sleep on the mattress on the floor and I on the remainder of the bed. It will be interesting to see who is the more uncomfortable.

With the exception of my one drunken bout on Thursday I have stayed in my room since you left – I have no desire to be anywhere public without you. There was some party on in Earl's Court last night that I said I would attend but I just did not wish to go. I stayed awake last night until six o'clock this morning re-living last Saturday night. It was a poor substitute for the real thing, but better than nothing.

There is so much I want to tell you and then again paradoxically, so much that I am afraid to say, in case I presume too much on your love or friendship or in case you feel that you are being driven into a corner…

My darling Denyse I love you so much, I cannot believe that I could love someone the way I love you. I want so much for you – more, probably than I can hope to give you. All I know is that I love you and that I will do all in my power to make you happy and if you are content, then so will I be happy.

I love you my darling.

Always, Your Don.

Reading his letters made me feel close to him. In previous romances, I had never received a love letter before. Working for the Lamdins at Twitten House in Newick I had time to think. I enjoyed being with this family finding Mr Lamdin sincere and fair. His business kept him in London for the week. He was relying on me to drive his pregnant wife to the hospital should he be away when her time came. The day I arrived he said, "Take one of my cars for a drive, Denyse, not the *Jaguar*."

I chose a car from his fleet of five. Driving his four-year old son, Paul to and from nursery school, enabled me to bond with this little chatterbox. Exhausted after my second day as an *au pair* for the Lamdins, I turned off my light and pulled the covers over my ears.

"Denyse! Denyse!"

Drowsy, I heard my name being called. Could this be the call I dreaded? I ran to the main bedroom, barefoot and in my pyjamas.

"Denyse hurry. My waters have broken. Grab my case and put it in the car. I'll go downstairs. Carry Paul and put him on the back seat. Cover him with blankets."

Mrs Lamdin was red in the face. I did as I was told. On a freezing-cold winter morning I drove along the winding, narrow, bumpy country roads. Holding her tummy, she gave me directions interspersed with, "Mind the bumps. Turn right! My contractions are...Ow! Hurry!"

I avoided thoughts of delivering her baby and concentrated on driving safely. We had to reach the hospital in time… Before she was wheeled into the labour room, she said, "Please phone my husband when you get back."

"I will."

I carried Paul to the car. How would I find my way to Newick without Mrs Lamdin's directions? Driving endlessly along the twisting roads and with no sign of Newick, I stopped at a filling-station. A policeman came up to the car. I wound down the window. The cold air hit my face. "Run out of petrol, *luv*?" As he spoke curling warm vapour like cigarette smoke, spewed from his mouth.

"No. I'm lost."

"Where're you going?"

"To Newick."

"You're going the wrong way, *luv*."

Not accustomed to being addressed as *love,* but grateful for his directions to Newick, we arrived at *Twitten House*. I tucked Paul into his bed and telephoned Mr Lamdin. My call was too late. Mr Lamdin answered, "Denyse, we have a darling daughter."

"Congratulations Mr Lamdin!"

"She was born twenty minutes after Gillian arrived. Both she and the baby are fine."

"Excellent."

"Is Paul asleep?"

"Yes, I'll take good care of him."

"Thanks Denyse. I'll be back on Friday."

Other than jamming the washing-machine with a pair of my knickers, I managed to run the household and care for Paul single-handedly. I was relieved to have Mr and Mrs Lamdin home. Paul was excited to see his baby sister, Claire. When Mrs Lamdin napped, I pushed Claire in her pram. I looked at her. She was beautiful.

I had become a part of this family and it would be hard to resign. When, I wondered, would be the right time to tell them? I joined Don on my weekends off, except the weekend Claire was born. When I stayed with Don over these weekends, my conscience warred within me. My strict Catholic upbringing told me I was immoral. My emotions told me falling in love was erasing my sorrow, pain and fear which had engulfed me since I was widowed. I went to Mass on Saturday evenings, but never took communion. I avoided the confessional box. These persecuting thoughts never left me.

I planned a six-week tour of the continent with fellow South Africans to give me time to work out my conflicting feelings. Mr and Mrs Lamdin accepted my resignation but the day I left, Paul contracted measles.

"Please stay another week," Mrs Lamdin begged.

"I'm truly sorry, but I'm committed to tour."

Mr Lamdin drove me to the station. I promised to return after my holiday...

Don joined my fellow travellers in a pub before we left in a *Microbus* on 14 July. I wrote: *Seven girls and three guys squashed into the Microbus left Earl's Court at 8.15 pm. Crossing the channel from Dover to Calais at 2 am, we drove through Dunkirk, Niewport, Middelkerke to Ostend.*

My journal captured our tour: *15 July, visited the Heinekin Beer factory: 20 July, prostitutes at the Rieperbahn revolted me; 23 July, played touch rugby. I cooked meatballs, mash and carrots; 24 July, Stockholm, male and female wore long hair: 25 July, Stockholm, went to flick, we swam in the sea; thoughts with Donal, my tall dark Irishman...*

Wednesday 26 July, Uppsala, saw the historical Viking mounds, saw the famous Yew tree on which villains were hung; 28 July, Oslo, visited the Kon Tiki Raft and met up with Margo Flynn, a South African friend from the ship, Africa; 29 July, Gulsvik, bought two Norwegian jerseys; Icy cold, but June, Diana and I swam under a suspension bridge. 30 July, journeyed over snow-covered mountain passes to Kinsarvik; a goat hopped into our van; 1 August, missing Donal; on route to Copenhagen, camped at Saljord.

After a guided tour of the *Turborg* Beer Factory in Copenhagen, we sang on the stage for the crowd. After the second tour, we were each given *Turborg* T-shirts. Wearing our T-shirts we were applauded after our rendition of the SA anthem, *Sarie Marais, Ag Pleez Daddy* and the *Knock-Knock Beetle* song or *The Click Song*. This Xhosa wedding song, performed by the late *Miriam Makeba,* has difficult palatal clicks: *Igqira lendlela nguqongqothwane,* The diviner of the roadways is the knock-knock beetle. *Igqira lendlela kuthwa nguqon-gqothane,* The diviner of the roadways is said to be the knock-knock beetle. *Sebeqbelele gqithapha bathi nguqongqothwane* It has passed up the steep hill, the knock-knock beetle.

We over-indulged on free beer which had disastrous after-effects: *We drank too much and were sozzled. Di and I fell against the hot water pipes in ladies. We burnt our arms and scorched our T-shirts. We passed out in the van after Di and I vomited into brown paper bags.* We had a terrible *babbelas* when we woke up. Today I am ashamed of myself when I remember this disgraceful behaviour.

I was treated for blood-poisoning and a bee-sting on 5 August before we drove to Berlin arriving the next day. We toured East Berlin. I crossed through *Checkpoint Charlie* on my own. Seeing the Berlin Wall, watch-towers and trenches, I wondered how anybody had ever escaped. Driving through Berlin the next day, I saw a *Microbus* like ours with the word *Zulu* on the back. We followed it and met up with fellow South Africans. Joy and I exchanged experiences and arranged to meet at Earl's Court. Our tour headed for Munich. *On Tuesday we visited a beer hall and joined in the hilarity and singing...*

From Munich I returned to London alone using an open rail ticket. 'Nine in a *Microbus*' continued their tour and soon I would be with Don. He was happy to have me in London. He asked me to live with him. My new home was Flat 7, 5 Westbourne Gardens, London W2. I felt secure and warmed to Don's love.

Not wanting to waitress or to be an *au pair,* an Employment Agency found me work 'temping'. I earned little and was bored. Practising my shorthand and typing skills the Agency tested and issued a certificate confirming my 35wpm typing and 120wpm shorthand.

I secured a permanent position with accountants, Morrison, Rutherford & Osborne, 5 Queen Street, London EC4. I was thrilled. Mr Osborne, my boss, was strict, understanding and patient. The girls in the office became my close friends. I confided in Sheila. Don welcomed me home after work. We chatted about the day's events whilst preparing our evening meal. Don was a better cook than me. His curry was delicious.

On Saturday mornings we shopped at Queensway; put our washing into pay-as you-go washing machines; stopping at a pub, Don had a *Guinness* and I enjoyed a beer shandy. We frequented restaurants. A violinist serenaded me at a candlelit table one evening. Don beamed. I never understood the French song, but the intonation of his voice and body language said it all.

Travelling in his maroon *Cortina,* we holidayed on the Welsh coast, visiting his school in Taunton on the way. I learnt Don was an only child, born in Dublin, of Protestant parents who had both died. On idyllic days Don fished and I enjoyed the sunshine and fresh air. Just as my life was normalising, another shock awaited me...

Knowing my feelings about living together, Don said, "I'll love and care for your Denyse, but marriage... I don't believe in it. It's old-fashioned." My dreams were shattered. In order to resolve this problem, we made a pledge to take each other as man and wife privately. From then on, Don introduced me to work colleagues and friends as his 'wife'. This eased my conscience, believing in the eyes of God, we were man and wife. Our 'marriage' was consummated.

On winter evenings I knitted a pink dress for myself in front of the television, watching *Coronation Street,* my favourite programme. Don brought work home. I admired his neat handwriting. His work involved a 'computer' something I knew nothing about. We walked in the parks hand in hand. He taught me to use chopsticks at Chinese restaurants. He showed me the sights of London. He bought me flowers and said very meaningful things to me. One day he scooped me into his arms and held me high. He bought me an ice-cream. I felt safe and loved with him.

One evening at the theatre I felt unusually bilious. I could not face a drink. The next day I confided in Sheila. She said, "You should have a pregnancy test."

"What's that?"

I was naïve. Sheila had a daughter, Jane. I took her advice and had the test. Some days later the phone rang in our office.

"It's for you Denyse."

"Thanks."

My pregnancy was confirmed. For some time I had secretly longed to be a mother. If I saw a young mother pushing a pram I became broody. I pricked myself to confirm that I was not dreaming. I could not wait to tell Don he was to be a father. That evening as I peeled potatoes in the kitchen, Don picked up on my exuberance and said, "You're happy tonight. Got a promotion at work?"

I hesitated before saying, "Don, we're going to have a baby." It was as though I had thrown a bucket of cold water at him. He froze. The look on his face said it all. He was *far* from happy.

"You're pregnant?"

"Yes, I'm carrying *our* baby."

"No!"

"No. What do you mean?"

"I know where you can have an abortion."

His reaction cut me to the core. His murderous words pounded in my brain. Before I broke down, I left the room. I could not believe he could he even think of something as brutal as that? I was carrying our baby. I battled through the evening. The tension between us was as taut as a tightrope. I woke exhausted.

With a heavy heart, I set off to work. I decided to keep my secret from the office staff. It was difficult to concentrate. Sheila was the only one who knew. She suggested I tell Mr Osborne. He was understanding and concerned. He told me how to claim maternity benefits, which I did. I swapped my milk coupons each day and enrolled at a maternity clinic for regular check-ups.

I braved the question of marriage with Don. Placing emphasis on giving birth within wedlock, I hoped he would soften. He simply said, "I do not believe in marriage."

Mr Osborne arranged for Marriage Counsellors to visit us. They failed to convince him. I had told nobody Donal had suggested I have an abortion. I procrastinated about breaking the news to my family in South Africa for two reasons. I did not want to disgrace the family. I doubted they would feel happy like I did and I dreaded their rejection. With enough money for an international call to South Africa, I dialled the number. I heard my mother's voice on the end of a crackling line.

"Hello. Is that you Neyse?"

"Yes... Hi... mom."

"Is everything alright?"

I wondered how my mother, so far away, knew something was amiss.

"Yes mom."

"That's good."

"I've got some good news. I've got a special Christmas present for you. You're going to be a granny!" It was out. The silence stretched on longer than waiting for an alarm clock to ring. The call devoured my money as time ticked on. Then the world seemed to stand still in those few seconds.

"When's the baby due?"

"In July, Mom."

The call ended. My Mother showed no emotion. Was she mad or upset? I hung up. I left the telephone booth. My mother and I corresponded regularly. I kept it a secret that I lived with Don. She knew I had met and fancied an Irishman. Her next letter confirmed her motherly concerns for me. She offered advice. My grandmother arranged for me to visit a Catholic priest in London. She told me to prepare myself to marry Donal, whatever that meant. No mention was made of how my mother felt or questions asked of how I was coping. If only they knew…

I kept the appointment. I went on my own. I rang the doorbell. A sombre Catholic priest, in his long brown *Franciscan* robes, ushered me into a gloomy, sparse reception room.

"Take a seat, child."

"Thank you Father." I sat on the nearest chair facing him.

"How can I help you child?"

"Well, Father," I began, knowing full well he had been briefed by the Kokstad priest.

"I've been living with a man. We're not married. I'm expecting his child. I love him, Father…"

It was my turn to experience the *bucket-of-ice-cold-water-thrown-at-me* feeling. He answered in monotone, "If you confess to me now, you will be forgiven child. While you live ith this man, you're living in sin. You're nothing more than a *whore* and your unborn child is a *bastard…*"

I was dumbstruck. I fled the room hardly seeing where I was going. Salty tears streamed down my cheeks. My nose ran. I sought help, understanding and love. I received the opposite. I felt bitterness and hatred towards the Catholic Church and the holier-than-thou priests, who dished out nothing but insults. I was having none of this. My baby had been conceived in love. How dare some old priest say this to me? What did he know of love? Had he no idea of how I felt before adding insults to injury?

What would I tell Don? My life was like a whirlwind spiralling out of control.

"I told you so," Don said when I told him. A deep wedge was driving us further apart. Don treated me kindly, but he was not home to welcome me anymore. He popped into the pub, coming back inebriated and falling asleep.

As the days passed, loneliness surrounded me. My boss, friends, Billy and Eileen supported me. I dreaded my sister's arrival in January. She and her friend, Pam planned to tour Europe. I promised them accommodation. My clothes tightened around my waist. Uncertain about my future, I held on to my meagre savings for more urgent needs. I made do… I counted the days…

13

WHAT NOW?

As the policy of deportation of Blacks from white towns took effect, the number of prosecutions under the pass laws rose sharply, reaching 700,000 in 1968. Migrant labour with migrant workers circulating continuously between black homelands and white-owned enterprises in urban areas, was seen by the government as a means of reconciling the white need for labour with its own determination to prevent permanent black urbanisation.

WHAT now? The answer to my question became apparent when I responded to the ring of the security phone, "Who is it?"

"It's your sister, Topsy."

"Hi Tops, I'm opening the door."

The dreaded day was here. Their faces said it all as they surveyed the bedsitter. I was confronted with, "Where are Pam and I expected to sleep?"

I was lost for words. There was no place. No beds. No linen.

"We'll make a plan," I offered, "But, sit down. Cup of tea?"

Whilst I made the tea I heard them whispering. I sensed the disappointment and shame my sister felt for me in front of her posh friend, who was a doctor's daughter. I ached for support, but braced myself for more rejection.

We struggled through the first night. When I returned the next day, they had bought a small van which was parked outside the flat. They used our kitchen and ablutions when Don and I were at work. My family had briefed my sister beforehand. She wasted no time in laying down the law which came naturally with her domineering personality.

"You must move out... You're a disgrace..."

She forced me to move to a communal flat with them. I returned the next day. Our tempers ticked like time bombs. Topsy and Pam left on their European tour. A relief to me, but, I asked myself, what now?

After Don refused Marriage Guidance counselling, I told him I planned to return to South Africa. His immediate reaction gave me hope.

"I'll join you as soon as I can."

He was kinder to me. I packed my possessions into a huge blue trunk, which he promised to ship out to South Africa. I resigned from my job. I would miss my boss and my friends. They gave me a beautiful wristwatch with large Roman numerals, which I nicknamed *Big Ben*. I gave my upright piano to Sheila's daughter, Jane. My last days shopping in London with Don were enjoyable. I bought a white coat, gloves, shoes and a handbag to wear on the flight home. My air ticket home included a ten-day stopover in Madrid. I did this hoping Don would ask me to return to him from Madrid.

With my traveller's cheques and a baby matinee jacket pattern, needles and wool, I was ready. On the 10 April, I clung to Don at Heathrow Airport. Arms entwined, we kissed. Before we parted, he said, "Promise me *no* letters after our goodbye today…" How long would I wait before he joined me?

Those precious moments were gone, but remain embedded in my memory forever. Why was I forced to leave behind the man I loved, I thought, as we winged our way higher and higher into the sky towards Madrid? Many more unexpected problems would be heaped on my already stressed situation.

I remembered talking silently to my unborn baby, revealing my innermost thoughts, my faith and love in the midst of my crisis…

I love you. I thank God for giving you to me. You are very special. I long to hold you and to cuddle you in my arms. You are only a few weeks old now. Satan tried to steal you from me by deceiving your daddy, who suggested an ab…. I can't say that word to you, but to tell you that this heinous act was legalised in England in 1967. Darling, you are growing in my tummy. My very own baby!

When I was four and a half months pregnant I spoke to my baby again:

Remember my little one, I loved your daddy. Saying goodbye was painful and flying on my own, with an uncertain future, was nerve-racking. We're on our own now…

Landing in Madrid, I collected my luggage, took a taxi to the hotel, unpacked and walked into town. The shops were closed. *Siesta.* I needed money. Back at the hotel, I tried to cash one of my traveller's cheques with the receptionist. She apologised, "Sorry, I can't help you. Your cheques can only be cashed in England. They are stamped '*Negotiable in the UK or commonwealth countries only.*'"

Another blow! What now? It was time to think and have a cup of tea. I sat in the lounge, with my knitting, knowing the money I had cashed on the plane would soon run out. My spirits were lifted when, for the first time, I felt little butterfly kicks in my tummy.

You filled me with joy. I believe you were telling me, 'I'm here with you mom.'

A KLM pilot in smart uniform walked in and spoke to the receptionist. He immediately came over to me, sat down and asked, "Where are you going?"

"To South Africa."

Without any hesitation, I told him my story…

"Over the Easter weekend nothing will be open. I'll see what I can do."

I followed him to the bar. He ordered a meal for me saying, "I'll be back." He returned later.

"I've managed to change your flight. I'll settle your hotel bill. Take this," he said handing me a wad of money. "It'll be enough for the taxi to the airport which I've booked. Now take care!"

"Thank you so much, but…"

I was never able to repay this kind, caring pilot. He had saved me from an impossible situation. He gave me so much money I was able to buy a few souvenirs at the airport. I flew to Johannesburg and on to Durban where mom, Pop and Patrick met me. Too tired to worry how they felt, I fell asleep on the back seat next to Patrick. We travelled under a full moon.

I settled into the bedroom off the front verandah of their new home, 28 Strachan Street. In my absence, the farm had been sold and they lived in Kokstad now. The community were kind to me making my plight easier. Letters, connecting me to my past, flooded in. I never gave up believing Don *would* follow me…

Father Antonine Kelly, once a parish priest in Kokstad, resident at the Franciscan Friary, Laurence Street in Drogheda, wrote to me on 13 April 1968.

My dear Neyse

I have just had a letter from your gran telling me of the news from London and that you are flying home on the 24th and I want you to know that I sympathize very sincerely with you in your ordeal and that I am thoroughly ashamed of my countryman. But of course it is not the first time I have had cause to be ashamed of our nationals – at home as well as abroad. Please believe that I have not one word or even syllable of censure for <u>*you*</u> *and I suppose I shouldn't have any for him but I'm afraid that is not the case: for his fall I have no blame, but for his present attitude I cannot find words strong enough to describe my feelings.*

For you just now I have great admiration. You are doing the very right thing. There would be no end of complications if you delayed to return home until you had to ask for two names on your passport and I'm sure you are aware of the callousness of newspaper hawks in these regions when they get on the track of what their foul minds would call a "scoop". No sense of decency or privacy deters them.

I am also ashamed of my fellow priest whoever he is, who behaved in a way so contrary to that of his Divine Master and I shouldn't like to be in his shoes: for who knows when he will need sympathetic understanding of his own trials. Please, Neyse, don't go to the trouble of answering this. I fully appreciate how disturbed you must be at the moment.

And believe you will have a big share in my prayers and masses.

With very sincere regards,
From, Fr. Antonine.

I broke my promise and wrote to Don, hoping he would be the person I believed he was. My mother for different reasons, tried to establish communication with Don through a Catholic priest in

Hatch End. His letter, written dated 9 July when I was nearing the end of my pregnancy, revealed how desperately this priest had tried to contact Don.

Dear Denyse

Thank you for your letter just received and please thank your mother for hers of about three weeks ago. I am very sorry you have been so ill but glad that you are now well again and that you have benefited so much from your stay at the coast.

My reason for not writing sooner was that I wanted to have some definite report or news to give, but all attempts at contacting Don have failed and he has not replied to any letter. Tonight I shall send one, in a last attempt, to the flat in the hope that he will at least answer the queries about the luggage.

I think, Denyse, that by not answering he really has given the answer we requested. This sounds cruel, but if he had the slightest intention of standing by either you or the baby, he would have shown signs of it long before now and would at least have replied to simple queries.

In view of his present attitude and neglect, one can only say that, while one is sorry for you, very sorry indeed, one must also be glad that you were not inescapably united to him in marriage. The man, who could be so callous now and so selfish and neglectful, would have made a very bad husband indeed. So while offering you sympathy, one must also offer you congratulations on your liberation from him.

If I hear from him or succeed in getting a meeting with him I shall immediately let you know. Please explain to your mother why I hadn't written in reply to her letter – I kept hoping each day that some definite news would come from him.

With my blessing for you and the baby and for all the family, and asking the Lord to make it all up to you in some wonderful compensation.

I never received the letter I longed for. Sister Mary Bernadette my favourite Primary school teacher, a short rosy-cheeked Irish nun, wrote to me.

Holy Cross Convent, George

My dear Neyse

I heard that you are expecting your baby soon and want you to know that I am thinking about you and praying daily at Holy Mass for you. It will be lovely to have your baby, to have someone to love extra specially and I hope you are looking forward to its arrival. I was glad to hear that you are with your mother. She will love and care for you as only a mother can. I came across the enclosed snap. I thought you may like to have it.

I've just returned from Cape Town where I had a check-up on my ears and to my great disappointment another operation in Sept. We are closing our Secondary School, due to shortage of teachers, and will move our Primary classes up to the Secondary classrooms. It's a good excuse for renovating, as we are having a noisy time hammering and plastering and paint pots all over the place…

I've been teaching Sub B and Standard I since I came here. A lively crowd but I love them. I never realised that I am getting old! Now, Neyse I must close, remember I'm keeping you in my heart and in my prayers and do hope you'll write to me and tell me your plans.

God bless you

Much love, Sr Mary Bernadette

In my eighth month, feeling uncomfortable and scared, I fought the reality of Don's deliberate evasiveness. My lawyer tried to enforce a Paternity Claim, but this failed. Don rejected my love… Don rejected his responsibility… Don rejected our baby…. Father Lucius's letter, dated 19 July, made me realise the truth at last.

Still no word from Don as obviously he has no intention of doing anything, or of even telling us directly, that he has none. I am sorry for you in all of this, but I am glad that you do not feel bitter. The baby who will do so much in your life was conceived in love and it is wonderful that the love remains and that you will be able to pray for Don.

It is so much better thus. Please God you will have a safe and easy confinement and all will be well. One thing is certain – your baby is coming into a loving family and will thrive on all the care and attention and affection that await it. And on its part, it will compensate you for everything and bring a new joy and happiness into your life. You have been endowed by God with great love and what a fortunate little baby this is.

With my kindest regards to you and your mother and to Mrs Brown and with a great big blessing for you in your confinement and one awaiting our baby when first you see it.

Keeping up the prayers and grateful for a place in yours...

***

Towards the end of my pregnancy I had X-rays taken. Twins were suspected. The pictures revealed my baby lying in the breach position. No twins. Because I went over my due date, I was given the 'castor-oil and bumpy car ride' treatment, which did not help. I was put into hospital and labour was induced with a drip.

Because my contractions started but ceased when the drip was removed, a Caesarean section was set down for Monday 20 August 1968. Chandrè Pegeen, weighing seven pounds eight ounces, a beautiful, healthy baby, was God's gift to me. Her second name, Pegeen, was a combination of her grandmother and great-grandmother's names, Peggy and Eileen.

"Did I have a boy or a girl?" I asked when I came round after anaesthetic. Sister Groom placed my baby, wrapped up like a cocoon, on my chest. She had a mop of long black hair, soft as down, blue eyes and fat cheeks with a cute button nose and a rosebud mouth. I loosened the blanket staring at her wee hand, with teeny dimples. She curled her tiny hand around my little finger.

"I love you precious Chandrè."

"Congratulations Denyse," my doctor said smiling at us.

The Kokstad community showered us with love, gifts, cards and flowers. To this day daffodils are a reminder to me of Chandre's birth. I recorded her progress in a Baby Book:

She lost twelve ounces in her first week. Gran-gran held her. I heard her hiccough. I bathed her on 27 August for the first time, but struggled to put on her bootees as she kicks so much. We left the hospital on 29 August. Margy was godmother at her baptism on 1 September. She cried when she had her first diphtheria/whooping cough injection and three Polio drops...

She was registered as Chandrè Pegeen Smith. Fulfilling my maternal duties, I put to use blankets, cot sheets, baby nighties, bootees, cotton-crochet bibs, woollen mittens and bonnets made by her granny.

Our room was equipped like a nursery with an enamel baby bath on a wicker stand, nappy buckets under the changing table and a nappy bag holding towelling nappies. Her pram, doubling up as a carrycot, was a gift from her great-grandmother. Knitted toys, a bunny, a gollywog, a soldier and a kitten, I made filled her cot. Letters of congratulation arrived from my former boss, Mr Osborne of Morrison, Rutherford, Osborne & Co, Chartered Accountants, 5 Queen Street, London EC4, dated 6 September:

> *I am delighted to hear you have such a beautiful baby girl and I hope all will go well with you both and that you will be very happy.*
>
> *I have telephoned Donal on numerous occasions and written to his private address. I thought he was avoiding me but on Tuesday I received a letter, a copy of which I have sent to your lawyer. Apparently your luggage has never left England and Donal says he has now returned it from the dilatory carriers and is making other arrangements for its despatch. He has just gone on three weeks holiday. I hope he dealt with the luggage before he went and that it will not be long before it reaches you. I am glad your sister had no difficulty over this.*
>
> *I don't know if you are receiving letters from any member of our staff but in case not I will tell you Maureen Jones has left and is expecting her baby next week Elaine's is due in October. Mrs Potts and Miss Macquarie are on holiday. Miss Morgan (the coffee lady) has just got back from a visit to her*

son or daughter and their family in Canada.

I trust everything will now run smoothly.

My love to you and a kiss for Chandrè Pegeen.

R. Osborne.

Father Lucius's letter dated 10 September 1968 read:

Most sincere congratulations to you and a huge loving welcome to dear Chandrè Pegeen. What lovely names and what a lovely baby she must be. And how good it is to know that you and she are safely through it all and that all are so happy. I'm truly delighted for you and for her. She is a special baby (what the Irish call a love-child) and what love surrounds her from her mother, her grandmother, her great-grandmother!

It is marvellous. When that photograph has been taken I want a copy, please. May the Lord look lovingly on you and your little treasure and may He send you all that will make your life and hers secure and complete.

I'm glad Don has seen your sister and that the things have been sent on to you. It was good that Jennifer could contact him, as this seems the only practical way of getting any word from him. If you don't mind my interfering a little, Denyse, do have a word with your lawyer about the matter of what rights Don would have over the baby if he contributes to her maintenance; it would never do if he could suddenly appear on the scene and whip her away from you. It is not likely, I know, but in these legal matters one does well to see it from all angles.

Take care of yourself now – no need to tell you to take care of Chandrè. You will both be in all my Masses and I'm so grateful for a place in your prayers. Some day when she is older, you must tell Chandrè about a priest called Father Lucius.

With a great big blessing for you both and with my love.

Delightedly your, Denyse,

Father Lucius.

I valued his advice but had difficulty divorcing myself from devoted friends in England. My friend, Sheila Potts, to whose daughter I had given my old-fashioned piano, typed me an interesting letter on office letterhead paper.

> *I'm glad you are enjoying Chandrè. For all the hard work, children are a pleasure. I know with Jane, although sometimes the responsibility hangs heavily upon me as it will be with you in the future, the joy she gives takes care of all the lonely and depressed times. Jane often asks about you and when I told her about your baby she was all questions. Is it a girl or boy? How old is she? How much did she weigh at birth? Jane is and never has been content with an explanation; she has to know everything.*
>
> *So sorry to hear of your long labour and all the illness. I think probably you had had so much worry whilst in England that everything closed up on you when you got home. Still it was fortunate you were in good hands and at home. I'm sorry to hear about Don. As you say when you love somebody so much it is so much harder to bear, when they seem so heartless. I'm very glad you are going ahead with a Paternity claim. If he doesn't feel the responsibility himself I think it will make him more aware of your plight if it is forced upon him. I don't think I shall ever understand what makes most men tick...*
>
> *Glad to hear your plans for setting up home. I'm sure you will settle once you get independent. Your car sounds super. If you do get to the UK soon please don't forget to come and see us. Mr Attfield and all the boys send their regards. In a couple of weeks the Lord Mayor's Show will be on again. Do you remember last year and what fun we had, you standing on that chair and taking your photos. We will all miss you this year when we come to the office to watch it again.*

Letters from abroad made me cry, linking me to my past. Spring cheered me. The gardens were bursting with blossoms and buds. Before breakfast I pushed Chandrè in the pram and on one of these walks, Ralph drove past and waved. He and Nolyn were returning from golf and I learnt much later Nolyn asked Ralph, "Who's that?"

"Neyse. I boarded with her gran, Mrs Brown. Neyse was head girl of the convent. She had a crush on me!"

A Christmas card from Mr and Mrs Lamdin in Sussex gave news of Paul, Claire and Miles. Their offer for me to join them moved me to tears. Would they feel the same when they knew I had been dumped and was an unwed mother?

Thank you very much for the photos. How are you? And what are you doing now? Do let us know how you are getting on. Claire is growing fast, crawling everywhere! Paul is very well, just getting over a cold though doing well at school. Just beginning to read now. We are having a quiet Christmas here with the family and Miles. Mrs Lamdin.

Denyse, would you like to come down over Christmas?

I am trying to arrange for Gill and the children to go on holiday after Christmas to find some sunshine, would you like to accompany them, at my expense of course.

Mr Lamdin.

I wrote to them. They were true friends as their reply of 25 October showed:

Dear Denyse

How are you and how is the baby? I have been meaning to write to you months ago, but time has flown by and I realize your little baby is a big bouncing baby now. Do send a photo and tell me all our news.

We are all well here, Claire is a dear little girl beginning to talk and getting into mischief all the time. She is nearly 20 months now and a big girl for her age.

Paul is doing very well at school and is reading to me nearly every night now, before he goes to sleep. Miles has passed his 'O' levels and is wondering what career to take up being a big boy of 16 now, but still at boarding school for another year.

We have found and moving at the end of November to a beautiful big house with grounds near Tunbridge Wells. And

I wondered if you are still wondering what to do if you would like to come back to England and make a life with us and your baby. Think about this and let me know. Our new address will be, Knowles Bank House, Pembury, nr Tunbridge Wells, Kent.

I am sad to leave Twitten House but it has become a bit small now with two growing children. Mr Lamdin is well – very busy in his work still. I have a horse now, and have enjoyed some lovely rides this summer.

Love to you, from us all,

Gillian Lamdin.

I never returned to England. Don might reject me a second time. Billy and Eileen were Don's close friends. We socialised with them in London. Eileen gave birth to a son on 19 July. Saddened to think how differently things had turned out for me, I faced the truth of Eileen's letter of 23 October 1968:

27 Kelvin Avenue, Palmers Green, London W1

Dear Denyse and Chandrè

I know I should have written you ages ago but to be quite honest I never seem to have a moment to myself. I settled down to write last week and then I thought that I would hang on until this week as I was expecting Don for dinner, but I am afraid that the gentleman never turned up. I was furious!!!

My sincerest congratulation. Don does know as apart from your writing him, Billy told him. If I were you I would forget him. He really is not worth your love.

Thank you very, very much for your gift. The boots did fit the baby for the first few weeks, but now he has outgrown them.

Oh! I forgot to tell you. I had a boy, Fergus Patrick, 8 lbs 7 ozs, normal delivery. It is hard to imagine him at that size now as he was born on 19 July which now makes him three months old and he weighs 16lbs 4ozs. He looks very like Billy. We are taking photographs...I will send you one. Please forward one of yourself and Chandrè.

At the moment we are busy decorating. We have just finished the baby's room... We put Walt Disney wallpaper up. Yes, babies do keep you going don't they? It seems to be a continual wash and Billy does not arrive home until about 7.30 pm and makes it a long day.

Did you ever get your luggage? Billy did say it to Don but I don't think he took any notice. I am glad that your family and friends stood by you. You do need someone, as possibly at first you felt very unwanted. Also, I do know that when Fergus was born on about the 4th day I felt very depressed so it must have been far harder for you. But God is good and I feel sure that you will get on very well as now you know you have somebody of your very own to spread your love on.

It is now 11.45pm and I am just about ready for bed. I will write again before Christmas. Until then, God bless you and your little one and thanking you once again.

All our love,

Billy, Eileen and Fergus.

I struggled with rejection. I struggled to put Don out of my mind. I struggled to put finality to this saga. Death was final, but life held hope. Donal, alive in England, the father of my baby, was my thread of hope...

My friend, Ann from the office, wrote to me.

113 Waterloo Road, Romford, Essex.

Dear Denise

At long last I have sat down and write to you. Thanks you so much for your lovely gift for the baby – in case you haven't heard from Sheila, I had a boy 7lb 4oz.

First, I want to say a very late 'congratulations' on the birth of your little girl. I can imagine how pleased you must be, especially as I hear from Sheila that things were a bit difficult and you had to have a Caesarean. I hope you like our gift for your little girl and I hope it fits. Don't babies grow fast! Do please write telling me all about Chandrè and how you are coping with motherhood – from your letter you seem to be getting along fine. Any photos?

My little terror is at the moment lying in his carrycot cooing to his teddy. He is absolutely beautiful (of course!!) with lots and lots of black hair. His eyes at the moment are dark. I think they may change. He was born on the 23 September, 10 days late. This date is such a big day in my family as it is my parents' wedding anniversary and also my sister's and the twins' birthdays, so you can imagine the excitement. We have named him Neil Alexander. He was christened last Sunday and Sheila and Jane came. I stayed on at work until practically the end of July, but gave up when we had a rather nasty car accident as my nerves were bad for a while. It was a miracle we were not badly hurt, just cuts and bruises. After the car was repaired, Allan traded it in for a Cortina and is pleased with the swop. I must say it is a very comfortable car.

The level of coverage by the TV companies of the Olympic Games was very high. We thoroughly enjoyed it all. I suppose Sheila told you about our friend Elaine – What a hoof!! She still has not had her baby. It's the longest pregnancy I've ever heard of!

Mr Attfield has apparently expressed a wish to come and see me and 'my young man'. He has some money for me and is saying he will give it to me personally. It will be just like him to call unexpectedly so Sheila is keeping an ear open so she can warn me. Before I left work he took Sheila and myself out for a meal one evening. We thoroughly enjoyed it – the food was gorgeous (I think the bill came to over £12!)

We had no luck with selling our house, so are stuck here for another couple of years.

I don't mind really, especially when I think of the place we were going into. The lounge area was beautiful, but the bedrooms and kitchen were so small. It was ridiculous. All the new houses seem to be like that now. The builders were also going to put up the price of the house another £200, making it over £6,500 for a terraced house!! They have built another section of houses on the site and these are going for £7,200.

Hasn't this year flown by? It seems a few months ago we were all together celebrating last Christmas. Such a lot seems to have happened this year. Allan is really looking forward to Christmas this year and to putting up the decorations on the tree. The shops are now full of all sorts of Christmas décor and it all looks lovely and cheery on these cold days. Your mother will be especially happy this year to have you home and Chandrè will be an added pleasure.

I hope I am not treading on a tender spot when I ask you what is happening with regard to Don. I only hope things are not too difficult for you at home and that you are now able to lead a happier and fuller life with your little girl. I am looking forward to hearing from you again with details of how Chandrè is getting on. Don't forget the photos!

My best wishes to you both. You are always in my prayers.

Love, Ann

Though we shared baby experiences through our letters, Chandrè had no daddy and this made us different from my friends. Correspondence with my friends ended after a Paternity claim failed. Reminders of Donal were severed when Mr Osborne's letter of 2 December read:

Last month I received a letter from Mr Pfaff, telling me that they still had heard nothing from Mr Clarke and asking me if I would take the matter up with him again. In view of your letter, I have not done anything further, and I have not replied to Mr Pfaff's letter. Some weeks have now gone by and it is possible that Elliot & Walker have managed to clear things up through their lawyers in London.

I do hope that everything is now in order and I should appreciate a line from you letting me know. If I can be of any further assistance, I shall be only too pleased to help you…

I kept these letters all these years. Today as I read them again I am transported back in time. Could my next goal be tracing each one and catching up on many lost years?

Donal never wrote. Neither did he come to South Africa as promised. I closed the door on him and devoted myself to loving and caring for my precious daughter, Chandrè Pegeen.

14

CHANDRÈ PEGEEN WILD

Black townships in 'white' South Africa were kept as unattractive as possible. In 1969 in Soweto, the township serving Johannesburg, the average number of people living in a 'matchbox' house was thirteen.

FOR two nights my mother looked after Chandrè when I went to Durban to buy a wingback lounge suite, an oak cottage-style dining room suite, *Red-Riding Hood* material for her nursery curtains, lounge and dining room curtaining and carpets. I was moving into *Kildare* in January 1969.

In December my College friend, Joy contacted me from Pietermaritzburg where she taught, saying "I'm longing to see your baby."

"She's beautiful, Joy."

She visited over a week end, persuading me to join her at a Tennis Dance.

"I'll look after Chandrè," my mother offered.

Joy was free but I felt self-conscious. An unmarried mother was frowned upon in those days. No young man would dance with me, I thought. Those *wallflower* days came back to haunt me. Mingling into the crowd, Joy danced with Barry Mail. I eyed a tall, blue-eyed blonde young man dancing with my cousin, Eileen Slabbert. To my surprise, he returned Eileen to her seat and asked me to dance. I got to my feet before he changed his mind. We danced the evening away. Nolyn asked, "May I give you a lift home?"

"Thanks, Nolyn, but Joy and I came by car..."

"Well..."

Rudely butting in I asked, "Would you and Barry care to join us for coffee?"

"We'd love to."

They arrived at 28 Strachan Street where Joy and I giggled like two schoolgirls. She was keen on Barry, but their friendship fizzled out. To avoid being hurt, I pushed any romantic thoughts from my mind. The forthcoming holiday with my parents at Umsikaba was a perfect escape route. I never expected Nolyn to take up the offer. He did and arrived at Umsikaba in his blue *Anglia*.

Our friendship, tinged with romance, made me put up my protective barriers. For the present my plans were for Chandrè and me, the two of us. We returned to Kokstad and on 14 January 1969, I moved into *Kildare*. Chandrè slept in her own bedroom, the room I had shared with Topsy when I was eleven.

My furniture and wedding presents were used for the first time. I was pleased with what I had bought, turning this house into our home. Memories flashed back: watching this house being built; Margy spilling *Gentian Violet* over herself and the bath; parading in my mother's cocktail dresses; the mouth-watering smells from the kitchen where granny in her pinafore, cooked or baked. Living on my own was lonely and difficult. What did *Kildare* have in store for us?

I taught at the Kokstad High School, having trained Millie a black maid, to look after Chandrè. Brenda, a teacher at the same school, boarded with me, sleeping in what was once granny's room. She loved Chandrè.

My confidence returned. I played social tennis taking Chandrè with me. She slept in her pram in the shade of an oak tree. Millie had time off. Nolyn visited us. He marked books with me in the evenings. We played canasta with friends, Ralph and Vivienne. Brenda babysat when we went out. One evening we held hands. I threw a birthday party in March and my young friends attended. Nolyn gave me a Percy Sledge LP record, '*When a man loves a woman.*' The words 'I'll give you everything I've got....trying to hold on to your precious love...' led to our first kiss, which ignited a fire. My parents warned me, "Nolyn's after your money."

One day I checked up on Chandrè at tea break. She was crying her heart out. There was no sign of Millie. Holding her close to my breast, I pacified her, changed her nappy and put her into her carrycot. I drove back to the school where Mr Kopke, the principal, accepted my twenty-four hour resignation. Millie had been to the tuck shop. She was fired.

I opened a small crèche in the garage, looking after six little ones on weekdays. They loved Chandrè. Agnes a new nanny was a gem. The children in my care were happy. Chandrè was safe and I had an income.

Soon after my boarder, Brenda, also a teacher announced her engagement to Barry Sonneman, Nolyn drove me to meet his mother and grandmother who lived in Cumberland Street, Umtata. He only just managed to fit the pram and baby paraphernalia into his car.

"What's all this stuff?" Nolyn had a lot to learn after all towelling nappies alone took nearly a suitcase! Chandrè slept in her carrycot on the back seat.

We arrived. Nolyn parked in the driveway. I settled Chandrè and joined them in the lounge. Neither woman made me feel welcome. They ignored me. Smoke hung thick in the air as his blonde blue-eyed mother Winifred Ruth Wild, called Ruth, with a lined face and tight thin unsmiling lips, chain-smoked. She, a teacher, sat in *her* chair exuding superiority. Gogs, his grandmother, short and fat, wore old-fashioned shoes and a shapeless frock. Although calculating, she was friendlier. The room was depressing. Heavy, brown velvet curtains kept the cold out. The furniture was shabby and worn. They hogged the heat of a small electric heater between them. I was cold, bored and welcomed my bed.

The next day I met Cheryl, Nolyn's sister, attractive but spoilt. Nolyn played golf and I was left with them. Cheryl ran a bath at 3 pm soaked for two hours using all the hot water. Next she threw a temper tantrum when she lost one false eye-lash. Her mother and grandmother groped on all fours, searching for it.

I washed Chandrè, warming a little water from the kettle. I left nappies folded, a bottle of *Gripe* water and a spare dummy on hand, making it easier for his mother who agreed to babysit my daughter. Nolyn came home. His mother and grandmother fussed over him, saying, "It's miserable out tonight. You'd be better off here. We don't see much of you."

I was angry because, I had spent the afternoon alone and had taken the trouble to look my best. In the end, we went out, but not for long.

"Nolyn do you mind taking me home?"

"What's up? You're the one who wanted to go out."

"Yes, I know. But now I would like to go home."

I had a hunch something was amiss. No sooner had we entered the house when my suspicions were confirmed. My baby's cries filled the house. She was not in the lounge. In the dark, cold bedroom we shared, my red-faced baby was ignored. I cuddled her, changed her nappy and kissed her. Sucking her dummy, she fell asleep in my arms.

His mother told me the next day, "I lit match after match. She was quiet. But I ran out of matches!" I was furious. How had she raised three children? The time to go home could not come soon enough. In Kokstad Nolyn helped me with the luggage. No more was said. It was good to put my head on my own pillow in our home.

Despite warning signs, this romance blossomed. Because Nolyn was a keen golfer, Pop suggested I learn to play the game and buy the necessary equipment. I took his advice.

Chandrè had a strange habit. She pulled and stuffed the fluff off the blanket into her nose. My baby, with a mop of blonde hair, jabbered away in baby talk and tip-toed in her first pair of shoes. My ten-year-old brother, Patrick blew out the candle on her first birthday cake, which her granny baked.

Nolyn returned from his holiday and questioned me about a note he had written me before he left:

Dearest Neyse

The inevitable has happened! I've got a flat in Umtata from 1.8.68. What do you think is the best plan? Just thought I'd let you think it over until I get there.

Fondest love.

His application, selling Life Insurance for the Old Mutual in Umtata, had been accepted and he announced, "I've been offered a flat from the 1 August. Are you coming?"

"No, we're not coming."

"Well we can get married."

I never replied. Was this *his* way of proposing to me, I wondered. I needed time to think this over...

***

My second-time-round wedding was imminent and the arrangements were underway. An open wedding invitation, put in the Kokstad Advertiser, triggered a predictable reaction from the community as they gossiped on every street corner,

"Must be a shotgun marriage.

He's after her money.

I hear they're leaving town.

Peggy will miss her granddaughter."

Several non-conventional wedding plans got underway – the ceremony would be at *11 am* on *Thursday* rather than 2.30 pm on Saturday, as was customary. Although an elegant cream suit was suggested, I wore apricot culottes under a full-length Swiss lace jacket, with a petalled bonnet instead of the conservative veil. Margy, my bridesmaid would wear a matching waist-length jacket over white culottes, trimmed with apricot. My mother sewed for hours to make all these ultra-modern outfits. How would the local press cover this wedding?

Granny's proverbial advice, *time waits for no man,* had friends volunteering the catering, the flowers, photography, hair appointments and visitors' accommodation. The convent Girls' choir offered to sing, *O Perfect Love.*

My crèche closed. Brenda found alternate boarding. We worked round the clock. Chandrè, a proper little chatterbox, enjoyed the hubbub of activity around her. Abandoning her toys she played with scraps of material in her imaginary world. It was time for my first grown-up talk with Chandrè.

"Mommy's getting married tomorrow, my darling. You'll have a *daddy*. Mommy still loves you. There'll be mommy, Chandrè and daddy." I continued as I lifted her three chubby little fingers one by one, counting, "One, two, *and three*. Then there'll be three!"

"*Free*, mommy, *free*!" she lisped, smiling. She never understood.

According to plan Nolyn and I stood at the altar of St Patrick's Cathedral on 23 August 1969 just three days after Chandrè turned one. Nolyn, looking handsome in his dark suit, faced me to take our vows.

I tried not to think of my marriage to Don Smith on 20 November 1965,when I had stood in the *same* place, took the *same* vows in the *same* church. The words, "*Till death us do part...*" disturbed me.

I fast-tracked my thoughts to Chandrè. She ran a temperature. We were pronounced man and wife by Bishop McBride and Father Baptist O'Toole. With arms linked we walked down the aisle between smiling faces, pausing at the door for photographs. Hugh Preston, Nolyn's close friend, was best man. My granny, in her blue outfit teamed with white accessories, gave us her blessing, "God bless you and keep you happy, today and always!"

After all the time-consuming preparations, our wedding was over. It was hard to leave Chandrè in my mother's care. We honeymooned in East London, a coastal resort producing pineapples. We drove to George, situated on the slopes of the Outiniqua Mountains. Staying in a dingy hotel, we looked forward to playing golf on the prestigious Cape Province Amateur Golf Championships course.

Kitted out for golf, we drove in Nolyn's *Anglia* to the George Country Club. I relied on my caddy, who was thrilled to play with my brand new clubs. Tucked out of Nolyn's sight my caddy said, "*Wag n bietjie, merrem!* Wait a bit, madam!" With that he whacked the ball straight down the middle of the fairway or pitched the ball six inches from the pin! There was nobody more surprised than Nolyn!

On the way back we stayed in Umtata with Nolyn's mother and grandmother. I was treated with the same contempt. I could not wait to leave. In Kokstad I was re-united with Chandrè. We headed straight for Durban where we stayed at the Plaza Hotel. From 8.30 am until 5 pm daily, Nolyn attended a ten-day Life Insurance training course. Chandrè and I spent happy days on my childhood playground, Durban's Addington beach. Chandrè played with her bucket and spade in the sand and I remembered: sitting on my dad's back as he lay on the white sand; laughing together on our bumpy *rickshaw* ride; proudly adding silver charms to my bracelet with each lucky packet he bought me and also, his visit to the Royal Hotel with a message for my mother, '*Remind her of this date, 22 December.*' It seemed just yesterday.

I bought Chandrè her first frilly knickers and trained her to pull them down and wee. This started as a game, but had the desired result. No more nappies during the day. One day I drove to Hillcrest to visit an old school friend of mine, Pat Gwalter. Her three-old son shared his toys with Chandrè. Pat and I drank cups of tea, exchanging stories of schooldays and motherhood. The day passed. It was time to return to the hotel.

Chandrè, sucking a lollipop, sat on the passenger seat. Baby seats or seat belts were not compulsory in those days! It was rush hour. Concentrating on the traffic, I drove bumper-to-bumper down West Street. Approaching a *robot*, the lights changed. The pedestrians stepped into the road immediately. I braked. The brake pedal flopped against the floorboards. The car moved forwards. Realising I had no brakes, I yelled, "God help me!"

To avoid hitting an elderly lady in front of the car, I swerved sharp left. The tyres squealed. The back of a bus loomed ahead of us. I missed hitting the bus by swerving right and pulling up the handbrake. The car landed on the island separating the two lanes. Amidst hooting and swerving vehicles, I removed the keys. It was a nightmare. Quite unperturbed, Chandrè sucked her lollipop, her hands covered in sticky syrup trickling down her chin onto her pretty dress.

"Mommy's had an accident."

Picking her up, I climbed out the car. Help arrived. A stranger approached, offering to remove the car. "I'll have the brakes repaired tomorrow," he said. He carried her push-chair and baby bag, I followed him to the safety of his shop. He called a taxi. I handed him the car keys and we left. Nolyn was at the hotel when we arrived.

"We've had a horrible accident."

"Where's the car?"

He was more concerned about the car than us. Still shaking and needing a comforting hug, he admonished me, "What! You left the car with a complete stranger. You honestly don't know his name or the name of the garage!"

"Yes. I couldn't think straight. I was shocked."

"How could you? You'll never see the car again!"

The stranger kept his word, saying, "Your car was out of petrol!"

With new brake-pads fitted and a full tank of petrol, we left Durban to begin the next phase of our married life. Nolyn was motivated and keen to work. I was excited. Disjointed pieces of my life were slipping into place. I had a husband. Chandrè had a daddy. We had a dog,

Spatts. Moving into our new home it was a time of new beginnings.

We settled into a one-bedroomed flat, storing excess furniture. Agnes, my new maid, accompanied us. Chandrè loved her. My contentment ended the day the manager called a dog meeting, saying, "Spatts must wear a bell whenever he leaves the flat, to protect my Chihuahuas." I ignored him. Spatts never wore a bell.

Below the lounge windows, a flat roof made an ideal play area for Chandrè. Agnes passed Chandrè to me through the window. I played with her in the sunshine and Agnes cleaned the flat. The manager heard of this and forbade me to use the flat roof. Margy visited us in December. She doted on Chandrè. Daily we cooled off from the sweltering heat in Chandre's paddling pool at Cumberland Street.

Despite Nolyn's cynicism I opened a crèche, the first in Umtata. I hired the Scout Hall on the Recreation Grounds. My handmade posters, hanging in shop windows, produced a resounding response. Spending little on the outlay, I was in business. The children enjoyed art, educational games, stories and singing. Mid-morning Agnes fetched Chandrè for her nap. These meagre earnings supplemented our income.

Nolyn worked hard. He found the Old Mutual typist incompetent which meant I spent evenings typing quotations using a portable typewriter. Life was full. With so much to do Nolyn's late home-comings were less obvious. As time went on, these nights alone occurred more frequently and lengthened.

This drove me to the first of many temper tantrums. Nolyn came home late after drinking too much. He tried to charm his way out slurring his words, saying, "And *howze* my *slittle* family?" I was not impressed. Fine time to ask how we were, I thought.

"You're late *every* evening. You never see *anything* of Chandrè. I sit *alone* in this flat night after night, typing for you. I've had enough!"

"Shame, I'm working my butt off for you and when I come home, all you can do is *moan and groan...*"

That did it. In the kitchen I opened the cupboard housing my red tea-set, a treasured wedding present from my marriage to Don. In a blind rage, I pelted the entire tea-set against the far kitchen wall rendering sharp, shattering sounds throughout the flat. I looked. Shards of broken glass lay strewn on the floor. My anger intensified when Nolyn put his head around the door and said, "You'd better clean up your mess. I'm going to bed!"

My fury turned to self-pity. Tears streamed down my cheeks and blurred my vision. I regretted my outburst and shocking behaviour. I disposed of the debris, finally creeping into bed where Nolyn slept soundly. No more was said about this incident and my unresolved anger, like a festering wound, simmered unseen, deep inside me.

My suspicions were confirmed. The doctor told me I was pregnant. My baby was due in June. This time it would be different, *normal* like everybody else, I told myself. I imagined Nolyn's face beaming with pride and joy as he drew me into his arms and told me how much he loved me. When he returned home late, I showered him with love.

"I've some good news."

"What's that?"

"We're going to have a baby ....in June!"

His reaction was not what I had imagined. No smile. No hug. No love. Instead he was deathly quiet. His face turned to stone, hard and cold. I waited for ages before he said, "But we decided *not* to start a family immediately!"

I kept my thoughts to myself. I knew nothing of birth control.

"I know, but it's happened. I thought you'd be happy..."

He laid the practicalities bare. The flat could not accommodate a baby. His advance of R100 (£50) per month barely supported the three of us. Clearly we could not afford a baby. He had started a new career involving long hard hours.

There was truth in what he said, but I felt hopelessly let down. Who would understand me? Turning to my daughter the next day, I said, "Chandrè, my angel, you're going to have a baby sister or brother." She put her arms around my neck, planting a slobbery kiss on my mouth. Her love enabled me to overcome the hurt I felt, but never showed.

Our money ran out at the end of most months. There were no credit cards. We visited my parents. We enjoyed hearty meals with tea and cake in-between. Nolyn filled the car with petrol at *Daddy Bros & Johnstone* on account. Before returning mom gave us *padkos* and included home-made jam, bottled fruit, banana bread, freshly-baked *crunchies* and ginger biscuits and fruit and vegetables from her garden.

We needed money for bread and milk. As we drove back one time, I shouted to Nolyn, "Stop the car! Stop!"

"What's wrong? What for?" he replied applying brakes. The tyres screeched.

"Reverse back a bit. I've found our bread and milk!"

He gave me that look – my wife's gone mad – but reversed.

"Okay, stop now."

I jumped out to collect my booty.

"Somebody's dumped all these lemonade and coca cola bottles. The refund on these will buy milk and bread for two days."

"*I'm* not going to the Greek café with those filthy bottles!"

"Don't worry, I will after I've washed them."

"Careful, don't put them against my golf bag!"

With more than twenty bottles in the boot, we headed home, where the cleaned bottles were exchanged for cash. I felt rich. We had bread and milk. We struggled financially. I balanced income against expenditure each month. We lived frugally. My financial worries diffused when Chandrè said her prayers, *'Gentle Jesus, meek and mild,* ending with, *God bless mommy. God bless daddy. God bless Spatts. God bless grandpa and granny, Binky,* their dog, *Aggie,* her nanny, the butcher, butterflies, and so on.

The flat could not accommodate a baby. We needed a house urgently. An old house situated near the golf course came onto the market. We arranged to see it. I could see the potential. My parents inspected the house. My stepfather was horrified, but we bought it for R7,000.

We borrowed R300 from mom to meet the transfer costs. Agnes helped me pack up the flat. I knew how to improve our new home, 31 Blakeway Road, but we needed money to do this.

Aboney, Agnes's husband joined us as a gardener and lawns and flowers-beds replaced a plot of potatoes. Spatts, our corgi, loved the freedom of a garden. Chandrè followed Aboney saying, "Annie p'ease, carrot for Chan." He dug up a carrot and washed it for her. She followed Agnes in the house fluffing a feather duster before saying, "All done, Aggie!"

Feeling big and waddling like a duck, I prepared Chandrè for the arrival of a baby brother or sister…

15

BRENT LYNDEN EVERITT WILD & BYRON RICHARD EVERITT WILD

In 1971 the black consciousness movement, instigated by Steve Biko gathered momentum, but the government struck back.

NOLYN'S brother, Ruthven, married to Kathy, lived in East London and worked for the UBS, United Building Society. Kathy a blue-eyed, red-haired radiographer was born in England. She gave birth to their first son, Adrian. My mother-in-law, wanted to see her grandson. She asked Nolyn for a lift to East London. When we picked her up on Sunday, three adults came to the car. Without telling us she had invited Mr and Mrs Green.

The passengers sat in the back and lit up their cigarettes. The car was transformed into a nightclub. I opened the vent and window. Throughout the three-hour long journey, Chandrè slept on my lap against my eight-month pregnancy bulge.

We dropped off our passengers in East London. We spent a memorable time at Marina Glen above the Eastern Beach, with its well-kept lawns, gnarled shade trees and miniature railway. We enjoyed a ride on the train as much as Chandrè did before we had lunch at the SANTA tearoom overlooking the beach. Pushing Chandrè in her pram, we walked 2 km along the esplanade, enjoying the sound of the waves and seagulls and aware of the smell of seaweed and sea spray. Passing the aquarium, Chandrè laughed at the penguins splashing and diving.

It was time to collect our passengers and journey home. Chandrè fell asleep on my lap despite the non-stop chatter. My mother-in-law, dominating the conversation, said, "He's *so beautiful*. He held my little finger and smiled at me. I think he looks like Ruthven."

"Please don't smoke. It makes me nauseous," was ignored as she chatted on. Chain-smoking she sneered, "What *drivel*? I'm not listening to *her.*"

The cigarette fumes made my eyes water. It was mid-winter, far too cold to open the windows. I opened and then shut the air-vent because cold air was blowing directly onto Chandre's perspiring head. She would catch her death of cold.

"Please open your vent, Nolyn."

"No. Why must *I* be cold?"

"Your mother's smoking. We need *some* fresh air."

"Open *your* vent if you want fresh air!"

"I can't. The cold air blows onto her head."

From what began as a simple argument, ended as a *shemozzle*. My mother-in-law not only sided with Nolyn in the commotion, but she slated Chandrè and me in front of strangers. Her words targeted my most vulnerable emotions.

"You're unreasonable... always want your *own* way. You wouldn't allow Nolyn to drive his *own* sister to Durban when *we* needed his help. You're so *self-righteous*!"

"I opposed the motive and *you know that*."

"Nolyn was stupid to marry..."

"Stop butting in!" I was fuming. Remembering *my own* mother's words, '*You have your father's temper*' heightened my rage. Trying to get a word in, "I'd always help but ..."

"There you go again," she interrupted.

"*My* car was not being used to assist in *Cheryl's abortion...*"

"*Who* do you think *you* are? I'll never know what *my* son saw in you... *Hussy* sleeping around with foreign men! *Brazen* enough to have an *illegitimate* child..."

This mud-slinging made Chandrè cry. Hatred welled up in me. She knew how sensitive I was about my past, but being pregnant made it worse. She was truly evil and would stop at nothing. I thought this was bad, but this was a foretaste of what was to follow.

"Please stop the car Nolyn."

"Selfish and manipulative, that's what you are," she added sententiously.

Nolyn had also had enough. The brakes screeched. The car stopped.

"I'll drive now. Hold Chandrè on your lap and I'll open the vent on *my* side," I said.

We swapped places. Before I started the engine, I stared at my mother-in-law. With my face full of hatred I spat out the words, "This is *my* car and if you want to *remain* a passenger in *my* car, I don't want to hear another word *from you*. If you start up again, I'll stop the car and put you out in the middle of *nowhere*. You'll have to find your *own* way home."

I drove off. The tension made the journey endless. My revengeful mother-in-law connived and schemed in the uncomfortable silence. Nolyn and Chandrè were both fast asleep when I stopped at Cumberland Road. I'll get rid of the miserable old bag first, I thought.

"Nolyn, won't you walk me to the front door," she asked sweetly, climbing out. No goodbyes or a thank you. Nolyn put Chandrè on the passenger seat before following his mother down the driveway. We waited and waited. Ten minutes dragged on to twenty. Mr Green volunteered to find out. He returned to say, "Nolyn's mother opened the door and said, 'Nolyn's gone to bed,' and then she closed the door."

Feeling belittled, bewildered and bitter, I gritted my teeth, saying, "I hate you!" Looking at Chandrè asleep where Nolyn had laid her, I wept. I took the passengers home. Afterwards when I reached our house, I could not open the front door. I drove back to fetch Mr Green. He opened the door but refused a lift home saying, "You've enough problems of your own!"

Chandrè was asleep in her cot. I made a cup of tea and noticed how cold and empty the house felt. Would he come back tomorrow? Was his mother contriving more evil? Nolyn returned early the next morning. I was still asleep. Before leaving for work, he remarked, "My mother's not impressed with your behaviour last night."

I did not care what his mother thought. I never replied. I decided there and then to avoid her like the plague. Unresolved anger and hurt filled my already bursting pot of warring emotions. Putting the incident behind me, I focused on my blessings – I had a supportive family, good health, a hard-working husband, an adorable toddler and a baby on the way.

***

Nolyn initiated adoption papers through the Magistrate's Court. One day handing the documents to me, he announced, "Darling, look, she's my legally-adopted daughter, Chandrè Pegeen *Wild*."

"Thanks my love, you've made me proud of you today!"

Home, 31 Blakeway Road, Umtata was good. Chandrè enjoyed the freedom of the garden. She splashed in a plastic pool, scrunching up her nose and closing her eyes. She said, "Look mommy, Chan's swimming." Aunty Molly gave her a two-seater swing, which had belonged to her daughters. With her doll she trundled around the garden or rode her tricycle. Three weeks before Brent's birth, Nolyn arrived home with alarming news.

"Neyse, the *Old Mutual's* arranged a ten-day course in Durban."

"Oh no! Can't you change this? I'll just be home with our new baby."

"No, darling, everything's arranged. I'll see you and our baby before I leave."

There was no point in arguing, but this was a huge disappointment. I was having a baby in wedlock and expected my husband to visit me in hospital and more importantly to bring us home when we were discharged. I had been denied this with Chandrè's birth. Surely he could have arranged this differently, after all the date of my Caesarean section had been decided some time ago. He knew the operation was booked for 19 June.

There was nothing I could do. Chandrè, excited about having a baby brother or sister, would stay with my mother. I was admitted to hospital and Nolyn stayed until the baby was born. My sadness dissipated seeing my precious baby son. His tiny fingers coiled around my little finger, he yawned and smacked his wee lips then opened his blue eyes.

He looks like Nolyn, I thought. Brent Lynden Everitt weighing seven pounds eight ounces, a beautiful healthy baby, brother to Chandrè, was in my arms. Lynden was my idea, a combination of Nolyn and Denyse. To keep the peace, Everitt, his paternal grandmother's maiden name, was added. In Umtata Nolyn celebrated on home-made brew before returning to fetch us from my parent's home in Kokstad. We drove to Umtata, the car full of baby paraphernalia, gifts and flowers. Chandrè peeped into Brent's carrycot, pointing her finger, saying, "*My* baby, B'ent!"

We had barely unpacked when Nolyn left for Durban. What was happening in *my* world? Why was nothing *ever* normal? *When* would things change?

A week later I joined Nolyn in Durban. I packed pots for sterilising bottles, nappies, *Milton* solution, the pram, Chandre's doll and doll's clothes. I drove to Kokstad with Chandrè and Brent on the back seat. There were no car seats for children in those days! We spent Sunday night with my shocked parents. They begged me to stay, but I refused.

The following day, with Brent fed and asleep in his carrycot and Chandrè alongside him on the back seat, I drove off. At Richmond, halfway to Durban, I stopped for lunch and bought fresh milk for Brent, hoping to arrive before the rush hour traffic in Durban. I was exhausted. Carrying Brent with Chandrè holding on to my skirt, I signed in at reception before a porter brought our luggage to the room. A cot was delivered. Chandrè explored her new surroundings. Brent slept and I unpacked. I lay on the bed, waiting. Chandrè heard the approaching footsteps, saying, "Daddy's coming!"

"What on earth are you doing here?" was his shocked reaction when he saw his family. I could tell Nolyn was not only surprised, but displeased.

"I've come to be with you, my love."

"You must be mad. I'm on a course all day. It makes no sense."

"But you finish at five and then we'll be together."

"You just don't get it, *do you*?

I was too tired to argue but longed for a hug. Perhaps I was wrong. What drove me to embark on this outlandish venture? Was it intuition? Was I imagining the worst?

"I'll have to arrange a baby-sitter. I've arranged to see the movie, *Airport* with the crowd. I'll be back."

Leave them with a stranger? What about *us* being a family together? In a quandary, I kept busy. This had helped in the past. After bathing Chandrè and ordering her supper to the room, I washed, changed and fed Brent. Chandrè tucked in. I was exhausted when Nolyn entered, accompanied by a middle-aged, balding man.

"This is David. He's prepared to look after the kids. Aren't you Dave?"

I had not been consulted.

"What time are you going out?" he asked. I observed his rather large beer paunch.

"We're meeting in the foyer at 7.30 pm, Dave."

"Okay. I'll be back at 7.25 pm. Cheers."

I faced a dilemma. Feeding her dolly, Chandrè copied me.

"You'd better get ready, Neyse," Nolyn suggested.

"I'll finish feeding Brent first."

Brent finished his feed. I burped him over my shoulder. Giving him a gentle kiss, I placed him on his side in his carry-cot, with a nappy supporting his back. I folded three nappies prepared a bottle for Brent before putting Chandrè on my lap. I read her a bedtime story. After saying her prayers she hopped onto Nolyn's lap and gave him a slobbery kiss.

Hurriedly I pulled on a dress, too tight around my middle. I had only just brushed my hair, put on a bit of lipstick and perfume and kissed my two little ones goodnight, when there was a knock on the door. Our baby-sitter arrived on time, with a book under his arm saying, "Don't worry. They'll be fine with me." It was dreadful leaving them like that, but...

We walked into the foyer of the hotel and were confronted by a hubbub of smartly dressed men and women. This must be *the crowd*, I thought. Why, I wondered, were *some* of the wives accompanying their husbands. Nolyn received an overwhelming welcome, yet he never introduced me to anyone. I smiled feeling out of place.

Suddenly I felt cold. Nolyn fetched my jersey from the room. He had barely gone when a young blonde sauntered towards me and said, "Hi, I'm Sandy. I believe *you're* going out with Nolyn tonight?"

"Nolyn happens to be *my husband*," I snapped. I was mortified when I realised my arrival had ruined the fling my husband and other married men planned with these tarts. Silence ensued. The looks from the assembled crowd said it all.

We left in taxis for the Playhouse Theatre. I was distracted by the plush carpeted floors and upholstered seats. Bioscope was not this grand in the Kokstad Town Hall with its noisy, wooden floors, dilapidated seats and the occasional breakdown of the projector. The lights dimmed and so did Nolyn's mood. He eventually held my hand, but it meant nothing to me. I was thinking of my babies.

I shivered then sweated. I stripped off my jersey and put it back on again. My head felt thick detached from my body. My eyes could not focus on the screen. The noise amplified and thundered in my head. My mouth was dry. My knees knocked. My teeth chattered. I gripped Nolyn's hand in fear as my forehead dripped with perspiration.

"I'm so hot, Nolyn."

"Shush, you're disturbing the movie."

"I don't feel well. My head's throbbing."

"Come on now. Watch the movie."

"I'm cold. I feel dreadful."

"Are you going to go on like this the *whole* evening?"

I tried to be normal. After a few minutes I knew I had to get out. I needed help. "Nolyn, please call a taxi for me. I'll go back to the hotel. I'm sick."

"Can't you *wait* until the interval?"

I tried. I decided to leave on my own, but could not stand. Nolyn was forced to help me out of the cinema. He reminded me how much he had been looking forward to this movie and how I had spoilt it for him. I was too ill to reply. David was shocked to see us back so soon. I collapsed onto the bed, begging, "Please call a doctor."

A doctor would only come in the morning. I was delirious with fever the whole night, saying, "I think I'm dying."

I survived. In the morning Nolyn went off to his course. A doctor examined me and diagnosed flu and prescribed *Paracetamol*. I phoned for a porter. He arrived immediately. Harry, a tall kind smiling Indian, saw the desperate situation I was in and said, "Don't worry. I'll look after your children." Without instructions he took charge – boiled the bottles, changed nappies and fed Brent. Whenever I opened my eyes, Harry was there, playing 'mother' to my little ones. The next two days were a blur. Harry cared for both me and my helpless little ones. One day Nolyn reminded me before leaving, "I'll be back at 5 pm. See you're ready!"

"I'll be ready."

He had no idea how I felt. My body ached. My head spun. I was lifeless. I valued Harry, as nanny, errand boy, nurse and playmate. That day the doctor called.

"You've still got a high fever. You'll never make the journey to Kokstad in your present state. I'll give you an injection."

He bent over and fumbled in his bag on the floor beside my bed...

What made me say this, I'll never know, but these words saved my life.

"We're only travelling at 5 pm this evening, doctor."

"The injection will've worn off by then. You'll need strong antibiotics. Take two tablets with your first dose. Then take one tablet every six hours. That should sort you out."

The doctor, in a hurry, handed me the prescription and left. Harry came back from the chemist with the antibiotics. I was asleep. The sound of plates clattering and smell of food woke me. It was Harry feeding Chandrè. Brent was asleep. The towelling napkins, piled on a chair, had been laundered.

"Your pills, Mrs Wild," Harry said, putting a glass of water next to me. I sipped, but never took the two pills. I dozed fitfully. I woke and asked, "What's the time Harry?"

"It's 4.30 pm."

"Harry, please pack everything."

Shortly afterwards Nolyn walked in and looked around.

"Well, did the doctor come?"

"Yes."

"And..."

"He prescribed antibiotics."

"Have you had them?"

"No."

"What's wrong with you Neyse? Where are the pills?"

Nolyn was clearly not impressed. I swallowed the two tablets before he helped me to the car. We had not travelled far, when I had difficulty breathing.

"I'm choking Nolyn... I can't' breathe... Help me, love..."

I gasped for air. I felt my neck. It was swollen. Nolyn slowed down and pulled the car off the road. He stared at me for a few seconds. Without saying a word, he drove like a getaway car after a bank robbery. I did not resist his reckless driving. The sooner we arrived in Kokstad the better.

We arrived. Nolyn rushed into my parent's house. I remember being carried by my stepfather; Nolyn carried Chandrè in one arm and Brent, asleep in his carrycot, in his other hand. My mother phoned the doctor. He arrived shortly. The next thing I was in hospital. I was given oxygen and an injection to counteract the penicillin. A day later the doctor told me how I had narrowly escaped death.

"Had the doctor in Durban given you the penicillin injection, you would've died within three minutes of him leaving the room."

I never knew I was allergic to penicillin. The synthetic penicillin tablets had had a devastating effect on my health. I spent a fortnight with my parents. My temperature came down, the swelling in my neck normalised and the red welts gradually disappeared. My mother cared for her grandchildren. Nolyn returned to Umtata. I made a good recovery but my deeper emotional wounds festered. I feigned happiness and kept Nolyn's infidelity to myself. My new role 'keeping-up-appearances' began to keep us together.

Did he still love me? Was this a one-off flirtation? Was something wrong with me? My self-esteem was damaged. Nolyn said he was innocent and that the woman had lied. Our lives moved apart, his with business colleagues and mine in a domestic role. Our worlds met when clients were entertained at home.

Picking up the pieces brought fresh challenges. I had not seen my mother-in-law since the last debacle. I was a recluse. Society challenged my self-worth. Anger, hurt, mistrust and rejection joined simmering emotions I had never dealt with. It took courage to accept Nolyn's invitation to join him at the golf club where things took a different turn.

In South Africa men drank in the bar and ladies sat in the lounge. Nolyn brought me a drink and joined his friends. Was I imagining it or were my friends looking at me strangely? Conversation steered towards children, maids, recipes, fashion, *Tupperware* parties and bits of innocent local gossip.

"Have you heard so-and-so is pregnant?

What's her name?

The new redhead will be asked to play league."

Daphne, a golfer, followed me to the toilet. She asked, "Could I see your wrists?"

Why did she want to see my wrists, I wondered.

"It's no use *denying* it. Nolyn saved your life when he found you in the bathroom with *both* your wrists slit and blood draining into the bath."

"What *are* you talking about?"

"Mrs Everitt, Nolyn's grandmother, who works at the surgery, *knows* what you did."

"Look at my wrists. *No* bandages. No *scars*. Are you satisfied?"

Seething with anger, I slammed the door. I squeezed past the men in the bar to Nolyn. "Have you heard the rumour that I slit my wrists and you found me in time?"

My outburst silenced the men in the bar. Some craned their necks to see Nolyn's reaction. Taking his time to reply, he placed his beer on the counter, "Yes, I know, but *this* isn't the *place* to talk about it."

He always had an excuse. Fed up with being put on hold, I raised my voice, "Have a look. Can anybody see scars on my wrists?"

Edged out the bar by my embarrassed-looking husband, I broke away from him and blurted out to an astonished audience of women, "Have a look." Pulling up both my sleeves, I continued, "Not a single scar on my wrists? I hope you're all satisfied?"

Nolyn took my arm and led me to the car. At home, he said his mother had started the rumour and had deliberately passed it on to a gossiping music teacher. He kept it from me never expecting the rumours to spread like wild fire.

I stewed over the slander. On Monday I confronted the gossip-mongers, my mother-in-law, Gogs and the music teacher. My words never scared his family, but at the thought of being sued for defamation of character, the music teacher said, "Ruth told me and I believed her. Please don't press charges."

"After what I've been through!"

I received a distressed telephone call from the doctor, "My patient's in hospital. Her blood pressure is dangerously high and she has heart palpitations. You've threatened to take her to court. I strongly advise you to stop or the repercussions could be fatal."

I heeded his warning. I buried the gossip. Thereafter things were going well. Nolyn's loan of R8000 from the old Mutual had been granted to fund desperately-needed improvements to the house. These renovations were underway when Nolyn came home with the news.

"I've bought a new car. Come and have a look!"

Stunned, a brand new, yellow, diesel *Mercedes Benz* stood in the driveway.

"Come for a ride."

He opened the door. I saw joy and pride written over his face. I never felt the way he did. I had not consented to selling my car. It was gone.

"I love the smell of a new car," I said trying to sound enthusiastic.

"It'll hold the dirt roads better than the *Ford*. Diesel's more economical than petrol!"

"Have you bought it?"

"Yes, of course!"

On this maiden drive in the new yellow *Mercedes* Nolyn was in his element but I had mixed feelings. How could he afford it? My car was new. Had his mother prompted him into owning his own car? I had no transport. How long would I have to wait for the second-hand car he promised me? More shocking news was coming.

I discovered he used the building loan to buy the car. Faced with escalating debts and an unfinished building project became my problem. The alterations limped on. I scraped together enough money to pay the labour costs. Our already high account at *Buffalo Timber*, the hardware dealers, mounted. The small amounts paid off monthly had little effect. I had sleepless nights worrying about our mounting debt. There was only one solution. I needed to work and applied for a job. I buried more bitterness, jealousy, anger and frustration.

My children were always my first concern. Chandrè loved Brent, chatted to him and popped his dummy into his mouth. The pram took strain, laden with shopping. Chandrè hitched a ride on the pram to and from town. Blacks admired them. They were fascinated with Chandrè's two pigtails, tied in pink bows. Brent listened to inquisitive conversations from his baby seat, moving his head from side to side.

"What's that?"

"A sprinkler," I explained.

"Why does the sprinkler wet the garden?"

"So that the plants don't die."

"Why do the plants want to die?"

"No, the plants don't want to die. The water makes them grow and gives them food."

These conversations reminded me of their favourite story, *The Angel of Rain*. I bought Chandrè a watering-can. She watered the flowers saying, "Lift up your heads, f'owers," which she quoted from the story.

***

I worked as an invoicing clerk at *Sparg's Wholesale* to reduce our debts.

At this time we were invited to two weddings. Nolyn was best man when his friend, Hugh Preston married Sylvia Muir. Her sister, Jenny, had been friendly with Topsy. An enormous double wedding, sisters Sylvia and Jenny, both with long blonde hair, and one I will never forget. Hugh and Sylvia settled in Umtata. Nolyn and Hughie, as he was called, were keen golfers and fishermen. We became good friends.

My youngest sister, Margy married Eddie Reichmuth in Kokstad on 19 December. Chandrè, wearing a Victorian dress with pantaloons, was her flower girl. Topsy and I were bridesmaids. We wore full-length pink Victorian dresses and carried parasols. My marriages, of 20 November 1965 to Donald Smith and 23 August 1969 to Nolyn Wild in this church, came back to me.

By December our house alterations were complete. Looking at the quaint dining room, previously a bathroom, pride swelled within me. White curtains at two small windows against red wallpaper had made this an intimate and perfect place to entertain prospective clients.

Before our holiday to Umsikaba, Dr Clarke took me off the pill saying, "Enjoy your holiday and remember, be careful. You can't have another baby for at least a year..."

"Yes," I replied thinking how unnecessary this advice was. Our friends Arthur and Heather de la Mare and baby son, Craig accompanied us. Nolyn showered me with more affection than I had expected. Chandrè developed a trusting loving relationship with Nolyn. I watched them build sandcastles. She tirelessly fetched water in her bucket, poured it into the moat where it disappeared. We spent lazy days in the sun, sand and sea. I dipped into rock pools to keep cool. I regained my self-worth as Nolyn and I drew closer.

After a refreshing holiday Nolyn pursued his insurance career. The year got off to a good start. My doctor's words, "I've taken you off the pill because of your allergic reaction to it. No falling pregnant for at least one year," came to me. He also said, "It's a miracle you carried Brent with no major problems," after my second Caesarean section.

I knew I was pregnant... This time it would be different. I procrastinated telling Nolyn until I could hold out no longer. He took me to the doctor. My suspicions were confirmed. I was happy. I wanted six children. Nolyn was unhappy, totally miserable. My friends, Heather and Sylvia were also pregnant. Through Arthur and Hughie, Nolyn learnt to admire my blossoming shape and treated me well. He volunteered to buy me grapes when I had a sudden craving. But how quickly things changed!

Friends and nannies gathered for Chandrè's third birthday. August produced frosty mornings but clear and warm days. I was taken by surprise when Nolyn introduced me to the new doctor's wife, Liz. She stared at me rudely and responded, "Heavens, I've never seen anyone so huge. You're ENORMOUS!"

Her rude words and unfriendly manner left me speechless. Nolyn supported me, "Her baby's due in three weeks!" He gave me a knee-melting wink and a kiss before leaving.

Liz, tall and slim, with waist-length hair, swaggered off to join the mothers outside. She sat down on the *only* cushioned chair. I refused to let her presence spoil this birthday party. I deliberately avoided her and was relieved when she went home. Something about her niggled me. What was it? I would soon find out…

I swapped my job at *Sparg's Wholesale* with Sylvia, for a teaching post at the Umtata convent but had to work off my notice in the afternoon. My day began at 5 am putting the washing into the twin-tub machine. The children clamoured for my attention when I arrived home exhausted at 5 pm. When they were tucked up in bed, I had lessons to prepare and books to mark. I was unable to keep this up and resigned for health reasons.

The old pram was replaced with a new modern high pram. I made a second nappy bag and filled it with new towelling nappies and liners. I hoped to keep Brent's nappies separate from the new baby's. Nolyn and I watched Brent take his first steps on his first birthday.

Some nights I knitted listening to *Money or the Box* and the *Springbok Hit Parade*. Nolyn fancied Elvis Presley and strummed on an imaginary guitar, singing *Hound Dog* and *Heartbreak Hotel*. Our collection of vinyl LP and 45 records had grown. Five records, stacked and played consecutively on our radiogram, was high-tech for those days.

Chandrè and Brent stayed with my mother when I was admitted to the Umtata Hospital. We signed papers to have my Fallopian tubes tied at the same time on the doctor's recommendation. On 18 September Byron Richard Everitt, weighing seven pounds eight ounces, came into the world. I saw him briefly before he was taken to the Nursing Home run by nuns because there was no maternity section at the hospital.

When Nolyn said goodbye to me, I choked. He rang my bell. Nobody answered. He rushed out and found my doctor, who came to my rescue. "I can't stay here," I pleaded.

Thinking I would never get into a wheelchair six hours after my operation, he said, "If you're able to get into a wheelchair, you may go to the nursing home!"

Despite the pain, I forced my legs over the edge of the bed and supported by Nolyn, I sat in the wheelchair. I am still shocked today realising what a risk we took. Nolyn drove with one hand on the steering wheel and the other holding the drip above my head. At the nursing home the nuns expected me to arrive by ambulance. They radiated love and I knew I would be safe.

Nolyn left for his course in Cape Town. This was my last pregnancy and my last chance to experience what I had missed out on the previous births, a husband to visit me and to bring me home. With my dreams shattered, I fought on. Treated like royalty with trays of delicious attractively-arranged meals, I was content. One nun, giving Byron to me for his feed, asked, "Do you have a little daughter?"

"Yes sister. I have a daughter and a son."

"Well, she continued, "Your baby's so beautiful. If you dressed him in pink woollies nobody would be any the wiser!"

Bonding with my new baby, I showered him with the same love I had given Chandrè and Brent at birth. I was sad to leave the nuns, when my friend fetched us. She prepared a supper dish for me. Alone with Byron, I longed for Nolyn. Byron slept well on his first night. So did I. The telephone woke me at 7.30 am.

"Neyse, I'm glad you're home. I've arranged a lift to Umtata for Chandrè and Brent. They'll be arriving at about 10 am. Are you there?"

"Yes mom. Did you say 10 am?"

"Yes. How's your new baby?"

"Fine. Who's bringing the children to Umtata?"

"I don't know the couple, but they're willing to take the kids to Umtata."

"Thanks mom. Bye."

What was the rush to send Chandrè and Brent back? Was my mother not enjoying her grandchildren? How could she send my children on a two-hour journey with strangers? A three year-old and a fourteen month-old! I rocked the pram with my foot, sipping tea all the while looking through the net curtains for a car. Spatts barked bringing me to my feet and to the front door.

"Hello, we've brought your children home," a stout man said.

"Mommy, mommy," they called both wanting to be picked up.

"Thanks so much."

"I'll fetch their luggage," he said, returning with a suitcase.

"Well, thanks again. Goodbye."

He left. Chandrè and Brent rushed towards the pram. Brent poked his finger at his baby brother, waking him.

"No, Brent, naughty," Chandrè scolded.

Chandrè helped me with two babies. Nolyn returned from Cape Town and fell into his work routine. Preparations began for our annual holiday to Coffee Bay in a caravan. Spatts and Pandora, our white cat would come with us and two maids. I took the challenge in my stride…

At Coffee Bay both maids came in early to look after Brent, aged eighteen months and Byron, three months, in answer to Chandrè's request to join her daddy on a rough-and-ready nine-hole golf course on the cliffs of Coffee Bay.

"Mommy can we play golf with daddy tomorrow?"

"Yes, my love. You'll have to wake up early."

"I can mommy."

Photos captured these happy times at Coffee Bay, which got its name from a ship, wrecked there in 1863, depositing its cargo of coffee beans on the beach. This remote seaside resort boasted two popular hotels, the *Ocean View* and the *Lagoon Hotel*. The easily accessible kilometre-long beach with white sands sat below towering cliffs. The golf course stretched along the tops of those cliffs.

The photograph of Nolyn's facial expression as he was about to strike the ball, depicts deep concentration which made him a scratch handicap player. His good tournament temperament and determination were the key to winning many trophies and prizes. As Nolyn struck the ball I remember the sound of the club swishing through the air, followed by a sharp crack as the club connected with the teed-up ball. Chandrè, three years and four months old, remained dead still, honoured to hold his wood. She watched in admiration. Herds of cattle grazed lazily amidst golfers and sometimes, these would-be targets were chased off the fairway. We started at 5 am because, as the sun rose higher in the blue sky, so the heat intensified scorching our fair skins.

Caravanning on a friend's property, we drew water from their water tanks and accommodated our maids in their servants' quarters. Nolyn snorkelled and fished and I took the children to the beach. Chandrè carried the beach umbrella; Brent carried the buckets and spades and I carried the rest – Byron in his carry-cot, his bag of baby paraphernalia, sunhats, sun cream and refreshments. Our Corgi, Spatts, trotted along loyally as part of the entourage.

Those days felt like yesterday. What bliss they were. Today I would think twice about putting my baby in the hot sun protected only by a beach umbrella! Sitting in the shallow water, I watched Chandrè and Brent splashing and jumping over the waves. Spatts cooled off in the shallows with them but returned under the umbrella, to protect Byron.

Before noon we gathered our sandy belongings and began the long hot trek to the caravan. Water, a scarce commodity, meant half a bucket to rinse the sand off everybody and to rinse the bathing costumes. After a nap we returned to the lagoon, where the children played in the incoming tide. Our family was complete when Nolyn joined us. The telephone lines to both hotels were more down than up, we had no mod-cons, no hot or cold running water. A trading store supplied the basics. Day after day we relaxed in the fresh sea air, waking at sunrise and retiring when the golden sun sank in the west…

I remember three significant events of this holiday. One Friday night we braved the rain and muddy roads and joined friends for drinks at the *Ocean View Hotel*. This meant crossing a causeway. When we returned it was impassable. The river was in full flood. We were stranded. The hotel owners permitted us spend the night on sofas in the lounge. I could not sleep. Were my little ones safe? Were the maids with them? Had the children woken to find we were not there?

At dawn I walked to the river mouth hoping to cross. I hitched up my skirt and waded out. The rushing water almost buckled my legs, forcing me to retreat. Nolyn was furious when he got wind of what I had done. "You could've been swept out to sea!" he chided me.

Dishevelled but determined to reach our children in the caravan, we drove to the causeway. Watching enormous uprooted trees being swept along in the raging waters, we shouted back and forth to the crowd gathered on the other side.

"Are the children safe?"

"Don't worry they're fine."

"We'll span a rope across the causeway to get you back."

"You'll have to hang on tightly to the rope!"

At 11 am, holding the rope suspended across the causeway, we waded through fast-flowing waters, cheered on by the crowd. The maids and friends had kept our family safe.

The next memory makes me laugh, today. I bought two fowl from the local *Xhosa* people. Chandrè and Brent fed them daily and regarded them as pets, not knowing why they were tethered to the caravan and fattened. To their surprise, there was only *one* fowl to feed on Christmas Day. "Somebody stole our chicken," Chandrè exclaimed. Brent followed close at her heels. How could I say I had roasted one of *her* chickens for our Christmas Dinner? What would she think? What was the answer?

"I think the chicken went home to his family for Christmas, Chandrè," Nolyn suggested, which met with her approval. She decided to let the other fowl go home too. She released it. This meant no roast chicken for us on New Year's Day!

It rained incessantly for a week. We were holed up in the caravan with wet nappies and crying children. Tempers frayed. Nolyn and I learnt to play bridge using a *Teach yourself bridge'* kit I had bought at an auction. In later years we enjoyed regular bridge evenings with friends in King William's Town.

Our holiday ended. Friends gave conflicting advice on how to tow the caravan up the steep narrow cutting on a gravel road.

"You'll never make it with a *Ranchero*!

Get your speed up first. Then make a run for it!

If I were you, I'd borrow a tractor, safer."

Our unforgettable exit began. As hotel guests and cottage-owners watched through binoculars Nolyn gave me his final advice, "Okay, Neyse. Off you go. Whatever you do, *don't* stop on the way up!"

"Of course. Bye, my love."

With Chandrè, Spatts and Pandora in the yellow *Mercedes*, I left. We climbed the S-bend of the steep cutting effortlessly. I slowed down, pulling over for an oncoming car. While changing gears I panicked. I stalled the car in the wrong gear. Try as I did to start and take off on this steep gravel incline, the tyres spun and the car skidded closer and closer to the edge of a sheer drop. I lost my nerve. I pulled up the hand brake. I left the pets in the car and Chandrè and I climbed out.

It was too late. Towing the caravan, Nolyn ascended the steep cutting. He could not see what lay ahead. The van was struggling to pull the caravan in first gear. Three-quarters of the way to the top, he saw the motionless *Mercedes*. He could not overtake on this narrow road. He was forced to stop. A dangerous situation.

"I told you *not* to stop."

"But..."

"Hurry, walk to the top of the hill and stop any oncoming vehicles, but before you do that, put some *huge* rocks behind the caravan tyres."

I was used to taking orders and knew this was for his safety. This precaution prevented the vehicles running backwards. Below anxious onlookers sent a tractor to our rescue. I stopped cars at the top of the hill and the tractor pulled the truck and caravan helped by locals wanting a *basela*. Every holiday told a unique story.

16

FIGHTING FOR MY RIGHTS

In 1972 Steve Biko abandoned his medical studies and became a full-time political organiser. In 1973 he was restricted to King William's Town and over a three-year period, he was arrested and detained twenty-nine times.

AFTER a happy month at Coffee Bay, some of my deep hurts had healed and Nolyn had shown the children fatherly love. By revealing our true feelings and spending time together, our relationship strengthened. Chandrè befriended Alice, next door. She spoke Afrikaans, but soon learnt how to speak English.

"*Asseblief,* Chandrè, "Please, Chandrè," was met with, "Yes, Alice you can play with my dolly!" Followed by, "*Wag, ek wil my poppie haal. Ek is nou-nou terug.* Wait I'll fetch my doll. I'll be back soon. "

Chandrè and Alice shared dolls. Brent played with trucks and cars alongside them. They loved their small tent. Sitting at six months, Byron was included in this game. A see-saw, a double swing, a sandpit and tricycles provided the children with healthy outdoor entertainment in our own huge garden. As toddlers Brent and Byron collected *songololo* and *goggas* putting these in their pockets.

Whenever I met Liz, she put on her false smile, saying, "I bumped into Nolyn today!"

"Did you now?" was my standard reply. Sometimes I ignored her, giving her a curt hello. Should I have paid more attention to those repetitive words? Her husband, Billy, was our doctor. When I left the surgery one day, the receptionist whispered, "Seems you've some competition with Billy's wife these days!" I remembered when Nolyn first introduced me to Liz and her hurtful words. Unsuspecting, I asked the receptionist, "What do you mean?"

"They're inseparable, those two..."

I knew exactly what she meant. I would fight for my rights. Before accusing her, I sought reliable witnesses. Liz's maid, not knowing I was Nolyn's wife confirmed, "Nolyn visits Mrs Liz at the house often and Mrs Liz tells me to take the children for a walk..." It hurt Norma, my trusted friend, to admit she had seen them together, saying, "Liz was having more than a friendly chat in his *Mercedes*..."

My bottled-up emotions surged – hurt, anger, bitterness, disappointment, worthlessness, jealousy and sadness. My fighting spirit took over. My mind was made up. I would end this, once and for all... An invitation to dinner at our home sounded normal. They accepted. My emotions churned. Trying to remain calm, I prepared a roast chicken with trimmings. By 8.45 pm. Billy and Liz, expected at 8 pm, had not arrived.

"Nolyn phone and see what's happened to them."

"They'll come. Stop flapping."

"The meal's being ruined and I'm starving, Nolyn. Please phone."

I listened as Nolyn spoke to Liz on the phone. Controlling my anger was becoming more difficult by the minute.

"Liz says Billy's just finishing a bed he's making. They'll be along soon."

"What *rude* people. They'll not get a second invitation from me," I hissed.

"Don't be like that!"

When Nolyn supported them, he exacerbated me. They finally arrived. I served the meal which was dried out. Nolyn and Billy talked golf, but not even a few gulps of wine eased the stilted conversation. I was not the normal charming hostess. Billy sensed something was wrong. He avoided a confrontation. Nolyn thought he had got away with it, but...The evening had a specific purpose. It was time to get to the point.

"I'm glad you could *both* come," I began, "although you *were late* and the roast was *ruined*. I thought it best to say this with all four of us present."

I paused. My eyes of hatred were fixed, first on Liz and then on Nolyn. I continued, "You two are having an affair." The room felt cold, like a morgue.

"You *can't* deny it, because I've *several* reliable witnesses. Billy, I'm warning you to control your wife. If not, I'll attack her. Liz, no wonder you were always *'bumping into Nolyn today'* as you told me. If *you* continue this affair with *my* husband, I will pull *every* hair out of your head. You've been warned. Leave *my* husband, father of *our* children, *alone*." Liz burst into tears. The two men looked at each other in shocked silence.

"May I take your plates, please? Nolyn will serve liqueurs in the lounge."

I collected the plates and stalked out. In the lounge Nolyn put on a Dionne Warwick LP record which played, *Walk on by*. They did not stay long. My confrontation had the desired effects. Fighting for my rights was a first, but this would not be the last.

***

Nolyn purchased a two-roomed shack at Coffee Bay. It needed to be enlarged. I drew up the plans and kept a tight rein on the finances. Every week I drove to Coffee Bay in the *Ranchero* to oversee the build. Driving back and forth at low tide, I loaded the truck with sand. Once I overloaded the van and was unable to drive up the steep incline from the causeway. The excess sand was off-loaded. This meant another rushed trip for more sand before the tide came in.

***

Ruth, my mother-in-law, broke up Percy and Louise's marriage. On her teaching sabbatical she planned a six-week holiday overseas. She bragged about this long before the time. Louise could not afford this holiday but Ruth paid for everything so that Louise could accompany her. But, before they left, their friendship ended. Ruth had *then* fallen in love with Percy, Louise's husband. A holiday destined to be a disaster from beginning to end.

Prior to this, my mother-in-law coerced me into attending a séance. She and Gogs, Nolyn's grandmother were spiritualists. Sitting in a circle with uncrossed arms and legs in the dark, she spoke through three spirit guides, a Texan, an Irish nun and a Scotsman, the night I attended. The accents were perfect. The Texan said my first husband, Don Smith, was standing behind me.

The lights were switched on. I wanted to run home, but there was more to follow...

Ruth asked. "Whose hands are hot?"

My hands were like burning coals. I owned up.

"Denyse, you've the gift of healing hands," adding, "You'll come back, won't you?"

I chose my words carefully, "Umm... I'll think about it."

I was pleased to escape the evil in that room. I had sinned. I had to get to confession. I would *not* be going back...

***

My mother-in-law returned from her holiday with Louise, who re-located to Natal with her children. Ruth married Percy. I was committed to hosting a reception in our home for twenty people. Six months later Ruth's marriage to Percy ended. She refused to accompany him to South-West-Africa, Namibia, on promotion. After this Percy and Louise were re-united as a family in Natal.

Nolyn and I took pity on her. She pleaded poverty having given up a teaching post she had held for forty years. He made his mother manager of his newly-acquired dry-cleaning business with very modern machines. Whenever I saw her she harassed me to attend another séance. "I'm not interested, thanks mom!"

Glowering at me, her wrinkled face grew uglier. A counter-attack usually followed...

Ruth arrived with Christmas presents for Brent and Byron *only*, saying, "I've brought the Christmas presents."

There were *two* presents in the bag. She continued, "for *my two* grandchildren."

Chandrè, deeply hurt by her words, never understood why she had been ostracised. Ruth had had her revenge.

"Don't worry. Yours is coming," I told my daughter. It never did...

Next we visited Nolyn's dad, Jack, his wife, Joan and half-brother, Terry. They lived in Koppies in the Orange Free State. Another love triangle opened. Jack, a biker, keen fisherman and good businessman, was a womaniser. He owned the only hotel in Koppies.

Joan said, "Ruth divorced Jack. She begged Jack to marry her before she gave birth to Cheryl. Jack honoured her request. Then they divorced a second time. Jack and I married and moved away," she concluded. Divorce was rampant in this family. His grandmother was a divorcee. She told me about Nolyn's brother...

"Ruthven divorced his first wife in Rhodesia. He has a son, Troy from that marriage. A few years on, he met and married Kathy, a radiographer from England. As you know they had two children, Adrian and Christine."

I told Joan we were there the day Ruthven told Nolyn, "I'm leaving Kathy. I've met another woman." He walked out on her that evening.

It seemed only yesterday we had walked along the esplanade with our children. I photographed this so-called happy outing with the wreck of the *SA Oranjeland* in the background. This SA freighter was built in Hamburg in 1969 and, after leaving the East London harbour in a gale, was wrecked off the Esplanade on 13 August 1974.

Kathy, Adrian and Christine returned to her family in the UK. I took more photos of Kathy and the children on board the *Union Castle* ship in the East London harbour. We watched the boat sail out the harbour taking Kathy, Adrian and Christine to England. It was awful to see them go… I missed them.

Before this a forthcoming wedding had distracted me. My sister, Topsy and William Botha, known as Bill, planned to marry on 1 September. Topsy met this tall dark handsome man in Johannesburg where they both worked. Margy, in a long blue dress, was bridesmaid. Chandrè in a matching dress was a flower girl. Blue-eyed blonde Brent wore a white satin shirt and blue velvet trousers as the page-boy. My two children were about to make this wedding one we would not forget. During the ceremony a posy tug-of-war between Chandrè and Brent with their assertive words, ensued:

"Mine!" Brent declared.

"No, Brent, *my* flowers, not yours."

"I hold them *little* bit, Chan'."

"*No*… let go…"

Chandrè desperately held on to posy, but Brent grabbed hold of it defiantly.

"*My* f'owers!" he shouted.

"Mommy, Brent's got my flowers."

My mother intervened. When the flowers were taken from him, Brent said, "I *not* naughty, granny." Nobody argued with granny. Chandrè cried. My mother comforted her. Brent and I left the church. Amidst this fiasco, Topsy and Bill took their wedding vows.

I pondered the events of the past year: I ended Nolyn's affair with Liz; I hosted my mother-in-law's wedding reception and supervised the building of our cottage at Coffee Bay. We holidayed in our almost-complete cottage over December. Nolyn invited guests, one of his traits I found difficult to accept. I looked deeper to understand myself and Nolyn.

The gentle easygoing young man, who once swept me off my feet in Kokstad, was now a driven businessman. He was nicknamed *Lizard* by Ralph Hilligan because he blinked his eyes like a lizard lying lazily in the sun. To me Nolyn had become a race horse determined to win every race, working with the same determination to sell more and more insurance policies.

I believed I was the only one he loved, but I was wrong. His difficult childhood without a father and no love from either his mother or grandmother, brought up by servants, shaped who he was. He and Ruthven were unwanted babies. His mother wanted a daughter, planned to call her Ruth, but switched his name to Ruthven. When she had a second son, her Lyn became Nolyn. When Cheryl was born she doted on her daughter.

Nolyn's friends taught him valuable life-skills. Deprived of so much as a child he strove to be rich. Nolyn dressed immaculately, spoke politely and kept abreast with world affairs. He relaxed by playing golf or fishing. His good relationships with clients were the foundation of his success. His friendly phone-calls and being a good listener cemented mutual trust. Nolyn was adventurous. He had flying lessons taking the children with him. He was unable to keep up the flying hours so he never got his wings.

If only – two words used in hindsight – our marriage had had stronger foundations and pre-conceived expectations of each other were more realistic. I loved Nolyn deeply and valued his positive characteristics, but I resented rejection and hated not knowing where he was and when he would return home. Neither nagging nor passivity solved the problem.

Often I telephoned the police at night to find out if an accident had been reported. My life of worry, lonely nights, imagining the worst, made me a nervous wreck. If I challenged Nolyn it resulted in physical violence excusing away bruises and gashes with lies. Looking deeper,

I wrote poetry to relieve my pent-up emotions. I had changed for the worse. My fiery temper and abusive words had stolen my joy. I fell deeper into a chasm of depression.

On not being wanted (dated 6.6.71)
Fingers feeling, reaching, searching
A heart longing, yearning, wanting
To find only rejection!
A kitten, playful and joyful
A fire, warm and powerful
Without any appreciation!
A child, needing and pleading
A mother's task, never-ending
Alas always contradiction!
With every second of each day
Two people close, now faraway
All because of separation!
Oh cursed be the man
Who brought this painful plan
To bear on civilisation!
Nerves reeling, pitching, breaking,
Fears gripping and imprisoning
Silently in reclusion!

Love (dated 1.1.1972)
Love is laughing and giving
Love is a way of living
Living to love, and to be loved.

Hurt (dated 10.1.1972)
Being struck openly
Not through deeds, but rather words,
The pain penetrates, lastingly.
A seething pain
Creeping in my mind
Not through deeds, but rather words
The hurt bites, increasingly.

Tomorrow (dated 6 .6.1972)

Why want for tomorrow? It will be here too soon
Perhaps bringing sorrow before the afternoon.
Want rather for today – tomorrow once it was–
A while is here to stay, before it too shall pass.
Tomorrow's a day unknown: Today has tasks begun
Of varied pleasures amidst laughter and good fun.
Want rather for today bring joy to young and old
Tomorrow's on its way as memories unfold.

I worked again doing clerical work at *Blakeway & Leppan Attorneys* and marketed *National Airways Corporation,* a company with four and six-seater planes flying between Umtata and Durban. When Chandrè accompanied me, the small aircraft shuddered, rattled and bounced through turbulence. She loved it but I was scared out of my wits.

One day Mary my work colleague and I issued car licences. The counter was clearly visible from the street. Being month-end, Nolyn had given me my house-keeping allowance. I stuffed the cash into my bag before I returned to work at 2 pm. I slung my handbag under the counter. At times the crowd was six deep with people queuing at the door. We balanced the money and handed it to the boss at 5 pm and I reached for my handbag.

"Mary, have you seen my bag?"

"No. You threw it under the counter."

"It's not there."

We searched. It had gone. In our busyness a bag-snatcher had taken it from under our noses. I lost my money, the house keys and photographs of the children from Topsy. I learnt, like fellow South Africans, more would be stolen from me in the future…

***

I surveyed the scene of our newly-built seaside cottage at Coffee Bay. Red gingham curtains brightened the country-style kitchen; pots and pans hung above the gas cooker; a large paraffin fridge stood in one corner; a work table beneath the window and underneath, two buckets of water in readiness. Linoleum covered the floors. The water tanks were full. The leather chairs occupied the enclosed section of the verandah leading to the guest room.

Ralph Hilligan and Dougie Pohl, Nolyn's work-mates, occupied this room. Their late nights meant breakfast was delayed. At night I watched as they drank bottomless bottles of beer. During the day they fished off dangerous cliff edges. I secretly worried about them. Chandrè and Kim, aged seven from next door, made friends. They discussed what to wear to the movie at the *Lagoon Hotel* that evening, before scampering away. My sons fell asleep. Nolyn, Dougie and Ralph turned in early. I wrote a letter waiting for Chandrè. I heard voices. Peeping through the curtains, I saw three torchlights in the dark.

"Mommy it was lovely," Chandrè said.

Kim left with her brothers saying, "I'll see you on the beach tomorrow."

Chandrè did not have to be told. She was in her pyjamas and in bed waiting for me to kiss her goodnight. The 16 December was a hot summer evening. The windows were open. Because Chandrè was scared of the dark, I lit a candle and put it on the wardrobe. This done I tip-toed to bed. I had barely fallen asleep when I heard, "Mommy I'm *hot*."

"Kick off your blankets."

I dozed off, but not for long...

"Mommy FIRE!" woke me. This time I jumped out of bed. It was not a dream. Flames leapt across the doorway of the children's bedroom. I ran down the passage and drenched myself and a towel under the shower. Dripping wet, I hurried to the doorway, screaming, "Wake up Nolyn, FIRE! FIRE!"

There was no time to waste. I must save my children. With eyes closed, I ran through the flames. I saw Chandrè, knees buckled under her chin, petrified, sitting at the top of her bed clutching her doll. Mesmerised, she screamed, "*Mommy, help*. Fire! *Help!*"

My sons were asleep. Their beds, on the further side of the room, were enveloped in smoke. The curtains and the bottom of Chandre's bed were burning. The wind came up and fanned the flames. The room was hot. I gathered my sleeping sons under my arms. I tucked them under the wet towel. With Chandrè holding my arm, her face turned towards my body, we escaped the blaze. Dawn broke outside as my bare feet trampled the dewy grass.

Carrying my little boys with Chandrè clinging to me, we arrived next-door. On the way I bellowed, "FIRE! HELP!" What sounded like gunshots made me look back. Flames shooting through the asbestos roof caused this noise. Kim's father, also Ralph, opened the door. Jean, his wife, was beside him.

"Fire, please look after my children."

Jean pushed past Ralph taking hold of my bewildered little boys. Ralph took Chandrè into his arms. My children were safe. I ran back to help Nolyn. In the pandemonium, we never saw Chandrè returning. Ralph and Dougie moved their vehicles from the burning cottage. Nolyn unlocked the water tanks. Raging flames devoured our cottage, minute by minute. Throwing buckets of water through the window did little to calm this inferno. Neighbours and hotel guests fought the fire with us. Ralph Hilligan asked, "Neyse, where is Chandrè? She's not with Ralph and Jean next door..."

"She *must* be. I left her there."

"She's *not* there, Neyse."

"Well, I'm going in to find her."

"You *can't*."

"She's *my daughter*. I will."

"I'll come with you."

Ralph and I slithered on the floor. Blinded by smoke, we made our way towards the inaccessible bedroom and then down the passage to the kitchen. By then I could hardly breathe. My eyes stung. Where was my little girl? Unnoticed by us, she had slipped back to fetch her doll, which lay where she had dropped it. She could not unlock the kitchen door. We found her, clutching her doll on the kitchen floor, in a room slowly filling up with smoke. Ralph picked her up. We escaped into the fresh air.

"My darling," tears of joy ran down my cheeks as I hugged her. I still have panic attacks reliving those horrific moments... Chandrè was safe with her brothers once more.

Daylight brought more helpers. Possessions were thrown out of the cottage in panic. It was decided to work in two teams forming lines from the water tanks. One line passed water to the person on the roof and the other to the bedroom window. The fire was extinguished two hours later. Blackened timber and walls smouldered. The smell of smoke permeated the air. It rained and without a roof, our cottage faced further damage.

The shock of the fire impacted on me much later that day. We had come very close to being burnt alive. That dreaded candle, I thought, had started the fire. The wind knocked the candle over and the curtain caught alight. The fire was fuelled by a box of wallpaper on top of the wardrobe. My thoughts went deeper. Material things can be replaced, but not life. God had spared our lives.

Friends gave the children clothes; the hotel manager lent me bedding and cottage owners found sheets of corrugated iron to patch the roof. Chandrè and I bought bedding and clothes in Umtata. Our visitors from Durban arrived and shared our heartache. We got by. It was not the Christmas I had planned, but we counted our blessings.

17

BRECHANBY

In 1976 the South African troops were withdrawn from Angola. It was then that Blacks celebrated the defeat of white power quite noticeably. In 1976 the Transkei, 42,870 sq. metres of undulating pastoral land studded with white-washed rondavel huts, occupied mostly by Xhosas, became a sovereign independent state.

SLOWLY we climbed the social ladder. Mixing with the upper echelons of society – doctors, lawyers, judges, authors, political leaders and business tycoons – I wondered where we stood in the hierarchic system of the day. Although not acknowledged by my husband, I found my own niche. I became an expert at entertaining and had no qualms mixing with the hoity-toity. They, bored to tears, welcomed my innovative and fun parties.

These varied. Formal three-course dinners, hors d'oeuvres, two different roasts with crispy roast potatoes and a selection of vegetables, followed by a choice of three desserts. I used our best *Noritake* dinner service, silver cutlery and cut glass wine glasses. A centrepiece of fresh flowers and candles completed the elegant table. From a *Hi-Fi* set, a long-playing record provided background music during this carefully prepared meal enjoyed by guests attired in suits and long evening gowns. We sank into armchairs in the lounge listening to Mantavani. *After Eight* mints and liqueurs were enjoyed followed by mocha in dainty coffee cups to conclude the evening.

Then there were my theme parties, casual and different. At a hippie party, guests dressed in tight jeans and T-shirts with flowers in their hair; drinks flowed like the Victoria Falls; music thumped loud enough for the entire neighbourhood to hear as barefooted couples gyrated and cigarette smoke wafted towards dimmed lights. I wonder how our children slept through this racket. Or did they?

An unexpected knock on the door was disconcerting. Nolyn opened it to unexpected visitors, two policemen in full uniform. The tall arrogant one looked down at his stocky, balding companion. Smiling he said, *"Goeie aand, meneer*, Good evening, sir," above the sound of *Hound Dog* blaring from the *Hi-Fi* set. They peered past Nolyn, glee in their eyes as they both summed up the scene. They believed their suspicions were justified. This party was more than noise and drink. These party-goers were smoking *dagga*.

"What can I do for you?" Nolyn asked.

Opportunely recognising the local doctor and the judge in hippie disguise, he replied, *"Jammer, meneer. Sal meneer die musiek asseblief sagter speel.* Sorry sir. Will sir please turn down the music?"

"Certainly, but it gets the party in the mood," Nolyn answered.

"Geniet die aand. Totsiens, meneer. Enjoy the evening. Goodbye, sir."

The two policemen left. Everybody laughed when they heard how narrowly we had escaped being hauled down to the local *tronk*.

At exclusive yoga classes in the home of Mr and Mrs Bruce, my double-jointed legs intrigued her. From a headstand position I easily curled my feet over my thighs into the *lotus* position and remained balanced on my head for several minutes, before unwinding my knees and feet and curling back into a kneeling position. When she heard my spine had been broken in two places, she found this feat incredulous.

Shamefully this feat did not end in the yoga class. After I had had a drink at our parties, Nolyn announced, "We have a floorshow," and he jokingly continued, "I bet you R50 that not one of you can repeat the act! Come along now. Place your bets. Who'll start the bidding? I have R5 in the front. R10 from you sir. At the back, R20 from you sir. Who'll give me R50?"

This was my cue to perform the *lotus* position balancing on my head to the hush of intrigued guests. Money never exchanged hands nor could anyone equal my performance. They looked forward to their next surprise party. With guests seated on the floor of the spare bedroom, I threw a daring fondue party for forty guests. Boards balanced on bricks were tables, twelve inches off the floor. Eight fondue pots holding boiling oil were placed on those tables. Bowls of raw liver, steak and chicken stood strategically amidst various dips, garlic bread, salads and bottles of wine. One accidental nudge could upset the table top with devastating consequences. This fondue party was never repeated but the smell of boiling oil rekindles the memory.

Newspaper cuttings and photographs are evidence of our steps up the social ladder. Outwardly I met the criteria – long evening dresses, elbow-length gloves and a bouffant hairstyle – but inwardly I felt threatened. Nolyn danced very closely with women. I feared the worst, which released my worst personality traits and dropped me in a deep hole of depression. While these thoughts ate into me, I bottled up jealousy, bitterness and anger. I sat alone watching, chain-smoking, pretending to be happy, agonising silently.

Rather than remain a wallflower I flirted my way on to the dance floor. As I fluttered my false eye-lashes, we moved closer in time to the music. I was riddled with guilt and realised this did nothing to appease my jealousy. I feared playing Nolyn's game in case it encouraged him. Deep down I longed to trust Nolyn. Would the ever-enlarging chasm drive us further apart?

***

During 1975 Margy Crossman and I started golf together. Her husband, Tony said, "You're a natural, Denyse." I learnt to drive, chip and putt. Middle-aged women dominated the club, but not for long. My advert in the local paper had the desired effect:

Appeal to golf widows

> *If you are tired of being a golf widow and meekly listening to your husband's post mortem of a weekly golf round – don't try to beat him, join him.*
>
> *The country club is on a drive to recruit more women players even complete 'rabbits'. The women's captain Neyse Wild said: 'We are starting a regular golf day on Thursdays to encourage women golfers who have not played for ages, and create an interest for new golfers. The competition will be over nine holes, teeing off either at 9 am or 2 pm. Each four-ball will have an experienced golfer in the team, who will coach the rest as they play. The competition will be cancelled in foul weather,' she said.*

The club has contacted 45 women, but any others, who would like to try their hand, should phone Mrs Wild 1154. DDR, Daily Dispatch Reporter.

Young blood livened up the golf course, ushering in a modern dress code. The 'oldies' disapproved of shorts, midriffs showing, sleeveless T–shirts and jeans. A notice in the ladies locker room read: *Beach wear is strictly forbidden on this golf course. All blouses must have a collar and sleeves. Jeans do not meet the required dress code.*

As captain of the Ladies Section of the Umtata Country Club, I arranged weekly competitions and ran a beginner's group. My name appeared in the press.

Denyse Wild won the Silver Division of the women's section with a score of 194. Daphne Colyvas came second with 195. Denyse and Daphne played in the same four-ball. Denyse had a good start. After the first nine holes, Daphne was lying seven strokes behind. After 18 holes she narrowed ahead after 33 holes. Daphne, who promptly three putted making them suddenly all square. They teed off on the last hole and both lay just short of the green for four. A branch of a tree caught Daphne's club as she chipped and Denyse took the hole and the championship by one shot.

I should have been happy with three beautiful children, a lovely home and notable achievements. Was I running away from something or searching for more? I remember Byron hated having his photo taken. He sprinted out of sight. The days with my children were my happiest. A Catholic priest took photographs at the Umtata Golf Course and gave me a copy of *Revue Missionaire Marianhill*, dated Sept Oct Nov 1976. The picture titled, *Rendre Neuve L'Humanite*, contrasted the lives of the *haves* and the *have-nots* in South Africa, showing Chandrè watching a barefooted black boy holding his home-made golf club.

I listened to outsiders say: "They've done okay. A house in Umtata, a seaside cottage on the Wild Coast, two *Mercedes* and a *Land Rover*." We had more pets. Spatts shared our home with two boxers, Caesar and Augustus; two cats, Pandora and Trevor; a budgerigar and two bantams – Benny crowed all day whilst Betty listened, scratching the parched earth. There had been a white rabbit, Cottontail, which hopped around indoors, amusing the cats. Nolyn inadvertently ran over him on the driveway when the rabbit was blinded by the car lights. The children heard the true story years later. Our possessions had doubled as we discovered shortly.

What more did I expect from life? Nolyn had become a successful Insurance Broker. He owned a modern dry-cleaning business which was doing well. I had opened the first crèche in Umtata; had succeeded as the first pre-school teacher; initiated golf for ladies and captained the Ladies Section. Supported, I raised children, socialised and furthered Nolyn's business, built a cottage at Coffee Bay and turned a rectangular house into our dream home.

Success came at a price. Mine was an insecure marriage. Separated from me by necessity of Nolyn's commercial trips, Nolyn drank in pubs promoting his business and stayed in private homes. Other women enjoyed his company. Jealousy ate at me. My lonely nights were spent knitting. My needles clicked away rhythmically, turning out identical jerseys for my children, which was therapeutic and rewarding. Strangers commented, "What lovely jerseys?" I expected more from life. I lived a world far apart from Nolyn.

His competitive business world sapped his energy and drove him on. I solved domestic problems on my own. Our social demands united us briefly. Nolyn won a sponsored trip to Cape Town and another to Rhodesia. In Rhodesia we stayed at the *Monomotapa Hotel,* 54 Park Lane in Salisbury. While we were there we met my cousin, Jeanette, married to Michael called Mac, and a friend from Umtata, Chrystal Sparg and her husband, Clive. Six adults squashed into one car to go to the movies. One afternoon in Salisbury Rhoda Leary Tony's wife, took us to a game park with her sons, Sean and Brett. Regrettably I never saw Tony. He worked for *Tobacco Sales* and was on a business trip.

Having climbed the social ladder I hated who I had become. What had happened to *Nolulum,* the one who never gets angry, my *Xhosa* name given to me on the farm, *Strathneva* almost twenty years ago?

Brechanby derived from *Bre'*, Brent: *Chan'*, Chandrè and *By'*, Byron was the name of our home in Umtata. A newly-built high brick wall fortified the house from unwanted visitors with an arched-over front gate and driveway gates.

I became an expert at wallpapering, fashionable in the seventies. I attempted to wall-paper the main bedroom ceiling. There were no Health and Safety rules in South Africa and I had no fear. A stepladder and petrol drum supporting a wide plank was the make-shift scaffolding for me to reach the ceiling. Precariously walking like a trapeze artist toe-to-heel on the plank, I pushed the wallpaper onto the ceiling.

John, our garden boy, assisted me. He passed me the glue-dripping brush or wet sponge. But, I stepped on spilt glue. My slippery foothold slid me helter-skelter along the plank, happening as if in slow motion. Teetering for a second, I crashed, landing with my bottom in the basin of glue on the floor. John stared too scared to speak. I burst out laughing. Relieved, John said, "I thought you hurt madam. John very worried!"

"Tonight I'll feel it, not now John. I've got work to do. Give me your hand."

We laughed like two children with no inhibitions as he pulled me up with the basin attached to my rear end and glue dripping everywhere. We mopped up the mess. I walked the same slippery trapeze and wallpapering continued.

Besides sport, auction sales sparked a new interest for me. I was on firstname terms with the auctioneer, Neil, of *Klette & Son*. Our house was filled with bargains and antiques. What I could not find in the auction rooms, I sought in the district, taking the children and John with me in the *Ranchero* truck. Stopping randomly on a dirt track off the main road, I interrogated local Blacks with John's help. I spoke *Xhosa* fluently which clinched cash deals or replaced my modern furniture with antiques. My collection grew. The garage became an antique workshop. Our dining room suite was replaced by an antique table and eleven chairs.

Influential townsfolk flocked to the new antique dealer at *Brechanby*.

Nolyn's business boomed. We extended our home. We vacated when *Harveytile Roofing* replaced the old roof, moving into the Tennis Club changing-rooms. We slept in one room divided by wardrobes. No hot water, two plug points! I cooked on a hotplate. We showered at the golf clubhouse. We had no privacy. Bouncing tennis balls and laughter woke us daily. Four weeks living like this turned into three months because the roof trusses were made incorrectly. During this time the children had chicken-pox and birthdays.

The old roof was removed and we hoped for dry weather. Returning after a weekend at Coffee Bay, the house was a mess. It had rained. Wall-paper peeled off the walls, built-in cupboards oozed water and the floors were a mud bath. With patience, perseverance and determination we finally moved back into our *Harvey-tiled* home. The passage, the boys' bedroom and a bar used up an oversupply of tongue-and-groove pine ceiling boards.

Our dream home was complete to Pop's amazement, after his earlier remark, "You're surely not going to buy this house?"

***

After the fire at our Coffee Bay cottage, we returned a year later. The children and I enjoyed the warm sunshine and the rolling waves on the unspoilt beach. On 16 December, Mr Sparg, a well thought of businessman from Umtata in his seventies, his son, Hughen and Nolyn went fishing and were returning, when… Bush telegraph brought the shocking news turning tranquillity into trepidation.

"They've sent for the doctor from the hotel.

A *Land Rover* went over the cliff!

Nolyn's *Land Rover* was headed in that direction.

Hotel guests have rushed to the scene.

Survivors…injuries…

The hospital's so far away…"

I had to find out more. Bundling up our belongings, we bid a hasty retreat. On the way Mrs Sparg, wearing her apron, rushed towards me, saying, "Denyse have you *heard*?"

"*Whose Land Rover* was it? Do you know what happened?"

"I hope *my* Philip's alright," she replied discounting her worst fears.

"Come in, Denyse. Wait with me," she said wringing her hands.

"Thanks."

Time passed slowly as we listened to the clock ticking. The children were unusually quiet. A vehicle approached. We peeped through the net curtains. A *Land Rover* skidded to a halt. Rushing out, not knowing what to expect, we heard, "Nolyn's *Land Rover* went over the cliff, but all three men jumped out in time. The brakes failed. Nolyn was unable to engage the *Land Rover* into low range gear. Trying to avoid the steep descent to the causeway and to slow down the runaway vehicle, Nolyn turned off the rough track into a ploughed *mealie* land. His plan failed.

The vehicle gathered speed bouncing over the contours of land like a rabbit running for its life. He switched off the ignition, shouting to his companions, 'I'm jumping out now. You must jump too!'

'You must be mad!' Hughen answered as Nolyn opened his door and jumped. With brute force and adrenalin pumping, Hughen broke the fishing rods forcing open the passenger door. He grabbed his elderly father, shouting, 'Jump dad!'

They made it just in time. The *Land Rover,* heading towards the cliff edge, gathered speed before it was airborne. It burst through the top of a *Coral* tree before it disappeared. The three *gillies* were locked in the back as it plummeted headlong off the cliff before falling several hundreds of feet to its final resting place, an outcrop of rocks a few yards from the Indian Ocean."

It was later decided the tree had saved the vehicle from landing in the waves. It was now cushioned, nose-down, on this bush-covered ledge of rocks.

"How are they?" Mrs Sparg asked.

"The doctor's with them. They were lucky. They've only sustained minor scratches and bruises. The *gillies* are still trapped inside."

"Can they be reached?"

"A team of men, with abseiling experience, volunteered to rescue the *gillies.*"

The story unfolded. One by one the *gillies* were brought to the cliff top. They had been tossed about like rag dolls during the accident. A doctor attended to their lacerations and bruises.

"What did you think when this happened?" Nolyn asked them.

"We thought we'd not see Christmas this year..."

Nolyn spent more time with us on the beach. A rescue team salvaged *Land Rover* parts and the number plate. The Insurance Company, not believing our story, investigated and settled our claim. We said a sad goodbye to our *Land Rover* CCY 632, which, to this day, rusts out of sight to man, near the unceasing sound of the waves...

***

My grandmother had been staying with each of her married grandchildren. At last it was my turn. Our house was ready for her visit. Granny spent a fortnight with us. The guest room, with a bedside light, a chamber pot under the bed, a dressing table for her powder puff and hairbrush, a glass to soak her false teeth, all had been made comfortable for her. A little vase of freshly-picked flowers added a homely touch.

Granny liked two pillows and a rug, for snuggling under for her afternoon nap. My children peeped in, saying, "Gran gran's snoring mommy." She snored alright. The children called my mother, *granny* and my grandmother, *gran gran*. Nolyn's mother was called *googie* and his grandmother, *Gogs*.

Granny slept in every morning. Nolyn was at work when I tiptoed in, drawing the curtains to let shafts of sunlight filter onto her bed. I put a cup of coffee, with two sugars and hot milk, on her bedside table.

"Morning granny. It's a lovely day. Did you sleep well?"

"Mmm... Morning my child. Yes, very well thanks."

Granny smiled unaware her hairnet was bunched on one side of her head.

"Enjoy your coffee. I'll be back to give you a hand."

"Not too much water my child," she reminded me. This was the daily routine. I ran a bath for gran whilst she sipped her coffee and said her prayers, kneeling at her bedside. After her bath, she padded back to the guest room in her dressing gown and slippers. A little later, she called, "I'm ready for you, my child."

I began to do up granny's corset and powdered her back with a powder puff. I was pleased I did not wear such uncomfortable garments. This time-consuming task, hooking the corset from the top, required patience. Halfway down the hooks undid themselves. I started again. Her stockings were fastened into the suspender straps, before a bodice and petticoat were pulled into place. Granny emerged, face powdered, a light hairnet holding her hair in place, a brooch offsetting the collar of her dress and smelling of *711,* ready for the new day.

"Where are the little ones?"

"Chandrè is at school gran. Brent and Byron are in the garden."

Looking through the window, granny enjoyed her breakfast, watching her grandsons racing down the driveway on their tricycles.

"Full of energy, they are," she would say.

It was a pleasure having gran stay with us. Helping me in the kitchen, she wore her apron and moaned at me for not wearing mine. Sitting in the lounge, gran did my mending – she sewed on buttons, put up hems and darned socks. Granny played the piano and sang *Confidentially, Melodie D'amour, A Nightingale sang in Berkeley Square, Amour Amour* and many other well-known tunes. She read the children a bedtime story before they said prayers, which ended, "God bless gran gran."

Granny had a heart of gold. She never sat idle but was busy, knitting and crocheting. Gran loved card games. We played *Canasta* or *Rummy* with her. She upheld her strong Catholic beliefs, saying grace before meals, morning and evening prayers, attending Mass, Rosary and benediction every day. She was well-respected. Young and old, loved Eileen Brown. We were sad when she left us to visit her next grandchild.

In her letter, which I kept, dated 27 June 1976, she enclosed three *Rand* notes:

> *Dearest Neyse*
>
> *Going through my writing box I find I had not enclosed Brent's birthday money - also another fleeting letter that should have been posted on that same date. I'm sorry Neyse – just hope that Brent did not realize I had not sent him anything. The other was to a dear priest friend of mine. Please put it down to unintentional forgetfulness. I am off tomorrow with Ann – who is up to take HER own car back – so taking the chance to go to Margy who is expecting me for a time and then proceeding to Viv and Heather – only to return when Kokstad warms up. I've never known such cold.*
>
> *I've missed mom so much and now will not see her as Joan says they will be home coming weekend. It seems from weather reports that they have even had snow down there. Hope they all come back better. I've heard no news of you but always remember your darlings in my prayers. Anyone buying your house yet? Hope you and the children are*

keeping well for a change. There is so much I would have liked to hear about you all. Up to my eyes packing now.

God bless and protect you all. Fondest love and big kisses for the young ones.

Lovingly from

Gran Gran

I treasure a letter dated 19 July 1976 with more banknotes:

Dearest Neyse

At last your letter has caught up with me. Thanks so much. I had a big post yesterday. It is nice to be home again. When you are sick there is no place like home, although all my grandchildren did all they could for me. I must say they are marvellous. It gave me so much pleasure to see them all so nicely settled in their homes, each one so homely with the individual touch that makes a home.

I could have had such a wonderful time with them all (also Theo and Kathleen) had it not been for the after effects of Kiwi flu. I don't know when I have felt so weak and dizzy. I am sorry to say I have not got rid of the dizziness yet, so I am seeing doctor again next week. I certainly am getting the quietness and rest out here that Doctor told me to have. I don't even miss the phone.

I had a surprise this morning when Mom, Pop and Patrick came out to see us. Mom is always so cheerful. She and Pat, also Buzzy, are coming out tomorrow to spend the day. Pop is going away for bowls. I am sorry, dear, to see you have to undergo another operation. What bad luck. I sincerely hope this will be an end to your troubles now. You've certainly had your share of illnesses between you lately.

Thank goodness Jeanette is over her operation now, (Lopoma) growth about the size of a walnut. I have never heard of this growth. Thanks for letting me know about birthdays. I still haven't got my birthday calendar, but mom tells me Chandrè's and Byron's are due. Please give them 'Happy Birthday' greetings. I am enclosing money for them.

The weather really has been miserable since I got back, such a sneaky wind. I feel the cold so much these days. Tragic news of John Stubb's early death only forty-three...

The girls are playing hockey and netball at Ixopo today. Stewey has taken some of the convent girls down and won't be back until this evening. Molly's poultry yard is coming on nicely, getting about six dozen eggs now so she is getting a bit of return for eggs, after so much paying out. I'm absolutely shivering so must stop. Keep your chin up my dear child. Things must take a better turn soon.

God bless, fondest love to you all.

Gran Gran.

My grandmother was an inspiration to me. Even today, she remains so much a part of my life. Amongst other things she taught me never to waste anything, to care and help other people and to live my life in the fear of God. Had I lived my life with this in mind, things might have been so different.

***

The winds of change blew in South Africa. White households enjoyed the luxuries – modern appliances, servants and garden boys, exclusive sporting facilities, movies, restaurants and hotels. Blacks adhered to *apartheid* laws, travelling in *blacks-only* buses and taxis, never sitting on *whites-only* benches and accessing *whites-only* homes and buildings as employees. Already many white-owned trading-stations had been taken over by black traders.

Verwoerd envisaged South Africa as a prosperous white state living in peace with eight newly-established black homelands. In 1959 the Transkei had been earmarked as one of the homelands. How would this affect our lives? Would it be safe to live in the Transkei? If not, where would we go?

This growing concern was debated amongst Whites:

"I heard the Blacks are *not only* taking over the rural trading-stations, but white-owned stores in the villages."

"If the Sparg's sell, others will follow suit."

"That'll be the end of the trading stations, mark my words."

"They plan to make the schools multi-racial!"
"I'm not having my child sitting next to a Black!"
"We're selling our house, before prices drop."
"There'll soon be a glut of properties on the market."
"Can you believe it? Stan was paid R75 000 for his house!"
"There are tough times ahead."
"The Transkei's changing. To what extent, waits to be seen!"

In the 1960's South Africa surprised the world experiencing the highest rate of economic growth in the world, second to Japan. When 250.000 white immigrants flooded into the country between 1960 and 1970, the white confidence grew and it crushed the black resistance, for a while. Could the Government continue to meet any contingency with emanating fresh stirrings?

Nolyn and I discussed the future of the Transkei. Nolyn, born and schooled in Umtata, considered himself a true Transkeian. Our once humble home was now our dream home. We had loyal friends. Our children were happy. We owned a seaside cottage.

When our closest friends, Eddie and Annette, Lyle and Joyce, John and Cynthia, all put their homes on the market, we made up our minds. As white families left, this huge exodus was felt. A *For Sale* board signalled our pending departure. Friends left for Durban, Cape Town, East London or Pietermaritzburg. An era of a life whites had shared in the Transkei – *braaivleis* on trading stations, card evenings and parties, golf and tennis tournaments in the rural villages, Engcobo, Mqanduli, Mount Frere, Idutywa and Butterworth, would soon be gone forever.

Chandrè severed her seven-year friendship with her first and closest friend, Alice. Brent and Byron lost childhood friends. Their pet bantams, tucked under John's arm, they feared would end up in his cooking pot.

We paid R7,000 for our house and sold it for R45,000. Needing a new home, Nolyn and I met an Estate Agent in King William's Town. After viewing several properties we bought two. Nolyn bought the 6 Galloway Road property and I bought 9 Stanford Road property as an investment. Leaving the Transkei, *the area beyond the river Kei,* and Umtata, (renamed Mthatha in 2004), was hard. *Brechanby* had been our home for seven years. We moved in September 1976. We would view the changes in the Transkei from a distance …

18

MAIDS AND GARDEN BOYS

Verwoerd restricted Black education saying, 'What use is it teaching a Bantu child mathematics when it cannot use it in practice? There is no place for him in the European community above the level of a certain form of labour.'

MAIDS and garden boys, affordable by all white South Africans, worked for us from my childhood years. One of the earliest maids I employed was Agnes, who retired to Matatiele due to heart surgery. Unable to bear children, she loved my children as her own. She called Brent, *Buti boy* and Chandrè, *Sisi*. I sent them money regularly but her husband's letter dated 5 April 1976 distressed me to know how they were struggling.

Nkosazana and Nkosana, Madam and Master

Agnes is much better. I can leave her to look after herself. I want you to give your boy a month notice this month so that there will be no trouble when I come. I am sure that on the 3 May I'll be there. We are starving in our house. I never work since 1972. There is no money so there is no peace in this house. Please help me with R2 for the bus.

Yours faithfully,

Abney Mgibanyoni

And in the same envelope, there was a letter from Agnes telling me, *Granny from Kokstad told me you want to leave Umtata because the children are always sick. Where do you want to leave to? What about your house? Nkosazana please forget that God is everywhere. You can't run away from death. Stay there. God will help you and your children. If you leave to anywhere, we will be there. We won't lose you. You're our good madam. Every time you are in our thoughts.*

Thanks very much for the money. Oh, I am dying to see you again and my

Chandrè; she is my Sisi and Buti boy. Byron is your little 'songololo', last born.

Their love for us bounced off the paper. Agnes had faith and determination. Their written English was good considering their restricted education. Our white children were unfairly favoured by the Nationalist government who, in the early 1970's, spent sixteen times more on white education per pupil than on black education. I held Agnes and her husband in high esteem, we lost contact.

South Africans called maids, *'girls'*, and gardeners, *'garden boys'*. These live-in servants were supplied with overalls and were paid a minimal wage. Employers helped towards their servant's children's education, medical and transport expenses. Servants were given second-hand clothes and curtains. A white man was called *'master'* or *'baas'* and a white woman, *'madam, missus* or *Nkosazana*. Whites called servants by an English firstname, regardless of age.

Apartheid operated in our homes. They used separate toilets, ate separately from us and sat on the floor. Their meals of *mealie* meal porridge for breakfast, *samp* and beans for lunch and bread at supper, were eaten on enamel plates with cheap cutlery. Maids had time off in the afternoon.

Families trained maids according to their personal needs. Daily routine included; bed making; sweeping, dusting, mopping floors, window cleaning; furniture polishing, brass and silverware polishing; hanging out and bringing in the washing; (maids tended to yank the washing off the line!) ironing; child minding; meal preparation; setting and clearing the table; washing up; opening and closing windows and curtains. When children got in their way, they shooed them away like chickens as they completed a demanding and responsible job!

Young and pretty Clementine, a maid the children loved, soon let me down… I felt uneasy one night when she babysat our children.

"Please love, let's go home. I've a hunch something's not right."

"You're usually right and I'm tired. Let's go."

The smell of peppermint liqueur and brandy hit us the moment we stepped inside the lounge where, spread-eagled like a starfish, Clementine lay, out cold.

"Clementine!" Nolyn bellowed, but she was motionless. He kicked her gently to stir her. She never budged.

"Are the children alright?" my fear translated into words. I ran to them. They were asleep. What would they tell us in the morning? Nolyn enraged that his liquor cabinet was looted, phoned the police. They arrived.

"*Wat's die probleem*? What's the problem?"

"*Kom binne. Jy sal sien,* Come in. You'll see."

Unable to rouse her they dragged her out. Halfway down the steps they let Clementine go. She tumbled to the bottom. I entered the liquor-reeking room.

"They threw her into the back of the police-van like a bag of *mealies*," Nolyn told me. In the morning Chandrè added, "Mommy, Clementine and her boyfriend poured dad's drink into empty *Coca Cola* bottles. I was scared."

Clementine was found guilty and served a short sentence.

Florence was my next live-in maid, assisted by a half-day maid, Sunshine. She was responsible for the washing, ironing, cleaning windows and polishing and Florence coped with meals and general housework. This worked well, until... The guest bedlinen and towels were washed after visitors stayed with us. When I checked the linen cupboard the bedlinen and towels were missing. "Florence, where did Sunshine put the washing and ironing today?"

"Mmm..." she hesitated, not wanting to blow the whistle.

"Well..."

"I see her. She put something under her overall. I not sure, madam."

"Where does she catch her bus?"

"At police station, madam."

With this information I took the children with me in the *Land Rover* to the bus stop outside the police station. I stopped. Walking to the bus driver's window I asked for his permission to search the bus. The bus, jam-packed with weary passengers anxious to get home, emptied. I cringed under their stares of contempt as I examined each passenger. Oppressed for years, hatred for whites like me was apparent. Sunshine was not on the bus. No words of apology could appease the disgruntled passengers as they squashed back into their seats on the bus. I feared they might take revenge.

In the police station I was advised, "Lady, you phone t'morror when Sunshine comes to yourrr place. Jus' you *kerry* on like nothing's wrrrong. She mus' know nothing. Then you phone me and you says,

'Hello,' like you talks to your *pel*, pal., and you asks her, *'You likes to 'ave coffee wid, me?'* and we be there."

I followed the instructions when Sunshine arrived. She denied theft when questioned by the police. I joined two policemen in their police *Land Rover* as they searched hut after hut in the black township. Petrified occupants had the same answer, "*Andiyasi,* I don't know," when questioned, "Did Sunshine sleep here?"

Guilt overwhelmed me. Why was I doing this? Did I understand poverty, cold, hunger, what it must be like to have no shoes or a toy? Never before had I seen such large-scale poverty. Scantily-clad children with runny noses ran around freely: thin old and infirm women hobbled towards three legged pots stoking up the fire with bits of wood; mangy rib-showing mongrel dogs sniffed scrounging for a morsel of anything edible and chickens scratched the dusty ground snapping up a find.

Despite this deprivation – no sanitation, no running water, electricity, telephones and as many as ten sleeping in one hut – everybody smiled. I had so much, yet I was chasing a few sheets and towels!

Sunshine outwitted us until the police searched the servants' quarters on our property. From under a bed, they pulled out a suitcase and flung out not only my towels and sheets, but LP records, silver, jewellery, cutlery and toys. Sunshine was arrested and discharged the same day because the 'stolen' goods had not left the premises. Nolyn dismissed Sunshine and my shame is with me today.

On another occasion a maid inadvertently dosed Byron on calamine lotion and *Friar's Balsam* when I was on the phone to my mother. She had seen me give him his medicine, so I presumed she knew what to do. When I heard Byron gagging, I slammed the phone down, "Bye mom."

I picked Byron up. With him losing his breath, I drove to the surgery, where the doctor gave him a stomach pump. I assisted.

"Byron could suffer brain damage," the doctor warned me.

By the grace of God, Byron survived without brain damage.

Louisa, arrived at *The Gables* sobbing, "A bus.. it kill Miriam… she come out the bus… bang… dead… driver no stopping… she...her... four children… no mammy!"

Pain seeped deep through her whole being. Drawing her blubbing body towards mine, I felt her anguish with each agonising throb. My words, "Louisa I'm sorry," were futile words in the midst of such intense pain. Her daughter Miriam, my live-in maid and mother of four, was dead. After discarding her drunken adulterous husband, Miriam had been the breadwinner of this family.

"How can I help you?"

"Me work for *medem*... Please?"

In her late sixties with heart problems, Louisa worked for me. She became the sunshine in my cloudy world, showed me courage in adversity, conquered sorrow with joy and replaced hatred with love. Louisa overcame a second heartache when her son Saul died in prison without his asthma pump. With her bandy legs aching and struggling to walk, she retired to Port Elizabeth to be nearer Molly Yali a relative. We wrote letters to each other for many years.

Two of my loyal garden boys, John and Michael, met with tragic deaths. Today I am indebted to my servants. They had little and never complained. Their cheerful smiles brought hope to me in times of despair. Their simple philosophy of life showed me how to forgive, to love, to share and to fight on. Whether white or black, we all experience joy, sorrow and hardship in this, the land of our birth.

***

We had lived in Umtata for seven years. We were not only leaving behind memories, but familiar Transkeian towns – Magusheni, Qumbu, Libode, Nqgeleni, Viedgesville and Lusikisiki home to Khotso Sethuntsa a witchdoctor millionaire, with 24 wives. I hoped to bury past hurts caused by my *skinnering* mother-in-law as well as Nolyn's infidelity which had caused arguments and had triggered jealousy, bitterness and hatred.

"We're on an adventure," I told the children on the day we left. Chandrè and I were in the white *Mercedes* packed with pot plants and pets. Nolyn, Brent and Byron waved goodbye. We were on our way to King William's Town in the Ciskei to start a new life.

"What's our new home like? Where's my school? Will I make new friends?" were questions Chandrè fired at me before the usual one, "Are we nearly there yet?"

"No. Let me tell you about King William's Town. It lies on the upper reaches of the Buffalo River and was started by Rev John Brownlee in 1826."

"Are there buffaloes in the town, mommy?"

"No, but hundreds of years ago, buffalo roamed freely here."

Southward bound on the N2, we bypassed Viedgesville before winding through the cutting and crossing the Bashee Bridge. We drove through Idutywa and then Butterworth. We snaked through the treacherous cuttings crossing the Kei River, which divided the Transkei from the Eastern Cape. On to the R63 we drove towards Komga. Major Hans Garret Moore won the first *Victoria Cross* on South African soil, in Komga in 1877.

We drove into King William's Town and stopped at 6 Galloway Road, a newly-developed residential area. Cool from the air-conditioner, the sudden heat hit us. I unlocked the front door. Chandrè waited in the car still registered with CCY number plates. My footsteps echoed in the empty house as I locked the cats in the guest room, leaving the fanlight open.

"Hello," a voice called.

An attractive lady with brown hair, a radiant smile, no make-up and wearing a skirt and pretty blouse, stared at me from the front door.

"Hi, I'm Denyse. This is my daughter, Chandrè."

"I'm Annamarie from next door. Would you like a cup of tea? Come over when you're ready."

We put the pot plants in the shade and went next door. Chandrè rang the door-bell.

"Come in."

We followed Annamarie into a TV lounge kept cool with drawn curtains. "Mommy, they've got a television." Chandrè exclaimed.

"Yes, I hope ours works here."

She poured tea into dainty china cups from a silver teapot and offered us home-made biscuits. Our conversation flowed like a rippling stream. Her husband, Vernon, owned a thriving business, *Mayberry Estate Agency*. When the pantechnicon arrived, we left. Annamarie offered us her help. I had already made a new friend.

This town was hotter than Umtata. Boxes and furniture cluttered the house by the time Nolyn and our sons arrived. Disappointment was written on their faces – a modern house, smaller rooms, exposed to the street; no trees to climb and nowhere to kick a football. What had we done? When a second pantechnichon arrived, the neighbours wondered how everything would fit into the house. The double garage bulged with boxes.

The highlight was unpacking the television set which had never been used. There was no signal in the Transkei. The children helped Nolyn in the lounge.

"It's my turn Brent," Byron yelled pushing his brother.

"Dad, Byron's pushing me."

"Behave boys. There's no need to shove," Nolyn admonished them adding, "let's enjoy doing this together."

A huge *Telefunken* television with faux mahogany panelling, bought from *Denis Stores* in Umtata, emerged from the packaging. The Government controlled SABC & TV with broadcasts alternating in English and Afrikaans. Television has developed since those days when the only Blacks seen were servants or spectators at a football game. Today almost everyone on television is black, with pronounced accents difficult to understand. We learnt later our arrival had caused quite a stir. "The Wilds in Galloway Road …the talk of the town….they not only own two *Mercedes* but also a *Land Rover*… they bought two houses… must have money…" Little did people know that behind this supposed wealth, the television was an escape from loneliness. Nolyn travelled to the Transkei spending even more nights away from home each month. When we lived in the Transkei he travelled to the Ciskei. It did not make sense. I doubted all his nights away were purely business.

Chandrè and Brent attended Hill Crescent Primary School, run by the nuns. They adjusted to their new teachers and pupils. As I shortened curtains, Byron played with his cars on the carpet, a change from collecting *goggas* and stuffing them into his pockets. Then he said, "Mommy, take the pin out of my leg, please." It was not a pin but a sewing machine needle embedded across his knee. Keeping my calm, I ran to Stephanie, a neighbour.

"I'd take him to the doctor," she advised. I did and a sewing needle was removed from his knee under local anaesthetic at the surgery. We had a family doctor.

Annamarie's twins, Stuart and Lindsay, visited one afternoon.

Lindsay, blonde, barefoot wearing shorts, was a tomboy. Stuart, sturdy with a deep voice, had a naughty twinkle in his eye. Their older sister Shelley, befriended Chandrè. Martin, an adopted son, Byron's age, joined in. Soon after we settled into our house, the Mayberry family moved to a mansion on the outskirts of the town.

The porta-pool was moved from my property 9 Stanford Road to 6 Reynold's View. I hired a bulldozer to level the front lawn removing an established garden to the shock of the neighbourhood who were struggling to create their gardens. Nolyn met friends through the Golf Club. We entertained twelve couples at a dinner party. Women wore long evening dresses and men dressed in suits. We danced in the lounge to taped music from a *Hi-Fi* set. *Lady in Red,* a popular tune, made me blush as I swirled around in my full-length figure-hugging red dress. This successful social evening promoted us to *Round Table* membership.

We had new neighbours. A doctor Eric and his wife, Dawn Kaplan and their daughters moved into the Mayberry's house. I welcomed them as Annamarie had welcomed us. Heidi, their youngest daughter and Chandrè became friends. I felt uncomfortable in their house.

"Come for a spin in my *Land Rover,"* Eric invited Nolyn and me when we visited them. It was fitted out with an all-round audio system. Eric drove at high speed. I thought it was our last night. Screeching to a halt, he said, "Have a go, Nolyn. Put your foot down."

Nolyn drove fast, but not as recklessly as Eric. To me we played with death.

I suspected Dawn was taking drugs but Nolyn disagreed with me until she passed out on the sofa in our lounge for two hours one day. My suspicions were confirmed. Drugs!

"Denyse please run me to the surgery," Eric asked me a week later. He climbed into the car holding a tin of peaches in one hand and a banana in the other, saying, "I'm late, Denyse." As I drove, he tossed the tin out of the window, followed by the banana skins. I shuddered to think that two weeks ago he had removed my thumbnail under anaesthetic.

"What am I to tell my patients, Denyse? I'm late."

"I don't know," I said, feeling uncomfortable. Was he also on drugs?

'Dr Kaplan's been struck off the Doctor's Roll,' a rumour circulated. To help this couple I looked after their daughters, unnoticed by either of them. I visited Dawn. Using the telephone directory she was compiling a fictitious list of patients' names to match the drugs her husband had supposedly ordered for his patients.

"Eric's not well," she said.

"I'm sorry, Dawn," not realising then a horrible drama was about to unfold. That same night three gunshots woke our quiet neighbourhood. People gathered around the Kaplan's house. The ambulance and police arrived. I was shocked and saddened to hear:

"Eric asked his wife, Dawn, to shoot him. In her drugged state she fired two shots killing her husband. She then turned the gun on herself. She's been rushed to hospital. She might not live... Heidi's with a neighbour. They're waiting for relatives from Johannesburg. The older daughter's with her boyfriend."

The Drug Squad asked Stephanie and me to collect all the drugs in the house. Dawn survived. She thanked me for being her friend and gave me a glass teapot. Years on, I learnt she had been acquitted of murder and re-habilitated in Israel. I lost contact with Dawn.

This tragic event and dogfights pre-empted a move to 9 Stanford Road. I pondered the last six months. Life was full of unexpected challenges. Exclusive residential areas were not safe havens. Would the move into 9 Stanford Road be our last?

My property bordering on an open piece of land provided an unbroken view overlooking the town and hills beyond. A short, steep driveway led to a double garage with an attic above, an ideal indoor playroom. We installed a swimming pool with brick boundary walls, a barbecue with a deck and established a vegetable garden in the private back garden.

One hot afternoon the children swam and I watered the garden. I was wearing three-inch high heels. "Time to get out," I called. Brent and Byron wore armbands because they could not swim properly. They feigned drowning in the deep end with armbands floating alongside them. I panicked. Dropping the hose and kicking off my shoes, I flung myself into the pool, fully-clothed, to save my sons. It was a prank. I gave them both a hiding and a severe warning. "Don't you *ever* do that again. A genuine call for help could be ignored!"

On another occasion I hacked off Chandrè's long wet plaits rather than laboriously loosen millions of tangles in her hair. My poor daughter's hair was in a terrible mess.

Thinking we had rid ourselves of the school nurse who had leeched on to us in Umtata, Chandrè announced, "The school nurse, Peta, was at our school today."

"She's the one from Umtata," Brent butted in.

"Shush Brent. I'm telling the story."

"She asked me where we lived. I told her," Chandrè confessed.

Peta, a short, fat, rather masculine old maid in her fifties with a strong German accent and whose two Alsatians were her pride and joy, arrived in her van that afternoon. Her dogs were the best, winning medals at every competition. Whenever she spoke, nobody got a word in. Eating and talking, she revealed the half-chewed food moving about in her mouth.

"Hello Peta. It's good to see you," I lied when she arrived. Politely I asked her in for tea. Having wolfed down all the tea eats and re-filled her teacup, she never got the message when I said, "I've a load of letters to type for Nolyn." She followed me up the stairs. In competition to my electric typewriter, she rattled on. The children escaped into the garden.

On another occasion, Byron, jumping on a pile of building sand, bit through his lip. Blood poured from his mouth. It took six people to restrain him when his mouth was stitched up at the surgery. He remained my accident-prone child. Early one morning, Brent woke me.

"What's the matter Brent?"

"The bottom of my bed's wet."

"It can't be."

"It is."

Brent was right. Our cat, Trudi was giving birth to the last kitten in a litter of four. Trudi licked her tiny, rat-like kittens clean in the bottom of Brent's wet bed. "I've got kittens in my bed!" he shouted, waking everybody to view the new arrivals.

Life went on happily at 9 Stanford Road, the boys played soccer and at their first practice, both teams chased the ball in a huddle. Then a train hooted. Brent and Byron abandoned the game to watch this engine shunting up and down, belching out smoke. They had never seen a real train before. Chandrè started ballet and Spanish dancing lessons. Ferrying the children to these activities was tiring and time-consuming.

We spent a weekend with Margy and family in Kokstad. We exchanged parenting skills and our children bonded. Chandrè pushed

Kirsten in her push chair and played with Jecca. My mother now had five grandchildren.

Our next holiday at Qolora Mouth, on a rugged sub-tropical coastline broken by numerous rivers with deep gorges and spacious lagoons, is unspoilt and truly wild even today. We nicknamed our hired caravan, *Teapot*. The worn-out, past-its-sell-by-date caravan looked out of place bouncing along over pot-holed gravel roads behind the *Mercedes*.

Arriving at our destination, we pitched camp on the edge of the river. There were no amenities. We used the *long drop* belonging to a cottage owned by Hughie Preston's parents. We drew water from their water tanks. We slept, dressed and stored our provisions in the *Teapot*. We enjoyed open-air showering and brushing our teeth and spitting into the ripples of the river. We had no electricity, running water, TV, radio, telephone, toilet, hand basin, stove or sink. We slept in a tiny space and woke at sunrise.

Our children enjoyed this *Huckleberry Finn* experience. They caught, scaled and cooked their catch on a fire they made on the river's edge. Living in bathing costumes, we swam, and collected shells as the sun browned our skins darker each day. This primitive holiday recharged our batteries. How would Steve Biko's death on 12 September affect our lives? Would the new lease of violence and fury on the streets continue? Were the rumours of the Ciskei's looming independence true?

In 1978 we met up with Eddie and Margy in East London where Eddie worked for *Mercedes*. At the zoo the children enjoyed a pony and trap ride. Brent held the reins, Byron stood at the rear and Jecca, Chandrè and Kirsten sat in front like three little princesses.

Before we sold our cottage at Coffee Bay, the school nurse invited herself along with her Alsatians. Torrential rain forced me to hang the wet washing on the verandah overnight. Peta was furious when her clothes and ours were stolen overnight. She left, saying, "I'll never come here again!" The headman found the culprits, who denied theft until Nolyn fired a shot into the air and our clothes were returned from where they had been hidden.

***

When Nolyn won a fully paid holiday for two to Europe (through his firm Financial Planning Services), Topsy and Bill looked after our children. We had a press photo taken at the airport in East London. From Johannesburg we flew to Brussels on our *Spring in Europe* adventure.

Boarding a luxury coach bound for Paris we visited the *George Pompidou* building, *Notre Dame*, the *Opera House, Arc de Triumph* and *Ponte Neuf.* We viewed Paris from the *Eiffel Tower.* We cruised the Seine seeing more famous Parisian landmarks. FPS paid for us to visit three night clubs in Paris. Dining alone, we discussed this.

"Please Nolyn, don't sit near the front."

"Why?"

"The performers entice men in the front rows to dance."

Nolyn's face lit up, saying, "What's wrong with that?"

I pictured him bragging to his friends, "I danced with a gorgeous French performer."

"You *know* the reason." I retorted.

We ate in an uncomfortable silence, aware of a couple a few tables from us conversing in French. I continued, "The first night club's a bit sleazy, but thereafter the clubs improve."

"Is this where *I'll* be asked to dance?"

"Yes, but *please…*" I began and switched to, "We'll also be warned that men should avoid being picked up by girls on the street, because the vast majority of these women are actually male…"

"You can really talk a load of rubbish."

"You know how prudish I am. I can't watch women baring their bodies. I hope this is not what's in store for us tonight."

"The *Moulin Rouge* is classy and huge…" is all Nolyn offered. Did he know more?

We stood up to leave. Passing the French couple, they said in perfect English, "Enjoy your evening!" They had understood *every* word of our conversation. I blushed bright crimson. We set off in high spirits.

On the bus the tour guide welcomed us. Summarising the evening events, he said, "A warning to the men on the bus. Don't get picked up by the women on the street. They're really men…" Nolyn laughed, saying, "I'd have been conned."

Much to my relief Nolyn did not dance on the stage of the first smutty club. The *Moulin Rouge* performance, with excellent choreography left me feeling uncomfortable as ostrich feathers waved about, revealing a stage full of bare-breasted women.

The next day a coach took us to Calais where we boarded a *Hovercraft* to Ramsgate. Crossing the English Channel in forty minutes at an average speed of 80 mph we had 250 passengers and 30 vehicles aboard. My postcard dated 2 May 1978, read:

Dear Chandrè, Brent and Byron,

We are sitting on the beach in France at a town called Calais. We will cross the sea in this Hovercraft to England. Do hope you are all well and listening to Bill and Tops. How are Spatts and my kittens? Soon we'll be home with you.
God bless. Lots of love,

M & D

The Hovercraft crossing was a first for both of us. In 1967 I had lived in London, but had forgotten how enormous it was. Rows and rows of identical houses reminded me of where Donal and I had lived. Nolyn's remark, "It's a concrete jungle!" ended my reverie. Our coach weaved through terrifying traffic – red London buses and hundreds of black London cabs– and stopped at the *London Tara Hotel* in Kensington.

We attended an Award Dinner on 3 May 1978. The wines on offer were *Chateau Clairac, Senator's Rheinwein White (Medium), Goldener Oktober Liebfraumilch (Dry)*. By 11.30 pm our party had consumed 328 bottles of wine. I doodled on the programme, bored with the never-ending Toasts and Replies. When Nolyn received a shield for the *Best Cape Recruit,* I felt proud.

I explored London on my own. In Kensington I bought brass-ware, a coal scuttle, a shovel, bellows, a *Paul Kruger* money box and two candelabras. We were heavily-laden with gifts when we reached Heathrow Airport. On this long flight home I smoked, no longer permissible today. On a domestic flight from Johannesburg the cabin crew objected to our excessive hand language. "Don't think you're going to stop me now. I've travelled from London with this and *nobody* complained. Excuse me." Nolyn made his way to his seat.

Our children were excited when we arrived home and Topsy had tales to tell. "I've trained your children. See you keep this up now, Neyse," Topsy told me as we waved them goodbye. What did *she* know about training children! They had no children of their own. Our children told us what had happened.

"Put your shoes in that corner of the kitchen.

Put your sandwich box and cool drink bottle in the sink.

Put your dirty school shirts and socks in the laundry basket.

Put your blazer on a hanger.

When you've changed I'll have tea ready.

It's time to do your homework; time to brush your teeth; bedtime!"

My children had been regimented like robots. They were delighted with their gifts, a pen with a moving *Hovercraft* when tilted; a miniature *Eiffel Tower* and lead soldiers.

"We visited Aunty Kathy, Adrian and Christine. Your cousins hardly remembered us. We cherished the memories and settled down to our normal routine once more.

19

GRANNY AND THE GABLES

In 1977 the death of Steve Biko as a result of police brutality, shocked the world. PW Botha became Prime Minister in 1978 after John Vorster retired. 'Free Mandela!' a banner headline in a Soweto newspaper 'The Post', started a campaign in March 1980 demanding the release of Nelson Mandela.

GRANNY meant a lot to me even when I was a little girl; I was aware of her presence. For her the end of each year was a particularly busy time. She wrote down the measurements of her eight granddaughters: waist, waist to hemline and waist to shoulders. She calculated the exact yardage of material she needed before meeting a traveller at *D M Brown's* to examine samples of fabric. Before placing her order, she stated categorically, "I *must* have the full order by the *first* week in November."

Her sewing machine hummed day after day as she laboured on relentlessly to complete this time-consuming task. At this time her sewing room was out of bounds. When I was fitted with a blindfold over my eyes, I felt the fabric with both my hands, wondering what colour my new dress would be and, being very aware of the smell of new material in the room. Topsy, Margy and I were always given identical dresses. Sometimes she embroidered fancy zigzag patterns in different colours along the edges of the white collars, using special machine attachments. The completed garments, which we called our *Sunday* or *party frocks*, were her Christmas presents to us. One year mine was a powder-blue nylon dress with a blue satin petticoat. This was my favourite.

Granny never wasted a thing. Scraps of material were sewn into dolls' clothes. Wrapping paper, empty toilet rolls, empty cotton reels, used envelopes, scraps of wool and lace, bottles and buttons, granny hoarded them all. Gifts of toilet sets, hankies, perfume and stationery sets which we had given her, went back and forth from one family member to the next. She sometimes received the same gift second time round! We teased her when she painstakingly opened her gifts trying very hard not to tear the paper before flattening it ready for re-using. I, too, cannot rip open a present. I love the paper as much as the gift.

My grandmother, who lived in Kokstad for about sixty years, had a heart of gold and was never idle. She sewed, knitted and crocheted. I am pleased that granny had the patience to teach me to crochet brightly-coloured squares, which I then sewed together to make snuggly blankets for my children. Gran enjoyed card games and I remember many evenings Nolyn and I played *Canasta* and *Rummy* with her.

She upheld her strong Catholic beliefs; she always said grace before meals; she knelt at her bedside saying her morning and evening prayers; she attended morning Mass and evening rosary and benediction daily, whatever the weather. As President of the Catholic Women's Institute, head of the Legion of Mary and in charge of the annual Catholic bazaar, she gave generously to the Church over and above her Sunday collection in the plate. The beautiful *Stations of the Cross* which adorn the inside of St Patrick's Cathedral in memory of my beloved *Dafoo* were donated by her. She was kind, honest, hardworking, never complaining, once a good tennis player and a fantastic cook. She had many friends amongst the farmers and townsfolk. Young and old, all loved Eileen Brown.

She was very fair. In her will she stipulated: *Starting with my eldest daughter, Joan, each one to wear my diamond ring for one year only, passing it down to Peggy, Ruth and then Molly. My last-surviving daughter keeps the ring.* My mother outlived her sisters and granny's exquisite ring became hers. Would she adopt the same strategy as her mother? Years later, the destiny of this ring resulted in heartache…

Granny and I stayed in a hotel in Durban once when I had more treatment on my eyes. On my birthday we took a bus from the Berea into central Durban to visit the toy department in *Stuttafords*, a leading upmarket store. She said, "Choose a birthday present, my child."

I immediately spotted the toy I wanted – a small wooden figure of a mother pushing her pram with a baby inside. When put on a slope, the toy became alive as the mother stepped forward setting her pram in motion.

"No my child, rather choose one of these dolls," granny coaxed me.

"No thanks granny. I *want* this," I said, holding the toy tightly.

"Look at *all* those pretty dolls. Which one would you like?"

"*Please* granny will you buy me this toy?" I would not be persuaded and clutched this cherished item. To my sheer delight, she picked up the prettiest doll dressed in pink and bought me both for which I rewarded her with hugs and slobbery wet kisses.

I was just thirty-three when my grandmother passed away in the Kokstad hospital on 23 January 1979 at the age of eighty-five. She was born on 2 October 1894, the eldest of six children. Her sisters were Mary and Mavis and brothers Havelock, Joseph and John. The wedding day on 23 August 1893 of my great-grandfather, John Theodore Pohl Hart, born 3 February 1862 to Ruth Margaret Davoren, born on 25 October 1872, was the day Nolyn and I married seventy-six years later.

I recalled much more when I stood at her graveside, listening to the priest say, "For as much as it has pleased Almighty God in His great mercy to take unto Himself the soul of our dearly beloved Eileen here departed, we therefore commit her body to the ground; earth to earth, ashes to ashes... Amen." When her coffin was lowered into the ground alongside that of my beloved *Dafoo*, warm tears trickled down my cheeks.

Today my grandmother lives on in my life through the smells – of incense when an altar boy swings the thurible like a pendulum – or of her favourite sweet peas; through sounds of sturdy footsteps on a wooden floor and the sound of her melodic voice calling, "Coo–eee! I'm coming!" and of lessons she taught me, her little pearls of wisdom, which I call to mind in my time of need.

***

Before rushing off to fetch the children from school, I admired our garden. The vegetable garden produced radishes, tomatoes, beans, lettuces, carrots, rhubarb, herbs too: chives, mint and basil. Flowers flourished and the palm trees along the front driveway were tall. Our home, where the kittens climbed up and down my curtains while I worked in the office upstairs, was a happy place. We were all content.

Fetching the children from school one day, I parked outside a beautiful gabled house set far back from the street. I was early. I opened the gate. There was a flagpole to my left and an enormous *Jacaranda* tree in lilac bloom on my right. *Agapanthus* nodded their blue heads in the shade of the pink *Frangipani* trees oozing sweet fragrance as I passed by. Crossing the manicured lawn I walked up the steps to the front door. I rang the doorbell. I was amazed when a tall pretty young woman opened the door.

"Hi," I said, not knowing what to say next.

"Hi. Do I know you?"

Her question made it easier. After introducing myself I said, "I admire your home every day. I wish we lived here."

"That's funny. Alan and I were thinking of moving."

"What did you both have in mind, Louise?"

"A more modern house."

"Could I look around?"

"Certainly Denyse."

I was smitten with the house, the ornate tiled fireplaces, sash windows and high ceilings. I had only ever dreamed of living in a house like this. There was enough ground to build two houses at the back.

"It's lovely. We have a property which might suit you," I suggested.

We swapped telephone numbers deciding to leave it to our husbands.

"Please pop in again Denyse," Louise enthused as I left.

Into the bargain, I had a new friend. Nolyn contacted her husband, Alan a pharmacist and they viewed both properties after which they agreed to swap homes legally. I believe we had the better deal. We moved again taking our additional cats, Trevor, Timothy and Ootsie-Lulu, with us. I had a pool built with a bougainvillea-clad pergola and a bar, made a new driveway winding between two palms to a double garage and carport. The old driveway I transformed into a sunken garden with tropical plants and ferns.

Using prisoners who had raped, murdered and assaulted, was a risk. This cheap labour enabled me to change the existing kitchen into an en-suite bathroom and laundry and also, install a new kitchen in what was once a servant's toilet and store-room. The *brookie lace* wide verandas surrounded the house which had six chimneys and two gables.

Inside *The Gables* my collection of antiques made a wonderful display.

***

Having sold our cottage at Coffee Bay, we hired a cottage at Kei Mouth for three weeks in June one year and invited my parents to join us. On the day we left I could not find my rings.

"Beauty!" I called. My maid arrived guilt written all over her face. She spoke without pausing for a breath, "*Medem*, they tell me they *take* my lounge suite if I not pay. I have plan. I sell *medem's* rings. She not wear them. She not miss them for *long* time. She good. She understand. Last week I get money and pay to *Lewis Stores*. He happy. He not take my things. Please, my *medem, not* be cross!"

If only Beauty had asked me to lend her money. Who was wearing my wedding and engagement rings now? Enraged, I spat the words, "Who bought them?"

"*Andiyasi*! I don't know!"

Nolyn, who had sold his *Anglia* and used all his savings to buy me the rings, was irate. "We'll never get your rings back. Let's go."

A nightmare journey began, with Pop in front with me and my mother and Chandrè in the back. Spatts settled at Pop's feet. Pandora and Timothy, sedated, lay on the back shelf. My rings remained on my mind as the cats miaaowed and jumped from the back on to Pop's lap. He smacked them with his newspaper, which made them screech and claw his legs. Arching their backs, they jumped away. To add to the commotion Spatts growled.

"You told me your cats slept in the car," Pop grumbled. He never liked cats, regarding them as useful ratters in barns on the farm and not house pets.

"I can't think why the sedatives haven't worked. We're nearly there."

We arrived ahead of Nolyn and my sons in the *Land Rover*. I stopped at the village store, where a friendly middle-aged, balding store-keeper handed me the keys.

"Do you know where to go?" he asked.

Village folk have a way of wheedling information from strangers. He had perfected this. Giving directions to the cottage, he scrutinised the passengers. I drove off and we arrived, expecting a seaside cottage.

"Look! Books! May I sleep here?" Chandrè asked.

With panoramic views, outdoor living and privacy, we could ask for nothing more. We relaxed; lazy lunches under the trees listening to the waves and squawking seagulls soaring overhead; rock fishing and exploring rock pools; swimming and walking barefoot in the sand dunes all in the glorious sunshine. One morning I gave in to my mother's pleas for me to have a go at fishing. We drove to a remote fishing spot with flat rocks.

"This is ideal," Nolyn assured me as he put down the fishing bags and baited up for me. He walked to the water's edge and cast into the sea. He gave me the rod, saying, "Hold the rod with the tip pointing skywards. I'll be back."

He fetched his rod where the children were preparing to fish in a gulley. I rested the rod in the bucket strapped around my waist. The waves looked huge and sounded like thunder, crashing mightily against the rocks not far from where I stood. I was cooled by sea spray as splashes threatened to drench me, but just as quickly, sucked back in a retreating rush. Nolyn returned with his rod. I had been frightened on my own.

On my right was a narrow gully into which I saw and heard the surge of waves. Reeling in his line after casting out, he warned me, "Whatever you do, don't run. Brace yourself. Hold your rod. I've got you."

His right arm tightened around my waist. I watched in horror as a freak wave, twelve-foot high still curling, hurtled towards us. It broke a few yards from our legs. The strongest force of water hit the rocks before pounding forward furiously with a mighty roar. We only just managed to withstand the force of water as splashes reached above our heads.

"Where are the children?" I looked round. On a pinnacle of rock our three defenceless children clung to each other as the raging sea swirled around them. They were safe. The receding water dragged bait bags, jumpers, hats and buckets into the sea. We were safe. This was the first and the last time I ever fished. Comforting the children Nolyn said, "The wind's switched direction, a bad omen. Let's go home."

***

The shrill sound of the telephone disturbed my daydreaming, something I did often those days. Staring into space my thoughts distanced me from reality.

"Hi Neyse," Margy's voice sounded as if she was in the same room, continuing, "'I phoned to tell you our plans."

"What's happening?"

"As you know we're emigrating. Eddie will go ahead and stay with his sister, Anita and her husband, Chiko in Switzerland while he looks for a job and a home. We're moving in December and staying with mom in Kokstad. Could we visit you in January?"

"That'll be great."

We chatted on. Margy did most of the talking. I had seen very little of them when they lived in Pietermaritzburg. When would we see each other again? Could we afford to visit them in Switzerland? Would they ever come back to South Africa?

Before heaping more concerns on my existing problems, granny's pearl of wisdom rescued me: *why worry about tomorrow, today has enough troubles of its own*. I would make the most of their visit.

Over Christmas in Kokstad we shared gifts, time, laughter and joy. We reminisced about our own childhood. The children played together. Today as a grandmother, I understand how much it meant to mom and Pop then, to be surrounded by Patrick and all three daughters, their spouses and five grandchildren.

My preparations for Eddie, Margy, Jecca and Kirsten's visit were complete. I had baked biscuits, stocked the pantry and deepfreeze and spring-cleaned the guest bedroom. My children put some of their toys and books on their cousin's beds saying, "All their toys are packed. They can play with ours." A small vase of sweet peas on the bookshelf scented the room.

Counting the number of *sleeps* before their cousin's arrival, my children's excitement was tangible when I announced, "No more *sleeps*. They're coming today!" The crunching sound of tyres on the drive brought my children out to meet their long-awaited cousins. They said nothing, sizing each other up. Eddie said, "They'll thaw out."

Their visit was a tonic with uninterrupted days of family togetherness around the pool and in the garden. We watched the children take turns blowing glistening bubbles from a wand, dipped in a soapy solution.

Jecca, five and Kirsten, three, loved the cats: Trevor, Trudy, Timothy, Pandora, Ootsie-Lulu and Schnoekie. They fed them each evening.

Nolyn enjoyed Eddie's company. He was a perfect host and husband. If only we could be like this forever. All too soon it was time for our goodbyes. We followed their car to the gate, waving until they were out of sight. The next day the house was deathly quiet.

Brent's question, "Have they gone now mommy?" a stark reminder to me of how far they would be from us soon.

***

I remembered Uncle Stewey who died on 19 March 1979. He had driven me to church in his car on both my wedding days. I had worked for him invoicing motor parts. He and Pop were both Kokstad councillors and had lengthy discussions. I would miss him…

***

Before our holiday in Mauritius, I had bought a new wedding band and had a diamond put into Aunty Marie's ring which my mother had given me saying, "It's not worth much. Do you want it? " This ring, I learnt later, directed the fate of granny's diamond ring…

Joining friends, we flew to Mauritius staying at Club Mediterranean, a paradise. Waves lapped sandy palm-treed white beaches where turquoise water and a coral reef stretched up to an azure sky. To keep cool we lived in bathing attire and dipped into the sea or pool. We revelled in the late night entertainment.

Nolyn went scuba-diving. I won the Women's Singles tennis tournament playing tennis in a bikini in sweltering heat. Every day we participated in beach activities, but when a Frenchman paid me too much attention, Nolyn was annoyed. We learnt to windsurf. We lost all our holiday photographs when both cameras accidentally fell into the water when I was paddle-boating. This holiday nearly ended in a worse disaster.

On our drive home through the Transkei the car ran out of petrol. I chose to safe-guard the car and Nolyn hitched a lift on the back of a *bakkie* to fetch petrol. Sitting in the driver's seat, I prayed for his and my safety. I knew I was vulnerable in a fuel-less car.

Cars drove past. Time ticked by. Looking into the rear view mirror,

I saw a black man approaching. He stopped at the car. A pane of glass separated us. He bent closer to beg a cigarette from me. He saw my *Dunhill* packet. I opened it showing him it was empty. What luck, I thought. Undeterred, he begged for matches. The box was also empty. He wanted me to open the window and his attempts had failed which intensified his anger…

Keeping my composure I opened the *You* magazine and pretended to read. An approaching car forced him to walk away carrying his *knobkerrie,* but not for long. He swung round storming towards the car. He haggled me for money, saying, "I'm hungry."

"I have no money," I answered in *Xhosa.*

"You lie!"

"I'm not."

I could not face his red eyes, a sure sign he smoked *dagga*. Time was running out on me. He would break the window. My heart thumped. He tried the door handle. I was expecting glass to splinter when I heard car doors slam. Nolyn and Hughie's arrival had saved me. He trailed off down a footpath. I was shaking, but somehow Nolyn's scuba-diving stories dominated the conversation as petrol was poured into the tank.

Not long after this holiday, Uncle Slabs died on 27 June 1980. I will always remember his contagious laughter, De… hah…hah. De…hah …hah, which started everybody laughing; he paced up and down, the radio blaring a running commentary on a rugby match. Puffing nervously on a cigarette, he would shout, "*Skop die bal*" Kick the ball!"

***

Health problems demanded I have a hysterectomy. At 6 pm my doctor, wearing an eye-shield over one eye, said, "Denyse I've an eye infection and will not be able to operate tomorrow. I could arrange for a gynaecologist in East London to take over from me."

I agreed to have the operation in an East London hospital at a later date. I was then discharged from the King William's Town hospital unbeknown to Nolyn who arrived that evening to visit me. I was ready to go home. I wondered if this change of events had upset Nolyn's plans. I remained silent, knowing his unsympathetic reaction had a deeper significance...

Days later I was admitted to the *Mater Dei Hospital* under the care of a gynaecologist. The operation went well. When the time came for me to tell Nolyn I had been discharged, I was met with another disappointment.

"Sorry, darling, you'll have to wait one more day. I'll fetch you on Thursday."

Nolyn's golf was more important. I needed him. Suppressing my anger, I pleaded, "But Nolyn ...." was cut short with, "I'll fetch you on Thursday."

Helpless and frail, I was mortified. Avoiding humiliation I phoned Annamarie saying, "Nolyn's unable to fetch me. I was wondering if you could?"

"Of course I will. What time?"

Tears trickled down my cheeks making it impossible for me to reply.

"Denyse, are you there?"

"Yes, Would 2 pm suit you Annamarie?"

My friend willingly fetched me even though she was looking after our three children and six of her own. She had the time. She helped me into the house and promised to return my children the next day, saying, "You need a good rest tonight." In this silent house with an aching body, I realised Nolyn was never there when I needed him most.

High on his priority list were golf, business and fishing. Somewhere at the bottom, I featured. Past and present emotions festered deep within me. I longed to be loved and I longed for the pain in my body to ease. Nolyn came home at 10 pm and said, "I told you I'd fetch you tomorrow." This brought me little consolation. I went back and forth to the toilet during the night with excruciating pain. Nolyn pulled the pillow over his head and slept.

"Take it easy," he said, giving me a quick kiss before he left for work in the morning. My parents arrived later. My mother contacted the doctor. I had a urine infection and was put on antibiotics. Thanks to my parents I recuperated well before they returned to Kokstad.

***

Life went on. I joined an oil painting class with Annamarie in Berlin (SA). A talented eighty-some-thing Afrikaans lady, called *Tannie* took the lessons in her enclosed patio. She inspired me, teaching me to mix colours, use various brush strokes, perspective and light effects. These therapeutic lessons transported me into my own creative world. Alone in the evenings, I painted late into the night. *Tannie* framed our paintings at a small fee. My painting of *The Gables* holds mixed memories today.

Myra, a vivacious auburn-haired ex-resident of Johannesburg, an attractive go-getter, was married to Ivan Walters, born in Mauritius. They had four sons. Ivan left *Bernina Sewing Machines,* to start his own business, a pawn shop on the market square which developed into a second-hand furniture business. Nolyn and Ivan had a common interest, business. Myra and I developed a friendship through tennis. She once asked me. "Denyse are you English or Afrikaans-speaking?"

"English."

"You're bilingual. It's hard to tell."

I owed that to my maid who only spoke Afrikaans.

One day we had to stop playing tennis when my partner, Maggie, rushed to smash a lofted shot at the net. With her racquet poised, she slammed the ball with her mouth wide open and as her racquet contacted the ball her top dentures shot out and landed in the opponents' court. Hitting the hard surface, they split in half. Maggie retrieved her broken dentures. She was now toothless. Hysterical laughter followed the remarks.

"Maggie smashes at the net and loses her dentures!

Tennis players advised to have denture insurance!

Which do I hit, the ball or Maggie's dentures?"

I also played golf, but the ladies were snooty and the course was challenging. The children settled down at school. Brent achieved better marks, after we kept him back a year and he attended Dale College. After Nolyn gave the boys a computerised chess set, Brent represented Border Province in the Under 12 Chess competition, staged in Port Elizabeth. We were very proud of him.

Aunty Molly was hospitalised and my mother visited her daily. I phoned the hospital and my aunt, who had not spoken all day, said, "Pegs, answer the phone. It's Denyse!" Aunty Molly's son, David was present. When nobody answered, I dialled again.

"I've been praying for Aunty Molly, mom,"

My faith was growing and God was changing me. A few days later on 6 May 1987 Aunty Molly died. I knew she was with the Lord. Without warning uncles and aunts were going down like skittles and all I had left were my childhood memories...

***

I remembered the day my children accompanied me in the *Mercedes* to remove our personal belongings from our cottage at Coffee Bay. Two weeks' rain had made the dirt roads impassable. Turning off the tarred road, the car skidded on towards Viedgesville. Ahead of me, vehicles circled out of control, some stranded in the *veld*. Driving slowly did not help. We broadsided as the car slithered off the road. The locals earned money pushing the car back onto the road. When my money was gone, we rewarded them with sandwiches, fruit, sweets and biscuits until we had nothing left. I can say with confidence today that God's hand of protection was on us then even though I was not aware of it at the time.

Still without a seaside cottage, we bought a collapsible caravan. We camped at Xora Mouth again. I added a foot pump for showering, a portable loo, gas fridge, gas deepfreeze and zip-up pantry, to improve camping. Thieving *kaffir* dogs, a derogatory term for black-owned mangy, starving dogs, robbed us every night. "*Voetsak*!" did nothing to deter them. The prowlers sneaked into our tent nightly. Opening the fridge, they wolfed down bacon, cold meat, cheese, raw eggs, and even butter. The dogs opened *Tupperware* containers and ate my home-made rusks and biscuits.

Fed up, Nolyn waited up one night. A dog approached the tent in the dark. He fired a shot. Yelping broke the silence as it vamoosed into the night. "Got you!" Nolyn shouted.

Within a few minutes our friends, Boots and Wilma Kaiser arrived at our caravan, saying, "You've just shot our dog!" Their dog, a mongrel easily mistaken for a *kaffir* dog, survived and we remained friends.

After this a raging storm woke us in the middle of a night. Our tent billowed like an airborne hot-air balloon. The wind dislodged the tent pegs. I clung to the central tent pole as Nolyn anchored the rim of the tent flaps with heavy rocks. The jangling tent poles and flapping tent, a musical composition conducted by gale force winds, kept us awake. A calm sunny day broke the next morning, defying any signs of the storm we had survived…

We dreaded 16 December, the day of two previous disasters. The day passed without incident… I called the family for supper, "I'm serving dinner." Byron slept on his bunk near the fridge. I switched off the gas stove and saw a grey film falling to the floor. I smelt gas.

"Fire, Get out!" I yelled.

In the nick of time Byron jumped up and fled the tent. The escaping gas ignited on the flame of the gas fridge, exploding into a roaring furnace. The wind fanned the inferno. Nolyn disconnected the ten-pound gas cylinders as I stood, glued to the floor, clutching Pepe my poodle. Fire consumed our caravan around me. I was immobilised. It felt like a bad dream! Wilma grabbed me and led me away from the turmoil. Panic-stricken friends fought the flames, first with fire-extinguishers and then with water from the river.

Finally the fire was extinguished. Nolyn's legs were badly burnt. He stayed with Boots and Wilma. The children and I spent a restless night in a neighbour's tent.

When dawn broke it was clear how narrowly we had escaped with our lives. If the gas cylinders had exploded, we would have been blown up like a bomb blast with limbs scattered over the *veld*. The local dogs fed on what food remained. The Blacks gathered charred debris. We returned home with me towing the burnt-out caravan. Nolyn drove the *Mercedes*. His secondary burns healed in time.

A fire at Coffee Bay! A *Land Rover* over the cliff! A near explosion at Xora Mouth! All these events took place on 16 December! Had a curse been inflicted on us, I wondered...

***

Nolyn, focussed on his expanding businesses, the drycleaners and a property investment company. He wanted to run his own insurance firm. Single-handedly I ran the household and attended the children needs. Our socialising increased but Nolyn avoided my candlelit dinners for two at home. We had attended a Marriage Encounter weekend run by the Catholic Church hoping to improve our marriage. It helped for a while only.

One evening I snapped... All day I thought of nothing else but going to the movies with Nolyn. He, keen to see *Jaws,* would arrive home in good time. I read the children a bedtime story before curling my hair in rollers, painting my fingernails to match my new pink floral dress and painstakingly applying my make-up. I checked my reflection in the mirror as Beauty arrived to babysit the children.

"Wait in your room until I call you," I suggested. On many previous occasions Nolyn had let me down and I never called my maid back to babysit. Tonight I hoped it would be different. "Yo..Yo...yo! Medem, look pretty. Beauty, she like smart dress!" she said, doing her own dance step of jubilation. Clapping her hands, she sang. Beauty always came in on time. Her retreating footsteps and the rhythmic ticking of the grandfather clock bristled me. Where was Nolyn? It was 7.45 pm. Not wanting to be late, I phoned the Golf club and asked to speak to him. A voice on line said, "Hold on a minute I'll see if he's here."

I waited before being told, "Sorry, Nolyn left a while ago."

I slammed the phone down. The children in their dressing gowns and slippers joined me in the *Land Rover,* and I drove to the Golf Club with curlers still in my hair. I felt like a volcano about to erupt. Enraged and out of control, I allowed years of suppressed anger to burst and bubble out of me. I would put an end to all the lies I had been subjected to for so many years. I parked.

Armed with my *golden goose* putter I strode up to the main entrance in my high heels. I swung my putter at the window pane with brute force. Although the sound of shattered glass and destruction scared me initially, I could not restrain myself and something inside drove me to bash and smash one, two, three, four enormous windows into smithereens. Huge transparent panes lay in ragged shards around my feet. The noise alerted golfers, who had been on the booze. Grabbing my arms they wrestled the putter from me.

"It's my putter. Leave me alone," I bellowed.

"What do you think you're doing?"

"I'm teaching you a lesson."

An annoyed spectator with slurred speech, admonished me, "You fool – you've bro – ken the win – dow tothemain en – tr – nce oftheClub!"

"You're lucky it's *only* the door. I intended to smash your sacred nineteenth hole which keeps husbands away from wives and deprives children of fatherly love," I screamed.

"Listen to her. Stupid bitch!" a golfer with beery breath bad-mouthed me.

"Don't you call me a bitch? I won't tolerate your insults or your deceit. How dare you say Nolyn had *already left* the bar when he was still drinking with you, talking rubbish like the rest of you and consuming too much alcohol? You *lied* to me."

Nobody responded to my ranting and raving. I continued, "That's my putter. Give it back to me. I hope this teaches you a lesson. My children are in the *Land Rover*. Leave me. I'm going now…"

When I climbed into the car, Chandrè asked, "What happened?"

"I was angry and broke the door. Daddy will be mad with me, but we're not going home immediately. We'll visit Aunty Annamarie and Uncle Vernon."

It was late. Unannounced we arrived taking the Mayberry family by surprise. My children happily joined their's downstairs, where they watched a movie on television. Their startled faces reminded me of my curlers. I removed them and told my story. They listened wide-eyed. When I had finished, Vernon and Annamarie laughed, which broke the tension.

"Good for you. This calls for a drink. Sherry Denyse?" Vernon asked.

"Thanks Vernon."

The sherry settled my nerves. I knew this was not ladylike behaviour, but previous hurts drove me to do what I did. We drove home. The children were soon fast asleep. Nolyn, too, was asleep. He would not stir till the morning. Taking precautions, I slept in the spare room. Disappointed that I had missed the movie and had damaged the club I now faced the music.

On Sunday morning Nolyn was in a foul mood. How could he face the crowds participating in this golf tournament? The President of the club had already telephoned him and voiced his fury, "It's a disgrace. A big tournament and the entrance to the clubhouse boarded up with scraps of wood. Nothing can be done until Monday! What will the visitors think? You should control your wife!"

A ripple effect resulted with individuals giving their own version of this incident. Mine remained unchanged. I had prepared myself to watch a movie with Nolyn. His golf buddies had detained him. They had lied to me. He had only left after I phoned the club.

Nolyn paid for the repairs. No more was said. The incident of my *golden goose putter* striking glass would be rekindled under different circumstances in years to come…

20

MAJOR PHILIP HUGHEN LEARY, 'POP'

During 1981 the ANC guerrillas targeted fuel storage tanks at industrial plants, fired rockets into a military base and bombed equipment at a nuclear power station. In 1982 a police team led by a brigadier bombed the ANC offices in London.

POP had not been well for several years. He enjoyed his afternoon walks. He watched Mom play bowls although he could no longer play. His illness demanded more than one operation in Pietermaritzburg before he was moved into the Kokstad Hospital.

"I'm coming to Kokstad to be with you," I insisted.

"But..."

"No arguing mom, you need support. Chandrè and I'll be with you tomorrow."

"But I spend the whole day at the hospital."

"That's fine mom."

For once I was playing the mother role and asserting my authority. My mother needed me. She was not coping. The Easter school holidays began and plans were made.

"Brent and Byron will be fine at Mazeppa Bay with me," Nolyn said.

"What about the meals?"

"Don't worry; we'll *braai* most days."

I must trust Nolyn with the boys. Whatever they did or did not, would be his responsibility. They would have a *'boy's only time'* with their dad.

Shelley and Chandrè were inseparable friends. They joined me. The girls chattered all the way. Ivy, my mother's maid fussed over them when I left them at mom's home. I drove to the hospital. A smiling nurse directed me to a private ward. I opened the door and was shocked at what

I saw. Pop, lying on his back, looked thin and frail. His eyes were closed and his breathing was slow and heavy. My mother sitting at his side stroked his bony sun-tanned hand. I kissed his forehead. "Hello Pop."

Tears trickled down my mother's cheeks. She looked tired and stressed.

"Denyse will look after you, Pegs," Pop said slowly and softly.

We visited the hospital daily coming home after 8 pm. When my mother attended to matters in town, I stroked Pop's forehead, held his hand and re-assured him I was with him. On these days at his bedside, I told Pop how indebted I was to him for all he had done for me and my sisters, his three step-daughters. I thanked him for his influence on my life. He became weaker with each passing day, hardly able to eat.

I remembered our caravan holiday in the Kruger National Park in 1963. My sisters and I took turns sitting between David and Michael in the backseat of Uncle Stewey and Aunty Molly's car. The Johnstone family had joined us. Both cars pulled caravans from Pietermaritzburg to *Skukuza* (he who turned everything upside down) which was the name given to Lt Col James Stevenson-Hamilton by the tribal people, referring to his fauna and flora regulations, and now the name of a campsite where we stayed in the park. This sanctuary was begun in 1895 by President Kruger.

We followed dusty dirt roads scouring the *bushveld* for game. We saw *bushbuck* and elephant devour vegetation. Giraffe gawkily drinking at a waterhole and others glided with their heads in the clouds. Herds of bovine eland hurtled past. Ebony crested sable antelope with massive curved horns stared back at us. *Springbok* cantered off in the distance. We saw zebra, cheetahs, *wildebeest, secretary birds* and *lilac-crested rollers* in their natural habitat. Pop spotted lion resting in the shade of a tree. He stopped the car which enabled us to view this amazing spectacle through his binoculars. Our African safari, under a myriad of stars at a campfire by night and under blue skies on adrenalin-pumping drives by day, was a unique experience.

I remember the time we ran out of cigarettes at Umsikaba and we rolled *zols* in newspaper with tobacco bought off *Pondo* women. Pop had given me so many memories.

One evening when mom and I returned from the hospital Chandrè and Shelley said, "We have a concert for you." We watched their performance of song and dance, which was their way of cheering us up. My mother and I were deeply moved.

It was a shock when we heard Pop did not have long to live. We contacted Tony, his son in Rhodesia (Zimbabwe), Topsy and Patrick in Johannesburg and Margy in Pietermaritzburg. Tony arrived first. He was positive and longed to take his dad for a drive. This was not possible. With his family gathered around him, Pop, it seemed, surrendered to a losing battle. Mom and I walked in the hospital garden. Tony and Patrick were standing at their dad's bedside when he breathed his last.

This was a sad day, 6 April 1982. His well-attended funeral service in the Anglican Church in Kokstad took place a few days later. There was not a dry eye present nor was there one bad word spoken of Major Philip Hughen Leary. He was a loving husband, caring stepfather, Pop and a remarkable dad and granddad! He would be sorely missed.

I found these words he had penned for my mother:

Peggy my girl

Many paths we have trod
Sometimes steep and rocky
But two peas in a pod
To make our way easy!
Peg, now times for you are alone
You have done so much for me
You have shown me the way home
You, my girl, done all so lovingly!

Right to the end, you held my hand
You were always at my side
To listen, to soothe and understand.
All things difficult you defied.
For everything, Peg, I thank you
Knowing you have strength without me
To live, to enjoy, to love and renew
All we shared so devotedly!

With my love, Phil.

He idolised his youngest son, Patrick who was twenty-three at the time of his death. Pop wrote this quote taken from the wireless message broadcast on Christmas day 1939 by King George VI.

For Patrick on his fourteenth birthday, from his Father.

I said to the man, who stood at the gate of the year,
"Give me a light that I may tread safely into the unknown."
And he replied, "Go out into the darkness and put your hand into the hand of God,
That shall be to you better than light and safer than a known way."

He was a wonderful courageous kind man who loved life and worked hard as a farmer, councillor, father and husband. I felt ashamed of myself for resisting his marriage to my mother. Pop, an avid reader, encouraged me to read. He was generous. I bought a bookshelf and a set of encyclopaedias with the money he left me – a lifelong reminder to me of an honourable man.

21

FLEEING THE CISKEI

The most serious attack in South Africa's history was a car-bomb attack outside a military building in Pretoria in 1983, killing sixteen people and injuring more than two hundred.

WITH advance warning Nolyn told me he paid R100 (£50) for a ticket to attend a fund-raising ball on Saturday at the golf club. "But that's expensive," I reacted.

"We've a chance of winning R1,000 (£500)," Nolyn replied. In those days R100 was a huge sum of money, a whole month's groceries.

With preparations underway – a hair appointment, buying an elegant long pink evening dress and notifying Victoria, our maid, to babysit the children – Chandrè announced, "Mom I've a dress rehearsal for our ballet concert at 6.30 pm on Saturday."

Chandrè had practised her dancing for weeks. Her costume was made. We could not let her down. It would mean fetching her from the dress rehearsal during the ball. With no mobile phones in the 1980s, parents waited patiently. "Dad and I'll be there to fetch you."

I dropped off Chandrè before I slipped into my pink evening gown with a sparkling sequined bodice and long softly-pleated flowing sleeves. I kissed Brent and Byron goodnight, took one last hurried glance at my reflection in the long mirror and thanked Victoria, who was listening to her *FM* radio in the kitchen.

Nolyn looked handsome in his dress suit. We drove to the golf club, joining our party of twelve. Soon Nolyn and I were dancing like we did when courting, close and in love.

"We're going to win tonight," I whispered in his ear.

"Everybody thinks that," he replied.

We returned to our table, but not for long.

"Will everybody take to the floor? If you're eliminated, please hand me your ticket, before returning to your seat," the announcer said.

The overcrowded dance floor, with couples dancing in time to *Tie a yellow ribbon round the old oak tree,* was silenced with, "Will all the couples with ladies wearing black shoes, please leave the floor."

We danced and more couples left the dance floor until we were among the fifty remaining couples. It was time to fetch Chandrè. Dinner was being served when we left hurriedly. We reached the Town Hall and waited ten minutes before Chandrè appeared. She hopped into the car, pleased to know we could still win the prize. Parking the car in the driveway, Nolyn said, "Don't be long!" I accompanied her inside, saying, "Remove all your make-up."

Hitching up my long skirt, I hurried back to the car. Very soon we were back at the ball and I noticed desserts were served. I picked at my food. Once more we took to the dance floor. I enjoyed having Nolyn to myself all evening. Fifty couples reduced to forty, to thirty, until ten couples remained. We were among them. It was then my thoughts focused on how I would spend R500.

The music slowed until only one other couple remained on the floor with us. We clung to each other. I felt Nolyn's clammy hand in mine. His heart was racing. I told myself, we're going to win. The last dance went on forever. I could hardly bear to listen.

"Will the couple with… two children, please leave the floor."

We had three children and were the last couple on the floor.

"The winning couple is Nolyn and Denyse Wild!" was music to my ears. Banging fists on the table, stamping feet on the floor, our group celebrated with us. Mickey Webb presented Nolyn with a wad of money, saying, "You see Denyse gets her share!"

When we arrived home after midnight, we woke the children and gave them R10 each. Victoria received R20. She kissed Nolyn's hand in appreciation saying, "Thank you my master. Victoria happy. Thanks *medem*!"

I planned to spend my R425 wisely, but… On Monday Nolyn said, "I'll bank the cash. It's not safe in the house." On Tuesday he arrived with antique swords and knives.

"What's all that about?"

"I bought these at an auction."

"What on earth for?"

"I invested our winnings."

"You paid R950 for these battered swords in shabby sheathes?"

"More than that! They're collectables. They'll look good in the lounge and will be worth a fortune one day. This is…"

I had heard enough. Nolyn had spent *all* the prize money on what he wanted. The maid was better off than me. My joy evaporated. Negative emotions warred deep within me.

***

The mood in the country was changing rapidly. Bisho, developing as the administrative capital of the Ciskei, meant independence was imminent. We loved *The Gables* and did not want to move. House-hunting began.

"I've found a lovely home overlooking the Nahoon River."

"How much?"

"R100,000."

"You must be mad!"

Nolyn's reaction came as no surprise. If we had paid R40 000 for *The Gables* seven years ago, it was worth a lot more than that then. "This is a real bargain in a prime position. A good property investment," the estate agent said. Nolyn never missed a money-making opportunity. The sale was agreed. We rented *The Gables*. Again it was time to move.

Our *Mercedes* registration of CCY in Umtata had changed to CD 1200 in King Williams Town and would soon have CE number plates. With the grandfather clock wrapped up in blankets in the *Microbus*, CD 4402, for the last time Chandrè and I drove down the driveway under Jacaranda trees dropping lilac blooms. Whenever we moved we ordered in *Kentucky Fry* chicken. Our new house was very different from the home we had left behind. It would take hard work to make it our home.

On one level were three bedrooms, a lounge with fireplace, entrance hall and bathroom with separate toilet. Through the lounge door, stairs led down to an open-plan TV lounge and kitchen / dining room and more stairs led to three bedrooms and a bathroom. The rooms had panoramic views of the Nahoon River and at night reflected lights rippled in the river. The dated kitchen was soon replaced with a new one. I had my own study / sewing room. A steep driveway curved towards the double garage. A bougainvillea-covered patio led onto an enclosed pool. Deer roamed the sloping garden at dawn and dusk.

The children caught a bus to their new schools, Selbourne and Clarendon, a first for them. I waited at home fretting they would catch the wrong bus. Mom stayed with us at 9 Reynold's View as she adjusted to life without Pop.

***

Putting years of hurts behind me, I rejoiced with my sister who had waited ten years to have her first baby. David Philip Botha was born on 6 January 1983.

"I can't believe David is *our* baby," Topsy exclaimed. She idolised her baby. My mother welcomed her third grandson with knitted, crocheted and sewn baby bootees and clothing she had made him.

"Will you be godmother?" Topsy asked.

Honoured to be asked I flew to Johannesburg for David's baptism. He was a bonny baby with dark hair and long fingers. "He's beautiful, Topsy," I said examining his long fingers and dark hair as I held him. He smacked his rose-petal lips and gave me a windy smile. I had forgotten baby smells and noises.

"We'd love you to holiday with us at Mazeppa Bay," I said before leaving.

"We'd love to."

Good family news followed sad news when on 29 March 1983 Aunty Joan passed away in Durban. Death conjures up memories. Aunty Joan loved knitting; she hitched up her skirt to tan her legs; was a crafty tennis player, a home-maker and keen gardener. She had been a second mother to me when I boarded with her at 107 Hawthorn Street. Mom had lost her first sister.

Nolyn won a fully paid holiday through Bowring-Barclays in the Algarve between 22 May and 2 June 1983. We stayed at the *Hotel Alvor Praia*.

My postcard read:

> *Dear Brent,*
>
> *We left you so quickly and flew to Bloemfontein, then to*

Johannesburg. Bill was there and he took us to Tops's house. Little David has grown so big. We had tea and chocolate cake and then went back to the airport, late again. The plane was hot, crowded and stuffy. We watched a movie "Firefly" at 12.30. Daddy enjoyed it. I slept under my seat on the carpet.

Love you, Mom and Dad.

I puffed on my Dunhill cigarettes throughout the Presentation Dinner on Friday 27 May while dancers in bright costumes entertained us. On Sunday we hired motorbikes. Nolyn insisted I ride pillion. I clung to him, but when the bike tilted dangerously close to the tarred road around a bend, I swung the opposite way. The bike wobbled, but Nolyn regained control. We pulled into a garage.

"There's something wrong with this bike. It's the tyres. The bike careers out of control on the bends," he told the group.

Nothing unforeseen could be found with the bike so we proceeded. Approaching a sharp bend, leading downhill onto a bridge, I leant in the opposite direction again. From this vantage point I saw a bus approaching. We wobbled dangerously. I sensed danger. To avoid being hit by the bus, I tucked my head against Nolyn's back and closed my eyes. I clung on. Peeping briefly, I saw our left knees were inches off the tarmac, but we were still on the bike. This episode caused deeper concern. We stopped again.

"There's *definitely* something wrong with this bike. I've been riding bikes for years and I *should know,"* Nolyn stated.

"Tell us what happens, Nolyn," Brian asked.

"Whenever we take a corner, the bike wobbles out of control."

"That's funny because that's when I try to balance the bike by leaning the opposite way to you, Nolyn," I said.

"You stupid idiot!" he admonished me in front of the group. I was belittled not yet realising I was to blame. "What do you mean?"

The group laughed. I had been the one nearly causing a fatal accident.

"Hold on and move with me," Nolyn said as we drove off.

It was an exhilarating day climbing steep mountain passes, driving through tiny cobbled villages and smelling mouth-watering aromas of Sunday lunch oozing from the open windows. Smiling, black-clad women waved as we passed their white cottages decorated with red geranium flower-boxes.

One hot afternoon we experienced our first bull fight. I turned away to avoid seeing the cruelty. The enraged bull, blood dripping from where sharp spears dangled from its neck, was enticed by a matador who waved a red cloak and dashed sideways. How bizarre. How could intelligent human beings derive pleasure from such brutality?

In a postcard to the children I wrote about our guided tour of Lisbon, crossing the Tagus River and visiting the Statue of Christ the King: *The Algarve is beautiful, a bit like Mauritius. We took a lift to the top of the Statue. The next day we boarded a yacht and had six hours at sea exploring the coastline with its enormous rocks and caves. We anchored and were treated to a fish braaivleis and wine whilst the skipper sang and strummed on his guitar. The water lapped at the side of the boat.*

***

In 1983 my back injury finally caught up with me. The pain was so severe when I shopped, I deserted the half-full trolley and drove home where I lay on the carpet. My hips ached. Nolyn was unable to sympathise with me because outwardly he could see nothing wrong. I had always been active, carrying heavy items, golfing, gardening, playing tennis – so why was I hobbling about like a cripple?

"See the doctor," he offered.

Doctor Tarr referred me for X-rays. The radiologist said, "You need an MRI scan." These Micro Resonance Imagery scans with side and aerial views pick up abnormalities in the spinal cord, vertebrae, discs or nerves. Pleased to be out of the tunnel-like scanning apparatus, I was then told, "Your orthopaedic surgeon will contact you in due course."

Mr Smit, still practising in East London, knew the history of my back. He had treated me after my car accident in 1966. "The lower fracture in your spine has broken and those vertebrae need to be fused," he told me. He explained the full implications of a spinal fusion.

"Would this reduce my existing pain?" I asked.

"I cannot guarantee this, Denyse. As I said, every spinal operation involves a risk. The slightest damage to the spinal cord could cause paralysis and more pain. If the operation is successful you should have reduced levels of pain."

I had faith in God and faith in him. My mind was made up. I agreed to go ahead with the operation at the *Mater Dei* Private Hospital in East London in October. When I came round from the anaesthetic a lady was standing at my bedside. Her serene face radiated love. She held pink roses. I must have dozed off, because when I opened my eyes she was gone. I remembered her parting words, "I'll visit you again. God bless."

Who was she? Had I been dreaming? Why had the room lit up in her presence? Without a visit from the children or Nolyn I welcomed a second visit from this lady.

"I'm Rose," she said. We chatted and the same warmth from her previous visit engulfed me. This time I saw in her something I wanted – compassion, peace, understanding and love. Her ensuing visits to my home would change my life forever.

Bedridden for ten days after the operation, I studied Psychology lying on my bed. At the beginning of the year I had enrolled for a BA degree through UNISA, an internationally-acclaimed correspondence university. Before leaving the hospital, I was fitted with a steel corset which had to be worn day and night initially. I could not drive a car or sit for three months.

"Mr Smit could Denyse travel to the Wild Coast in December?" Nolyn asked.

"How do you plan to transport her there?"

"On a mattress in the back of the *VW Microbus*."

"Yes, but you'll be taking a risk. The gravel roads will cause considerable pain and could cause complications."

"I'll *drive slowly*, Mr Smit."

"Then it's at your own risk Nolyn."

Nolyn drove me home in the back of the *VW Microbus*. I lay on a mattress, but the smallest bump in the road sent me reeling and sweating as the jarring targeted my raw wounds. Arriving at home, Nolyn helped me up the stairs and onto the bed. "See you later," he said giving me a goodbye kiss. He dashed back to work.

I dozed off with Pepe my black miniature French poodle, curled up at my feet. I woke to the sound of my children's voices as they returned from school. Chandrè, Brent and Byron sat on the bottom of my bed showering me with love. They questioned me, "What's a fusion?"

"The specialist inserted a bone from each hip into the top and bottom of my lower spine, making it stiff."

"Did they cut your back open? Do your hips hurt?

Will your hip bones grow again? I'm glad you don't need a wheelchair.

How will you eat if you can't sit?

We're so happy you're home again, mommy. We missed you."

Each day was a little easier. I put a trunk call through to Pretoria to advise UNISA of my predicament, saying, "Could you arrange a bed in the examination hall for me because I'm unable to sit?" Never before had they had a request like this, so I waited for them to call me back.

"We'll send an examiner to your house, 9 Reynolds View. You must put up notices, '*Examination in progress. Do not disturb.*' on both your front door and the door of the room in which you will write the examination. Disconnect your telephone. The house must be kept quiet for the duration of the two-hour paper on both days."

I received a confirmation letter. The examiner arrived promptly on two separate days and sat in the bedroom with me whilst I wrote both Psychology papers with difficulty, lying on my back feeling hot and uncomfortable in a steel corset. I never expected to achieve high marks under the circumstances. My results made me realise a University degree was within my reach. I enrolled for two more modules, Sociology I and Psychology II, commencing in January 1984, not realising after this year my studies would soon be put on hold...

We left for Mazeppa Bay with me lying on a mattress in the back of the *Microbus*. It was a nightmare journey. I felt every bump in the corrugated, pot-holed gravel road, which in parts was covered in huge rocks dumped by the inefficient Transkei road works in an effort to maintain the roads. It took days to recover from this three-hour journey.

The children went to the beach. Nolyn went fishing. Wearing a steel corset not only protected my spine from harmful movements whilst the bones knitted, but it prevented me from scrambling over rocks, swimming in the waves, snorkelling in rock pools, relaxing in the sun and building sculptures in the sand, all of which I had previously taken for granted. Loneliness hung over me as I remained isolated in our cottage. I watched from a distance.

On the cool front verandah I captured the sweeping view on a small canvas in oils. The distant horizon separated the azure blue sky, dotted with cotton wool clouds, from the turquoise Indian Ocean. The thunderous, towering waves built up before stretching, arching and crashing as white foam against the rocks at the bottom of a grassy slope below our cottage. To the right of the sandy white beach, the white, frothy, foam-edged waves raced towards the shore.

Cattle walked in single file along the water's edge. A swing bridge, supported on each end by two blue steel pillars, connected the mainland to the grassy island, where several pathways marked the trails to popular fishing spots, where fishermen sat in groups with rods held high waiting for fish to bite. Overhead, seagulls squealed. Beaded, blanketed local women returned home carrying bags of mussels balanced on their heads. I lay on the cool grass next to the water tank, resting. Brent is the proud owner of this oil painting, today.

22

MY LIFE CHANGED FOREVER

Thousands were left unemployed when South Africa slumped into the worst economic depression in fifty years. This caused tensions to intensify in black townships throughout 1984. A method of killing, 'the necklace' – a tyre filled with petrol thrown over a victim and set on fire – an ANC trademark was practised in 1985.

AFTER our holiday at Mazeppa Bay I became impatient and isolated. Unable to drive, I had lost my independence. I longed for Nolyn's company, support and encouragement. With the children asleep and oblivious to my feelings, the nights dragged on depressingly. Louisa, a Godsend, watched television with me falling asleep most evenings. Her presence comforted me.

One day Rose Blakeway, immaculately dressed, visited me.

"Hello Denyse. Do you remember me?" she asked in her Irish accent.

"Hello Rose. Yes, I do. Do come in. Thanks for the flowers," I said accepting her posy of pink roses. Little did I know my friendship with Rose would change my life forever.

***

Looking back I realised the Marriage Encounter weekend had not salvaged our marriage. I re-read postcards from Nolyn when Byron was born in Umtata.

Hi Loafer

Hope you're keeping fit and well. How's the new son and the rest of the family? Write sometime. Course is fine – too much work!

Played 12 holes yesterday.
All my love,

Nolyn.

And another he one dated 26 September 1971 was even briefer:

Dear Kid
Just admiring the view and thinking of you.

Love Nolyn

Nothing made sense. He had time for golf even on a training course! Was this a man's world? I pondered the solution when Rose, a regular visitor, smiled her way into our home. When she started on her pet subject, salvation, my hackles rose. I protected my staunch Catholic upbringing but her Irish charm worked on Nolyn. A part of me wanted her inner radiance but a part of me resisted the truth. I could not accept I was a sinner – after all I went to confession. I needed a friend to understand, encourage and advise me. Lately my prayers seemed to be bouncing off the ceiling.

"Nolyn, I know just the person you should visit," Rose said.

"Who?"

"Paul. He's also an insurance broker. You'll get on well with him."

"Sounds good to me," Nolyn replied.

Nolyn attended church with Deon and Sue Stevens who lived over the road from us. He forfeited golf. Two hours after the children and I returned from the Catholic Church, Nolyn came home, as happy as a lark. He said, "Lovely people. I'll go again."

The more he attended this strange church, the deeper I dug my heels in until he asked, "Why don't you join me this Sunday?"

"Hmm... Okay I'll come but just once," I answered, thinking my suspicions would be confirmed. Arriving at this modern building I noticed drivers darting for a parking. Others dashed inside. At the door a couple welcomed us with love and radiant smiles, before we entered into a hall with tiered horse-shoe-shaped seating. A large wooden cross hung on the front wall of a central stage. There were no statues, candles, *Stations of the*

Cross, organ, altar or tabernacle. People chatted, waved and laughed like a family get-together.

"Nolyn, when do we go into the church?"

"*This* is the church."

To add to my confusion musicians played drums, guitars and a piano as the congregation stood and sang at full throttle, *This is the day that the Lord has made...*" They clapped, waved their arms about and some danced. The words were projected on the front wall. There were no hymn books and no Latin recitals. Defying this free worship my body stiffened. I was even more embarrassed when Nolyn joined in. From a podium in the front a man dressed in a suit said, "Please sit down. Let us pray."

His prayer was a reverent conversation expressing his love and gratitude to God as though God stood beside him. An hour-long sermon followed. I was hooked from the start and words from the Bible broke down my barriers. I absorbed every word like a sponge soaking up water. I wondered how he knew me so well. After all everything he said was meant for me personally. As we left Rose greeted us, "It's good to see you. Bill's such a good teacher."

How odd, she called the priest, Bill. Driving home in contented silence, love encompassed us, a love superseding human love. I hungered for more. Rose kept her word. She introduced us to Paul and Mary the next week. We entered a lounge with white furniture and a glass coffee table. Immaculate! It was a little piece of heaven.

"Take a seat," which meant I lay on the sofa. They were easy to talk to. They steered the conversation towards our personal Christian beliefs. In the miracle of the moment, both Nolyn and I were born again. Through the Holy Spirit we understood the words of John 3:3 *'Jesus declared, "I tell you the truth, no one can see the kingdom of God unless he is born again."* and John 3: 16 *'For God so loved the world that he gave his one and only Son that whoever believes in him shall not perish but have eternal life."*

We were children of God. They prayed for us. We cried tears of joy. They gave us each a Bible. That night I had the best night's sleep I had had in years. I woke the next day knowing we had been taken out of darkness into light. We were no longer spiritually blind or deaf. For the first time I understood the Bible, God's written word.

Our lives had changed forever. For a while I attended the Catholic Church with the children on Saturday evenings and joined Nolyn on Sunday mornings. Before long we all attended the Full Gospel Church. Our faith grew through the exemplary teaching of Bill Price. The devil wasted no time in sowing seeds of doubt. An unseen spiritual warfare waged in both our lives.

***

With me engrossed in my studies and Nolyn in his job, we drifted apart. After passing Psychology I, Education I and Sociology I through UNISA I felt fulfilled. Nolyn added a partnership in the Wavecrest Hotel and a Property Investment Company to his ever-expanding business portfolio. Our communication broke down. All it took was one incident to tip the scales...

"We're all going out tonight. Can we come in?" Byron and Arlene Sparg were at the front door and caught me unaware. Nolyn had not told me. I was a mess. I had to transport the boys to and from chess that evening. I made the first wrong decision. "No. I'm not going out," I replied and quite out of character I closed the door on them, knowing what I did was wrong, but not caring.

"Come on Neyse!" Nolyn begged when he arrived. I refused. He left without me. The devil controlled my mind. One bad decision led to another. I telephoned a lawyer in King William's Town blurting out, "Hi Miccie. I want a divorce. I can't live with Nolyn anymore." I could no longer hide Nolyn's infidelity from my teenage children and I felt sinful. I took Miccie's advice and put the furniture into storage.

"It'll only take two months," the lawyer advised.

Our home was dismantled and put into storage by *Stuttaford Van Lines*. It felt all wrong and haunts me to this day. I cried like a baby. My mother could not console me. The children were sad and angry. Nolyn returned from a business trip to an empty home. Bandit, our bull terrier left all alone, greeted him. I was unable to cash a cheque for R1,000. He closed our joint account. We were penniless. Nolyn arranged to meet me at my mother's flat. I was petrified. Would he murder me?

"Neyse why?"

"I've had enough. I can't take anymore."

"Please come back. We can make it. I never wanted a divorce."

"It's too late. I've been hurt too often."

He left without a fight. My decision had terrible consequences. Nolyn retrieved the furniture from storage. Denise Webb, his lover, took my place on a trip he had won through Bowring Barclays. The children battled through year-end examinations. We moved into an unfurnished townhouse in time for Kathy's visit from England. She was shocked to see the predicament we were in. Previously dumped by Ruthven for another woman, Kathy fully understood. She bought my children Christmas presents I could not afford, before she, Adrian and Christine flew back to England.

A month later traffic noise forced a move to Ayre Place. Nolyn kept to himself. We struggled on. Would my prayers be answered in 1985? Forgive me Lord. I prayed, and thank you Lord for making a four-bedroomed house with a pool in Ayre Place available to us. I rented this house in a *cul-de-sac* with the proviso that I furnished it after the pending court case.

In the interim with few clothes and *less* than the basics lent to us, we moved in. Bedding, a kettle, an electric frying pan, four spoons, knives and forks, four plates and four mugs, a broom and dustpan were lent to us. My mother's television in the lounge helped. Somehow we coped. I drove the children to school. I worried. Nolyn threatened to hi-jack the *Microbus*. Each journey was tense. Louisa, my friend and maid, washed the clothes and swept the house. With nothing to dust and nothing to polish, she spurred me on. My days in the pool were interrupted by visiting estate agents.

"Are you moving out?" prospective buyers asked the same question over and over.

"No. We've just moved in," I answered.

They were confused. Louisa and I laughed when they left. I swam and she sat in the sun, watching. "Can you swim Louisa?"

"No, I'm scared of the water. Madam, be careful that engine not catch you in the water," she said laughing. She referred to the *Creepy Crawly*, which the removal firm refused to store. It was invaluable to us, vacuuming the bottom and the sides of the pool daily, until... We arrived home one day and the *Creepy Crawly* had disappeared. Alarm bells rang. How much longer would I keep the *Microbus*? My newly acquired faith and coping mechanisms came to the fore. I mustered indefatigable determination to conquer unimagined challenges.

There are two days when we lived at Ayre Place which stick in my memory. The day Margy invited me to a ladies' prayer meeting. Buried deep were my desperate feelings which wrought unpredictable fractious behaviour in me. My bedraggled appearance, rumpled tracksuit, my hair pulled up in a ponytail and without make-up. I puffed frantically on my cigarette and complained to my sister as we arrived, "I can't understand why I'm *not* allowed to smoke inside this house!"

Margy admonished me, "Shush, Neyse, we're at the door. They'll hear you!"

"See if I care."

Inside a group of ten well-dressed ladies returned my stare as I, smelling like a dirty ashtray and looking completely dishevelled, took in the scene. Everyone had a smiley care-free face enhanced with make-up, wore fashionable clothes, boasted manicured finger nails, flattering hairdos and dripped with expensive perfume.

When curly-haired Sybil, with kind brown eyes, picked up her guitar, the excited chatter died down. She strummed the strings. The group sang, *Oh how happy I am Jesus lives in my heart.* I haphazardly mouthed the words feeling unworthy, unclean and weak. Sung consecutively, these choruses had words, it seemed which spoke *only* to me. We sat down. Latin prayers from my Catholic background were meaningless; *Hail Marys* repeated using rosary beads and specific prayer responses read from a Missal were all I knew. Why, I questioned did *prayer* need an explanation?

The lesson began. I was hooked from the start. I memorised the sequence: P= praise, R= repent, A= ask and Y= thank You. Several women prayed aloud. I listened. The prayers said for Ann, who I had misjudged as *Miss Perfect* and who had terminal cancer, made me cringe ashamedly. Margy took me home.

"Thanks Margy," I said, too proud to tell her how I *really* felt.

This outing was about to transform my life for the better. That night, sitting on my bed, which consisted of two continental pillows on the floor, I puffed on my last cigarette of the day. I thought of the day's events as I smoked it right down to the filter. I stubbed it out in the smelly, butt-filled ashtray on the carpet next to me. I watched the last curl of smoke waft above my head.

I would put the lesson on prayer to the test. This was new to me but I tried, praising God then I repented. "Dear God forgive me for all my failures and my sins. I am wretched. I cannot hide anything from you." I had already decided to ask God to help me quit smoking, which I knew would be *impossible*. After all I had tried *everything* there was to quit smoking. I had even had acupuncture. Nothing had worked. I quit for a while, but once I started again, I smoked more than ever. On bad days, which were frequent, I smoked sixty cigarettes.

With a real *need* to be helped but not yet convinced that my prayer would be answered, I began, "Lord please help me to stop smoking," and instantaneously the words I had sung that morning played in my head. A gentle voice asked me, "How can I live in your heart, Denyse, with your filthy cigarettes?"

"Is that you Lord?"

The longest prayer I had every prayed began in my two-way conversation with God. It was just as if God was in the same room. Well-practised in listing my fears for not breaking this dirty habit, I spat these out convincingly, "But, I'll put on weight; I'll become bad-tempered; I'll have withdrawal symptoms; my cigarettes calm me down in these difficult times." Each time God answered with three words, *"Trust in me."*

Not yet convinced I challenged again, "Lord, how do I know I'm not hallucinating or making all this up? Will *you* give me a sign?"

"My love and my peace, which only I can give, will fill your whole being. Trust in Me," was the reply from God. Without fully understanding what that meant, I ended with, "Thank you Lord," switched off the light and fell into a deep sleep.

Like clockwork each morning I reached out for my cigarettes when I woke. This time I never lit up. Instead, carrying my cigarettes to the kitchen, I switched on the kettle. Ah! I thought, I'll light up with my mug of coffee. Coffee meant I reached for my cigarettes. My hand stopped in mid-air as I heard the sound of heavenly music around me, playing, *Oh how happy I am, Jesus lives in my heart*. I stood glued to the kitchen floor where I felt love and peace filling me up to overflowing. I thought I had been transported into heaven!

I shoved the cigarettes and matches on top of the kitchen cupboard, just in case, and got on with the day. Since Valentine's Day, 14 February 1985, I have never had any desire to smoke, neither have I been tempted to smoke nor have I ever smoked again. That was twenty-seven years ago!

"Mom, how come you're not smoking anymore?" Chandrè said three days later. Friends who knew me as a chain-smoker, passed the same comment. My testimony to a miracle was repeated often to astonished listeners. I emphasised how God had honoured all His promises to me that day. I never gained weight; had no withdrawal symptoms and my bad-temper and frustrations eased. Today I give God all the glory and all the thanks for doing the impossible for me.

I have a vivid memory of the day of the court case. I believed God would undertake for us. The children were at school when Nolyn visited and said, "I won't be in court today. I must warn you, I'll win the case."

"We'll see about that. You and I *have* to appear in court." I answered.

"I won't be in court," he said, smiling as if tasting his victory. This intimidated me. He left. Later, I drove to the courthouse where I was introduced to the barrister representing me. This was a Supreme Court case. I was marched into the courtroom. There was no sign of Nolyn. In hushed silence I took the stand. With my hand resting on the Bible, I swore to tell the truth. I was interrogated and replied truthfully. I returned to my seat. The moment I had long waited for, had arrived. The judge gave his verdict. It was not what I expected. I asked the barrister to repeat the verdict: "The entire household of furniture is to remain with Nolyn Wild..."

My mind leapt into rescue mode. I begged the barrister, "Please ask the judge if we could each have a bed!" My request was granted. I was oblivious to the world around me when I walked to the *Microbus*. I drove to my mother's flat. What would I tell the children? Why had God *not* answered my prayer? How did Nolyn know the outcome before the hearing? My mother, anxious to hear the result, was waiting. Beforehand she had offered to unpack, hang curtains and arrange furniture. I stopped and saw her face at the window. She waved. I waved back.

I hooted three times and drove back to Ayre Place where *Coloured* workmen were painting the television room. I parked and rushed inside. Louisa greeted me. Her cheery smile melted away when she heard the awful news.

"Just a bed each, Louisa."

"I sorry my madam. I make you tea. You not cry. God help us. You see."

I walked into the television room. It smelt of paint. The bare walls were a stark reminder to me of failure. Flinging myself on the floor, I screamed as though I was being murdered. I rolled on the floor, screaming louder and louder, on and on. The neighbours rushed over thinking I had been attacked. I heard them speculating between themselves:

"She's gone mad.

Is this some type of fit?

Don't touch her. She could be dangerous!

She's demon-possessed.

Should I call a doctor or the police?"

Louisa greeted my mother when she arrived and her words, "Just a bed each!" was *all my* mother needed to be told to know what had happened.

"She'll be alright now. I'm her mother," she told the distraught neighbours, who left the room at her request.

"Calm down Denyse. This will get you nowhere!" my mother said.

I sobbed uncontrollably, asking for my GP. He came.

"Please sedate me doctor. I need to sleep this off. You do understand?"

A nod and an injection gave me time before I faced my children. I slept round the clock. I apologised to the neighbours. I told the lessor we would vacate the house at the end of February. With our few clothes the move was easy. We moved back into my mother's flat. I programmed my mind to blot out thoughts of my paintings, sewing machine, books, photo albums and jewellery, to alleviate additional persecution. I put my trust in God. I prayed that He would find us a place to live…

***

Staying in my mother's flat became unbearable. The children and I listed an ideal property to rent – *affordable, in a quiet street with a fenced-off garden for the dogs, a bedroom each for us and rooms for Louisa.* This is what we prayed for day after day.

"I was given the telephone number of someone wanting to rent his house," my mother said returning from bowls. After supper I called the number.

"Hello can I help you?"

"Yes. I heard you'd like to rent your house. Is it still available?"

"Yes, it is."

"What rental were you asking?"

I declined his offer saying, "The rental's too high. If you decide to reduce the monthly rental, please let me know." I left it there...

My mother was more disappointed than I was. Having taken over her flat, her lifestyle was compromised. Brent and I shared the spare room, Chandrè shared my mother's room and Byron slept in the lounge; our clothes hung from the picture rails or were in suitcases under the beds. Homework with three teenagers seated at the dining room table, my mother watching television and me cooking, was bedlam.

The properties we liked were unaffordable and the affordable ones were unsafe. One evening my mother answered the phone saying, "For you Neyse. A man!"

This lessor came back to me with an offer I could now afford.

"Are you still interested?"

"Yes, I'll definitely take it. Go ahead and draw up the Lease Contract."

"But you haven't seen the property yet?"

"I don't need to. I'll take it."

"Fine. Will 5 pm tomorrow suit you? My address is 9 Annandale Road."

"I'll look forward to meeting you tomorrow."

My mother eavesdropped from the lounge, asking, "What was all that about?"

"I've rented a house and we can move in next week."

She was flabbergasted, replying, "You have not *even seen* the house?"

"God has answered our prayers. The house will meet all our needs."

As arranged I drove past the castle to a quiet cul-de-sac and saw the house set back from the road. A driveway, flanked by a rockery on the right and lawns on the left, led to a double garage from where steps led up to the front entrance.

Neil, short and dark-haired, greeted me in his English accent before I followed him into the house. He was easygoing and ticked off the inventory list attached to a clipboard. The house was fully furnished and even had a piano and a television. After signing the relevant documents, he gave me his UK contact telephone number and I left. Joy bubbled out of me. I raced back to tell the children. They were excited to move into a furnished house with a garden.

Once we were settled in this lovely home with panoramic views of the Nahoon River, Louisa reminded me, "You see Louisa tells you God is help us!"

My faith grew. Chandrè, Brent, Byron and I were taken into Stirling Full Gospel Church membership on 1 September. We were given the Bible verse from 1 Corinthians 15, 58: '*Therefore ... Beloved... be steadfast, immovable always abounding in the work of the Lord, knowing that in the Lord your labour is not in vain.*'

I took in a schoolboy, older than my sons, to help a friend. I started a Ladies Prayer Group which Bertha Yazbek, a Catholic friend attended. I was mixed up with weird people posing as Christians, whom I joined for a weekend at Hoggsback, before I wised up.

Best of all, Nolyn returned the windsurfer and paddle-ski. We spent most weekends on the Nahoon River which cost nothing. We relaxed in the sea air. I stood on electric eels, was rescued by a boat when strong winds swept me towards the river mouth almost out to sea. I regained my self-confidence. Bijoux, my miniature poodle, sat between my legs on the paddle-ski, to the delight of passing surfers when I paddled up and down the Nahoon River.

Keeping within my budget was challenging especially when unexpected financial demands were made. I could not deprive a child of a school outing. This meant we often ran out of food. I could improvise for two days with little but it was an impossible task for longer. Already painfully thin, I felt the pangs of hunger. I prayed. My friend Marie arrived with two food parcels, saying. "The Lord laid it on my heart to bring you some food."

On another occasion I was depressed seeing the children walk to school in the pouring rain. No umbrellas and no raincoats! I had no petrol. They had no sandwiches. I knew when they returned home there would be nothing for them to eat. I had one tea bag and some milk, nothing else. Ann, whom I had not seen for a while dropped in for tea. We chatted. She marvelled when she learnt how I had quit smoking. She asked me to pray for her to quit.

"Let's have another cup of tea?" Ann suggested.

She followed me to the kitchen and opened the fridge to fill the milk jug as I filled the kettle. The fridge was empty.

"Denyse, what's going on?"

"We've no money until next week. Extras have crippled my tight budget."

Ann gave me money. She put petrol in the car and bought us groceries saying, "I was paid today. I was meant to visit you. *Now* I know why."

"Thank you Ann. You're a true friend," I said giving her a hug.

"You'd do the same for me, Denyse," she said not expecting any acknowledgement. Her next visit was fraught with adrenalin-pumping activity and amusing consequences.

Through life's ups and downs I learnt to trust God. Words in the Bible leapt off the page at me and added valuable meaning to my life.

With endless visits to Joe Yazbek my lawyer who never accompanied me to Grahamstown, Nolyn and I were divorced on 5 December 1985. I felt bereft. Was this what I wanted? It was too late for regrets. Maybe I had now been sufficiently broken for God to start changing me from the inside…

Part Three

1986 - 2012

IN HIS LOVE

Luke 10:27-28
*He answered: '**Love** the Lord your God with all your heart and with all your soul and with all your strength and with all your mind,' and, '**Love** your neighbour as yourself.'*

George and I are wed at Blaauwklippen 31 May 2008

Left to right: John Larkan and Margy, George and Denyse, Pastor Henry Heyns, Peggy Leary, Topsy and Bill Botha

Below: Chandrè turns 21 with, clockwise, Nolyn, Denyse, Eddie, Margy, Shelley, Joy and Trevor Trussler

Above: Members of the Fish Hoek Friends of Music Society - Chris Pemberton, Unknown, Helen Crida, George Hill, Louise Elliot, Denyse, Pat McCrindle, Chris Schultz, Jill Fitnum. Sitting: Carole Loveday

Left to right: My grandchildren Matthew, Peter, Jordyn, Adrienne, Jaime

Above left to right: Alyson, Jordyn, Anton, Chandrè, Jaime, Adrienne, Brent, Liesel, Peter and Byron meet on the white cliffs of Dover 2003

Below: Christmas at Hordle. Clockwise: Pat, Peter, Alan, Sheena, Jack, Sam, Mark, Margaret, Ellen, Peter Thomson, Linda and George

23

WE NEED A HOME

In 1986 Pass books are done away with. Between 1984 and 1989 a state of emergency was declared in a spiral of revolution and repression. International sanctions increased.

IF ever I needed a miracle in my life it was after my divorce. This had not eased my unhappiness. My hopes were shattered. In ways I could never have imagined, material possessions would again be ours. All we possessed was a cheap, cane lounge suite. Nolyn had access to the children, but I had custody. His life with a live-in girl-friend had changed very little.

The *VW Microbus* became his, despite the fact that I owned a brand new vehicle when we married in 1969. I bought an affordable second-hand *Opel Berlina* from a car dealer, George Heath. Before leaving 9 Annandale Road, I booked a chalet for a fortnight at an Eastern resort, Glen Eden, which overlooked the broad rocky mouth of the Bulura River. This sparse chalet, set amongst fifty others, did not match our cottage at Mazeppa Bay.

My thoughts drifted there. What was happening in *our* cottage? *Who* was with Nolyn? Would *my* linen, crockery, games, books and carefully packed pantry be respected? Before my thoughts ruined me, I focussed on productive plans. We needed a home. I needed a job.

After our holiday at Glen Eden I inspected a house in an unsavoury residential area. "The Quigney's undergoing a facelift. This is the time to buy. Property prices will double in value," the agent assured me. I signed the *Offer to Purchase* document. With no front garden, the house boasted a seaview squashed between towering seafront hotels. The large rooms, with dated wall-paper peeling off the wall, smelt musty.

A young couple rented the outbuilding. "An additional source of income," added the estate agent.

The inevitable happened. I never expected the bank to grant me a mortgage. Overnight I owned a property I did not *particularly* like. I gave notice at 9 Annandale Road and with our few possessions we moved into this *Coronation Street-type* neighbourhood. Women, with curlers in their hair sat on plastic chairs on the *stoep* or pavement puffing on cigarettes and pointing at us. They laughed and shouted to friends on the opposite side of the road. The neighbours sought prime positions to watch us unpack our goods from a hired lorry in the street.

Our hatred for this house grew. Sinking floorboards, cracked walls, rattling windows, dirty carpets and a linoleum-floored cupboard-less kitchen stared back at us mockingly. The smelly toilet and chipped turquoise bathroom suite, long past their sell-by-date, repulsed me.

That evening, overtired and depressed, I responded to a knock at the door with Brent and Byron close at my heels. Two intoxicated unsavoury characters breathed their alcoholic fumes over me. Whilst the bearded bushy-haired man looked on, his short toothless unshaven accomplice spoke, "*Wil die pragtige jong vrou n dop saam met ons drink?* Would the pretty young lady join us for a drink?"

I did not need this. Rudely, I slammed the door in their faces. Brent and Byron secured the house for the night. Exhausted and unhappy we went to bed. We were seated at the breakfast table in the kitchen the following day when I opened the blinds of the kitchen window overlooking our neighbour's back garden. I could not believe my eyes. A man pranced around stark naked in broad daylight. I closed the blinds. My children witnessed the scene. We vented our anger: "This is the worst ramshackle, filthy place I've ever slept in."

"These *dagga*-smoking, *dopping* drunks drive me dippy!"

"Clatter-bang! Rattle-bang-clang!"

The noise had kept me up all night.

We made a unanimous decision to leave this house immediately. Whenever I needed help I went to my mother. But would she take us in *again*? Without a telephone connection, I left the children to wash up the breakfast dishes and drove to mom's flat. She was surprised to see me. "You look terrible my girl. What's wrong?"

"I never slept a wink. All through the night, big vehicles reverberated over steel manhole covers in the road. Two drunks asked me to join them for a *dop*. Today we saw a naked man prancing about in the garden. I can't possibly let the children return to this neighbourhood after school when I start work." Unburdening myself had made me feel better and so, I continued, "When my maid, Louisa came in, she said, 'Madam, the people at the back, they smoking *dagga*.'"

"You poor girl," my mother was shocked to hear of our ordeal. But I had not yet finished. Without stopping I blurted out what I had wanted to say, but had been unable to verbalise, until then. "I *hate* that house. I wish I'd *never* bought it. I *hate* the Quigney. I'm scared and depressed. I'll put it back on the market on Monday. We just *cannot* live there."

So much hatred spilled out followed by an outburst of tears which gave tremendous relief. I had *finally* let go. Hugging me, my mother asked, "Would you like to come back here Neyse?"

"Yes, please mom."

I hurried back to tell the children who were exceedingly happy to be leaving. Again the entire neighbourhood took up prime positions as we moved out. This took several trips backwards and forwards with our clothes piled high in the car.

From then on we pronounced the Quigney, *Quinn-nay,* a posh derivation. Louisa and my two dogs, Pepe and Emmy, lived in this house safeguarding our cane lounge suite and four beds from uninvited guests. The next hurdle was to secure a job.

After an interview with Ted Walsh, the Director of the Greater East London Publicity Association (GELPA), I was appointed Personal Assistant and tour guide and given a uniform. The next week I started work for GELPA at the Town Hall, Oxford Street. My next challenge was to find somewhere more *permanent* for us to live...

***

Without furnishings to hide the mess and with very little money to spare, we worked every Saturday pulling off wallpaper, filling cracks and holes in the wall before painting the walls cream. The house was scrubbed. The carpets were cleaned professionally. The *For Sale* sign went up and I wondered how long I would have to run between two properties.

I bought provisions, cooked, and transferred clean and dirty washing from the flat to the Quigney. Louisa ironed and walked the dogs. We chatted about the day's events and how she brushed off prowlers, saying, "Master not want you come here!"

My dogs hated the separation but dogs were not allowed in the block of flats. Their barking alerted Louisa to lurking vandals adept at ransacking unoccupied properties. As a single mother, working all day, living in a cramped flat and renovating an unwanted property, I was amazed I had time for suitors.

The first, George Heath, caught me on the rebound of a disastrous divorce. This was short-lived. I was vulnerable. He found me attractive and different. His visits to Glen Eden gave me adult company. Well-built, kind, but unintelligent, this Christian man filled a gap. Our friendship moved too fast. He spent too much time at 9 Annandale Road. His company gave my self-confidence a boost, until…

George, the children and I were seated in the lounge after attending a Sunday evening church service when there was a knock at the door. A plump angry-looking woman towered above me, shouting, "I want to speak my fiancé, George." It was as if a bucket of cold water had been thrown at me. As I dashed inside I heard loud crashes.

George appeared and shouted at his fiancée, "Stop breaking the pot plants. Please!"

George apologised and left. We looked at the damage; six enormous pots of flowering geraniums lay in smithereens. The children's comments added to my unhappiness:

"Did you know he was engaged, mom?"

"Common woman!"

"Make them pay for the damages!"

He returned for his belongings – and that was the end of George!

After this Ben Trevelyn, employed by *Mercedes Benz* in East London, bought my house in the Quigney. Caught again by a feeling of indebtedness to him, a whirlwind romance began. An evening of dining and dancing at *Move-n-Pick* restaurant followed an invitation to his shack at Hamburg on the coast. This proved an eye-opener to me; he and his friends were not my type. Another friendship ended.

Next I bought a house at 17 Balfour Road in Vincent. I met an intelligent, kind tall man, Dick Arnold. I regained my self-worth. He never criticised or ridiculed me. He was divorced with no children. He got on well with the boys and Chandrè. Talented at woodwork he made me a *Stinkwood* bowl with a lid, which I still treasure today.

***

What a year it had been. On the 4 April 1986 Aunty Buzzy died from cancer. Before this Aunty Joan her eldest sister had died. My mother had lost her mother, her husband and her sisters. With so many deaths taking place and the muddle of my life, my little world seemed to be collapsing around me. How fragile life was.

***

We were settled in a three-bedroomed house in Vincent. This modest house was home. Although sparsely furnished, Louisa and our beloved pets were with us. Our fragmented family tried to normalise. Walking away from marriage was never easy...

My lawyer phoned me one day, saying, "Denyse, please call to see me. I've some good news for you."

Good news was scarce. During my lunch break I called to see my lawyer who said, "I've got a cheque for you – just over R6,000. Spend it immediately; otherwise Nolyn will claim the money."

"R6,000! A windfall! We need so much," I said examining the cheque.

The children were thrilled. Armed with our priority list, we bought a *Sony* television, a fridge, lounge suite, second-hand dining room suite and a glass-top electric stove the very next day. We stacked the plastic garden table and six chairs in the car and at home, put them in the lounge. We felt like kings. Not surprisingly Nolyn phoned me on Monday.

"I heard you've been paid R6,000. Where's the money?"

"We spent it!"

"That's *my* money. You couldn't have spent it so soon."

"As I said, we've spent it."

The silence was deafening and I asked, "Are you still there?"

"I've got to go now. Bye." The phone went dead.

This was not the end of it. Arriving back from work, I noticed

Nolyn's *Range Rover* parked outside our house. Approaching the front door, I overheard Brent say, "It's true dad. We're all so excited. Tomorrow our goods will be delivered."

Nolyn saw how happy the children were to have plastic garden furniture in the lounge and how they longed to set up the television. After this he returned their games, books and toys and two of my paintings. He invited the children to a *braai*. Being alone was hard. Harder still was accepting that my children were with his girl-friend and her four-year-old son. Denise, a tall and thin woman with waist-length brown hair, an ex-Zimbabwean, worked at the United Building Society. She went to Mauritius with Nolyn – a prize he won through his job.

Where I worked in the City Hall meant bumping into her often in Oxford Street. I held fast to the Bible verse, *Greater is He that is within me than he that is in the world.* With Jesus in my life, I learnt to overcome bitterness and hatred.

I got on well with my boss, Ted Walsh. My job included taking minutes at the GELPA meetings; transcribing shorthand notes; using an electric typewriter with a corrective ribbon; duplicating on the photo-copier; using the telex machine; transferring incoming calls from the switchboard to various offices and dealing with telephonic queries.

As a tour guide on regular Pineapple Tours I spoke over a microphone on the bus telling visitors, "Oxford Street is lined with elegant church spires; the museum, has the world-renowned prehistoric coelacanth and an egg of the extinct dodo; the Queen's Park is a 34 hectare botanical garden; the zoo has 150 different bird species." And crossing the river I continued, "This double-decker bridge, road and rail, crosses the Buffalo River with a view of the dolos-protected sand-dredged harbour, the only river port in SA with a huge grain elevator which can load 1600 tons per hour."

After a tour on the pineapple farm we returned via the Buffalo Pass, and I announced "This steep-sided heavily wooded area known as the *Umtiza* Forest, protects a rich wildlife – forest weavers and crowned eagles, blue *duikers*, bushbuck, blue samango and vervet monkeys. The *Umtiza listerana,* Buffalo thorn is endemic to this area."

After *Buck's Fizz* at the Ann Bryant Art Gallery, we returned to the City Hall. My job revived my self-confidence. It was easier to be alone when the children visited Nolyn, but when they spent a weekend away at Mazeppa Bay, I was devastated. Sometimes it was difficult not to badmouth Nolyn in front of my children.

Nolyn phoned like clockwork, every Monday evening. Our shared parental role was stressful. We lived frugally but Nolyn lavished luxuries on the children which I could not afford. My treat for them was a soft-serve at Marina Glen on Sunday. We licked our ice-creams listening to fluorescent-glinting waves rumble shorewards.

Nolyn never experienced *our* lifestyle. Chandrè, Brent and Byron, once accustomed to luxuries and a good life, were now deprived of the bare necessities. Often we struggled to survive. I understood hunger pangs as did my boys forfeiting lunch often. They shared a small bedroom. Chandrè sewed her own clothes on my *Singer* sewing machine a far cry from the fashionable clothes and accessories once bought in exclusive shops. We had both completed a *Grooming and Modelling Course* with Dee Vogel and were fashion conscious.

My children had no pocket money and never asked me for anything. We got by with little. The pleasure in buying a red broom, a dustpan, a bucket and a mop with my first salary cheque, was indescribable! Material possessions took on a whole new meaning.

Nolyn and I had been through rough times. Young and in love, we had laughed at the same daft situation. I believed we were meant for each other. How had it all gone so horribly wrong? Sharing the children took courage. I hoped, although separated, Nolyn and I would always love our children. No amount of money could ever replace this love...

***

My mother made my daughter's Matric Farewell Dress and Brendan's matching cummerbund. They made a very handsome couple. Chandrè, an academic achiever, was accepted to study law at the University of Port Elizabeth (UPE). Would her friendship with Brendan survive the separation? Another frugal Christmas followed but the children found student jobs earning much needed pocket money. East London bulged with holiday-makers from the Transvaal, nicknamed *Vaalies,* derived from Transvaal or "*Kyk daar!* Look there!" as they repeated pointing fingers at interesting things.

Taking Chandrè to this predominately Afrikaans-speaking university and settling her in was hard. She shared with Carla. Would she withstand peer pressure? When would we laugh together again? Would her faith endure?

"I'll write often and phone you," I promised. Trying to conceal my tears, I drove away with a hollow feeling. I sang to taped music which softened the pain of separation, but it was a long three-hour journey home on my own.

Michelle Webber, who lived with her grandparents in Balfour Road, continued to get a lift to school and church with us. She flirted with Brent and Byron. They shied away from her. She had a mother-figure need which I tried to meet. She called me 'mom'. Due to her mother's immaturity, Michelle had had to play mother to her siblings.

I visited Chandrè in Port Elizabeth after my car had been serviced. Suzie, a friend, came with me. The car overheated and the engine ceased near Peddie which spelt danger for two women alone. I flagged down a car. Harry the white driver, said, "I hope there'll be something left of your car Denyse," loading our luggage into his boot. "They'll even strip the wheels." Harry's words added to my misery but we were safe. He stopped in Grahamstown and made arrangements for my car to be towed away. In Port Elizabeth things got worse...

My precious daughter, who meant the world to me, had been led astray by her friends. I caught a bus back on Monday and arrived late for work and utterly shattered. My easygoing boss was annoyed. The garage in Grahamstown reported a loose radiator cap had caused the water to leak from the radiator and burn out the engine.

Waiting for a re-conditioned engine, Nolyn lent me his *Mercedes*. Anxious to bring Chandrè home, Brent and I drove to PE. Byron remained home alone. At 8.30 pm with Chandrè and her two rowdy friends we made the same journey home. I fell asleep at the wheel. Brent grabbed the steering wheel, jerking the car back onto the road. He prevented us from plummeting down a steep gorge. Chandrè drove and made me nervous. From Port Alfred I took over and we finally arrived home. That night I thanked God for sparing our lives.

Chandrè wrote: I'm coming home for the summer holidays, making me happy. She had gained weight. I booked a slimming treatment and aerobics classes for her. My letter dated 17.11.1987 lay on her pillow:

It is wonderful to have you home again with us... You have been missed in our home. We love you so much. We can share our love with you now for 2 months. That's wonderful. I hope you will relax and get strong in every way.

Welcome... We love having you here with us. We shall enjoy every minute of the holidays being with you. God bless you today and each day.

With our love, Dad and mom, Brent and Byron.

Love, I knew, was the core ingredient to binding families together and we needed a double dose right now...

***

With few possessions and unable to afford curtains for privacy, I wanted more than anything to make 17 Balfour Road a proper home for us. My friend, Ann, who once gave us petrol and food when we were starving at 9 Annandale Road, came up with a suggestion I could not refuse...

One Saturday afternoon when the children were out with friends, Ann and I drove to 9 Reynolds View, the six-bedroomed home we vacated in 1985 and where Nolyn lived with *all* our furniture. (He had legally had the furniture returned to 9 Reynold's View from storage.) This was the first time I had returned since taking my lawyer's rotten advice, "Put your furniture into storage and sue for a divorce."

Ann drove down the steep driveway and into the garage. With the car hidden from view inside the garage, we tiptoed to the side door... Nolyn was at Mazeppa Bay over the weekend, but were his friends inside?

When I opened the door from the garage leading to a courtyard, Bandit, our Staffordshire terrier bounded over me. He slobbered a warm welcome as I patted him fondly making me feel guilty. Did he think I was returning? Was he being looked after properly? Nolyn loved Bandit, but who fed and cared for him when he was away on business trips and weekends at Mazeppa Bay?

I tried the door to what was once *my* study. It opened. We entered the house stealthily. What I beheld no longer resembled *my* home – the disarray of furniture, paintings and cluttered ornaments. Nothing was remotely like it used to be. A shambles! My precious antiques, Persian rugs and collectables so garishly arranged. I agonised realising some strange woman now abused *my* valuable possessions.

Ann brought me out of my reverie whispering, "What do you want? Hurry Denyse. We can't afford to be in the house for long."

What shall I take? I saw and grabbed my three embroidered pink cushions, my *Paul Kruger* brass moneybox and my *Kenwood Chef* from the kitchen. This was dear to me, bought with my inheritance money from my grandmother. I grabbed the silver biscuit barrel which granny had given me before she died.

"No," Ann said, "it's impossible to take the bookshelf and encyclopaedias. I've found a cutlery set though."

I wanted my paintings but they were too big. We gathered a few practical kitchen items, my two brass candelabras and a *riempie* stool. The boot was full.

"Let's go," Ann said perspiring with fear.

Bandit's eyes gazed into mine pleadingly as I patted his head lovingly and promised, "Goodbye old chap. Be good Bandit. I'll be back..."

Before Ann hid this hoard in her house, she reminded me. "Remember you only took what was yours!" She would return the goods to me when it was safe to do so. This was to be *our* secret. I was home before the children returned.

As I surveyed my sparse surroundings, I felt the love, almost tangible, around me; the scent wafting from a vase of flowers in the hallway; a handmade *Thank You* card stuck on the fridge door; our freshly ironed laundry on the clothes horse bathed in the afternoon sun and Pepe and Emmy wagging their tails, waiting to be fed. Try as I did to push the present shambolic scene of my former home from my mind, it haunted me for days. Did Bandit feel the way I did? Deserted and unloved.

It was ten days before Nolyn noticed anything was missing. He telephoned me at work and snapped, "Where are *my* pink cushions? I know *you* took them."

"What are you talking about? *Me* taking *your* cushions!" I retorted. His accusation was partially correct. I had taken the cushions which were *mine,* not *his.*

"I'm coming to fetch *everything* you took."

"You're welcome. Goodbye Nolyn."

I chortled to myself realising I had the victory for once, as small as it was...

As anticipated, Nolyn was already questioning the children, when I got home. Brent said, "Dad, mom *never* took your things. They're not here,"

When I came in, I was met with, "Hello, I *know* it was *you!*"

"Hello," is all I offered ignoring his further allegations.

Nolyn left confused. I, in turn, would have to wait a very long time before my few treasures could come out of hiding, but, I was prepared to hang on...In the humdrum of daily life I forgot the secret Ann and I kept.

Ruth, my mother-in-law now living in East London alone after her mother had died, soon put me to the test. She needed a friend and relied on me to buy her cigarettes, medication and toiletries. She moved into a boarding house and coerced Brent and Byron into hanging up the pictures of her three guides, an Irish nun, an American Indian and a Scotsman. My sons muttered to themselves as they unsuccessfully attempted to drive the nails into the wall. This was a relief to us because evil emanated from those pictures.

Ruth joined us for tea most Saturday afternoons. On one occasion several Christian friends visited. She detested their uplifting conversation and joy. Her sulky mood turned to anger. Interrupting the chatter she demanded, "Denyse I want you to take me home *now*!"

"But I'm about to pour the tea for everyone *now*, mom."

With no concern for anybody but herself, she blurted, "I *must* go now." Her face was red. Her blood pressure rose. To avoid an outburst of unrestrained fury, I said, "Okay, mom. I'm sure my friends will excuse me. Let's go."

What followed next shocked me... I opened the front door for my mother-in-law. She walked to my car. I called to my friends, "I won't be long," and closed the door. My neighbour's friendly black cat usually brushed up against my legs and purred when I passed by. The cat slunk towards me. It stopped. Cruel, threatening dark eyes glared at me...

This once-friendly feline had transformed into an aggressive predator and sprang at me, clawing a front paw deep into my arm. In self-defence, I turned my face away as the second front paw swiped my face but missed, drawing blood from my neck. I pulled the cat off me and dumped it on the grass. My mother-in-law sneered from the car.

"I won't be a minute," I called to her before disappearing into the house with blood streaming down my neck and arm.

"What's happened mom? You 're bleeding," Brent asked when I bumped into him on the way to the kitchen.

"The cat! Grab the first aid box from the bathroom please."

"What cat?" he asked in disbelief.

I told Brent what had happened as he helped me clean the deep scratches on my neck and arm. He applied *Germolene* before covering the wounds with gauze and strips of *Elastoplast*. "Thanks, Brent. That'll do for now."

Try as I did to be cheerful whilst I drove my mother-in-law to the boarding house, she ignored my wounds, muttering and moaning, "Terrible friends... All that religious chatter... Every second word Daphne said was Je... I feel ill."

She could not say the word, 'Jesus'. I ignored her hurtful, derogatory words spoken with derision. I knew it would not be long before she whinged on the phone to me about how badly off she was. We struggled financially but I gave her whatever she asked me for.

"I feel ill," she repeated rushing in without even a thank you and I quickly drove off. I was pleased to be back with my friends in a relaxed happy atmosphere. These friends, encouraging and loving me through thick and thin, were my lifeline. Much later Trevor Goddard, a wonderful Christian friend and one-time Springbok cricketer, told me, "Your mother-in-law, steeped in spiritualism, empowered the cat to harm you through her satanic power. Pray the blood of Jesus over yourselves and your home and you'll come to no harm."

His advice worked and Ruth never harmed me or my children again. With each passing day her anger and frustration festered but my faith and trust in God flourished.

24

TEACH ME TO LOVE

Apartheid's grip on South Africa began to give way. F W de Klerk replaced P W Botha as president in 1989. On 5 July 1989 a meeting between P W Botha and Nelson Mandela took place in the basement garage of Tuynhuys, a Cape Dutch mansion in Cape Town.

WAS our love reaching Nolyn? Did he *need* our love in his life? Who knew what the year ahead would bring? Hoping to re-kindle our love I wrote:

> *Another Christmas, another year gone by, another year of division! Wishing you a blessed Christmas, full of joy and peace and love...You are part of us and we are part of you...the joy, peace and love cannot be full when one-fifth is separated from four-fifths. Divorce robs children of joy, steals what is rightfully theirs, a loving father and mother; kills motivation and self-ego; destroys security and financial stability.*
>
> *Love is the greatest ingredient to overcome all transgressions. I will love each one of them forever with all my love. I will do for them as much as I can. I will never put people or events before them but stand true to my word as they are swallowed up in love, saturated, so they can love again... each one has a problem here. We never set an example for them.*
>
> *May you feel love, sincere and from the heart, as you read this note; may you open your heart to receive our love, which does not come in fancy wrapping-paper; may you soak up our love which has no price-tag and cannot be valued in Rands.*
>
> *Our love flows to you freely, fully, faithfully and binds us*

together as one. Our love is all we have to give you, if only you would open your heart and accept our love. We always keep giving you our love. When will you give us yours? We give all our love to you over Christmas Nolyn and more of our love to you each and every day of 1988. We believe you do love us. We love you more and God loves, all of us, the most.

Neyse, Chandrè, Brent and Byron.

Many unanswered questions dangled in the air, but rather than make New Year resolutions I reflected on changes which had affected my life and Nolyn's. During our sixteen-year marriage, rejection had plagued me. Who had Nolyn ditched me for? Was he safe on the Transkei and Ciskei roads, where cattle, horses, goats and sheep roamed freely on the *highways*? How much longer would I have to struggle to win back his love?

With many odds against us, Nolyn and I had achieved our rags-to-riches dream. Yet, at the pinnacle of success, our love had died. Swamped in our greed, we wrangled over money and possessions, as couples do. I hated myself when I retaliated like a lunatic, becoming a person I barely recognised.

Why did I still love Nolyn? Was reconciliation a pipedream? Deep down I resented the women who had hurt me and made a mockery of *our* marriage. When I was his wife, I lived a double life. I supported and smiled at his side on social occasions, but at home I cried and fought for his love. I reminded myself I was the woman who belonged to Nolyn. I learnt to live helped on with the words...

Teach me to love
Oh Lord, so often as I go I blunder unthinkingly,
Into the chilling thought that shrivels dawning joy
As frost will blacken tiny tender buds
Or just the slightest careless touch
Will mar the feathered wings of gorgeous butterflies.
Teach me to love
That little children's eyes may light
With confidence and joy when they meet mine.

Teach me to love
That neither look nor act nor attitude of mine,
May take from those I meet
One single bit of peace, one particle of joy.
Teach me to be so radiant with love
That I may pass in safety to and fro
Nor leave one wistful thought in hearts I leave behind.
Teach me to love
That saddened eyes may smile,
That weary backs may straighten from the touch of sympathy,
And so dear Lord, that I may be a blessing whereso'er I go –
Nor hinder any slightest thought from finding Thee.
Teach me to love.

(Source unknown)

In 1988 my hopes were raised. My sons said, "Denise has left dad!"

"Maybe you'll get back together now?"

Nolyn's ego was damaged. I saw his deep hurt. He never expected a second woman to walk out on him! He came back into my life, popping in to chat and staying for supper. We dined out, watched videos or had a *braai* at his home. We shared old friends. These together times were special, but could I trust him again? Could we love each other unconditionally? Could life ever be what it had once been? One thing was certain I never wanted to be hurt so badly again. I asked God for wisdom.

***

Nolyn offered the cottage to me for two weeks in June. He was softening. My friend Dick joined us and Chandrè invited her new boyfriend, Anton. On this holiday it bothered me that Chandrè and Anton remained at the cottage. Discovering Chandrè was taking the pill, I challenged her. "You don't need this? What are you taking these for?"

Justifiably my daughter was angry. I had invaded her privacy. She never upheld her Christian principles and this made me furious. A row ensued.

"Let's go, Chandrè," Anton said pulling her into the bedroom and closing the door. That did it. I wanted the best for her. I exploded. My words of wrath caused irreversible damage. I watched them as they walked out carrying their bags. Rushing back to the beach I poured my heart out to Dick.

"There's nothing you can do. They'll come back!"

"I'm so upset. She's my daughter."

I waited. They never came back. I walked to the Mazeppa Bay Hotel and saw them sitting on their luggage on the kerb of the dusty road. Chandrè lifted a beer can to her mouth and flicked ash off a cigarette in her other hand. Anton thumbed a lift at a passing car. This was not my daughter. I caved in with sadness...

"Please come back," I begged, "We can talk."

They ignored me. I left, not knowing what would happen next. The pain I felt that day was to last a long time. Chandrè and Anton hitched a lift to Gonubie. Nolyn took them in. From that day Chandrè ignored me completely. My letters were not acknowledged. When I phoned I was told she had moved out. Where was she? She came to East London but never visited me. When would I see my daughter again? I ripped open a letter dated 17 July 1988 from Dick hoping he had news of her.

9 Shabani Road, Kragga Kamma, Port Elizabeth.

Dear Denyse

Sorry that the first letter got lost. I still don't know the correct address. I think it is Avalon Road but I do not know the road number. Thank you very much for sending my leather jacket down to P.E. I don't often wear it and I had completely forgotten about it.

I really enjoyed Mazeppa Bay very much. It was the only part of my holiday that was really relaxing. It was just far too short. One of the tricks I learned there was to use a combination of ordinary tea and Rooibos tea. I am really enjoying it. I made it in the teapot you bought me. When I spoke to you a few hours ago, the clouds were coming up from the west.

Now it is pouring. We have had almost continuous rain since I returned from East London.

I made you something for your new home, but I was not satisfied with it, so I have not sent it. The main problem is finding a decent piece of timber to start with. I refuse to work with pine. Next time I am in Knysna I will try to get hold of some decent wood, Stinkwood or Yellowwood. I am rapidly learning how to use my computer. I have a choice of 16 different type styles. This one is called 'Courier'. This is typed using a word processing package. The big advantage is that it is not necessary to keep copies of any important documents. They just get stored on a floppy. Enjoy your week.

Lots of love, Dick (Arnold)

***

Through the church, I joined a tour to Israel. My mother came too. Touring the Holy Land for ten days increased my faith. I had walked in the land where Jesus was born, died on a cross and rose again, to redeem Jew and Gentile alike.

Brent and Byron, in their final school year, had coped in the townhouse without me, but when I returned dirty dishes were piled high in the kitchen sink!

In December Chandrè and Anton worked at the Wavecrest Hotel, a business Nolyn had bought on the Wild Coast. She was living with Anton. I longed to hear her voice again. I yearned for her company. I ached to have her back. How long would I have to wait?

If ever there was a time in my life that I needed to feel loved, it was in 1988. *Teach me to Love,* helped me love Nolyn in a way I had never loved him before. My roller-coaster ride through life plummeted to an all-time low. I missed Dick a friend I confided in.

In June Chandrè vanished into a void, coming to East London and never even contacting me. I hoped I would bump into her. I never did. What had happened to my fun-loving, caring and considerate daughter? Overnight she had changed into a contemptuous, detached and insensitive young woman. She smoked cigarettes and drank beer. Despite this I loved her deeply and longed to have her back.

Just when I thought things could not get any worse, Nolyn met flamboyant Sharlene. Not only was she six years older than Chandrè, but she had a young daughter. Was he seriously thinking of marrying her? Was my last flicker of hope finally about to be extinguished? Would this, like the rest of his romances, fizzle out? I grappled at straws, being the ever-hopeful optimist.

One day a phone call from a woman, who sounded like a common hussy said, "Hi Denyse. This is Sharlene. Nolyn asked me to phone you."

I listened. Bewildered, I answered politely, "Hi Sharlene."

"Could you come round to the house and pick out some of *your* things? Nolyn says he'll decide what you can take. We're getting married in November and I need to make space for *my* things."

A deathly silence ensued before she asked, indignantly, "Are you still there?"

"Yes."

"When can you come over?"

I could hardly take it all in. Taking a deep breath, I replied, "Give Nolyn a message from me. If that's his intention, tell him I'll arrange for a pantechnicon to fetch everything. He knows only too well that when we got married, he had nothing. *Everything* in that house is mine. There's no need for *me* to choose. Goodbye."

Shaking with rage, I slammed the phone down and tried to compose myself. What a nerve Nolyn had, humiliating me through his young floozy. He knew we were struggling yet this trollop had the audacity to complain to me she had insufficient space for her things. If only he was giving me something with love, I would have been grateful. Life at times, I *thought*, could be so unfair, especially as this shocking situation started to unfold.

Nolyn sided with Sharlene. The day he fetched Brent and Byron for a *braai*, he told me categorically, "You'll never change! You were so rude to Sharlene!"

"I told her the truth, that's all!"

From that moment a bigger wedge drove us further apart. I felt sorry for our sons. They had to accept a new stepmother, yet remain faithful to their dad, and to me. I know how much they loved and admired Nolyn. Clinging to the words in *Teach me to love* I overcame the temptation to destroy their love for Nolyn. When they returned, their mixed emotions spilled out.

"Mom, Sharlene's only twenty-seven."

"She's got a daughter of four."

"Dad's bought the Gonubie Bottle Store with his cousin, Alf Wild."

"She smokes and drinks and... "

"Dad's invited us to their wedding. They're getting married in November!"

"It's bang in the middle of our Matric Exams!"

My sons' revelations deflated me.

"Surely you could wait until December and consider the children for once in your life?" I confronted Nolyn over the phone to change his wedding plans. He refused with an accusation, "Stop always telling me what to do!"

That awful day dawned. I drove Brent and Byron to 20 Tidewaters in Gonubie. We arrived as a taxi dropped off Chandrè and Anton at the big gates. My heart ached. My daughter looked elegant in a two-piece suit, high heels, carrying a wedding present under her arm. I wanted to chase after her, but she had slipped through the gates without even looking my way. I knew she had seen us arrive. The pain went deep. "Will you be okay?" Byron asked as I gazed at the two figures disappearing out of sight. I had not seen or spoken to her for six months. Today she had deliberately snubbed me, when I needed her so much.

"I'll be fine," I promised. "See you later. Goodbye Brent and Byron."

I started the car with hot tears streaming down my cheeks. The reality hit me. Nolyn was marrying Sharlene. He had finally rejected me. Arriving back at our tiny townhouse in Beacon Bay, I dreaded the next few hours on my own.

I flopped into an armchair and immediately, Je t'aime, my black miniature French poodle, jumped onto my lap. Emmy sat curled up at my feet. Sharing my grief, they nuzzled closer to me, whimpering as I continued to sob uncontrollably. Then the doorbell rang. Red-eyed, I opened it and Carol, my friend put her arms around me and said, "I've come to keep you company. You couldn't be on your own with the wedding going on."

I felt her genuine concern. Carol, a blonde divorcee, who had experienced the same pain in her life, put the kettle on. She tried to cheer me up, "You'll get over it."

"But, Carol I believed God would change Nolyn and restore our marriage."

"Those were your plans, but maybe that's not what God planned for you."

"Do you think they'll be happy?"

Carol's thought-provoking question, "Perhaps, but will it last?" made me think.

"Only time will tell..." I decided.

My mind warred with thoughts of, *"She stole Nolyn from me."* Carol left when Brent and Byron arrived, moody and unhappy. They stalked off to their rooms, where Byron buried his head in his books and Brent lay on his bed, his eyes closed, with pain etched on his face. My heart went out to my sons when they unburdened. Telling me about this awful black wedding which came at a most inappropriate time, they commented:

"It was evil. She's a witch. She wore black.

Everything at the wedding reception was black and gold.

Dad's mother caused a scene at the reception. Chandrè and Anton were there."

This wedding was the talk of the town. Wherever I went, tongues wagged about the evil black wedding. They claimed Sharlene was a witch. I felt wounded. Marriage had been wickedly misconstrued. Would Brent and Byron cope in their final exams? Could they empty their minds of all this malevolence? Would they still hold their dad in high esteem? The more I thought of Nolyn and Sharlene, Chandrè and Anton, the more I realised how I needed to love them. By forgiving them and asking God to forgive me, only then would our love for each other be restored.

Strangely, soon after his wedding, Nolyn invited us to Mazeppa Bay. Doubtful of how I would be received, we arrived. Nolyn welcomed us. Underneath his smile he could not conceal his hidden love. We offloaded the luggage together packing the perishables in the deepfreeze and fridge.

Slipping into beachwear, we walked down the narrow path in single file. We were a family again. Clambering over rocks we reached the wooden stairs where two blue pillars marked the entrance to the swing-bridge. Walking gingerly along the swaying bridge with our footsteps in unison, we clung to the handrails as the sea swirled below us. I had walked on this treacherous bridge many times before. Fear gripped me when I remembered how I had carried my beloved poodle, Pepe under my arm using one hand on the handrail.

Brent and Byron raced across slippery black rocks heading for a gully. Nolyn and I reached them. Sharing a smooth sun-baked rock with the familiar seaweed smells around us, we watched our care-free sons hurl pebbles into the sea. The sun beat down on our heads. I tasted salt from the spray as waves crashed against the rocks close by, cooling the hot African sun on our fair skin.

"It's funny to see you at Mazeppa again," Nolyn said. I remembered his words to the letter. I felt he was looking at me differently. Had he noticed I had changed? Physically I was now very thin, but the most noticeable changes were on the inside. God had removed my temper, anger, jealousy, impatience and foul language. Family relationships were important. I savoured this God-given time with Nolyn, wanting it to last forever.

"Thanks Nolyn. It means so much to me. They've missed these holidays!"

We said very little, but in the fresh air, under the blue skies and listening to the roar of the sea, we drew very close. Before this bliss ended, the fun-and-games began. Nolyn splashed water over me. Our boys joined in. Cooler but saltier, we returned to the cottage where another surprise awaited us. He brought out a tray of freshly picked oysters with accompanying *Tobasco* sauce and a second tray of mouth-watering mussels, my favourite. What a feast! We tucked in, disposing the shells into a strategically-placed plastic bucket.

"Beer shandy Neyse?"

"Yes, please."

"Beer, Brent and Byron?"

Enjoying his sense of humour they settled for a beer shandy. Barefooted and in bathing costumes, I sipped my shandy and was mesmerised by the view from our verandah. In front of my eyes, the picture I had captured on canvas after my spinal fusion, spilled out in breath-taking beauty. Sharlene arrived disrupting our togetherness with, "Hi everyone."

Her plump five-year old daughter retreated hastily. Displaying her tanned body, she brazenly sized me up and down. I returned her scrutiny. Her long light brown hair hung below her shoulders and her thick waist separated a tight-fitting tiny bikini. She put her arms around Nolyn drawing him closer. They held their embrace. She put her lips on his. I turned away. "Excuse me a minute," Nolyn said, following Sharlene inside. After a brief disagreement, she drove off in his *Mercedes*. Unperturbed Nolyn returned and took Brent and Byron with him to check if they understood how to lock up the cottage; how to disconnect the gas cylinders and how to pump water into the butt on the roof for the shower.

When they returned we said nothing, but warmed to each other. To ease his imminent parting, I said, "You're not leaving now?"

"I'm afraid it's time for me to go."

How often in the past I had heard those same words and had grown immune to the sadness of parting. This was different. His face portrayed *'I wish I could stay'*. We said goodbye and waved as his *Range Rover* disappeared in a trail of dust, leaving an uncanny emptiness behind. We had a wonderful holiday. Was there a part of me missing? Did Nolyn feel the same? Was it that Nolyn was not there, or maybe he was?

The news that Sharlene had left for South West Africa came as no surprise. By the end of January their divorce was final. Was this our time of reconciliation?

"Dad's hurting," my sons said. He felt the pain I had felt after our divorce. I knew since our divorce, neither of us had been happy. I scrutinised each word in Nolyn's letter. Was I too optimistic?

22 February 1988   5 pm

Dear Neyse,

Thank you for the letter – always nice getting letters.

I'm glad you enjoyed Mazeppa with the children – strange seeing you there again after all these years!!! Yes, I miss my family missed – growing up with them – something I've lost forever!! I often wonder what it would be like to be with you again whether we would just live together – maybe that is the problem and I wouldn't be able to settle down again? I got the PE garage to start on Chandrè's car after a lot of arguing. Hope they don't rip me off. Well, maybe the prodigal son will return one day. Who knows?

Love Nolyn.

He expressed emotion, joy and sadness. His doubts worried me. Was he the one making the unfair rules if they implied, *I must have freedom to do exactly as I please, no matter how it hurts or humiliates you?* Is this what he expected of me?

***

After selling 17 Balfour Road I rented a small townhouse, 16E Shamrock Sands, Beacon Bay, in a safe security complex. With two bedrooms and a bathroom upstairs, an open-plan living space and a third bedroom downstairs, it was affordable, light and airy. Byron won a bursary to study Computer Science at the University of Cape Town. Brent embarked on a business course at the Technical College in town. Tertiary education made both my sons exempt from the compulsory two-year SA army service.

My finances were depleted after buying the bare essentials for Byron. A telephone call from Nolyn relieved the situation, "I've arranged a lift to Cape Town with friends. We'll share travelling costs. Pack sandwiches for the journey!"

According to plan we travelled with another couple and their son. The next few days were one of the best and most memorable times I shared with Nolyn. I relied heavily on my faith. My purse held a paltry R4 (40p), the day we set off for Cape Town in a heavily-loaded *Kombi,* Microbus. Topsy accommodated us in Cape Town. The initial awkward moments soon disappeared. We slipped into familiar chatter. Nolyn called me, *'darl'*, for darling, like he always did.

At the toll road, I paid R2.50 leaving me with a mere R1.50! We stopped at *Matjiesfontein,* bulrush fountain, made famous by the son of a Scots railwayman, Douglas Logan. It was visited in its hey-day, by Lord Randolph Churchill, Cecil Rhodes, Edgar Wallace and Olive Schreiner. We admired its original Victorian glory as we quenched our thirst in this oasis in the Karoo. Shielded from the hot dry desert in the air-conditioned vehicle, we drove through Worcester and the 4 km-long Du Toit's tunnel. This cuts through the *Hex* River Mountains into a meandering valley famous for *hanepoort* and *barlinka* grapes. Table Mountain came into view and Cape Town nestled at its feet.

We headed for the university. Parking outside Leo Marquard Hall, Byron's residence for the next few years, he offloaded his luggage. Nolyn paid his fees. Bill arrived to fetch us. We drove through heavy traffic to Constantia. My sister welcomed us showing Nolyn and Byron to their room and me to mine. This did little to sever our close bond. Ivy, once my mother's maid now worked for Topsy. She was treated like a family member. My R1.50 was an inadequate tip. The day we left I prayed, "Lord, please remind Nolyn to give Ivy a generous tip! R10?" Seconds later, I heard: "*Enkosi,* thanks Ivy,"

"*Enkosi* master," she said waving a R10 note in the air.

My prayer had been answered. We hugged Topsy and Bill goodbye. Later, saying farewell to Byron saddened me. We stopped for coffee at the *Wimpy* in Rondebosch.

"Darl', do you have any small change on you?"

"Would R1.50 help?"

"Thanks, that's perfect for the parking meter!"

My money was gone. How would we survive the next few days? Inclement weather forced us to overnight in Port Elizabeth. Nolyn paid for everything. Arriving at Shamrock Sands the next day, Brent met us. Nolyn gave him R50, saying, "Here's some pocket money."

The more my faith was tested, the more steadfast my faith became. The house felt quiet. I missed my sons' bantering.

"I'm starving, mom. When are we eating?"

"Stop changing the TV channel! Give me the remote Byron!"

"Has anyone seen my school tie?"

With those lingering memories, I fed the dogs and went to bed. My thoughts travelled to Chandrè in Port Elizabeth and to Byron in Cape Town. I tossed this way and that, listening to the crickets. I remembered God's faithfulness and I was deeply grateful. Nolyn's written words, *Maybe the prodigal son will return one day. Who knows?* hammered in my brain keeping me awake. I counted sheep. Then gran's pearl of wisdom, *however long the night, the dawn will break,* soothed my troubled mind and I fell asleep.

***

Nolyn missed his family and their growing up years. So on my birthday he arrived at ITEC – Independent Teacher's Enrichment Centre, where I was personal assistant to the Director, Gerry Ledger. We sipped tea and chatted in my office, causing a stir amongst the staff who observed and chattered: "He's good-looking."

"That's her husband."

"*Ag*, oh, even if he divorced her, he still loves her."

That evening, Nolyn and I celebrated my forty-fourth birthday at *Le Petit* restaurant. Enjoying my favourite, snails in garlic butter and sirloin steak, we reminisced: Brent's battle with dyslexia and his success as a Border chess player; Byron's accident-prone childhood and his Mathematical brain: how Chandrè had transformed from a giggling girl who played *Charlie's Angels* into a lawyer-in-the-making. The evening slipped by as quickly it seemed as all those years. Was this the beginning of more happy times together? It was strange, Nolyn taking me home. He walked me to the front door. I went weak in the knees when he held me close and his lips met mine. My body drew warmth from his. Our eyes met in love.

"Thanks, darl'. You made my birthday very special. Coming in for coffee?"

"It's like the good old days. Thanks, I can't stay. I'll help towards Chandre's 21st."

Turning to leave, he added, "I'll be in touch soon."

We spent more time together. I mended his clothes. I trusted him. But...

***

I frequently visited my former boss from GELPA, Ted Walsh, who was also born on 20 March. That year I shared tea and cake in his office, a day late.

"So tell me, Denyse. What are your children up to?" he asked, fixing his blue eyes on mine. Plump and slightly balding, he was like my *dafoo,* immaculately dressed in a dark suit and polished shoes.

"Byron's in his first year studying Computer Science at UCT. Chandre's in her second year of an LLB degree at UPE. Brent's at Technical College doing a business course before he studies Architecture at UPE next year."

"They've inherited their mom's brains! How're you and Gerry getting on?"

"We're busy. Black schools need all the support they can get. We've started running one-day workshops. Many uninvited teachers turn up. Our workshops are designed for sixty. Travelling to the Transkei or Ciskei means leaving at 6.30 am and getting back at 7 pm. We run conferences for Principals at the Centre. She's roped me into gardening in high heels!"

Ted laughed. "That's excellent. I knew you'd fit the job when I arranged the interview. Gerry's a real go-getter. Now, Denyse, have you met anyone special?"

"Mmm... No," I replied thinking it better to keep Nolyn's frequent visits secret.

This highly intelligent, well-travelled man in his mid-fifties, although divorced, regularly visited his ex-wife in Dordrecht, but in East London he enjoyed the company of a younger woman who accompanied him to musicals performed by the East London Orchestral Society, to restaurants and business dinners. I admired his ex-wife's gentleness and elegance.

"Good bye Denyse. Thanks for sharing my birthday. Please visit again."

"Thanks for the tea and birthday cake, Mr Walsh. I'll be back. Bye,"

I never realised then that that would be our *last* shared birthday...

The year raced on. Before I knew it, it was August. I made plans for Chandre's party. She phoned me out of the blue. I was ecstatic.

"Hi mom. How're you?"

"Chandrè. It's you! I'm fine, thanks my girl."

Over the phone we decided on a guest list, the dress code and a menu. The day could not come soon enough. I marked off the hours.

Margy and her husband, Eddie, offered their beautiful home to us. They assisted with the catering. On the 20 August 1989 we were up at daybreak, transforming her TV lounge, with French doors opening onto a bougainvillea-clad patio adjoining a swimming pool, into a thirty-two-seater restaurant. Nolyn sent the *Gonubie Bottle Store* delivery van with drinks, glasses and ice. We set up a bar on the patio. Flower arrangements, candles, pretty napkins and place names finished off the table settings. Margy and I breathed a sigh of relief.

"It looks good!" Jecca and Kirsten agreed. They helped Eddie set up tables for serving food from the adjoining double garage. We were nearly ready.

My daughter and I were re-united in July. I recorded this event: *A year in a mother's life is a long time...for over a year you have not been home...I must look good... hair washed, hot curled, you know the procedure, you often looked on... Brent and I walked into the airport building... the arrival of your flight was announced ...rushed to the arrivals section...how precious to receive you in my arms... Deep inside I wanted to say, 'I'm so glad you came home. It's been so long, so very very long!'*

Chandrè would be at the townhouse. My heart soared when I saw her chatting to Brent over a cup of coffee. She was a young woman with darker hair, cropped short. Slim and beautiful. In our embrace forgiveness conquered our past hurts and restored our love.

"I'm so happy Chandrè. I love you my girl."

"Stop crying mom. I love you, too."

There was no time to chat. We dressed. Chandrè, wearing a blue tailored dress with elbow-length sleeves and a fabric flower accentuating her tiny waist, looked stunning.

"I've got all the pots in your car. I'm off mom," Brent called up to me as he slammed the door and drove off in my car. Driving Brent's car meant high knee-raising gear changes and re-starting the engine often. Chandrè and I were still laughing when I parked and walked into Margy's garden. The guests spilled onto the patio. Their chattering drowned the distant sound of the sea. Friends gathered around to hear Nolyn's short speech after which he handed Chandrè her 21st key. I looked on proudly. Chandrè thanked the guests. Brent took the photos. Trevor Goddard said grace when we were seated at tables.

A joyous mood prevailed throughout the evening. Looking at my daughter I pondered her life: conceived in England; rejected by her biological father; loved deeply and adopted by Nolyn, the only dad she knew; older sister to Brent and Byron; young lady soon to be a lawyer. Our daughter! I felt prouder than a dozen peacocks. After the guests departed Nolyn and Eddie chatted under the bougainvillea and Margy and I tidied up. Before leaving we expressed our gratitude to them. Nolyn said, "It's a pity Byron wasn't here!" I agreed.

On Sunday Chandrè returned wearing my diamond engagement ring Donald Smith had given me. I gave her this ring and an oil painting I painted of fishermen mending their nets, titled 'Come follow me', words Jesus spoke and which signified her Christian commitment. Shortly after this euphoric occasion, a dramatic event would rob me of my joy.

***

I answered Sharon's telephone call to me and heard, "Denyse, Mr Walsh was killed instantly when his *Mercedes* overturned. He was on his way to see his wife in Dordrecht. "

"No!" I exclaimed.

Seven days later, joining the throng of mourners assembled together in a packed crematorium, I paid my last respects to this prominent businessman. His wife stood in the front row with her son's arm on her shoulder. I admired her composure. Could I emulate such serene equanimity in these agonising circumstances, I pondered. Little did I know then, what lay ahead...

***

On 18 September Nolyn lent me his *Mercedes* before he flew to Cape Town on a one-day business trip. He invited Byron to lunch saying, "Dress properly, no jeans or T-shirt." Father and son celebrated Byron's eighteenth birthday, one Byron would always remember. On 20 September Nolyn collected his car from me saying, "Brent, I'm getting a new *Mercedes*. You can have this one." I watched Brent's face light up saying, "Thanks dad."

Nolyn and I embraced. Giving my ear a tweak, one of his distinctive habits, he whispered, "I'll see you on Friday. We'll have dinner together. Okay?"

"Sounds great. Give me another hug, darling." We hugged and our kisses re-ignited a flame of love which had been dead for many years. We waved as Nolyn drove off. I knew Nolyn felt the way I did, ecstatic. I would tell Nolyn how I felt on Friday night.

That evening I had agreed to give my testimony at a Bible study group held in Trevor and Joy Trussler's home. To Brent's astonishment I said, "Brent, go without me. Put in my apologies. I'm staying at home. I feel uneasy..."

"But you're giving your testimony tonight," Brent argued.

I refused to give in. When Brent came home, I was still awake.

"Are you okay mom?"

"I can't sleep. I'll be alright."

He walked upstairs to his room. I heard the click when he switched off the light. The shrill sound of the telephone disturbed the nocturnal silence.

"Who can that be at this time of night?" I asked myself.

Racing downstairs, I reached the lounge. I groped for the light switch on the wall. The sudden brightness made me screw up my eyes. "Hello."

"Hi Denyse."

"Oh! Hello Cheryl," I said, recognising my sister-in-law's voice.

"I've some really bad news..." and the line went quiet.

"What's happened? Is it mom? Dad? Has something happened to one of them?"

"No, Neyse. It's...Nolyn."

"What?"

Had we been cut off? Then she stammered softly, as if not fully comprehending what she was saying, "Nolyn's... had... a car accident. Neyse..." She paused before continuing, "Nolyn's dead!"

"Oh my God! Oh my God, help us!" I repeated.

Cheryl continued talking, but my mind was unable to take in what she had said to me. I kept saying, "Help us! Oh my God, help us!"

Dropping the phone on the cradle, I collapsed onto the sofa in a daze. My knees shook. I closed my eyes in an attempt to shut out what I had heard, but the words, *Nolyn's dead*, hammered louder and louder in my brain.

"What's wrong mom?"

I looked up and saw Brent in front of me. How could I tell him? Could I put it off a little longer? Why did this have to happen?

Confused, Brent asked, "What are you muttering about, mom?"

"It's bad news, Brent."

"What? Tell me. What's happened mom?"

"It's dad... He's had an accident..."

"Where? Is dad alright? "

The words I dreaded saying, "No, Brent... Dad... was... killed in an accident!"

"That's not true. Who told you that?"

"Cheryl."

"Phone her back. Now!"

I dialled Cheryl's number. Ruthven answered. Before I could speak, Brent snatched the phone from me and blurted out, "What's happened to my dad?"

It was as if Brent had solidified into stone. He was unable to speak. He did not hear what I said to him. He did not move after he had dropped the phone. Standing glued to the ground, Brent stared into space. I needed help. I telephoned Trevor and Joy. It was 11 pm. I cannot remember what I said.

"We're on our way Denyse." They arrived. Comforting us as best they could, they prayed incessantly throughout the long, sad night...

Unable to think, Trevor and Joy thought for me. In the morning they phoned my mother who, in her distraught state, comforted us. Joy telephoned my sister, Topsy in Cape Town. "Don't worry, I'll tell Byron and Chandrè. Yes, yes! I'll make arrangements for them to come home immediately." Topsy met Byron at his residence and broke the tragic news to him. She had already packed his suitcase. They drove to the airport. Grief-stricken and alone, Byron flew from Cape Town to East London. It was only two days ago that he had celebrated his eighteenth birthday with his dad. Now he was dead!

Topsy arranged for her friend, Zenobia, in Port Elizabeth, to break the catastrophic news to Chandrè. Overcome with grief she remembered celebrating her 21st birthday with her dad only a month ago. Anton accompanied her on the intercity bus to East London. He comforted her.

The phone rang continually. Friends and family commiserated. Cards and flowers poured in. People came and went. I saw the grief on Nolyn's dad's face and I felt his pain. Jack Wild had lost his son. "My son," he said, "He's gone!" I took his hand in mine. We never spoke. Nolyn's brother, Ruthven telephoned, saying, "Denyse please hold the funeral over for a fortnight. Des and I leave for Mauritius today. We can't cancel our holiday."

"I'm sorry Ruthven. It would be unfair on our children to wait two weeks!"

Brent, walking around like a zombie, had migraines and vomited violently. I tried in vain to comfort him. My own heartache was inconsolable. My sons gravitated together.

Chandrè was consoled by Anton who had recently lost his dad. I could not eat, sleep or think. In the midst of this deep anguish my daughter chose a smart black dress at *Edgars* for me. With tears in her eyes she said, "Dad would want you to look good for him!"

We were too grief-stricken to attend Nolyn's funeral service on Monday 25 September in the Anglican Church, Umtata, but our thoughts were there. Nolyn had been christened in this church. On Wednesday 27 September, we drove to the Crematorium. Eddie met us at the entrance. He took my arm and we walked to the front row of the overcrowded Chapel. I stood, where a week before, I had wept for Ted Walsh and had admired his brave ex-wife. Inside the coffin, covered in flowers, and so close to us, was Nolyn's dead body… I could not believe this was happening…

Nolyn, a prominent, well-liked businessman and competitive sportsman, drew young and old from all over the country, to pay their last respects to him. Men in dark suits spilled out of the side doors. We sang *Amazing Grace*. Our pastor Rob Lindsay paid a carefully-compiled Eulogy to Nolyn. The moment we dreaded arrived. His coffin slid through an opening in the wall and disappeared as the small doors closed again. His father and mother cried. We cried. His family and friends cried. A man loved by so many was gone. Why?

There was no immediate answer to my question. In one night, Nolyn's tragic death had turned our whole world upside down…

25

SHOW ME THE WAY

On 2 February 1990 F W de Klerk lifted the ban on the ANC, PAC and the Communist Party. On 11 February Nelson Mandela was released from the Victor Verster prison, after 27 years. In 1992 SA returned to the Olympics. In early 1992 the white electorate endorsed De Klerk's stance on ending white minority rule, in a referendum.

WE don't deserve this. I picked up the Daily Dispatch newspaper, dated 22 September 1989 and read the inaccurate account of Nolyn's death. Athol Wootton claiming to be Nolyn's partner inappropriately publicised his divorce and omitted his many life-time achievements. I was livid.

EL man dies in motor crash

An insurance salesman here was killed in a motor car accident on the Bashie cuttings between Idutywa and Butterworth late on Wednesday night. Mr Nolyn Wild, 42, (he was 43) had been driving to Umtata when his car crashed at about 11 pm on Wednesday his business partner, Athol Wootton said yesterday. Mr Wootton and Mr Wild were partners in an insurance firm, Gonubie Brokers.

Mr Wild was divorced and had three children. He was a keen golfer and fisherman. Mr Wild's mother, sister and brother were already in East London and his father would be arriving from the Free State today. Funeral arrangements had not yet been finalised.

I kept the two notices I had put into the Daily Dispatch:

Wild, Nolyn: Tragically taken from us on 20.09.89. Gone but never forgotten. Safe in the arms of Jesus. Neyse, Chandrè, Brent and Byron.

And:

WILD: *The family of the late NOLYN – next to God our heavenly Father, who knows each one of us even before we were conceived; who has numbered every hair on our head; who each day is our comfort and refuge at this time of great sorrow – extend heartfelt thanks to all family, friends and business associates everywhere, for their tremendous love and concern. Special sincere thanks to all who assisted at the time of the accident, to those who remembered Nolyn at a special Memorial Service held in Umtata on Monday 27.09.1989 and to those who paid their last respects on Wednesday 29.09.1989. We thank each one.*

Dad, Mom, Neyse, Chandrè Brent Byron, Ruthven, Cheryl and Terry.

On Thursday the Executor of Nolyn's Will, Mr Keyes met Nolyn's father and mother, his sister, Cheryl and her husband, Trevor Whitfield and my children and me at his Standard Bank office. The family hoped Sharlene was not included in his Will. In sombre mood Nolyn's Will was read out. There was no mention of Sharlene. Chandrè inherited money; Brent and Byron's inheritance was held in trust until they both attained the age of twenty-five. Nolyn provided for me on condition I did not re-marry. All his assets were to be reduced to cash, except his *Range Rover* and the two boats, which he bequeathed to his sons. Ruthven inherited some money and was appointed guardian of my sons.

Mr Keyes met Brent and me at 20 Tidewaters, Gonubie. He allowed us to remove Nolyn's personal items before the Public Auction, an emotional day. We packed his clothes, fishing tackle and equipment. Lying on his bedside table, I recognised the birthday card I had given Nolyn in May and a booklet expressing my love. The card dated 1989.05.10 read:

No Matter What, I Know We'll Make It Through

Things haven't been that easy for us lately, but I just want you to know...that as far as I'm concerned, we're worth every single thing it takes to keep our smiles and our lives together. I love you, Nolyn.

And that love is more important than any other thing could possibly be, and maybe things haven't been too easy for us, but I promise you that we're going to make it through...

Because I know how strong my love is, because I have faith in us, and because I've never known anyone as <u>wonderful</u> as you. HAPPY BIRTHDAY! Lovingly, Yours as always, Neyse.

I cried reading the words from the Song of Solomon: *Love is as powerful as death; passion is as strong as death itself.*

On the dressing table I saw the suitcase with the keys to our cottage at Mazeppa Bay and called out, "Brent look what I've found! The Mazeppa Bay keys!" Clutching the case, I turned round and bumped into Mr Keyes.

"What keys are those?"

"The keys to our cottage at Mazeppa Bay."

"Give that to me. That property will also have to be sold!"

"But..."

"You know what was written in Nolyn's Will, Mrs Wild," he sneered and walked off with the suitcase.

When I next called on Mr Keyes he announced: "I dislike you, Mrs Wild." I thought he was joking. Had I misunderstood him? Jokingly I said, "If that's how you feel, you could swat me like you would a fly, buzzing around your office?"

Following a hard cold stare, he droned on, "I *dislike* you Mrs Wild."

How was I to deal with this unsympathetic man? What had I done to him? Could he not tell I was grieving? Then he told me, "You'll have to remove your children from university. The Estate is frozen. The Bank will not be able to release any funds."

"Do you have anything more to say?" I questioned.

"You and your three children may put aside one item of furniture before the auction. Remember, full payment must be made within fourteen days of the sale."

"I shall *not* put more pressure on my children. I'm sure Barclays Bank will help me. Good bye, Mr Keyes."

I stalked out of the building like an enraged bull. Trying to suppress my anger was not easy. When I picked up the newspaper and read that *Perks Auctions* had been nominated by the Standard Trust to sell all the assets, I felt my world was slipping away.

Instructed by the Executors Estate Late Nolyn Everitt Wild, we will publicly submit to

PUBLIC AUCTION on TUESDAY 24 OCTOBER at 10 am.

1. *Riverside Gonubie residence*
2. *Household furniture & electrical appliances (including antiques, Persian rugs)*
3. *1982 Mercedes Benz 200, Manual, 260272 kms.*
4. *Firearms*

I phoned Byron. He wanted the grandfather clock. Chandrè selected the antique oak hallstand and Nolyn's recliner. Brent chose the music centre which he and Nolyn had recently bought together. My choice was the oak lounge suite and matching coffee table. Where would I find the money? Barclays Bank had given me a huge overdraft to pay the children's university fees, funeral and travel costs. I could not ask for a bigger loan.

***

Ruthless bargain-hunters at the Public Auction carried off our possessions with little respect or understanding of what these items meant to me. I watched the contents of my home disappear onto the backs of *bakkies,* into boots of cars and onto lorries. Gone forever! Should I have bought everything for R50 000? Soon the house was empty except for our few purchases.

During the sale Brent begged me to bid for Nolyn's guns and his golf clubs. I did adding these to my fondue set, paintings, bookshelf and encyclopaedias. How would these items fit into our tiny townhouse? A concern, but not for now… Leaving the house Brent and I walked through the echoing empty rooms.

Our melancholy was interrupted when a neighbour, Neville

Puttergill arrived. He called Brent aside, saying, "You're the head of the family now. It's your responsibility to look after your mom, Chandrè and Byron." He meant well but right then, this was too much for Brent. He started a migraine which dragged on and off for weeks.

We needed a bigger townhouse and so moved to Blue Waters, where the *Range Rover*, my sons' joint inheritance was locked up in the garage. They also inherited two ski-boats. One was stored. The other was sold.

In this lovely townhouse on the Nahoon River with a distant view of the sea I was out of work. Was I dismissed from ITEC because I had been too honest? I had enjoyed working for Doctor Coetzee but I resigned to re-charge my batteries. After this I worked in the Finance Department for *Eskom* in Beacon Bay.

Most afternoons my friend, Carol Fyfe and I walked the dogs on the beach. One day I exploded. My screams resounded above the roar of the waves. My throat felt like hot coals. I shouted, "God, why did you allow Nolyn to be killed?" I had believed God would restore our marriage. I yelled even louder, "Why, God?"

Words I had buried deep within me suddenly surfaced in a rage. This was followed by self-pity. "I don't want to live anymore!"

I said it all at last. Shame settled over me. I turned to my friend. Carol hugged me. In the comfort of her arms she said, "Good, you've let it all out! God understands. He will never leave you nor forsake you."

I was flabbergasted. Instead of reprimanding me or telling me to pull myself together like everybody else had, she consoled me. With my eyes closed, I listened to the screeching seagulls overhead. I smelt the washed-up seaweed at my feet. Surrounded by God's creation, Carol prayed. Her prayer was like balm poured into my wounds. In between tears of remorse and sniffs, I begged God's forgiveness for my relentless rage, false accusations and self-pity. When I opened my eyes, my heavy burden had lifted. I saw a beautiful rainbow spanning over the horizon of the sea and I knew then, I *could* go on...

***

Byron spent Easter with me and the townhouse felt more like home. My friend, Ann, returned my possessions which she had hidden in her house for two years. The cushions, candelabra and riempie stool, were reminders of a home we had once shared.

On his last day at home, Byron drove the *Range Rover* to draw cash from an ATM whilst I prepared lunch. He would not be long. Then the phone rang.

"Denyse, there's been an accident. Byron. Come quickly."

"Where?"

"Outside the Christian Centre."

"Is Byron okay?"

"That's all I know. They've called the fire brigade and the ambulance!"

Grabbing my car keys I jumped into my red *Honda* and raced to the scene of the accident. I parked on the hard shoulder and pushed my way through thronging onlookers, asking, "Where's my son?"

Nobody answered me. Tyre marks on the side of the road showed where a vehicle had veered off. The fire brigade were hosing down the *veldfire*. An onlooker said, "A *Range Rover* plummeted off the road. It's down there somewhere!" The ever increasing sound of sirens warned me of an approaching ambulance in the midst of this pandemonium. My heart beat faster. I was reminded of the night I had been rushed to hospital in 1965. Running down the embankment, I searched for my son. Then I saw a wrecked vehicle. Could this be the *Range Rover*? From behind the ruined remains he emerged, shocked, bruised and scratched. Byron was alive.

"Thank God you're alright!"

"It wasn't my fault… a *Ford Mondeo*… came across…there were girls in…"

"Don't worry about that Byron. You're safe."

At the scene of the accident the driver of the *Ford* admitted his guilt. In his statement to the police later he denied this, stating, "Poor visibility, caused by smoke from a *veld* fire on the edge of the road, prevented me from being able to see the approaching *Range Rover.*"

Byron reported the accident to the police. The AA towed the remains of the *Range Rover* to the scrapyard. I submitted a claim to the insurance company and learnt of the driver's denial of guilt. Byron had swerved to miss the *Ford Mondeo* with three young girls sitting in the back. We received a feeble insurance settlement, but everybody was alive.

Brent was devastated to learn of the demise of their joint inheritance. I had just fitted four new tyres and paid for the interior to be re-upholstered. Try as I did to cancel an all-day golf tournament in King

William's Town the next day, Mary, the captain would not hear of it, "You can't possibly back out now, Denyse. I'll pick you up tomorrow at 7 am."

I worried about Byron driving to Cape Town alone as Mary and I drove to the golf course. The incident of me 'striking glass with my putter', flashed into my mind on the way. It stayed with me when I walked into the clubhouse where staff recognised me.

I played 36 holes of golf with the same new ball. My adrenalin was on an all-time high. Could this account for my good golf?

"You'll need a trailer for all your prizes," quipped a golfer next to me, as my name was called out - *Best all day net*: Denyse Wild; *Nearest the Pin:* Denyse Wild; *Stableford Competition*: Denyse Wild, adding to the pile of prizes around my chair – huge ceramic vases, urns and bowls. Today I have this silver trophy, a reminder of that victorious day.

"Well done!" Mary said driving home, "and to think you wanted to pull out of the tournament. You've done the Gonubie Golf Club proud!"

Byron arrived safely in Cape Town. Brent came home the following weekend and on the way to the scrapyard, he said, "Don't be stupid! We'll be able to repair it." His face said it all when he photographed the wreckage, all that was left to him by his late dad.

***

Byron's letter dated 28 April 1991 revealed his concern: *I hope Brent had a nice weekend at home and managed to sort everything out – his car and the Range Rover. What was his reaction when he saw the Range Rover?*

Brent was devastated. The reality of not being able to fall back on Nolyn when life threw one hurdle after another at me, hit me hard. More often I turned to my faithful dogs. Their ears twitched as I spoke my troubled thoughts aloud: "We only paid Mr Wilson R12, 500 for the cottage. Mr Keyes has attracted nationwide buyers. A wealthy Johannesburg-based conglomerate, hiring a private plane, flew to Mazeppa Bay. They offered R100,000."

I slammed the file on the coffee table which made Emmy bark. Pepe leapt onto my lap and licked my face. Patting and nudging him closer for support, I picked up the file. Pepe listened, curled up on my lap. If only Mr Keyes had not heard me the day I found the keys, things might be different right now, I thought.

I could not borrow any more money. To lose our cottage would be catastrophic. Where would I find R100,000? I had to account to the Standard Trust for all the children's expenses posting the relevant receipts. I desperately needed a holiday. Remembering; *tackle one thing at a time,* another of granny's pearls of wisdom, I sipped my coffee. Then the telephone rang.

"Hi Mom. How are you?"

"Fine thanks Chandrè."

"I've some exciting news!"

"Tell me. What?"

"Anton and I are engaged."

"Engaged? Tell me more."

I was not expecting this news. I did not really know Anton. She was my only daughter and I wanted the best for her.

"I'm happy for you my girl. I'll put the announcement in the paper," I responded following in my mother's footsteps. There was one snag. There had been no family celebration. Hiding my true feelings I continued, "Have you set a date for your wedding?"

"No not yet. We'll make plans with you."

"You're getting married! Congratulations!"

The news lifted my spirits, but was followed by a bitter disappointment…

***

The next day Cliffie Phillips made a proposal, "My friends, the Stevensons from Burgersdorp are keen to share joint ownership of the cottage with you. What do you think?"

"I'll discuss this with Brent and Bryon."

He left. My phone bill rose with trunk-calls to Cape Town and Port Elizabeth. We discussed this proposal. They were not keen. Mr Keyes threatened to accept the highest offer. As time ran out, I scraped together R50,000 and bought into a partnership with people I had never met. I now faced another hurdle. I removed our personal belongings under the close surveillance of a Standard Trust staff member. When I put the oil painting I had painted in the car, my mind was filled with bygone memories.

***

The first anniversary of Nolyn's death fell during my second tour to

Israel. Would my children cope? Chandrè took in my dogs which were put on the wrong flight but finally arrived in Port Elizabeth. Brent's flight was delayed when security discovered an unlicensed firearm on him. It was confiscated until he registered the gun in his name.

I flew from East London destined for Tel Aviv the next day. This flight stopped at Luanda where we waited in a hot, airless lounge. Before boarding the plane passengers' names were called out and passports checked. I was detained with two fellow passengers. When our leader questioned this, he was told, "No more seats on the plane."

"The group cannot be separated. The passengers on the plane will alight and remain here with the three passengers you have detained."

The officials argued. I was handed a boarding pass and took my seat 27Y on the plane with the tour group. Two fighter jets escorted our plane through volatile airspace. War ships lining the Red Sea were clearly visible below. Several family members were not in favour of this holiday but my faith was growing. I remembered God's faithfulness: homeless, He found us a furnished house; starving, He supplied sustenance; He broke my smoking addiction and replaced deeply embedded hatred with love.

But my faith was soon to be tested. The 14 September dawned and I travelled on a coach to Masada. I imagined what was happening in South Africa. This was my daughter's wedding day. She told me of their intended wedding the day before I flew. I was too heart-broken to remonstrate. I wondered. What was Chandrè wearing? Who gave her away? Who were her bridesmaids? All I could do was to picture her as a radiant bride walking down the aisle to the sound of the wedding march. I longed to be with her. I got through the day.

On 20 September I remembered the night of that awful telephone call. Life can be so tough at times but knowing the Lord eased my pain. I toured Israel and Turkey with our church group. Afterwards Joan Meredith and I hopped on and off ferries from one Greek island to another. Idyllic. We flew from Athens to Cyprus for a further fortnight. With new experiences on this holiday I was refreshed spiritually, physically and emotionally. Joan and I became firm friends. Our friendship continues today.

Back home I telephoned Chandrè anxious to hear about her wedding. I learnt they had been married in the Registry Office.

Annamarie and her daughter, Shelley, Brent and Anton's best man were the only guests. No wedding gown, bridal march, confetti, garter or cake. Marrying outside the church haunted me for years. Depression gripped me whenever I thought I had been deprived forever of hearing her say, "I do!"

My joy returned the more I focussed on God's goodness which I experienced when I dropped my car keys in the sea-sand. Carol and I searched and prayed. "Lord, you know where I dropped my keys. Please help us find them."

The fading light and trampled dunes made it impossible for us to find the keys. I swung round. At my feet I saw something shining.

"Your keys!" Carol exclaimed. She saw them before me.

We thanked God all the way back to the car in the dark.

***

When Pepe escaped from the property and was run over, my mind was made up. I was leaving *Blue Waters*. I took two days off work recovering. Chandrè helped me overcome my sadness. "Hi mom," she said.

"Hi Chandrè."

"Has your puppy arrived?"

"No not yet. I'm so excited. Her bed, puppy bowls and an alarm clock under her mattress, are ready for her."

"What'll you call her mom?"

"Je t'aime, which means 'I love you."

We chatted on sharing the excitement. Soon I held my tiny black bundle of joy. Two small dark eyes looked at me. I not only fell in love with my new puppy but she became the centre of attention. Her puppy noises and smells were something I had almost forgotten. I heeded my daughter's advice in a letter she had written to me: *By this time tomorrow evening you will have your new little baby with you. She's such a sweetie pie but has a temper on her. This afternoon Nelson was playing with her on the brick paving and he knocked her over. You should have seen her. She ran after Nelson growling and barking. It was hilarious!*

Full instructions telling me how to care for my puppy followed, ending with her informative remark...*she's a pedigree French poodle but is not registered.*

When I left *Blue Waters* Je t'aime was three month's old and played with Emmy who had become both mother and playmate to her. Living true to her name, she showered her unconditional puppy love on everyone. My new home was now 21 Tenth Avenue in the seaside resort of Gonubie, which takes its name from the local bramble berries known to the Xhosa as *gqunube.* I bought the house from an elderly couple returning to England and who were auctioning off their unwanted possessions. This auction was very different from the one in 1989 at 20 Tidewaters. Flashbacks of that day were unleashed with accompanying emotional turmoil. I pushed these aside telling myself, life moves on yet new experiences conjure up old memories.

The auctioneer was kind to me, "All yours for R10, £1," he said.

"You mean *everything* in the room?" I queried.

A nod of his head confirmed my disbelief. Looking around the room, I realised I was set up for life with embroidery thread, cottons, wool, crochet hooks, knitting needles, pins, needles, patterns and unused craft sets. The tropical garden was beautiful. Two tall wild banana trees, a huge rubber tree, three jelly palms and three forty-foot Coral trees, (also known as *kaffir booms* whose seeds are used as lucky charms by the Blacks), covered in scarlet red flowers, created this park-like garden screening the house from the street. A long driveway swept down the side of the house leading to a double garage.

A games room off the garage had two huge windows which brought the garden into the room and absorbed the golden rays of the setting sun. Red and yellow poinsettias competed with pink, purple and scarlet climbing bougainvillea; crimson bottlebrush trees, two metres tall, sidled up against the taller evergreen monkey-puzzle trees, originally from Chile. (In 1850 a man in Bodmin, Cornwall, looked at this rare tree and remarked, 'It would puzzle a monkey to climb that." And so the name stuck.)

Multi-coloured rose bushes scented the garden growing alongside a heavily-laden lemon tree. Of an evening the lemon blossoms and the twenty feet high pink and white-flowering frangipani trees exuded an exotic fragrance. Honeysuckled archways flanked by flowerbeds of pelargoniums and agapanthus divided the garden into lawned rooms. Pathways led to fruit-laden banana and paw-paw trees, birdbaths and a garden bench. The wash-lines, in a suntrap, were hidden behind the garage.

French doors off the TV lounge opened onto a pergola, covered by a Golden Shower providing shade from the sun and shelter from the rain. Teas and lunches were served here with friends. On one such occasion, Bridget said, "I love the water cascading over the rocks into small pools."

"The goldfish hide under that ledge, but are quick to come up when I feed them," I said looking at the exotic palms, grasses, reeds and water lilies surrounding the fish pond.

"Your garden certainly attracts a variety of birds Denyse."

"I see the weaver birds have torn your palms to build their nests. "

"Have the hadedas caught any of your goldfish?"

"Not yet," I answered, "but their raucous cry wakes me early every morning. They're proficient at aerating my lawns whilst feeding on earthworms." Today I miss their raucous cries as they fly off in the early morning and return again in the evening.

Bridget and my other friends went home with cuttings from plants, paw-paws and bananas. Before I moved into the house, *Rentokil* fumigated to get rid of the cockroaches which came out at night in their droves. These hardy pests can live without food or water for a month. Using *Dyroach* spray I finally exterminated them. At night black *geckos* ran along the walls catching moths. Emmy and Je t'aime watched in quiet amusement from the comfort of their cushioned baskets.

My brokenness healed in this new-found refuge and prepared me for more catastrophic challenges! A five-bed-roomed house, main-en-suite; a private garden; screened by bougainvillea was my own quiet study shared with twittering birds.

I settled into the relaxed ebb and flow of life... From this tranquil oasis, I walked to the village for milk and the newspaper; frequented the library and Post Office. The beach was within walking distance and boasted a boardwalk.

Whilst working for *Eskom* and living at Blue Waters, I had resumed my studies through *Unisa* and now reached my final year. I had never taken Mathematics and now had to pass Statistics in two separate papers. Even using a calculator was foreign to me. I used images to retain information; psycho-analysed golfers, church attendees, pedestrians and cemented the knowledge in my brain. But would I pass? I was extremely disciplined and determined to get my degree.

I wrote the final exams and waited for the results. That moment of joy and relief dawned. I had passed ten credits and had my BA degree majoring in Education and Psychology. I achieved this in 1983, passing Psychology I; in 1984 I passing Sociology I and Education I. With no money and my life in chaos, I resumed my studies in 1991 passing Education II and Psychology II; in 1992 passing Biblical Studies I, Education III; and finally in 1993 passing Geography I, Biblical Studies II and Psychology III.

I graduated on 22 April 1994 at a Ceremony held in the City Hall of East London. Eddie and Margy were my two guests. What would I do with a degree at my age? Would it secure me a good job? Had this struggle been worth it?

Time would tell…

26

WHAT WAS OUR SECRET?

Nelson Mandela was sworn in as President on 10 May 1994 with FW de Klerk and the ANC's Thabo Mbeki as Deputy Presidents.

WHAT lay behind the tragic events of Coulter Street? My mother had narrowly escaped death on that night of horror...My father had come for her brandishing a knife... She escaped to the convent and collapsed... I had frozen from fear as I huddled my sisters under my arms... How could I get to know my biological father? Would he have been a doting grandfather and now, soon-to-be great-grandfather? Andrew's revelation to Margy and I would finally bring closure to a secret we had held for so many years...

In September 1974 we were living in Umtata. I received a letter from my mother on my way to tennis. I opened it and read. My mother always updated me on her bowls' achievements, family get-togethers and her gardening, but I was taken aback when, in the midst of her ramblings, she wrote, 'Your father died in Durban last week,' and in the *very* next sentence, she rattled on about her weekly activities. I stopped in my tracks and read the words aloud, 'Your father died in Durban last week.' My father, *dead*... No detail given... A one-sentence statement...

I phoned my mother, who already guessed what this call was about. When I asked her to tell me more, her answer was curt, "That's all I know. Enough of that now. How are the family? All well?"

"Fine thanks, mom. I'm just on my way to tennis. Bye for now."

I remained in a trance and frantically dug out the memories I had of my dad. I pictured us once again playing on the warm sands of Durban beach; heard his laughter on the many loving visits to me, when I was staying with strangers in Durban; and finally I re-lived the night of horror at Coulter Street and saw his anger in action. Yes, that was the last time I had seen my dad. Nineteen years ago! The reality sank in. Since 1955 I had had no contact with my father and from today I would never *ever* see my dad again. He was gone forever. Uncontrollable tears rolled down my cheeks.

In January 1994, twenty years later, Margy and I visited Andrew Lloyd, my dad's brother, who lived alone on the outskirts of East London. Over a welcome cup of tea, I was given a deeper insight into my dad's life. This was my first meeting with an uncle I had never heard of before. The likeness between Andrew and my dad was uncanny. I kept staring at him. I took courage and told my uncle, "Andrew, you look just like our father."

I never even knew when his birthday was until that day. Andrew gave me my dad's birth certificate showing he was born in Lusikisiki, on 26 September 1919; his Record of Service in the Natal Mounted Rifles (NMR) during the Second World War, when he was awarded medals during 1940-1943; his provisional Divorce papers dated 25 March 1957; his I.D. card 007945905. His death certificate dated 24 August 1974 disclosed that my dad died in an ambulance on the way to hospital. The cause of death was recorded as, "Coronary Infarction." A document detailed his cremation at the Stellawood Crematorium, Durban, on 9 September 1974.

My father was the third eldest of eleven children, Phyllis, Iris, Andrew, Percy, Doreen, Dennis, Keith, Trevor, Ronnie and Gill, as advertised in the death notice from a newspaper cutting. Andrew praised my dad for his bravery during the war, his kindness as a brother, and explained to us that the war had played a major role in my father's addiction to alcohol. The saddest revelation was when Andrew disclosed, "Your dad kicked the habit. Unfortunately, it was too late. He had spent his last years in a monastery, employed by the fathers as a handyman, and was given a room and food. As his illness intensified, Eric asked me and several of his siblings, to please contact Peggy. 'I want to see my three daughters once more…' he pleaded. I wrote and told your mother and I telephoned her in July at which time I made it quite clear to her that Eric did not have long to live."

My mother ignored every request. Sadly my father's dying wish was not fulfilled.

Understandably, my mother wanted nothing more to do with Eric after her close shave with death. She painted a dreadful picture of him. She had secured a Court Order in 1956, which prohibited my father from coming within a certain radius of Kokstad for her and our protection. But was my father all the things my mother had labelled him? A homeless drunkard? A jobless failure? A good-for-nothing?

Whatever views I had had of my father prior to our meeting with Andrew changed drastically that day. After all, he was my biological father, a daddy I hardly knew. I had never had a father-daughter relationship with him. Throughout my childhood and adulthood I never knew what it was like to have a father. But I decided then, that today and forever, my dad would have a special place in my heart!

We kissed Andrew goodbye and both came away emotionally drained. On the one hand I was happy to have met Andrew and to learn about the good side of my father, but I was very sad that I had inadvertently deprived him of the love he wanted to give me. My dad has missed out on my growing up years, my weddings and seeing his grandchildren. He had been deprived of what most fathers took for granted!

Andrew also told us how much my father *loved* my mother. He could not accept that my mother had a suitor. He wanted her and his daughters back in his life, so much so, that he had made an ultimatum: "Tell me you'll come back, Peggy. I'll give you time, until 22 December." Her refusal to give my father one more chance sent him out of his mind and fuelled by alcohol, he lost *all* control.

Margy and I parted, but not without her saying, "Please don't tell mom that you and I visited Andrew today. It will only upset her."

"I promise," was my reply.

And so all those years, we kept the secret...

27

ME, A GRANDMA!

In 1993 Vodacom, SA's cell phone was launched. After the Boipatong massacre in 1993, the ANC withdrew from constitutional talks. On 26 April 1994 Nelson Mandela said: "We, both Black and White, shall build a rainbow nation at peace with itself and the world."

MY daughter and I telephoned regularly. During these chats, advice on gardening, cooking and current affairs was swapped. We exchanged love and laughter closing the distance between us over a telephone line.

"How's Cape Town?"

"Wet and much colder than PE."

"Tell me about your new house?"

"It's small, but cosy. A log-fire in the lounge keeps the whole house warm. Properties are very expensive in Cape Town."

Little did I realise *then* she was longing to tell me something.

"Your house reminds me of *The Gables*. Do you remember our evenings around the fire?" I jabbered on, "It was a real treat for me to eat an orange and throw the peels into the log fire when I was a young girl growing up on the farm. I loved the citrus smell emanating from the ashy embers. Sorry, here I go again, rambling on about my childhood memories and the happy times I spent with you, Brent and Byron. Now where were we?"

"Mom… I've been trying to tell you. I'm pregnant! You're going to be a grandma."

It took a while for the news to register. My thoughts flashed back to the day I telephoned my mother from London twenty-six years ago, saying, *I've got some good news. I've got a special Christmas present for you. You're going to be a granny!"*

Suddenly my first pregnancy became vivid after all those years. Cruel words from the past stabbed my heart, *you're living in sin... you're nothing more than a whore and your unborn child is a bastard...I know where you can have an abortion...you're a disgrace...*

Before these devastating thoughts stole my joy, I deleted them.

"I'm thrilled for you. Tell me more," I answered.

We nattered on. I listened attentively learning about ultra-sounds, unheard of in my time. I broadcast the news accurately to family and friends. Baby boutiques attracted me. I studied all the mod-con gadgets and outfits for infants. How the times had changed. My baby-centred days included stockpiling baby garments and clicking away on knitting needles to make mittens, bootees and matinee jackets. Time raced on. My excitement accelerated. In December I stayed with Byron in a flat he shared with students. Knowledge, a flatmate from Nigeria joined us on Christmas Day.

Chandrè and I sat in the back of Byron's red *VW Fox.* Our scenic drive through Camps Bay and Llandudno soon turned into a nightmare. Every restaurant declared, "Fully booked, I'm afraid," which meant no Christmas Dinner. Hot, bothered and famished, we wolfed down pizzas in a shabby pizza parlour in Rondebosch, a poor substitute. I admired Chandrè, who never complained and endured the sweltering heat, 32 degrees, in a cramped car without air-conditioning.

A few days later my imagination ran wild: I wore a bedjacket, bed socks and a pink hairnet. In my toothless bespectacled state, I examined my dentures smiling back at me from a glass of water. Laughing hysterically I decided to be a 1994 grandma instead.

Then I fondly remembered how my granny had showered me with kisses, pulled a treat for me from her apron pocket and encouraged me with pearls of wisdom. Above all, she showed a willingness to help others especially family. I wanted to follow in her footsteps.

The big day arrived. Byron drove me to the Gardens Hospital and parked. I held my head high knowing I was about to see my first grandchild in that building. I leapt out.

"I'll wait here, mom," Byron said.

I hurried on to the reception desk, asking, "May I see Mrs de Jager please?"

"Certainly," a smiling brunette led me to her ward. Chandrè beamed at me. To this very day I remember the tears of joy we shared in our embrace.

"Congratulations Chandrè... I can't wait to see your baby."

"She's beautiful. Jaime Ashleigh weighed ten pounds."

A knock on the door interrupted us as a nurse entered.

"Would you like to see the new baby?"

This was what I had been longing for. I kissed Chandrè goodbye. At the nursery the midwife held up a wrinkly-faced baby with a mop of black hair and a rosebud mouth. Only a pane of glass separated us.

"She's beautiful!" I whispered not wanting to wake her.

It was time to leave. On my way out I bumped into Anton. Just about to congratulate him, he asked, "What are *you* doing here?"

"*Haw*!" an expression of disbelief is how I should have responded, but instead I answered, "I've just seen *my* beautiful granddaughter!"

No more was said. We parted. Telling Byron gave me some relief. We drove off.

Once more I remembered my granny and what she had meant to me. If only I had asked my grandmother to tell me more stories of her life... If only there had been more time... If only she could see her great-great grandchild...

I hoped my grandchildren would say of me: she spoils us, takes care of us, is always happy to see us, she catches us when we fall and tucks us into bed, she reads us stories and doesn't mind if we spill jam on her cloth or if our hair's a mess.

At a time when the new South African word, *Ubuntu,* means 'I am what I am because of who we are', becoming a grandma seemed apt. *Ubuntu*, incorporates a people who share, care, trust, respect and help. Jaime my first grandchild, born on 7 January 1994 the year of *Ubuntu,* would never experience *apartheid*...

***

How could I bury the past and live in the present when Nolyn was always in my thoughts? After five years his presence was still everywhere, but physically he was nowhere to be seen. A real emptiness targeted the pit of my stomach. Stark reminders – bananas, crayfish, *Castle* beer, *braaivleis*, rare fillet steak, golf, cars, people and places –

were unavoidable. I missed his Monday night phone calls; the smell of *Old Spice*; the car door banging and his footsteps walking up to the door. I longed to have him back.

I daydreamed about his life. I would be lying if I said I had no regrets. Had I failed him by running away? Why had I not got to read his Eulogy at his funeral? Would writing my life story compensate for many unspoken words? The tragic deaths of Donald and Nolyn were a stark reminder to me of the precipitousness of death. Treasuring the memories, I tried to live each day constructively as though my last.

For too long I had lived in Nolyn's shadow referred to as 'Nolyn's wife' or his 'ex'. It was time to change that. With resolute determination yet still vulnerable, Gordon my neighbour's son, captivated me. Eighty year-old Di Wood saw I was hurting. She knew her son had romanced me when he was engaged to another woman. "I would have warned you to keep away from my son. Gordon's been a womaniser all his life!" she exclaimed.

This brief romance was similar to the one with George Heath. Both men said they were Christians. Both were engaged to another woman. Both had deceived me. When would I learn? This humbling experience inspired me to move on.

"I'm planning a holiday in the Cape, looking at properties in Kleinmond. I'll stay with a friend in Greyton," I told Chandrè on the telephone.

"Drive carefully mom and let me know how you get on."

I duly arrived in Greyton named after Sir George Grey. This tranquil village, once a market gardening town with functioning water furrows and thatched cottages, was cradled in the Overberg Mountains. Too rural for me, I decided. The closer I got to Cape Town, the more spectacular the scenery. Majestic mountains silhouetted the skyline with waving wheat lands in the valleys below.

I looked at properties in Kleinmond at the foot of the Palmietberg. The nine-hole golf course reminded me of Gonubie. Not convinced I could live there, I drove on to Cape Town.

Byron and I drove to Fish Hoek one Saturday afternoon. Umbrellas dotted the golden sand amidst suntan-lotioned bodies soaking up the sunshine on brightly-coloured beach towels. Bathers frolicked in the rolling waves, diving, floating, jumping or splashing. Strolling along

Jager's Walk constructed on the edge of rocks and rock pools, I gazed across the bay where whales wallowed and spouted fountains into the sky. Mist rolled down the distant mountains. On the Clovelly beach local fishermen spread their nets on the sand near their rowing boat. This was a paradise and I wanted to be a part of it.

When I returned to the car Byron commented, "This is better than Kleinmond."

My mind made up I returned to Gonubie. In no time I rented my house and found a flat for Brent on the East London beachfront. A month later my household possessions were transported to Cape Town. Alone in my fully-loaded car, I drove for twelve hours to 17 The Glade, Fish Hoek. I arrived exhausted and grateful that Topsy had taken delivery of my furniture and made up my bed and made me some *bototie* for my supper.

Byron fetched my dogs from the airport. I waited. Without a mobile or landline, I worried. It was late. At midnight Byron and his girlfriend Liesel, studying medicine at UCT, arrived with my distraught dogs. He moaned, "I was unable to get Brent on the phone so tried granny who said, 'Brent was late taking the dogs to the airport. They missed their earlier flight,' so this is why we're so late."

"I'm sorry. Thanks for fetching Je t'aime and Emmy," I said relieved to have my pets with me. They bounded between boxes running into the small garden, sniffing in their new surroundings. Je t'aime ran into the sliding glass doors at which point Byron and Liesel left.

On my own I was at the start of a new chapter in my life with my own identity. I called my dogs inside and locked the sliding door. Exciting days lay ahead of me, but right now all I wanted was a good night's sleep. When I woke and walked into the garden followed by my two dogs, I noticed the irrigation system. A heavy fog hid the mountains giving a mysterious feeling to the day. My days were consumed with unpacking boxes, hanging pictures and curtains until this rented three-bedroomed townhouse felt like home.

In March Topsy organised my 50th birthday party. She reminded me, "It'll be the family only and I'm paying for everything!" On 20 March 1995 we drove to the Cape Town station. A champagne breakfast was booked in the dining carriage of the train enabling us to enjoy the panoramic seaviews and whales on a return trip to Simon's

Town. We parked. Topsy herded us along saying, "Hurry up! We'll miss the train."

This was a busy time with commuters going to work. We boarded the dining carriage. A steward asked, "Do you have a reservation?"

"The Botha party," Topsy replied.

"Come this way."

We were shown to our reserved seats, with one small snag… Our party of nine meant Byron, Liesel, Bill, David, Topsy, mom, Kirsten and Ann sat together, leaving me as odd-man-out seated with total strangers. "Open your present," Topsy suggested.

Surrounded by strangers who did not know if they should watch me or look out the window, I removed a gold chain with five gold rings from the wrappings.

"Put it on! It's from me, Margy and Patrick," Topsy said to me.

I wore it around my neck. This did not change how I felt. Alone!

All those years ago on my 21st birthday I remembered how I had let my family down due to the excruciating pain in my back. Would I want to remember my 50th birthday? The train chugged into the Cape Town station where I thanked Topsy and the family. I was quite happy to be home in the company of my faithful pets. It seemed they understood me better than humans at times.

The next champagne breakfast was a joyous occasion. Liesel and Byron announced their engagement on Saturday 8 April 1995 at 9 am at 17 The Glade, Fish Hoek. Byron, Liesel and I worked late into Friday night making the necessary preparations. In the morning sunshine we opened garden umbrellas around garden furniture seating thirty-six. Family members and university students arrived as the heavens opened. Everybody crowded indoors as garden furniture was hurriedly stored in the garage.

Our planned garden party became an intimate indoor stand-and-shuffle-between-guests party. The pouring rain did not dampen our spirits. The melon balls, muesli, yoghurt, Bucks fizz, fresh fruit, croissants, bread rolls and coffee quickly disappeared. Happiness spilled out of me as I carried one-year-old Jaime and listened to Byron's eloquent speech. Jaime clapped her little hands imitating the adults. They opened presents for all to see. I wished Brent was with us. Their engagement was made public in the paper: *Doctor Robert and Hadmud*

Moffett announce the engagement of their daughter, Liesel to Byron, son of Denyse and the late Nolyn Wild of Fish Hoek.

I explored Fish Hoek nestling between the Indian and Atlantic Ocean. This town was built around a central circle, 29 kms from Cape Town and nestling under the Silvermine Mountains. It was once the only teetotal town in South Africa. I made friends with Maurine Wood swimming in the waves. She also lived in Silverglades and like me, was a dog lover. Eileen Gourley a golfing friend from Gonubie lived and worked in Fish Hoek as an estate agent. My travelling friend Joan Meredith attended the Full Gospel Church and lived in St James. I joined the Baptist Church pastored by John and Averill Thomas. Choreographed by Ruth Britain eight of us worshipped in dance at the official opening of the new church.

I made more friends when I joined the Fish Hoek Friends of Music Society. With an active hiking group I explored the surrounding mountains. Emily, my hairdresser, George, the *Shell* garage petrol attendant, Marion, a librarian, Glenda, a pharmacist, Lorraine, a shop-owner, Jayne Wilde at *Whiskers Dog Parlour*, Maggie at the Laundromat, Victor, a handyman, and others, became my friends.

At home my phone rang often, friends popped in and I enjoyed my new identity. Through Eileen, 35 The Glen was bought with Brent and Byron as joint owners. The ever-changing views towards Chapman's Peak and golden sunsets enchanted me and my visitors to my home.

Lynne from Gonubie visited and we trailed a wine route. Carol Fyfe, the friend who helped me find my car keys in the sand, spent a glorious week with me. In Hout Bay she donned a sailor's cap when we ate fish and chips. Michelle Webber who called me 'mom' and now working in East London holidayed with me visiting the Castle, V & A Water-front, Bird World and Cape Point.

Lorna, a distant relation who had moved to Cape Town, was diagnosed with breast cancer and underwent a mastectomy. I invited her to recuperate in my home. A smoker and slovenly, it upset me to come home to dirty coffee mugs and butt-filled ashtrays strewn everywhere. My pastor, Peter Spoor visited her one day. She picked up her prosthetic breast, threw it on the coffee table and said, "I refuse to wear this!" Things got worse. One night she drove off in her car although she was prohibited from driving. I worried. The following day after a row, she left on bad terms. It worries me to this day that I never heard from her.

I nursed Lorraine O'Grady through bronchitis. Her then shaky marriage was restored and our friendship flourished. We celebrated our birthdays together. She shared my problems and I encouraged her. Sadly I lost contact with her.

Margy stayed with me when her husband, Eddie was critically ill in the Constantiaberg Private Hospital. He had fought a lung disease for twelve years. I was with the family, including his sister Anita and her husband, Chiko from Switzerland when he breathed his last on 23 July 1998. He was a family man, smiling and happy and ready to help. He no longer suffered and was with the Lord, but we were grief-stricken. Byron, Liesel and I had driven through the night to attend Eddie's funeral in East London. He was a man we greatly admired.

In Fish Hoek I found my own identity and my home was open to family and friends. It was here I discovered the Coloureds, brown people, who are different from the Blacks. I watched fishermen rowing ashore before pulling a trawling net on to the sand. They sold the wriggling fish, 'hardies' to bystanders. I listened with interest to the way they spoke:"*Dis lekker by die see,* It's good to be at the seaside," after a good catch. "*Jislaaik!*" when a meagre offer was made for a large fish, expressing outrage.

"He's my *chommie,*" or "She's my *tjerrie*!"

"*Moegoe*!" not complimentary and if termed *skelm,* you would not be tolerated but avoided...

My move to Cape Town had been expensive. I needed to secure the property with fencing. I needed a job. Unashamedly I told my friends. I am forever grateful to Maurine, who helped me achieve my goal...

28

THE JOAN ST LEGER LINDBERGH ARTS FOUNDATION

In 1996 the Truth and Reconciliation Commission chaired by Archbishop Desmond Tutu began hearings on human rights crimes committed by former government and liberation movements during the 'apartheid' era. Thabo Mbeki, known as the backroom operator, had a degree from the University of Sussex. He underwent military training in the Soviet Union and became President in 1999.

MAURINE questioned me on the phone, "Have you seen the job advertised in the Echo?" This free weekly newspaper kept me updated with local events. It lay unread on the coffee table.

"No, I haven't."

"You should apply. Let me know how you get on..."

I posted my application saying a prayer and hoping I had made the closing date, 3 May 1996. Now it was just a waiting game. A few days later, thinking it was a friend, I answered the phone causally with, "Hi, 7851154..."

A man's voice answered very formally, "This is Mr Hill from the Joan St...."

My heart raced faster as I listened to each word and agreed to be interviewed in Muizenberg. I scribbled the date, time and how to get there. Then I dialled Maurine's number. She was delighted to hear I had been shortlisted with two others. I prepared myself for the interview. A hair appointment with Emily, manicure, a classic suit, stockings and heels – transformed me from a country bumpkin into a city slicker.

"Down Je t'aime! You'll ladder my stockings," I pleaded with my excited poodle as I glanced in the full-length mirror before leaving for Muizenberg. His directions were clear and very soon I was parked outside the impressive *Herbert Baker* mansion, where I would be interviewed. Unaware that I was being watched, I teetered, as elegantly as possible, up the steps to the entrance. I had hardly rung the doorbell and taken a deep breath, when the door was opened by a tall good-looking fifty-something gentleman, wearing a suit.

"You must be Denyse Wild. I'm Mr Hill, the Director. Come in."

"Pleased to meet you Mr Hill," I responded as we shook hands and I followed him into a nearby office. "Take a seat."

Keeping up the formality, I sat facing him on the other side of an enormous desk. The interview began. As we spoke and he smiled, I relaxed and became the real me. Soon I discovered he had an identical twin brother, a doctor, practising in my home town, Kokstad, and his identical twin sisters were both primary school teachers, my true profession.

"I'd like you to meet Joan. She lives next door and is expecting us for tea."

George Hill told me Joan was the daughter of *CNA* magnate, AVL Lindbergh. Her only son had a brain haemorrhage and died soon after completing his degree leaving her bereft. Opening this business was her way of giving back to the community. I had no idea what to expect. As we entered her lounge, I saw how the other half live. Opulence! Sumptuous living only money could buy!

Joan, small in stature, heavily made up, with blonde hair and painted nails, sat in a corner armchair wearing an expensive jumper and leggings. Sitting near Joan was a large smiling redheaded lady, elegantly attired, dripping with expensive jewellery. Introducing me to both women, George said, "Meet Mrs Lindbergh or rather Joan, as she prefers to be addressed, and Daphne, Joan's secretary."

"Pleased to meet you Denyse," is all Joan said, her expressionless face gazing at me as I shook her soft hand. Before I had time to reflect, I watched from where I sat opposite Joan. Dressed in white, three angelic *coloured* handmaidens entered the room, carrying tea trays. Perfectly trained, they poured tea from a silver tea set into gold-rimmed china cups and served chocolate cake from a cake stand. As quietly as they entered, they disappeared. *Apartheid* was ingrained into South Africans and was evident in all walks of life. Whilst sipping tea and eating delicious cake, I struggled not to choke answering questions fired at me from three directions.

"Where do your children live?"

"How long have you been on your own?"

"Do you like me?" Joan asked her blue eyes staring at me. This direct question took me by surprise. I told her that I did, wondering if that was the right answer...

Her reply said it all, "That suits me, because I like you Denyse."

That was the signal to leave. I thanked them and said goodbye. Then George and I returned to the main building via the back door, where workmen were laying brick-paving. The inevitable happened. I looked up, missed the paving and plunged my foot into the sand, embedding my shoe. Standing off-balance, one shoe off and one shoe on, George rescued my shoe, shook off the sand and put it gently onto my foot. Feeling embarrassed in front of him and the workmen, I said, "Well Mr Hill, if nothing else, I've left my footprint behind."

On this more relaxed note I left with the promise that he would advise me within the next few days. Driving back I tried not to put my hopes up too high pondering upon my unusual experience. The next day the phone rang. I recognised the voice and answered, "Good morning Mr Hill," wondering what the verdict would be...

"Could you start on Wednesday?"

I put the phone down and exploded with excitement telling my captive audience, "Je t'aime, Emmy! I've got the job. I'll have to sort out my wardrobe..." My poodles shared my enthusiasm licking my hands and making doggie noises.

On my first day, Olga the tea-lady and cleaner greeted me, "Enjoy your coffee Mrs Wild." This kind gesture calmed my nerves. William, the handyman and driver introduced himself. He too was *Coloured* with a warm friendly nature.

Decorators hung curtains and lights; expensive ornaments were arranged; shelves were installed in the library; a computer network was cabled providing four internet computers for guests; crockery and cutlery were unpacked and stored. Distancing myself from the hubbub, I familiarised myself with a brand new computer and printer. I had a blank canvas. The administration of all documents and a filing system were my responsibility. Granny's wise words, *take one day at a time,* enabled me to tackle this daunting undertaking.

The occupants of *Sandhills,* Hector a decorator and Alastair an accountant, introduced themselves. Two quaint arched bridges, over large koi ponds lit by old-fashioned street-lamps, linked *Sandhills* and Joan's home to the Foundation. Daphne, Joan's secretary sent me this card dated 15 May 1996:

> *Dear Dynice,*
>
> *Welcome to the Foundation. I know you will be very happy here. I've been with Mrs Lindbergh for eighteen years and it's been a total joy working for her.*
>
> *Sincerely, Daphne Russell.*

Mail merge, indexing a library, designing tickets, posters and programmes were among the many things I had never done before. My sons helped me tremendously. George dictated letters to me which I transcribed from shorthand. Sometimes I typed them as he spoke. My office had a view of the sea. I watched migrating flocks of birds swooping low over the sea and wallowing whales.

The all-round sound system provided classical music in every room including the conference area upstairs. I became adept with the phone. Replies to attend the official opening poured in. This black tie evening attended by the echelon of society, Lords and Ladies, Earls and Countesses, Directors of leading businesses in and around Cape Town, caused a local stir. The *False Bay Echo* dated 6 September 1996 captured this momentous occasion with photos of Joan, Daphne and Sue Wardrop. Christopher Beatty was the guest speaker. *'Bringing back a sense of Cape style'* with a photograph of George and me, read:

> *Muizenberg's asset is the block of Herbert Baker designed houses in Beach Road and in particular, the one housing the Lindbergh Arts Foundation, the elegant venue for the promotion of the arts. The establishment of the foundation was the brainchild of philanthropist and artist, Joan St Leger Lindbergh, daughter of the*

industrious and successful AVL Lindbergh. The Foundation stages art exhibitions, music performances, lectures and poetry readings and serves as a venue for functions with a cultural component...

Managing director of this stylish venue is George Hill pictured with his secretary, Denyse Wild embody the elegant style of the Foundation. A function at this stylish venue is like no other. It is a polished performance where guests and members are greeted and treated with old school grace. They are offered good wines and specially prepared snacks, and while you would expect the atmosphere to be stuffy, it is not. It is formal but friendly and tends to bring out ye olde courtesy in all of us.

The Joan St Leger Lindbergh Arts Foundation attempts to re-introduce that sense of style which has been our heritage since the days of Lady Anne Barnard and well before – call it Cape style if you wish. We aim to create an elegant venue for the promotion of the arts, to promote promising artists and recognised ones in a celebration of cultural expression which has formed part of civilised society for many centuries. We wish to promote visual and performing artists and create an atmosphere of cultural club camaraderie among our members.

We upheld Joan's dream putting on morning and evening concerts, art exhibitions, book launches, conferences and private celebrations. The biography by Madeleine Masson titled, *'A Man of All Seasons',* tells the story of a Joan's father, Welsh schoolteacher who came to South Africa and bought a small corner shop called the Central News Agency. He and his partner Mike Davis expanded it to one of the largest chain stores in Southern Africa. Affectionately known as *AVL* he became the country's most successful exhibitor of Hereford cattle and was chairman of the SA Olympic and British Games Association in 1930.

We launched *'Her African Quest'* an autobiographical account of Barbara Tyrell's travels in South Africa researching and sketching. A *fundi* in this field and a talented artist, she became my friend.

As the Foundation succeeded and expanded, so my wardrobe enlarged to meet every occasion. George Hill, a man of few words and a former inspector of English in the Cape, wrote:

Dear Denyse *20 December 1966*

I cannot imagine what this year would have been like without your enormous contribution. You are a tremendous help to me, far beyond the confines of your job description. Thank you so much for your charm, efficiency, reliability, resourcefulness – I could go on and on. The Foundation has become an outstanding success, and much of this is thanks to you. I wish you and your family a blessed Christmas and much happiness in the New Year.

Sincerely, George Hill

This concluded 1996 with a fortnight's holiday having now achieved job satisfaction and financial security, which had eluded me for many years. Festive preparations and the arrival of my second grandchild took precedence.

On 28 December I drove Chandrè to the Durbanville hospital for her Caesarean section. Jaime and I returned to Fish Hoek. "Are we nearly there nana?" Jaime asked.

"No not yet darling." Driving to the hospital the next day, Jaime asked, "How big is my baby sister? Is she sleeping? Can she sit on my lap nana?"

Adrienne Kelsey de Jager, born on 29 December 1996, was showered with love. I longed to bond with her. I proudly watched Jaime holding her baby sister. I did not have to wait long. Driving a brand new *Peugeot,* Chandrè arrived at the Foundation during my lunch break with her two little ones. At a nearby restaurant I held my second granddaughter and listened to Jaime, a real chatterbox, who adored her baby sister. I would treasure those happy days forever...

***

Shirley Cloete was commissioned to make two glass octopuses for the Foundation. I watched in admiration as both were painstakingly mounted. Her glass, sought after by collectors, was displayed in a glass cabinet. I bought a glass paperweight to remind me of her.

Tessa Uys, an international pianist, drew a full house at her annual recitals and became a friend. I met talented and intellectual people. I knew more than 200 by name. I knew their likes and dislikes and seating preferences. The rich mingled with the less opulent diverse personalities. I loved them all.

One Saturday morning I woke up with a lopsided face. My taste buds had gone. My right eye was dry. I rushed to Sister Mary at the pharmacy in Fish Hoek. She sent me to the local hospital. "You have Bell's Palsy," the doctor informed me. "We must pump you with steroids to prevent your face from being permanently lopsided. Take twelve tablets to start with. Use the eye-drops as directed."

"I can't taste anything."

"That's all part of it. I've made you an appointment for Monday with an ENT specialist at Groote Schuur Hospital." Today I am deeply indebted to the medical staff.

The year ended with another letter of thanks from George Hill.

> *Dear Denyse* *December 1997*
>
> *Thank you so much for your wonderful assistance and contribution to the foundation during 1997. It has been a busy, successful year, and your able and gracious input has been invaluable to me. Thank you so much for assisting us to making a Foundation one we can be proud of. I wish you well over the festive season and for 1998. God bless you.*
>
> *Sincerely, George Hill.*

A third year got off to a flying start and again we featured in the newspaper this time the Cape Times dated 9 April 1998 titled:

> ***Nirvana in Muizenberg The Lindbergh a dream come true:***
> *Some people do yoga to relax. Those in the know float into the Foundation and effortlessly get very near to nirvana. A place to celebrate cultural expression...poetry evenings to classical guitar recitals...a library to immerse yourself in hidden lives...a local history room to view photographs of a bygone era...an Internet Room to escape into cyberspace... surrounded by art in its various forms, savouring tea and cake or contemplating the Koi fish...*

Material things never meant much to me, but success enabled me to enjoy some good things in life. Everything was going so well, but it would not last...

One morning George went to the bank. The vet, who attended Joan's two standard poodles, was expected. I ushered him and his wife in then answered the telephone.

"Joan passed away a few minutes ago Denyse. Where's George?"

"Oh no! George's at the bank. I'll tell the staff and put a sign 'Closed' on the door." When George arrived he was shocked to see the 'Closed' sign on the door. He entered a Foundation in mourning. I had switched off the music. I consoled Olga and William who worked at the Foundation with me. They wept uncontrollably. Later that day I knelt next to Joan's bed and prayed. Tears rolled down my face. Things were about to change drastically...

***

Joan's lifelong dream had been fulfilled. Her Arts Foundation was a resounding success. In July 1998 enormous vases of scented flowers turned every room into a spring garden. Life-long friends including an eclectic mix of dedicated hedonists, assembled to mourn her death at a Memorial Service in the Foundation. Her nephew Sean and two nieces were also present.

Syfrets managed her finances. Strange changes followed her death. One Monday morning we found the Koi floating in both ponds. A vet examined the poisoned fish. I, in my high heels and stockings, removed the putrescent carcases from the water. Following this, Hector's prized parrots were placed in strategic positions to maximise disturbance during our classical music concerts. This ended when Hector and Alastair, Joan's friends, vacated *Sandhills*.

Over and above the many extra tasks added to my profile, I arranged flowers weekly, which took 90 minutes to complete. I planned to ask for a small increment but first phoned *Flowers for Africa* for professional advice on flower-arranging fees. I ended the conversation saying, "Thank you," when Tina, a former proof-reader of *Lindlife Publishing* and presently working in an upstairs office as administration assistant, walked in and chatted to me.

On Monday George called me into his office and accused me, "Tina heard you speaking to *Flowers for Africa* in an acrimonious manner in front of several patrons. You will be required to attend a disciplinary hearing set down for 2.30 pm on Wednesday."

I never expected this. I had regarded Tina as my friend. I was not given a chance to explain.

Were they concocting a false allegation? Without legal representation, I attended the disciplinary hearing. A lawyer unfeelingly said, "Read the twenty-three allegations against you." I could scarcely take it in. My eyes settled on the words, "Your gross misconduct has forced the Foundation to sever your services with immediate effect." I had only just started to trust people!

But none of this is true, I wanted to say, but I already knew this would not reverse my predicament. I accepted defeat. I left the room. An alternative plan buzzed in my head. It just might work. I was hurting and humiliated as staff members watched me removing my personal belongings and leave. I drove away and parked out of sight. I dialled Sean, Chairman of the Board of Directors, on my mobile. He listened to my story. Aghast he said, "What utter rubbish, Denyse. Go back to work as normal tomorrow. I'm on my way to a Board meeting. This issue will be settled in your favour."

"Thanks Sean."

My return ushered in drastic measures. Tina was dismissed and Marina was employed as a wage-clerk. George worked from his home and I moved into his office. Sally Minor assisted me at reception. My workload and responsibilities increased, but the Foundation's interest was always prioritised. Sean took on a Director's role. He and his family moved into Joan's home. *Sandhills* was used as an art gallery and catering facility.

During Sean's reign, many staff were hired and fired – Tracy, Beulah, Daniel, Alex and Michelle, Gerald and Keith. The original staff members were offered a new contract determined on diminishing finances. Could this be the truth? An article in *Style* April 1998 claimed: *'Joan, CNA heiress, donated a million to the rebuilding of the burnt-down Masque Theatre in Muizenberg'.*

Previously Sean was the one who had saved me from unfair dismissal. Why did it appear that Sean was now forcing me to resign? As second-in-command, I could not accept status and salary demotion. I took my redundancy package after seeking legal advice. This decision was easier said than done. At the final concert I welcomed the members I knew so well, smiled at them and made sure they were happy, hiding my inner turmoil from them. I would *never* experience this again. This had been my life for *six* years. Why was this ending so *unfairly*? Music filled the air, but my heart played a dirge throughout the concert. Naming each member I smiled goodnight hiding my sorrow. Nobody guessed this was my *last* goodbye. I locked up the Foundation for the *last* time and drove home. In bed my sorrow spilled onto my pillow before I fell asleep.

I sent a letter saying goodbye to all the members of the Foundation. This parting from both staff and members felt like many deaths, so final. Stress and depression set in. For days I remained in bed with curtains drawn. In my darkened house, I crept deeper into my own gloomy world not wanting to eat. One day my mother arrived and said, "Pull yourself together girl."

"Just leave me alone, I want to *die!*"

I had hit rock-bottom. How would I be able to claw myself out of this mess? Where would my motivation for living come from? How would I survive without this income? Believing in the prayers and support shown to me by concerned family and friends, my world gradually lit up again.

Some members wrote me encouraging letters and some enclosed cheques to support me. Shirley Cloete famed for her two glass octopi, wrote: *I do hope you can find a suitable job that would be interesting and keep you in funds.* Naomi Harrison wrote: *I was devastated to hear you had left...For me you WERE the Foundation... It is simply not going to be the same, not seeing you... you were always such a gracious hostess, warmly welcoming...I cannot help but feel rather bitter towards the...*

I realised the more I harped back to my successful career pioneering a cultural foundation which had no precedent in South Africa, the longer it would take me to recover. Winding back the clock was impossible. I surrendered. That part of my life was over. I had to bury it, forget it and stop wishing to have it back.

'A heart at peace gives life to the body, but envy rots the bones (Prov.14:30), turned my life around. I accepted life could be cruel at times, but what counted was my attitude in adverse situations. Questions arose: Is there *ever* such a thing as job security? Could I *ever* trust again?

Denyse's varied skills and competence were a great asset in setting up an operational unit that would not only function efficiently internally, but also effectively publicise our objectives, and encourage people to visit the Foundation, attend our concerts, and become members...She single-handedly established data bases and introduced effective business procedures which became indispensable to us. Denyse set high standards and her presence at the Foundation set the appropriate tone and an example for us all to follow... She was well-liked... No concert was complete without Denyse's gracious presence and warmth... She combines a gentle humility and a sense of humour with acute psychological insight, as well as the appropriate assertiveness, and succeeded fully in ensuring that the objectives and ambience of the Foundation were effectively maintained and extended...She is extremely methodical, with a meticulous and creative eye for detail. ... a credit to the Foundation.

Even with such a praise-worthy testimonial from George Hill and with our friendship fully restored, how would I *ever* get back into the job market as a *white* South African with *black* empowerment so entrenched throughout the country in 2001?

29

FLIGHT

In 1996 Parliament adopted a new constitution. In 2000 Mbeki disallowed the use of anti-retroviral drugs in public hospitals. In 2001 thirty-nine multi-national pharmaceutical companies halted a legal battle to stop South Africa importing generic Aids drugs.

MY requested number of invitation cards arrived. *Dr and Mrs Robert Moffett request the pleasure of your company at the marriage of their daughter, Liesel to Byron, son of Denyse and the late Nolyn Wild at Kloof Catholic Church, 79 Main Road, Kloof, Durban on Saturday 8 July 1995 at 11 o'clock and afterwards at Thomas More School, Kloof, Durban.*

I added a personal note to some before sealing the envelope. I heard the dull thud as I dropped them into the letterbox. They were on their way. Topsy persuaded me to have an outfit made so we bought the pattern and material but my shapeless peach suit was most unflattering I discovered too late when I looked at the photographs.

I stayed with Liesel's parents a fortnight before getting involved in wedding preparations. On my first night before I retired I was warned, "Keep your windows closed at night Denyse."

Waking up in a strange house I wondered what lay behind the curtains. I pulled them aside. A troop of monkeys were swinging from branch to branch alongside my bedroom window. It was like a tropical jungle out there. I hurried downstairs to an empty house. Hadmud had gone to Mass and Bob to work. In the days that followed Hadmud, Liesel and I prepared for the wedding.

"I'm not allowed to go out walking alone," Teas, Liesel's youngest sister, a red-headed schoolgirl told me the afternoon she joined me for a walk. In this prestigious neighbourhood it was not safe in broad daylight for two women to be alone.

Liesel fitted her wedding gown. She looked stunning. Byron arrived. Brent was best man. Liesel's student friend, Juliet Baxter and Teas, in emerald green gowns, were to be her bridesmaids. One evening at Mass followed by a rehearsal the priest noticed Byron had not taken communion which caused an upset.

"Sort out your son, Denyse," Bob said.

"Byron's a man and quite capable of handling his own affairs."

Under duress the rehearsal went ahead and afterwards we shared a strained evening meal. Little more was said and I retired to my room but not for long.

"May we come in?"

"Yes,"

Byron and Liesel sat on my bed. We discussed the problem. "Byron, keep to your own beliefs when you receive Communion on your wedding day as part of the Nuptial Mass printed on the programme. God sees your heart and the hearts of those who believe differently from you," I suggested.

Byron agreed. We slept peacefully. I felt Nolyn's absence all the more as the day drew closer. At the reception it was arranged that I would sit on my own.

Liesel looked beautiful on her wedding day 8 July 1995 as the many photos showed. The marriage ceremony began at 11 am and went off smoothly. Re-uniting with family and friends was euphoric. Eddie and Annette van Zyl and John and Cynthia Hannocks, who had known Byron as a little boy, attended. Mom, Margy, Eddie, Kirsten, Vivian, Heather, Jeanette, Neville, Wendy, Jillian, Eileen, Derek, Chantal, Donnaleen, Doug, Scott, Sarah, Topsy and I caught up with family news. It was over too soon as we walked outside to wave goodbye to the newly-weds who drove off with cans clinking on the tarmac from the back of Byron's car advertising 'Just married.' I could scarcely take it in. My younger son was married!

Jeanette took me to the airport. I was happy to be going home. Je t'aime and Emmy welcomed me when I walked in the door. I confided in them: "I missed you, my darlings... Byron's married now... I have a new daughter... What a shame Nolyn was not with us… I hated being the bridegroom's mother without a husband!"

I pondered when Brent would also get married!

***

It was four years later that Chandrè, Jaime, Adrienne and I motored from Cape Town to East London for the celebration of Brent's marriage to Alyson Greenfield. We stayed at the Blue Lagoon Hotel overlooking the Nahoon River. The hotel was undergoing refurbishment. Noisy bulldozers belched black fumes below our room and woke us early. Dust filtered through closed windows and settled everywhere. An electricity power cut on Saturday forced us to a hairdresser further afield. On returning to the hotel, the water had been cut off. Chandrè telephoned the reception. She was told, "The builders have broken a water-pipe. The mains are switched off. We're hoping to have the pipes repaired before the wedding reception this afternoon!"

We cleaned the girls with wet-wipes. Chandrè carried Jaime from the hotel to the car. Jaime, in her long blue dress, white stockings and ballet pumps looked like a porcelain doll. She stood with Liesel at the church door, handing out confetti. We entered the church.

Despite the preliminary mishaps, a truly happy wedding ensued. Brent and Alyson made a stunning bridal couple. Rachel, Alyson's younger sister was bridesmaid, Byron was best man, Bradley was page boy and Jaime was flower girl. I felt proud of my son.

Margy and Jecca watched Jaime dance with Liesel whilst I rocked Adrienne in my arms. John and Jean Greenfield mixed with all the guests and made us feel part of the family. Their wedding day would be happily remembered.

A knock on the door at 5.30 am woke us. We were surprised to see Brent and Alyson. They said, "We've come to have coffee with you before you leave."

"Mommy, she's not wearing her wedding dress," Jaime said. We laughed enjoying this thoughtful gesture. After this memorable occasion, the newly-weds who were due to spend their honeymoon at Hoggsback, waved us goodbye.

On the journey I re-lived the wedding as I read: *Today we are gathered here to celebrate the wedding of Alyson, daughter of Jean and John Greenfield to Brent son of Nolyn and Denyse Wild. On Saturday 10 April 1999 at 4 pm*

in the Victoria Methodist Church 50 Inverleith Terrace, Quigney followed by reception at Sunset Restaurant, Blue Lagoon Hotel, Beacon Bay. I was happy as I hummed the tune of *Amazing Grace* to the words sung at their wedding: *As wedding music fills our hearts we hear the Word of Grace*
That when a home is built on love, it is God's dwelling place.
And as they now make covenant let us renew each vow
That binds us to the King of Love who stands among us now.

All my children were married. I had two granddaughters. What lay ahead?

***

Emigration, I was soon to learn, always brought pain to families. It tore loved ones apart in the struggle to survive and put food on the table. These words, from 'Awesome South Africa' by Derren Campbell, paint a picture of the necessity to emigrate in order to stay alive…

Every morning an impala awakes
Knowing that it must outrun the fastest lion it if wants to stay alive.
Every morning a lion wakes
Knowing that it must outrun the slowest impala or it will starve
It makes no difference if you are a lion or an impala
When the sun comes up in Africa, you must wake up running…

Was this the reason so many people were leaving South Africa? Would my children join the so-called 'brain drain'? Was there no *other* solution? "Mom, Liesel and I have decided to emigrate. We don't see a future for ourselves here." Those dreaded words were out. I had to face reality. Byron had graduated from UCT with an Honours Degree in Computer Science and held a good job in Stellenbosch; he'd bought his own house with a large swimming pool in Rondebosch; he drove a *Hyundai* four-door sedan with a *VW Fox* as a second car. He and Liesel had worked hard and renovated their home putting in a new kitchen, stripping out old carpets and sanding the pine floors. Their home, in peak condition, sold swiftly and they moved in with me.

Emigration demanded mounds of paperwork. I sensed their panic and stress to get work visas, passports and finances in order, but I enjoyed their company. During this time, Cape Town experienced eight mountain fires which burnt simultaneously, the worst ever. A ferocious south-easter, also known as the *Cape Doctor*, fanned the blaze. Helicopters scooped water from the ocean, dousing the destructive inferno in areas inaccessible to firefighters. All that remained afterwards were depressing charred sandy mountainsides stretching from the Groote Schuur Estate to the Cape of Good Hope Nature Reserve. Had the *dassies* and baboons survived? All the *Proteas* and *fynbos* were gone. Soot settled in our homes and the smell of ash hung gloomily in the air for months afterwards.

"I've sold both cars," Byron announced one day.

"Does this mean you'll be on your way fairly soon?"

"Yes, mom, if everything goes to plan."

Things went to plan and in April 2000, on a sunny day I set off with them to the airport, but there was no sunshine in my heart. They were about to fly miles away into the unknown, England, with nobody to meet them at the airport, with no fixed accommodation and no job. I dared not ask them about their finances as I was in no position to help.

"Byron please let me know how you're getting on. Email me from an Internet Café. Take care. I wish you both every success in your exciting venture."

We hugged. Tears streamed down my cheeks as I said, "I'll miss you. God bless."

With backpacks strapped to their backs, they waved, turned and disappeared through the 'Departure Gates' amidst thronging travellers. Parting would be difficult, but seeing that plane take to the air and knowing they were winging their way into the unknown, filled me with sadness. Returning to the house on my own was worse. Emptiness! They were truly gone! I learnt the full truth of their difficulties years later.

They only had each other; strangers in a huge impersonal London, where they struggled to survive, staying in youth hostels and battling the cold in unsuitable clothing. Byron wore a suit for job interviews and Liesel waited a distance away, with two huge backpacks, their worldly possessions! Feeling fragile and fed up with London, they travelled to Oxford to stay with Liesel's relative. On the train journey, Byron arranged a job interview in Coventry, which was successful. They rented a Council flat, used public transport and made do with little. It was far from the life they had left behind in South Africa a few weeks ago. All I was told then was, "We're fine. I've found a job and we're renting a house."

My daughter had been planning to emigrate too but, with two children, they had additional delays. For me this delay meant more time with Jaime and Adrienne until Chandrè announced quite unexpectedly, "Anton's been made an offer he cannot refuse... The company will pay for our flights and provide us with a furnished house in Holland."

"Holland! But you can't speak Dutch!"

Their Durbanville home, with pool, large garden and distant view of Table Mountain, sold quickly. Anton and Chandrè had worked hard, published a book in two languages, *'Farm Labour: A guide to basic labour law in the agricultural sector'* and lived comfortably with the help of a servant. They down-sized to a rented townhouse and from there, their possessions were crated for storage. Jaime and Adrienne spent the last week with me. This enabled Chandrè and Anton to complete their last-minute tasks without upsetting the two girls especially when the packers arrived and their world disappeared into boxes.

In December 2000, on a sweltering hot day, I wheeled Jaime and Adrienne on a trolley into the terminal building of the Cape Town International Airport. Topsy caught this on camera. My mother came to say goodbye. In the busy airport building we gathered as a family, savouring the last minutes together. Two-year-old Adrienne slept in my arms and Jaime, just five, with a sprained ankle enjoyed all the fuss made of her. Then their flight was called up. Unrestrained tears flowed as we bade them farewell.

"I hope she doesn't wake up," I whispered handing my precious bundle to Chandrè.

"Nana! Nana! I want my nana!" she screamed, flailing arms and legs about as she fought to get back to me. Chandrè, drained emotionally, tried to pacify her, but to no avail. This little family disappeared into the throng of travellers as Adrienne's screams faded away. I was later told she was still crying on take-off and for two hours into the flight.

Although I had programmed myself beforehand that this time it wouldn't be such a wrench, it was much worse. Four family members were gone. All that was left were the bleak reminders as I gazed at the possessions they had given me. Toys for Brent and Alyson's one year-old daughter Jordyn, pot plants and books were scattered around my home. Depression drowned my joy knowing there would be no more fun weekends with my granddaughters and no more meals with this family.

The only way to see them would be for me to travel to Holland. Impossible though it seemed at the time, I resolved to work, to save and to visit.As a white woman I was discriminated against in the workplace. I tended a property in Simon's Town and cared for Mrs Knoop who was disabled, when they visited SA for five months each year. I joined up as a beauty advisor for *Avroy Schlain* cosmetics to improve my monthly income.

Chandrè's first letter warmed my heart. Some emigration issues included: living in minus degree temperatures; a daily language barrier; driving on the *right* side of snow-covered and icy roads and deciphering strange food in supermarkets. Despite having to scrape ice off the windscreen each morning, the girls attended a Montessori school in a nearby village and picked up a few words of Dutch!

I consoled myself. Brent, his lovely wife Alyson and my little granddaughter, Jordyn, were still in the country. More time was spent visiting them in East London despite the distance, 1000 kilometres. But at the back of my mind the question lurked. How much longer would it be before *they* emigrated? They owned a new home, had a large circle of friends and Brent had been promoted in his IT job with the *Old Mutual*.

"Our house is on the market," Brent told me on the phone one November evening. He continued, "We're off to the UK. We can't take the stress and violence anymore. I have to think of Jordyn."

It was not long before Brent, Alyson and Jordyn spent a few days with me before emigrating. Byron and Liesel would meet and accommodate them initially. The days flew past. On their last day, my birthday 20 March 2002, we went to Ratanga Junction. I wheeled two-year old Jordyn in her pushchair whilst Brent and Alyson enjoyed adrenalin-pumping rides, which included the famous 'cobra'. After a fun day together we returned to 35 The Glen where Topsy and my mother were waiting. My sister said, "You can't shower now. You'll miss your flight."

Brent and Alyson ignored her. They showered, closed their cases, which they then dragged and loaded into the boot of her car and mine. There was too much luggage for one car. We drove to the airport trying to be cheerful. Saying goodbye to this family was the hardest of all. They were the last of my three children emigrating. A dark cloud of despair descended over me. How would I survive?

As a family we had fled the Transkei in 1976 and then fled the Ciskei when it too became independent. We wanted to always be a part of our beloved country. I consoled myself knowing I was not alone. I still had my wider family. Since 1991, 1,500 Whites had been killed and since 1994 250,000 Whites had emigrated. So many South African families suffered separation anxiety as they were divided in search of a better life in America, Australia, New Zealand, Europe and the UK. But, giving up your place of birth with no guarantee of success was no easy task. Severing the support of lifetime friends and family and adjusting to living in a servant-less world was only the beginning of stretching their coping mechanisms to the maximum.

Emigration, born out of need and not choice, had torn my immediate family apart. Left behind, I struggled on alone, encouraging all three families, as best I could, from a distance...

30

WILL THE PAIN EVER PASS?

Mbeki chose what he termed 'quiet diplomacy' when Zimbabwe's dictator Robert Mugabe began his terror to stay in power. Together they blamed Britain for not committing to financing land distribution and supporting its own 'white kith and kin' in Zimbabwe. In 2002 Gadhafi said to a crowd of 30,000 spectators in Durban, "Africa is our land!" He referred to the whites in SA and Zimbabwe saying:"...forgive the whites. They are now poor. You are your own masters... You are free! We are bigger than them! We are mighty! If they want to serve us, okay. If they want to go back, okay. Goodbye..."

WHAT made me do it? Was I driven by loneliness? Was it the fear of growing old alone? Or was I missing my children and grandchildren? Whatever the reason I made a huge mistake. It was when I worked as a beauty advisor for *Avroy Schlain* cosmetics, that Marie one of my clients, introduced me to her close friend, a widower born in Holland. She felt we were well suited. I fobbed her off saying, "I'm not interested," but she was not taking *no* for an answer. I was gardening one spring morning when the phone rang. I ran to answer it.

"Ja, I've spoken to my friend. He's keen to meet you," Marie said.

"No! I told you I'm not..."

"*Ag,* Oh Denyse, please join us for coffee at the Longbeach Mall. He's handsome."

I'm up to my elbows in dirt. I'm gardening and..."

"*Moenie* worry *nie,* don't worry. We'll see you at *Costa* at 11 am. *Lekker!* "What had I let myself in for? I arrived in a white blouse, shorts and sandals and saw Marie from a distance. Hair coiffured, perfumed and oozing with charm, her short plump figure moved towards me.

She drew me into her arms, flattering me, "You look smashing. Come and join us. Ton meet Denyse."

A sun-tanned slimmish man wearing shorts, a striped T-shirt and a cap, stood up and reached for my hand. He had bushy eyebrows and blue eyes behind glasses. He smiled at me, "I'm very pleased to meet you Denyse. Marie's told me all about you."

I responded politely. Coffee was ordered. During the ensuing conversation I learnt he and Marie had a lot in common. They had been in a relationship before she, a widow, married her present husband. They spoke Dutch. Before leaving I gave him my telephone number never thinking there would be any follow up, but there was.

I was content doing my own housework. I loved my home and garden so much. I wanted to end my days here. Ton visited me more often. I was taken in with his charm. He proposed to me. I accepted ignoring the warning bells: My pastor refused to marry us because Ton was not a Christian; my children would not be attending the wedding; I ended up in Constantiaberg Hospital with a twisted colon. He overcrowded my house with his possessions. He allowed his son, Lex and family who were struggling to move into his house at 50 Chebec Crescent owned by his Dutch in-laws. On 27 July 2002 we were married in the Kommetjie Catholic Church. A reception was held at Dolores' home in her *Montessori* school. He had six children: Hanni, Rene, Dolores, Ronnie, Lex and Tommy and eight grandchildren the youngest of which were twins.

A month later I flew to the UK and Holland to visit my children and to work as a live-in carer to survive. After re-marrying I lost the monthly income from Nolyn's Estate. I had no pension. When I returned, Ton said, "We've got to move to 50 Chebec Crescent. I'm the only person permitted to live there."

"If I'm unhappy could we return to 35 The Glen?"

He agreed. I spent money on picket-fencing, painting the interior, new curtain rails, shampooing the carpets, kitchen and garden improvements. The house looked like an auction room, chock-a-block after I moved in. It was tiny. Worst of all was the traffic noise. I was unable to sleep or even go outside. Day and night the traffic droned on and on. I could not live with this. I pleaded to move back. He refused and his doctor put me on *Prozac*.

My mother turned 80 in 2003. We celebrated her birthday at Topsy's house. I paid her this tribute:

My mother, born on 3 June 1923, grew up on a farm near Cathcart and rode to school on horseback. Money could never outweigh love. You were raised with love and received the labours of love – mielie-cob dolls hand-knitted socks and jerseys, home-sewn dresses, home-made bread and butter and home-grown fruit and veggies.

Disaster forced your family to leave the farm – a severe fire followed by drought a year later. You moved to Kokstad where 'D M Brown General Dealer Store' was started. You were educated at the convent... were taken under the wings of Jimmy Wardlaw. Nothing escaped Jimmy's notice and you had to own up to attempting to smoke with Ruth! Your fine pair of legs did not go by unnoticed and you were aptly nicknamed 'Legs!'

You inherited your love of music from your mother, who taught classical piano at the Queenstown Convent. Joan your elder sister played the mandolin, Molly played the Hawaiian guitar and Ruth played the piano. You had piano and accordion lessons. Your dad loved to sit at the piano with you. He played the left hand and you the right.

Your piano playing provided additional income. We sang 'Lily Marlene, White Cliffs of Dover, I'll Be Seeing You, and A Nightingale Sang in Berkeley Square' and others as you played. We shared hard times but happy times. You taught us to respect our elders, to obey without question, to eat everything on our plate, to be seen and not heard, to know right from wrong and to put on our Sunday best for Mass which we never missed. We grew up in a house of love and felt secure. You married Philip Leary and we loved our brother, Patrick. You gave me driving lessons.

You moved from Kokstad to 'Graydene', East London as a widow and pursued your love of bowls becoming a singles, pairs and trips champion. Besides being the Lady President for many years, you also represented Border in national tournaments.

In 1996 you moved to 32 Sycamore Crescent in Fish Hoek and enjoyed regular afternoons of 'Rummikub' and 'Scrabble' with friends. You always had green fingers and kept a colourful garden, all the year round. You were an example to us. You darned and mended, recycled everything, crocheted sunhats out of plastic shopping bags, bathed economically and never wasted food. God has blessed you as the matriarch of our family with a son and three daughters, six sons-in- law, six grandchildren and four great-grandchildren.

My annual overseas trips brought temporary relief but I dreaded returning. More and more demands were made on me to reduce his debt. I stopped this when I learnt how lavishly he lived and how Ton's debt remained unchanged. I also learnt later how he visited my mother and sister and he badmouthed me. Neither would allow him back into their homes. My life became miserable. I felt trapped and friendless. My own family deserted me making lame excuses as to why they could not attend my 60th birthday tea. When I believed things could not get much worse, the phone rang.

"Hi Neyse. Can you come over for tea?"

Just like my sister, indirectly telling me what to do!

"I'm knee high in mud. I'm cleaning the fish pond..."

"It won't take long. You can go back and finish cleaning your fish pond. You see, it's an opportunity mom's waited for – to have the three of us together."

"Are Margy and John already with you?"

"Yes, they had lunch with Bill, mom and me."

My hackles rose. I had not been invited. My anger intensified knowing I had been ostracised from family get-togethers because of Ton. It was understandable, but *I* was still family. "Oh, I see..."

"You'll need to come over now."

I felt like my sister expected me to come running whenever it suited her. My blood pressure rose. She never gave me a chance to reply.

"Surely you won't disappoint mom?" she was cleverly transferring the guilt on to me."I'll try to be there by 3.30 pm," I replied to keep the peace.

"Thanks. I'll tell mom. Goodbye."

She's done it again, I thought, slamming down the phone as Ton walked in. Although I knew he had been eavesdropping, he asked, "What was that all about?"

"Topsy's invited *me* to tea," I began.

"And you're going?"

"Yes, whatever it is. It's better to get it over and done with."

Ton had not been invited. His feelings showed as he watched me climbing into my *Hyundai Accent.* Alone I drove over the *Ou Kaapse Weg* shrouded in mist, which thickened as I ascended the steep Silvermine Mountain pass. Unable to enjoy the views of rocky coves or Lion's Head, I wound down my window slightly to savour the fresh mountain air, the *fynbos* and *Protea repens,* sugar bush, SA's national flower. When hiking in the Silvermine Nature Reserve, I had seen sugarbirds probing for nectar deep into the flower head, pollinating *Proteas* this way. My mood improved when I thought how blessed I was to live in such a beautiful part of the world.

I descended to the other side, now in bright sunshine. Electric fencing surrounded the prestigious golf course to my left, which contrasted starkly with the electric fencing and coiled barbed wire demarcating the *Victor Verster* prison boundaries to my right. Vineyards stretched up the lower slopes of the Constantiaberg Mountains giving way to pine forests higher up. I drove through the Tokai Forest and along Spaansgemacht Road into Vergelee Road. I parked in the driveway behind the double garage.

When I rang the doorbell, two *Jack Russells* bounded through the house towards the security gate, barking. Ignoring my greeting momentarily, Topsy admonished her dogs, "Shush Spot! No, Scamp!"

Topsy, hot and flustered, came down two steps and unlocked the gate. "Hi Neyse. Come in."

I made my way past her stylish lounge, only used on special occasions, into the open-plan TV lounge and kitchen where the family were seated. Bill greeted me from his chair, where he continued filling his pipe with loose tobacco. I hated the smell of cigarettes and smoke. I bent over to kiss my mother. Margy and John stood up, saying, "It's good to see you Neyse," which made me feel a little more welcome…

"Tea Neyse?" Topsy asked from behind the kitchen counter.

"Thanks," I said, finding a vacant chair and sitting down.

My tea arrived with an enormous slice of chocolate cake which I declined. My sister persisted, "Come on, it's delicious. I baked it today."

"*No* thanks!"

She plonked the plate with the cake down noisily, showing her annoyance. With the preliminaries over, it was down to business. A nod from my mother prompted Topsy to ask, "Shall I fetch them now, mom?"

"Yes please Tops," my mother replied which sent my sister out the room, but she soon returned carrying three large brown envelopes. She presented one to Margy and one to me with my name on it, saying, "Mom's given this a lot of careful thought to make sure it's fair. She'd like to give us our inheritance of jewellery today," Topsy announced, glancing across the room at Bill, who showed no interest.

A while back my mother told me she was dividing her jewellery. We spoke about granny's ring, a family heirloom. Had she included granny's ring? Surely not, since the three of us were in favour of sharing the ring, just as granny had arranged for her four daughters. The opening-of-the brown-envelope procedure dragged out. In turn we took out a piece of jewellery, admired it and thanked my mother until all three envelopes were empty.

Can you imagine how I, the eldest daughter, felt after this? Topsy admired my mother's diamond engagement ring on her finger and Margy held *granny's* ring. My disappointment vied with my rage for top position. I excused myself and stalked out of the room, red-faced, with the offensive brown envelope under my arm. My hurt went much deeper than the contents.

For many years my mother had worn granny's ring. I dreamt of wearing it one day, for a year maybe; of passing it on to my daughter, who would pass it on to her daughters; of sharing the family heirloom; of continuing the inheritance in the family.

When I returned my packet the following day declining my inheritance, Bill said, "Topsy and your mother are still asleep." I was hardly home when a telephone altercation followed between Topsy and me.

"You'll give mom a heart attack with what you're doing!" Topsy said.

"I'm only telling the truth. How can you honestly call this *fair*?"

"It *is* fair. It's what mom *wanted*."

"If it's fair, let's return our packets, shuffle them up and each choose an unmarked packet. Agreed?"

"Don't be mad!"

"But that would be fair!"

The phone was slammed down on me. My indescribable hurt, despite these words I found on an old card, has never left me...

There are times when you have been hurt so badly
That you become certain that the pain will never pass.
But it does...
Sometimes because of your efforts, sometimes in spite of them,
But always, always it goes away.
So hold on and know that tomorrow will come,
And with each tomorrow, it will be better...

Added to this pain, I faced having to put my beloved poodle Je t'aime, down. Maurine my friend assisted me before I flew back to England. My pain went very deep.

***

The day the phone rang and I spoke to a care manager, Charles from England, was an answer to prayer. "Denyse, a three-month caring position has come up in London. If you're interested you'll be interviewed telephonically by the client's son Peter."

"I'm certainly very interested. When would I start?"

"As soon as possible... two weeks from today. While I remember, Peter would like you to email him a photograph of yourself..."

Everything happened so fast. I emailed a picture of myself as requested, had an hour's telephonic interview with Peter and secured the job. The next few days were frantic – buying my return air ticket and making arrangements for my absence from home.

Ever since my family had emigrated, I had flown to Holland and England to spend time with them. This time there was one person who did not share my excitement. Ton unobtrusively did his best to hinder my preparations, but nothing would stop me now. Jobless, and with debts rising every month, this would solve our financial pressure. I said goodbye, promised to write letters, to text and to phone, little realising then how difficult this would be.

As I flew from Cape Town to London Heathrow my fellow passengers were relaxed and, in contrast, I was filled with foreboding with no notion of what lay in store for me. Soon I would be entrenched in hard work, and plenty of it, in an overpopulated world and yet I would feel lonelier than a single survivor on a desert island.

London conjured up past memories: Was Don, father of my daughter, still alive? Would I find him in London? Was he living with another woman? A part of me longed to see the man I had once loved so deeply all those years ago, to hear his voice again and to see his laughing smile, but a part of me was afraid to know the truth.

Having spent most of my life in wide open spaces looking up into starry skies at night, living in large homes with servants doing all the mundane housework and driving my own car wherever my heart desired, in trepidation I recoiled deeper into my seat. I took another sip of wine. The very idea of living in a claustrophobic flat surrounded by concrete and noise in a sprawling cosmopolitan metropolis of about 1600 sq. km, travelling in the fast-moving over-crowded *Underground*, sent shivers down my spine.

The plane landed. There was no turning back now. Carrying my hand luggage, I smiled at the air hostesses in gratitude before I thronged my way into the long 'Passport Control' queue for non-UK residents. I collected my suitcases from the 'Luggage Reclaim' and exited the bustling terminal building. Clutching my ticket, I waited to board a bus to meet Charles, my employer. After a sleepless night and my inexperience at airport navigation, my adrenalin rush maximised before all my energy was sapped from me. I arrived at High Wycombe, my destination.

"Welcome. *Hoe gaan dit?* How are you? Did you have a good flight? Coffee?"

"*Baie dankie,* Thank you."

Hearing Afrikaans spoken and Charles' familiar South African accent, settled my nerves. Sighing I plonked myself onto the nearest chair. We chatted over coffee. He wore a short-sleeved shirt but under my coat I wore three layers of clothes. To me, 13°C was cold.

We drove off and in no time had arrived at Cranmer Court in Finchley. Knowing I was about to come face to face with Trudi and her son Peter, I had no time to take stock of my surroundings. We took the lift to the second floor and rang the bell.

Ninety-something Trudi sat in a recliner bathed in sunlight next to south-facing lounge windows. Bald, tall and thin, Peter dominated the conversation as he fiddled with his spectacles. My mind absorbed important matters and discarded the rest like selective hearing. After this introductory meeting, Charles left and I felt as if I steered the ship alone. As it turned out, that is what live-in caring is like. On duty 24/7 gave me no time for myself. I had two seven-hour breaks on Wednesdays and Sundays, the legal weekly minimum.

Because I intend to write *'Memoirs of a Carer'* my caring experiences in London will be kept brief. I bought food and cooked, bathed, dressed and pampered Trudi, made beds, cleaned toilets, dusted, polished, hoovered, laundered, ironed, ordered in and unpacked incontinence supplies, phoned for medical and beauty appointments, drove Trudi to engagements, to see friends and for walks in various parks, lunching some days at the Golder's Green park restaurant. Between chores, I pushed her to the toilet and back in her wheelchair, gave her a foot massage, prompted medications and assisted with physiotherapy exercises. Chiropodists, reflexologists and physiotherapists came and went weekly. I kept a detailed report for the Care agency, documented a monthly income and expenditure report with relevant receipts and emailed a weekly report to Peter who lived in San Francisco.

I mailed the *Financial Times* and Peter's post weekly and conveyed messages from him to the housekeeper regarding the lease of his London flat. The smooth-running of white goods, heating and water became my responsibility. Weekly shopping trips to Brent Cross were fraught with energy-sapping routines – finding a disabled parking space, unloading and seating Trudi in the wheelchair, weaving through crowds of shoppers in the Mall and reaching a toilet in time. Exhausted I pushed her over-loaded wheelchair to the car, keeping Trudi dry during difficult wheelchair-to-car transfers.

To me Trudi came first. In her twilight years I vowed to give her quality of life as she battled heart problems, dementia, double incontinence and immobility. This required extreme patience, particularly after successive sleep-deprived nights. I questioned myself: How would you like somebody to treat you in the same circumstances? In this way I was able to overlook and forget her unpredictable behaviour. We had a good relationship. I treated her with total respect and dignity and she in return, trusted and enjoyed my company.

Charles phoned weekly. He gave me the telephone number of a SA carer called Elsie. Short, dark-haired with a guttural accent, we became firm friends. Also a carer she boosted my confidence, gave me invaluable advice and allowed me to sleep on her bed during my time-off. She showed me the wide open spaces of Finchley Park and Avenue House Estate. I shared my secret with Elsie – I had lived in London with Donal Clarke in 1967 and I had borne his daughter in SA.

We took a pink London taxi to Westbourne Gardens one day. Walking along the same pavement I had walked thirty-eight years ago when I fell pregnant with my first baby, I reached the stairs to the flat. Would Donal be in? Would he pick up the answer phone? Would he recognise me? I rang the bell and waited.

"Ring it again," Elsie encouraged me. I did. It was then we both burst out laughing. In all my excitement I had not noticed the building was under construction and was unoccupied. Had a meeting with Donal been prevented for my own good, I pondered. Trying to hide my disappointment, I said, "Too bad! We had our first ride in a *pink* taxi!" and Elsie sensing my sadness, had me laughing again in no time.

Before the three months were up Charles offered me an extension of my contract. I could hardly turn down this opportunity. Jobs in South Africa were scarcer than hen's teeth. When I asked Ton what he thought, I sensed he wanted me to return. He said, "You decide."

My decision had irreversible consequences. A week later Topsy phoned saying, "Ton's threatened to put all your belongings out in the street, on garbage collection days!"

The starving blacks ate rubbish and fed babies strapped to their backs as they scavenged in the filthy garbage bags. My belongings would be Christmas to them!

"Are you sure?" I questioned Topsy, never thinking Ton would stoop so low.

"I'm positive. It's the talk of Fish Hoek."

"I'll phone him and get back to you."

After my telephone conversation with Ton, I slammed the phone down in a rage. He told me he could not wait until I returned in December, ending, "I can't bear to see *anything* of yours in *my* house. It must all be thrown out *now*."

The prospect of losing all my possessions yet again opened up my past hurts. Nolyn had won the court-case and secured everything leaving the children and me with virtually nothing. His untimely death resulted in a Public Auction, when I agonised seeing my worldly possessions vanish into the hands of strangers. No, I refused to lose the little I owned for a third time. It would be a struggle. I could only return to South Africa in December.

I gave Topsy *Power of Attorney*. With great difficulty she took charge. *Stuttafords,* under her supervision, packed and moved my possessions and my car into *Storageland*. She simmered and boiled, argued and defended me as she gathered my things from the higgledy-piggledy mess.

With Elsie back in South Africa for good, I had lost the only friend I had to confide in. My personal problems were never disclosed in the workplace. My health suffered. Triggered by stress overload, psoriasis, red flaking plaques covered my entire body even my face. As if this was not enough when I smiled in public, people shunned me thinking I had a contagious disease. If they knew my circumstances would they have at least smiled back? I was homeless, put out into the street by my husband. I worked in a foreign country. I had no friends nearby.

Only *one* thing had not changed. The Lord still loved me unconditionally and my trust was in Him. I counted my blessings. I had a roof over my head, food on my plate, I could see, hear and walk. My brain functioned normally even though I concentrated hard to put toothpaste on my brush and several routines I had previously done automatically. The sun setting over the trees in the park, foxes jumping over the boundary wall at night and birds twittering at daybreak, restored my will to press on until December.

It was then I flew to Cape Town. My mother welcomed me with open arms and I knew she hurt for me. It was no holiday. I consolidated my possessions in *Storageland* from three to two units. I again nominated my children as beneficiaries on my Life Insurance policies, gave banks and businesses my mother's address and resigned as secretary of the Fish Hoek Friends of Music Society and as beauty advisor for Avroy Schlain cosmetics.

My mother tried to recover *The Last Supper,* a framed tapestry granny had made for me and some other sentimental items from Ton, but to no avail. With the money I had saved, I put down a deposit on a flat, 5 Kinrae Court in Fish Hoek, visited John and Margy in Kleinmond and spent a day with my friend Ruth before I flew back to London.

It was freezing cold in Finchley after temperatures of 32 degrees in Fish Hoek. I missed lying in the shade of the bottlebrush on my mother's lawn, reading and our competitive games of *Scrabble* as I chatted to my mom in the evenings...

Still covered in psoriasis, I believed things could only get better in 2007. For the moment I belonged in London: to work, to pay off my mortgage and one day, to unpack my few worldly possessions into my very own home. All the hardship I endured would *then* be worthwhile. Driven by loneliness I contacted Gail who once lived in Muizenberg. Ruth my friend, a carer in England, had recently introduced me to Gail.

"Hi Gail. Do you remember me? I met you through Ruth a while back."

"Of course I do. How're you doing Denyse?"

"Fine, but I was wondering if I could visit you on Sunday?"

"I'm moving. Would you like to help me?"

"I'd love to."

"Do you have a car?"

"Yes,"

Plans were made for Sunday. Her friend George would meet me at the Barnet Hospital. From there I would follow George's car to Enfield where we would both move Gail's belongings to Stevenage. George telephoned me to confirm the arrangements and asked, "How will I recognise you Denyse?"

"'I'll be wearing a pale green jacket."

I was the only person in the Barnet Hospital cafeteria, our meeting place, when a grey-haired man strode up to me and said, "Hello. You must be Denyse. I'm George."

"Hello George."

"Would you like a coffee?"

"Yes please."

I could not help but notice his gentle blue eyes which matched his blue shirt. I pushed what I was thinking from my head, after all, *he* was Gail's friend *and I* was a married woman. I returned to Finchley with a skip in my step, from helping a friend, I believed. George had other ideas. Weeks later he invited me to lunch. We got on very well, but I made it quite clear to him I was married and valued him as a friend.

All my life I had yearned for love and to give love. I tasted love briefly then it escaped me. I loved *Dafoo*, who died at my bedside. I loved my dad, but he became a person I never understood after that awful night of 22 December. The love he gave me was cut short. From his deathbed he begged to see his daughters one last time. His desperate effort to reach out to us in love was also denied.

Love came and went fleetingly. In 1966 Donald Smith, my first love, was killed tragically leaving me widowed, aged twenty. In London love swept me off my feet even breaking down the barriers of religion. The man I loved, Donal Clarke, never followed me to South Africa as he had promised. In 1968 that love was no more. I fought hard to love Nolyn, believing I could change him. In 1989 when our love was being restored, he died disastrously in a car accident. In 2002 love was blind when I married Ton, a miserable mistake. In the next three years he had labelled me a schizophrenic and had his doctor put me on *Prozac*. I was through with men for life. My heart had been broken too often.

How do you quench love? How could I walk away from true love? How could I resist George's gentleness, kindness, considerateness, patience, understanding and support. With George I could be myself and not try to be what I was not. He gave me red roses. He phoned me each night... He even searched and found a glove I dropped. I spent Christmas with my two sons in Dorking and gave George two shirts. He gave me a diamond necklace. This was the beginning of more than friendship, but...

After a break in Dorking, I returned to care for Trudi in Finchley. The day Peter flew back to San Francisco Trudi's toilet handle broke making it impossible to flush. I had this repaired, but Peter's reaction was unreasonable. I resigned. My relief carers, dark-haired eccentric Mona, my age, from Lebanon and Luba, in her twenties, from Slovakia, took over from me. I trained them in order to maintain the high standard of care when I left.

I hugged Trudi goodbye. "Please Denyse don't leave me," she begged. It was not easy to walk away...Charles found me a caring position in Bovingdon near Hemel Hempstead where George lived. Caring for Phyllis Deacon, Jennifer and Terry's mother, I tried to make Phyllis happy and comfortable, but her health deteriorated and she was hospitalised. I visited Phyllis in hospital. She, frail and weak, sang her favourite song for me. She touched my heart. How long did we have left to share these tender moments?

When I visited George on Sunday 10 February 2008, Luba phoned, saying, "Mrs Tausinger died at 2.40 pm today, outside your bedroom on the way to the toilet!"

"What happened? She was so well! Does Peter know? Are you alright?"

I telephoned Peter in San Francisco to offer him help and my condolences. He was overcome with grief. Mona, Luba and I met at Brent Cross in a quiet corner of a restaurant. We took turns giving her a last tribute over a cup of tea. My grief lasted days and days. One day it would pass.

It was time to take stock of my life. I took a break from caring. I decided to allow my marriage to become 'null and void' by living apart from Ton for five years. My friendship with George turned into love. In fairness to us, I found a divorce lawyer on the internet and my divorce proceedings began. I wrote a letter to Ton's six children admitting my guilt and asking them for forgiveness, but heard nothing back from them.

I was a free woman on 2 April 2008 despite resistance and a threatening email. George proposed and shyly slid a beautiful diamond engagement ring on my finger on 10 April. I was 63 and George was 78 when we arranged our wedding in South Africa over the internet. Steve Rowe of *Perfect Weddings* telephoned us regularly checking on the arrangements. "You'll love Henry the pastor," Steve said on the phone.

With our matching wedding bands packed, piles of documentation in order for our marriage to take place and to obtain a visa to re-enter England; with accommodation booked, we flew from Heathrow. Topsy met us and drove us to Fish Hoek where we transferred to my car in *Storageland*. I introduced my mother to George. They got on well but we had to leave for Stellenbosch. We stayed on a wine farm, *Aan-den-Weg* run by Petra and her husband. She, blond and tall, could not do enough to help us. The next day we explored Stellenbosch and visited *Blaauklippen Wine Estate* in pouring rain.

We woke to sunshine and rose petals on our breakfast table on 31 May. Petra shared our excitement, covering the bonnet of our car with roses... George looked handsome in his new suit. I wore a peach suit and cream shoes. Steve Rowe waited for us at *Blaauwklippen* and ran through the programme. Before introducing us to Pastor Henry Haynes, he presented me with a bouquet and George with a matching button-hole. Henry, rotund smiling and efficient, checked our documents and described the order of the wedding service. We commended Steve on his perfect arrangements.

Looking out to majestic mountains and nearby vineyards, Henry in the presence of my mother, Topsy and Bill, Margy and John, officiated. He presided over the ceremony reading from God's Word, before we took our wedding vows and shed a small tear of joy. With his blessing at the end, we signed the Register.

Standing in the shade of old oak trees amidst squirrels scampering about, we enjoyed a glass of champagne as informal photos were taken. Afterwards we shared a delicious meal in the museum exclusively for our wedding party. I wanted the day to last forever, but it was time to say goodbye. Back in Stellenbosch we changed into more relaxing clothing then George and I walked hand in hand, newly-weds, through the vineyards as the last rays of sun sank behind the mountains and flickering farm lights dotted the darkness.

We honeymooned at Arniston a remote fisherman's resort. We were treated to fresh fish in a tiny fisherman's village restaurant and the two brown ladies sang for us in Afrikaans. We explored Franschhoek and neighbouring wine farms, Boschendal and Spier. We visited Hermanus and Margy and John in Kleinmond. Idyllic days sharing our love for each other...

We celebrated mom's 85th birthday at Topsy's house together with Margy and John, Kirsten, David, Ann, Patrick and Bill. Topsy excelled as usual in the kitchen. Between securing a Spouse's Visa from the British Embassy in Cape Town; buying new light fittings for 35 The Glen and curtain rails for my flat, we played *Scrabble* with mom.

We packed. I was emigrating. Is this where Africa ends for me, I wondered. I looked at the familiar people and heard the proverbial voices around me. As I boarded the plane that would take me far away from Africa, a twinge of sadness tore at my heart.

At daybreak we landed at Terminal Five on 4 July 2008 as Mr and Mrs Halse. We returned to Hemel Hempstead on the *National Express* coach in a heat-wave. Plans were underway for a celebration with our families and friends in England. George's youngest daughter Pat, kindly arranged this at the Cannizaro Hotel. We languished in luxury accommodation the night before. The small flower arrangements I had made for each table were put in our room.

On 25 August 2008 both our families were united for the first time. George's three children: his son Alan and partner Sheena and Jason, Alan's son; his eldest daughter Linda and husband Peter and their two children, Ellen and Jack and his youngest daughter Pat married to Mark and their son Sam. Mark's parents, Brian and Eileen attended. They met my daughter, Chandrè and her daughters, Jaime and Adrienne who had flown over from Holland; Brent, my eldest son married to Alyson and their daughter Jordyn and my youngest son, Byron and his wife, Liesel and my two grandsons, Peter and Matthew.

My friends Luba and her Australian boyfriend, Ashleigh; Mona; Charles and his wife, Heather; Trudi's friends and mine – Walter, Jackie and ninety-eight year-old Hanni. George's sister-in-law, Joan and her husband, David and George's late wife's sister, Margaret and her brother, Peter joined us. They shared our joy and their presence made us happy…

George and I lived in our flat in Hemel Hempstead, convenient for the Baptist Church, library and shops, but we were already making plans for our future…

31

NEW LIFE IN THE NEW FOREST

In 2004 South Africa suffered from one of the highest crime rates in the world. Thabo Mbeki begins a second term as president and Mangosuthu Buthelezi is dropped from the cabinet. In May 2008 waves of violence directed at foreigners, hits townships across SA. Dozens of people die. Thousands of Zimbabweans, Malawians and Mozambicans return home.

ALTHOUGH I chose to leave South Africa a part of me will always be there. My childhood memories of the sounds, smells and the beauty of Africa will never be obliterated. They will go to my deathbed and rise up like the grey smoke of a candle when snuffed out, corkscrewing upwards.

George and I returned from South Africa to live in our flat in Hemel Hempstead. I was now Mrs Halse. My few possessions, shipped from South Africa, were put into storage because the flat was too small. This prompted us to house-hunt on the internet. With fond memories of a previous stay in the New Forest, Hampshire, we booked into a self-catering cottage in Everton for a week. Robert, an estate agent, showed us numerous houses. We liked a house in Hordle which we had seen on the internet. Our offer on 10 Charnock Close was accepted. Our flat was rented out. By 18 December 2008 we had moved into our new home.

Byron, Liesel, Peter and Matthew rang our doorbell and sang, "*We wish you a merry Christmas.*" They and Liesel's sister Teas, spent Christmas with us. Brent, Alyson and Jordyn laden with presents arrived on Christmas Day. A family togetherness was shared over a joyous Christmas celebration. After both families returned to Dorking George and I travelled to London for a second celebration at George's daughter Pat's house. I was overjoyed to be part of George's loving family: his son, Alan and partner Sheena; his elder daughter Linda and her husband, Peter Millard and their children, Ellen and Jack; and his younger daughter, Pat and her husband Mark Edmondson and their son, Sam; and Peter and Margaret Thomson, brother and sister of George's late wife, Jean.

Early in 2009 after my training at Blandford Forum, I started work for *Agincare* as a carer, a challenging and rewarding job. I was able to love the elderly in their homes in Bransgore, Barton-on-Sea, Milford-on-Sea, Lymington, New Milton, Ashley, Boldre, Brockenhurst, Hordle and Everton. I mourned those who passed away but I hold fond memories of them.

After frequent visits to Dorking, George became well acquainted with Brent, Alyson, Byron and Liesel. Jordyn, Peter and Matthew welcomed him as their grandpa showering him with love on every visit. These three had grown up as siblings but they hardly knew their older cousins in Holland. George met Jaime and Adrienne for the first time at the Cannizaro Hotel in 2008.

I remember the momentous occasion when my five grandchildren met for the first time in Dorking in 2007. (Before this, when Peter was a baby, the three families had met on the white cliffs of Dover in 2003.) Jordyn, eight, was excited to see Adrienne, nine. Those two were inseparable. Peter, four and Matthew, two were hyped up by Jordyn's enthusiasm. The two boys would see Jaime and Adrienne for the first time. I, like a mother hen with her brood, felt proud. This was my family, my children with their spouses and their children.

As grandmothers do, I remembered each grandchild from birth. Kind and sensitive Jaime laughed heartily from a young age. She loved animals. Adrienne grew into a social butterfly but was a *splash-a-holic* baby in the bath. On a sleepover when Adrienne was still a baby, she cried incessantly and Chandrè had to take her home at 9 pm.

I travelled to East London when Jordyn Courtney Wild was born on 12 August 1999 by Caesarean section. On arrival I had lost my voice. The chemist gave me medication saying, "It's not contagious." Happiness surged through me when I saw Jordyn in Alyson's arms. I marvelled at her tiny hands, feet and cute face. Returning to Fish Hoek with one photo of Jordyn gave me much to brag about.

When Liesel's pregnancy was announced, I planned to see my new grandchild in England. My flight was booked. Peter David Wild was born on 24 March 2003 four days after my birthday. I arrived in England with my suitcase bulging with baby clothes.

"Congratulations Byron and Liesel!" I announced to the proud parents. Peter was my first grandson. Rocking him on my knee, I admired his chubby face, long eyelashes and dark hair. "He looks just like you as a baby," I told Byron. Many happy times were shared with both families at *Apple Cottage* in Westcott getting to know Steve and Carol, the owners.

Two years on Liesel expected a second baby. Travel arrangements were made. Peter was a two year-old toddler when his brother, Matthew Benjamin Wild was born on 17 June 2005. By this time Byron and Liesel had bought a house in Ashcombe Road where Byron challenged me, "Change his nappy mom!" I was nervous, Matthew was so tiny.

Jordyn was the cutest angel in a nativity play at St Martin's Church. That month I drove her to gymnastics in Leatherhead and she asked, "Nana can you drive my mom's car?"

When Jordyn was five she played computer games, quite foreign to me.

One year I spent Christmas with Chandrè in Holland. Brent, Alyson and Jordyn joined us. Swimming with my three granddaughters and Alyson in a heated pool at the hotel with snow and ice outside, was fun. Jaime's tears flowed like a river in flood when it was time for me to leave. I could not hold back my tears when we drove off heading for the ferry at the Hoek of Holland.

Jordyn had amazing balance and stood on Brent's hand as a toddler. Holidaying with me in Fish Hoek Jordyn tramped around the garden in my high heel sandals. My goldfish intrigued her. Adrienne at that age draped my handbag over her shoulder, dragging it around the house. On holiday at Mazeppa Bay Jordyn enjoyed the waves.

During my visits to England I looked after my grandchildren getting to know them more intimately. In 2007 I photographed them from eldest to youngest. Jordyn shared her bedroom in their Dorking home with me when I visited. She was fascinated with my jewellery, make-up and shower cap. At night she woke me, saying, "Nana you're snoring!"

Peter is still the spitting image of his dad. He loved Jordyn, copied her and shared his toys with her. Adventurous fearless Matthew though younger, kept up with Peter and Jordyn. His vocabulary has always been way above his years. Matthew studied the finest detail. I wonder what were you thinking when you watched a snail on the chalk-drawn track of a cement slab! Five cousins spent many happy hours together.

In 2008 Chandrè, Jaime and Adrienne returned for our wedding celebration at the Cannizaro Hotel. I looked up and saw my smartly turned-out family. My five grandchildren looked so grown up. I felt proud when you opened our gifts during the celebration which you regarded as a proper party.

***

On 10 July 2009 I flew to South Africa on my own because my mother was giving up her home and moving into a care home. It was a sad time dividing her possessions between Patrick, Topsy, Margy and me. On 13 July we heard the tragic news. Vivian, my eldest cousin had passed away in Durban. Topsy and I attended his funeral. Vivian had been Headmaster of Westville High School where the service was held. Overhead pictures reminded us of his life. He was a much-loved and respected man and to me, the big brother I never had. Sad occasions bring families together. On this occasion Topsy and I condoled with Heather and family before exchanging family news and love with our cousins.

Returning to England after my fall out with Topsy and Bill over mom's welfare meant Kirsten took me to the airport. On 26 July I arrived in Dorking with gifts. The *Springbok* rugby jerseys were worn immediately. I snapped the rugby pose as all five said, "*Laduma*!" A raucous trumpeting of three *vuvuzelas* followed. Those moments, which no money can buy, stay with me forever.

My deep thinking and reserved Jaime, you are like a *protea* opening up to reveal your inner beauty when you smile. Flitting from flower to flower, touching and changing lives is how I see you Adrienne, my *Table Mountain* butterfly. Jordyn you to me are like a *springbok*, leaping joyfully into the air as you bounce over life's hurdles. Peter you are my caring and confident *chameleon*, weighing up the consequences before you (change colour) make decisions. Matthew to me you are an early bird, a *hadeda*, greeting the dawn noisily and seizing every opportunity with raucous enthusiasm.

My grandchildren begged me to tell them stories about their parents. We swam, cycled, hiked, climbed up into a tree house, baked and danced together. We laughed and chatted over meals at home and in restaurants. Afterwards we all felt *propvol*. They made me feel loved, vying to sit next to me. This has worn off as they have grown up but I trust our love never wears off. Each grandchild is very special to me. Each grandchild will always be loved by me. I will always be there for each grandchild.

Remember me when I grow old and frail, spare a little time for me, a phone call, an email, a visit and even a hug...

***

My life was going so well. I loved my husband George, who is devoted, kind, considerate and supportive. I felt secure in a beautiful home where our possessions complimented each other. Caring for others gave my life purpose. We had found friends through Ashley Baptist Church and the Hordle Short Mat Bowling Club. But trouble was brewing in Holland I discovered, when I phoned Chandrè for her birthday in August. As mothers do, I prayed and pushed any negative thoughts aside.

In November 2010 a *Schengen* Visa from the German Embassy in London enabled me and George to board the Eurostar from St Pancras and visit the Christmas markets in Cologne. Scary thoughts of being in a tunnel under the sea tugged at my emotions. Lunch was served on the train and before we knew it, we had left the tunnel.

After an exhilarating holiday I heard from Chandrè that Anton had been made redundant. Without a job, his work visa could not be renewed. During this time of uncertainty I felt her pain as they struggled to survive. Their worldly possessions in five cartons were shipped to us. I valued the prayers and support of my many friends. I leant heavily on George who stood by me. The counselling I received from the Citizen's Advice Bureau lessened George's load as I in turn, learnt how to handle the situation and to remove the guilt I had heaped on myself for not being able to do more for them.

Leaving Holland meant leaving behind their possessions, home and two cars. They flew to the Philippines and adjusted to the heat and third-world culture. I contacted them on my mobile phone. Each time we spoke, I thanked God for answered prayer. My family were surviving. When Lynne Volker my golfing friend from South Africa, a regular visitor, was with George and me my mobile phone rang. At that moment the three of us were sitting in an open-top bus touring the Isle of Wight.

"Hi Chandrè."

I listened. Her story unfolded across thousands of miles that separated us. I absorbed each word like a sponge soaking up water. Although the sun shone and birds sang, my world suddenly became a dark place without bird twitter. I tried to be cheerful but inside me worry ate me up.

Following this incident George and I took a bus to Southbourne where we found a much-needed *Western Union* Money Exchange in an Indian-owned corner shop.

"Yes, *jest* wait, I *cen* do *eet*," the cheerful owner told me as he lifted mounds of dusty papers off the top of his photocopier machine. His two inquisitive young children peeped in from the back of the shop. He sent them off saying, "Go to *memmy*!"

What seemed an impossible mission slowly materialised. He explained over the phone that he had misplaced his password. After successfully verifying his identity, he was given access to proceed.

"Your money *pleez*."

"I don't carry that amount of cash on me."

He scratched his head. I had no choice but to go ahead with his plan. He transferred money from my account into his own account. From his account he made the transaction with Western Union to the Philippines. He was happy and gave me a password for my daughter to use when collecting the funds, saying, "She can get the money on Monday."

The text message on my mobile, *Thanks, mom. We have the money*, brought relief. Modern technology is amazing.

A few days later Chandrè and family with two cats and a dog flew to South Africa. On 29 April 2010 Topsy kindly met them at the airport. She had prepared my mother's townhouse for them and has been extremely supportive and generous to them ever since. Jaime and

Adrienne started school in Fish Hoek. Anton secured a job. They had stability and a glimmer of hope for the future. Chandre's health had suffered. She had become very thin and developed high blood pressure. God, I believe, loves them and has a plan and purpose for their lives.

***

George and I have had wonderful holidays on the Isle of Wight, Norfolk, Okehampton and Ilfracombe. Our home is open to visitors who leave saying, "I'll be back!" We attend Ashley Baptist Church pastored by David and Alison John. We enjoy outdoor bowls at the Lymington Bowls Club. I joined an autobiography class through Brockenhurst College at the Community Centre in Lymington in 2010. Brendan, the tutor encouraged his students to enter competitions and to attend the Winchester Writers' Conference. Caryl and I completed and posted off our application forms.

My appointments were confirmed by email. The writing competitions closed on 31 May. I wrote in earnest spending hours perfecting my work. Deeply indebted to George and my friend Janet who helped me, I put my competition entry in the post.

On Saturday 23 June George waved goodbye to Caryl and me at the Brockenhurst station. We felt like children on our first day at school, apprehensive, expectant and fearful. In Winchester we took a taxi to the university campus where red, white and blue balloons bounced in the breeze. Inside the Stripe building, bookstalls bulged amidst bustling writers. "Look who's behind you?" Caryl said. Turning round I saw Alan Titchmarsh before we took our seats in the crowded auditorium.

"This is the 32nd …," Barbara Large, petite in high heels and flouncy short dress and pink jacket, began. Professor Joy Carter introduced Alan Titchmarsh's keynote address *How To Grow a Writer.* With wit and charm the words rolled off Alan's tongue. Thereafter jostling through the crowd and struggling up two long flights of steps, I entered the Tom Atkinson building and listened to Jane Wenham-Jones's talk, *Write What You Know.*

Caryl's first appointment had upset her. I was also disappointed but was soon chatting to an American writer, Sheila Maguire. She said, giving me her card, "Keep in touch on email. I'll buy your book!" I had a new friend.

Caryl and I scrutinised the prize-winners on the noticeboard. I spotted my name saying, "I'd be happy with a Highly Commended."

After lunch I attended appointments and more talks until my saturated mind closed down. At the prize-giving in the Stripe Theatre we applauded the prize-winners. Then I heard: "Life-writing. The Highly Commended are..."

"Caryl, that's Tony from our class! I'll collect his certificate."

"Third prize... Second prize a worthy winner, an interesting story even suffering a broken spine... Denyse Halse." I shook hands with Doctor Bernard Lamb and had my photograph taken. With our long-awaited day over we boarded the train to Brockenhurst where George greeted us. "How did you get on?"

Too tired to talk, Carly drove off. At home I told George the good news. All the while the reality had not yet sunk in even when I put my weary head on the pillow, drifting off to sleep, I was still thinking... Unbelievable! Second Prize!

***

Pattering raindrops on the window woke me early on 19 December. I crept downstairs and returned to bed with a cup of tea for George and me. I pondered the sequence of events:

A Spouse's Visa had enabled me to re-enter the country in 2008. An Indefinite Leave to Remain in 2009 had given me long-term stay. I applied for British citizenship after living in the UK for three consecutive years. Under the Nationality, Immigration and Asylum Act 2002, anyone over the age of eighteen who has successfully had their application to become a British Citizen approved by the Home Office must attend a citizenship ceremony. I applied and waited. A letter from the Hampshire County Council notified me: Wednesday 19 December 2012 at 11.30 am at Hampshire Register Office.

Joan my sponsor and George were to be my two guests. As arranged Jim, Joan's husband drove us to the Brockenhurst station in inclement weather.

"Thanks Jim. I'm sorry you're not able to join us in Winchester."

George, Joan and I were on the 10.15 am train to Winchester. I gazed at the ponies and the sodden countryside of the New Forest through the train window. Before I knew it we walked into the Register Office. The hall filled up. Jeff Martin the Master of Ceremonies, introduced Brigadier Henderson in his smart naval uniform and who represented the Lord-Lieutenant of Hampshire, Dame Mary Fagan.

Standing I took the Oath of Allegiance: *I Denyse Estelle Halse swear by Almighty God that on becoming a British Citizen, I will be faithful and bear true allegiance to Her Majesty Queen Elizabeth II, her Heirs and Successors, according to law.* We recited the Pledge of Loyalty together: *I will give my loyalty to the United Kingdom and respect its rights and freedoms. I will uphold and respect its democratic values. I will observe its laws faithfully and fulfil my duties and obligations as a British citizen.*

Everybody stood and sang two verses of the national anthem before each new British citizen was presented with a certificate, *on-the-occasion-of-becoming-a-British-citizen* pen and a welcome letter from Theresa May, the Home Secretary. Professional photos were taken. Light refreshments followed.

We left to be met by Jim in Brockenhurst. Today I became a British citizen, raced through my head as we drove to the *Hare & Hounds* restaurant. Outside the pouring rain could not dampen our spirits and inside the radiating warmth of a log fire brought colour to our cheeks, as did the glass of wine. My children phoned to congratulate me that evening and reading the words, *'Now you're truly one of us'* written on a card from my Short Mat bowling friend Beryl cemented the occasion. The following evening Roy and Mavis Atkinson (my second sponsor), friends from Ashley Baptist Church joined us for another celebration at the *Walhampton Arms* in Lymington. I had added my name to 1500 new citizens welcomed by the Hampshire County Council's registration service each year!

32

A TRIP DOWN MEMORY LANE

In 2005 President Mbeki sacks his deputy Jacob Zuma, in the aftermath of a corruption case. In 2006 former deputy president Jacob Zuma is acquitted of rape charges and is re-instated as deputy leader of the governing ANC.

AS for me I spent half my life trying to recapture my early childhood bliss, but from now on I decided to devote my time to bring happiness to the man sitting before me. After my trip to South Africa on my own in 2009, I planned a trip down memory lane in 2011 to show George my country, the places where I had grown up.

On May 11 we took the *National Express* bus from Southampton to Heathrow. We boarded a direct SAA, South African Airways, flight to Johannesburg, or *Igoli*. This became the *City of Gold* when George Harrison, a stone mason working on a farm, *Langlaagte*, discovered gold in 1886.

"We've landed on African soil," I said proudly. A cultural fiasco unfolded. No sooner had we loaded our baggage on a trolley when it was whisked away by a smiling black porter, who said, "No worry, me take you." We hurried after him to the domestic departure gates to board our flight to Durban. The smell of perspiration reached us as his strong arms heaved the overladen trolley onto the escalator with George and me behind him, hoping it would not topple over. In *Xhosa* our porter argued his way through barrier officials. He then smiled at us for his tip, R100, £10, daylight robbery. He was gone, but for us there was more to come.

Aboard the plane we relaxed, gazing out the small window as the plane taxied down the runway. In no time at all we were airborne winging our way to Durban. The knots in my stomach tightened. Suppressed fear surfaced as I remembered the many warnings from my family: To avoid being robbed or shot, stop away from a *robot*; give yourself a chance to pull away if necessary; be alert for *tsotsis*; thousands of white South Africans had not only lost their security, but a family member who never made it home, through carjacking. In 2011 the official murder rate was 58.5% per 100,000; excessive crime, driven by a shoot-to-loot mentality in my opinion, was a direct result of a 40% unemployment rate.

We landed at the *King Shaka* International, a new airport on the North Coast. Pushing our luggage-laden trolley, I bought a simcard for my *cellphone* requesting, "R50 please."

Unbeknown to us at the time, the black lady at *MTN* conned every customer, saying, "You'll have to wait a few hours before the card is activated and you're able to use your phone."

We left to collect our hire car, a red *Hyundai Getz* at *Europcar* and only just managed to fit two small cases and hand luggage into the boot. George depended on my navigation skills as we travelled on unfamiliar roads, in an untried hired car whilst applying unacquainted survival tactics in a crime-ridden country. In South Africa everybody travels with nothing in the car to avoid forced entry and carjacking. No wonder I drove off wearing my reading glasses dodging oncoming traffic and wondering why my vision was so bad!

Driving along the well-signposted motorway, we passed sugar-cane fields before the traffic increased. All vehicles exceeded the prescribed speed limit. Taxis doubled the legal passenger capacity to swell their coffers. After bypassing Durban, we drove along the once sought-after South Coast resorts frequented by affluent white society and now occupied by Nigerians, peddling cocaine, heroin or mandrax and supplying 'freebies' to corrupt cops to turn a blind eye.

Exhausted but safe, we arrived at our first night's stopover, *Treetops Bed and Breakfast* in Margate. This tropical garden setting, rich in birdlife, was fortified with barbed wire and electric fencing above a seven-foot boundary wall. The next day at breakfast I told the landlady, "We're off to Kokstad today."

"You can stop in Harding for tea," she suggested and gave us directions. Leaving the coast and heading inland, only the distant majestic mountains and valleys remained unaltered. Gone were the small herds of black cattle, traces of wood smoke from hut-flecked hillsides and women in tribal dress balancing firewood on their heads as they trod well-worn footpaths. Pedestrians in western attire tramped along the motorways, thumbing lifts from passing taxis; hawkers lined the roadside with their wares. The once jade-green mountainsides were discoloured with soil-erosion and overpopulated with zinc-roofed brick-walled houses boasting water tanks, TV aerials and *jalopies*.

We turned into Harding and out again, as fast as I could safely weave the car through a maze of pedestrians, taxis, dogs, chickens and goats. A definite 'no no' for an elderly white couple conspicuous in a sea of Blacks! It was non-stop travel to Kokstad. Mount Currie, unchanged, came into view.

My cousin David, his son Mark and David's wife Tiffy welcomed us at their thriving business, *Johnstone Motors* in Hope Street where we parked. "I've been in this business for forty years," David, distinguished by streaks of grey, said over tea.

"You've got guts to travel that distance, at your age," Tiffy said with a warning, "From Umngazi detour via Kokstad to avoid Umtata or you'll put your lives at risk!"

"Neyse, what are you doing here?" a surprised older-looking Myrna and her husband Francois, exclaimed when they called in for an impromptu chat. Over more tea, we shared how life had matured us. We joined David and Tiffy for a delicious meal in their home that evening. George tasted *biltong* for the first time and we exchanged family news, email addresses and love.

My mind churned struggling to acknowledge my childhood memories of Kokstad were something of the past. My safe-haven birthplace had turned into a dirty, third-world town, hammered by its uncaring, new occupants who had no appreciation of the pioneers who struggled to build and establish this once-pristine, oak-lined farming village. Anger and sadness overwhelmed me to see the neglect, destruction and filth in the streets. Informal traders sold coat-hangers, live chickens in boxes, raw meat off the back of dirty trucks, live sheep from another truck, and fruit and food even flies would not sit on. Outdoor barbers tended clients seated on plastic milk crates. Metal garbage bins were outdoor barbecues.

I was sickened by huge posters, "We offer same-day abortions..." and "Penis enlargement..." which were plastered all over the town and in residential areas. *Who are these people? Where did they come from? Who is poisoning their minds in this iniquitous town?* The *Royal Hotel* had been demolished, *D M Brown's* was now a hideous supermarket and Whites were conspicuous by their absence. Today ninety per cent of the population of Kokstad have *Aids;* innumerable orphans struggle to survive and teenage pregnancies are ever-increasing. My granny would be horrified if she were still alive. Was there any hope left for Kokstad?

The owner of the *Traveller's Lodge* where we stayed turned out to be Megan Dorning, nee Mundell, young widow and daughter of the couple, now deceased, who had managed *DM Brown's Store.* She telephoned Kippy Bryden's daughter, Gaye who agreed to meet us at *Strathneva.* Kippy and his wife, owners of the farm, were on a safari holiday. My spirits lifted to see the improvements to the farmhouse and garden. Gaye's daughters splashed in and out of a sprinkler on the lawn where I had once done headstands and cartwheels. It was nostalgic to see the same *Aga* stove in an alcove where Mom's chickens had kept warm in cardboard boxes. We were left to wander through the house and past the two silos and grazing livestock on the way to the dam where my sisters and I had once swum and skirted legavaans in a boat. It all seemed only yesterday.

Returning to Kokstad I stopped at 107 Hawthorn Street. A brick wall hid the house from view but from the driveway gate I caught a glimpse of a pool on the front lawn. The Coulter Street house was rundown and used as legal offices. Mom and Pop's retirement home, 28 Strachan Street, had been subdivided with a house built on what was once the orchard. The dam and avenue of trees Pop had planted had matured but the panoramic view was spoilt by a cheap housing estate beyond. The once tranquil corner property *Kildare* was unchanged from the outside, but boasted hideous tall street lights controlling incessant traffic.

George rested in the car as I traipsed through the convent grounds taking photographs. Little had changed. The swimming pool, now empty was the same, but the tennis courts were now park land. Walking back from the grotto, a smiling nun greeted me. She offered to unlock the cathedral after she had given three *Aids'* children clothing and money. "My granny donated the Stations of the Cross," I told her as she unlocked the wooden door and we stepped inside.

"Your grandmother?"

"Yes. There's a plaque on the wall over there," I said.

Suddenly I became a celebrity to her. She invited George and me to tea in what was once the Bishop's house and where the few remaining nuns now resided. She telephoned people I knew, saying, "Mrs Brown's granddaughter, Neyse is in town," and arranged for me to meet Lorna after Mass that evening. Grateful for the hospitality we excused ourselves.

I paid a fleeting visit to the Kokstad Bowling Club, now barbed-wired and remote-control gated and boasting eight bowlers. I entered the clubhouse in desperate need of TLC and photographed my mother's name on the Honours Boards now pushed into a side passage. As I approached the Kokstad Tennis Club it looked unaltered. Stepping inside the glass-enclosed pavilion I realised it was now home to three smiling Blacks, sipping tea from tin mugs. It would not be wise in the fading light, to visit my grandparents' grave in an isolated graveyard, I thought...

That evening with Vivian Lindsay in Lorna's sumptuous home over tea, I caught up with the Kokstad I once knew. I was saddened to learn how many stalwart Kokstad figures had passed away. Some had retired to Natal.

"Lorna, the evil posters plastered all over Kokstad shocked us!"

"There's nothing we can do. As fast as we pull them down, they put them up again," Lorna explained adding, "Practising witchdoctors and unqualified GPs are rife in Kokstad!"

Lorna and her late husband, Des Wicks had bought *Strathneva* from us before it was sold to Kippy Bryden. Tomorrow a new dawn with new experiences I thought falling asleep next to George.

Leaving Kokstad on Sunday, with mixed feelings, we filled up with petrol and headed for Umngazi. Crossing the unused railway-line, I took one last look at Mount Currie in the rear-view mirror and choked back my tears. I decided to cherish the Kokstad I once knew and lived in between 1949 – 1969 and blot out the hurtful images of the present.

"Are you alright?" George asked.

"Mmm...just reminiscing. It's Sunday so the roads should be quiet."

It was a blessing that George was oblivious to the unpredictable dangers of this journey. Animals roamed freely with drunk and dagga-driven Blacks on the road. Carjacking… I prayed God would keep us safe.

The road climbed through Brook's Nek Pass on the slopes of the 2,012m Nolangeni Mountains where we turned off into *Pondoland* heading for Flagstaff. This beautiful trading village derived its name from enterprising traders who flew a white flag from a flagstaff to inform *Pondos* there was no trading on Sundays.

That they no longer uphold this practice as was made evident the moment we drove into a dilapidated dirty town, trade in full swing. Filth and chaos dominated the scene. Driving slowly I searched for my uncle's trading store, *K N Rock General Dealer.* It was obliterated by buses, litter-strewing shoppers zig-zagging between hooting taxis on pot-holed garbage-covered roads.

We passed *Magusheni,* the place where a flock of the sheep had been struck by lightning and killed. Further on was Mount Nelson, the home of an eccentric herbalist millionaire, Khotso Sethunsta. He lived here with his 24 wives producing 200 children, until he died at age 90. I drove through Lusikisiki, a larger version of Flagstaff and again I felt appalled. This village once bustled with blue-blanketed *Pondo* tribesmen on horseback visiting trading stores, the labour-recruiting office and the Magistrate's Court. Gone were horsemen… Gone were the *Pondos* in tribal dress… Gone were the babies tied with blankets on their mothers' backs…

I remembered, *Qawukeni,* the Great Place of the paramount chief of the *Pondo* people. Even in times of modern road engineering, Port St Johns did not flourish as a port due to the difficult access from the hinterland. The road, following the Umzimvubu River, cut its gigantic cleft in the coastal mountains to reach the sea between two precipitous sandstone cliffs. The headlands formed the Gates of Port St Johns, rose 360 metres above sea level and were named after General Thesiger, west bank, and Commodore Sullivan, east bank. These men arrived to hoist the Union Jack after this area of the river had been ceded to Britain by the *Pondo* Chief, Nqwiliso, in 1870.

We drove south of Port St Johns through the indigenous tropical forest. Here in the shelter of some of nature's loveliest sanctuaries are the wild harebells, tree orchids, succulents and fern, and a profusion of birdlife. We followed the Umngazi River for 11 kilometres and very often I hooted at cattle in the middle of the road and goats and kids sleeping on the road.

"This is truly Africa, where children wander alone on the road; where *sangomas* in distinctive blue and white outfits parade on the roadside and dance themselves into a stupor to chat to dead ancestors; where African men drink beer under a shady tree and where womenfolk tend to children and brew beer on the hut-speckled hills," I said.

We arrived in a spacious lagoon and a sandy beach, an unspoilt wilderness and the haunt of fishermen from all over southern Africa – the Umngazi Bungalows Resort.

"The drive was well worth it," George said as we entered the gates, guarded day and night. The road interspersed with indigenous forest and thatched bungalows led to a car park. A smiling black hostess handed us a hot flannel and a welcome drink saying, "Relax and enjoy yourselves. The keys to your bungalow will be available at 2 pm."

The holiday atmosphere was tangible. Holiday-makers splashed in a sparkling pool, reclined on loungers soaking up the warm sunshine or sipped drinks under thatched umbrellas. Some, like us, savoured the scene and smell of the *braai*. The neatly mown lawns fell away into the river, which ran lazily into the sea. Steep sand dunes edged the far side where guests waited for the ferry.

"Let's walk along the river."

The footpath was bordered by *Strelitzia,* wild bananas, cannas, arum lilies, ferns, red-hot pokers and tropical palms. Small lamp-posts and garden benches, recessed into the garden punctuated the walkway.

"There's our bungalow. It's beautiful."

"Pity we're not staying a week," George said as we both savoured every new smell, African sounds and enchanting vista.

"Did you see that?"

I saw a fish jumping out of the water and making a sudden splash.

"Look at the herd of cattle on the sandbank!"

"Yes, I've never seen that before," George answered.

We listened to the rippling of small waves as the tide pushed in. The sky was cloudless and little birds twittered as they fluttered from a tree to the ground and back. Overhead a raucous sound, HAA-HAA-HAA-DEE-DAA, made me look up.

"What on earth was that?" George exclaimed.

"That's the sound made by the *Hadeda Ibis*, birds of Africa, when flying. Look there they go," I said pointing to the two large dark-brown, black-billed birds flapping their glossy green and purple wings as they flew distinctively across the blue sky. I remembered... This is where my father and mother spent their honeymoon. Time had stood still in this place. It was unspoilt. How amazing that we, too, could enjoy the same tranquillity and beauty that they shared sixty-seven years ago...

Excitedly, we strolled back. The smell of a *braaivleis* beckoned us. We helped ourselves to an assortment of attractively presented salads and to chops, *boerewors*, steak, chicken and sosaties. Sitting in the shade of a coral tree, overlooking the pool, lagoon and beach, we tucked into our lunch.

"What have you got there?" George asked.

"*Umngqusho,* something I've been looking forward to."

"What is noosh? Is it pasta?"

"It's the staple diet of black people made of samp and beans."

Neither of us could resist the delicious deserts. I heaped *melktert,* ice-cream and fresh fruit salad, which was made of *paw-paws,* melons, granadillas, guavas, bananas and *naartjies* onto my plate and enjoyed every mouthful.

At the car park, we followed a friendly staff member in his buggy to our bungalow where he kindly carried our luggage inside.

"*Enkosi,* Thank you," I said surprising him.

We both immediately admired our accommodation. A huge lounge, with armchairs, a coffee table and fridge had three steps which led into an open-plan bedroom. The panoramic views from outside poured in through the large sea-facing windows. The French doors from the lounge and bedroom opened onto a thatched verandah, overlooking the river and sea.

A dressing room led off the bedroom, with plugs galore, a dressing table and hair-drier, towelling gowns and a glass door into an open-air shower, from which you could watch the birds and waves. The bathroom, with enormous spa bath also had a magnificent seaview with two large hand basins and several mirrors. Cushioned chairs and a table invited us to relax on our private verandah. I checked my mobile phone for messages and discovered I had no money on my phone. I had been robbed in Durban along with so many others.

We unpacked the bare essentials wanting to enjoy every moment of this paradise. George scrutinised the ever-changing views through his binoculars. His next remark made me laugh, "William and Kate would've enjoyed a honeymoon here." We remembered the Royal wedding of 29 May.

The sound of three helicopters overhead seemed out of place, but we watched with interest, as one by one they landed in the estuary of the lagoon and switched off their engines. The whirring blades ceased spinning and again the stillness of Umngazi was restored. This was a safer and faster way to reach this remote spot. Families in boats, rowed gently up and down the lagoon, joggers waved as they ran along the footpath, *hadedas* swooped down onto the lawn, where they used their long, black beaks to dig for earthworms. The cattle started moving off the sand in single file. How did they know the sun would set in less than an hour? A faint mist spread over the sand and the sun sank over the hillsides, illuminating the clouds in pastel shades of peach and pink. Darkness fell and we retreated indoors.

This is a romantic place, I thought as we walked hand in hand along the moonlit path to the dining room. After another delicious, meal we cuddled contentedly in our King-size bed and soon fell asleep listening to the *to-ing* and *fro-ing* of the waves, accompanied by the lapping water of the lagoon running out on the outgoing tide.

Another perfect day dawned which made our parting from this piece of paradise more difficult. East London was our next overnight stop but which route should we take? We could be there within an hour or drive for eight hours inland to bypass Umtata.

"We'll risk it," I decided at the T–junction. I was on full alert.

"Look there!" George said laughing heartily and lifting my mood.

"What's so funny?"

"A man lifting his friend on the handlebars of his bicycle, riding down the *motorway*. It would never be allowed in the UK!"

"That's normal. Anything with or without wheels shares the road."

There was more laughter when George saw goats shading themselves under the steel barriers of the busy main road. Next I braked as a woman crossed the road pushing a shopping trolley laden with firewood; further on a black man trundled two children in a wheelbarrow. Without a doubt we *were* in Africa.

Without indicating, taxis swerved to a halt where there was no hard shoulder and picked up passengers. In this vein we entered my former home town, Umtata where every driver used his own unique set of traffic rules accompanied by hooting, swerving and screeching brakes. Focusing on the road ahead, we reached 31 Blakeway Road, unscathed.

An occupant of the property, an attractive twenty-something black girl, talking on her mobile, gave me a conducted tour of *Brechanby*. The house had weathered the passage of time well. The original light fittings, hand basins in the children's bedroom and wood-burning lounge fireplace brought back memories. I admired the protective white boundary walls built forty years ago.

From there we passed the golf course. Skirting the high street, we saw locals napping on the grass and meths-smelling vagrants occupying broken benches on a weed-strewn lawn decorated with fruit peels and whirlwinds of litter. We refuelled. The next lap took us through Idutywa and Butterworth more deteriorated than Kokstad, to the Kei cuttings, where we joined a backup of stationary cars. Whilst waiting for the oncoming traffic to pass through a single-line due to road construction, droves of hawkers plied their wares of sweets, chips and drinks on each side of the parked vehicles. Without thinking, I grabbed my hidden camera and stepped into the road. The driver of a 4x4 vehicle hooted at me. I jumped and saw his angry face as he bellowed, "Get into your car immediately!"

In a split second I was back beside George. I forgot that outside the car my life was in danger. In this isolated spot, ruthless have-nots were merciless. Lives were lost for the sake of a mobile phone. Life in Africa was cheap.

We journeyed on to East London, so different from when I lived here. At *Sea View B&B* in Beacon Bay we enjoyed a glass of wine while soaking up the vista of the Nahoon River mouth and the Indian Ocean. This spectacular panorama was equally as good from the open-plan bath in our bedroom.

The next day we met my golfing friends, Mary Jones and Maureen Fabri at the home of Vic and Lynne Volker. Although we had aged, our golfing memories were recaptured with youthful exuberance. After much hilarity we bid each other a fond farewell. From there I drove to the Gonubie Golf Course where those nostalgic days sprang to life. My next stop was where I once lived, 21-10th Avenue. Sadly my tropical garden had been thinned and the two *Coral* trees had been cut down. Driving off I spotted my curly-headed neighbour, Jo. I stopped. "Jo!"

"What are you doing here Denyse?"

"I'm visiting from the UK."

"Are you living there now?"

We fell into a conversation as though time had stood still. Jo had lost her husband, Vic at age 86 in 2009. Her son, Paul, a baby when I knew him, was now 25 and had recently married. She could not afford burglar-proofing or electric fences but trusted in the Lord's protection.

"I've given up teaching Maths at a High School in East London. The pupils have no respect for teachers. I teach Maths privately from home." I treasured this meeting ordained by God and snapped the occasion before we hugged goodbye.

Later sea spray and seaweed smells wafted to where we sat on a secluded bench on the Gonubie boardwalk and watched the waves pounding against the rocks. We dined in a seaside restaurant with the sun sinking and casting a golden glow over the ocean as fishermen trudged over rocks and gulls screeched overhead.

Monday was Election Day in South Africa, a bank holiday and by chance our hostess chatted to us at breakfast. She discovered I knew Boots and Wilma Kaiser, whom I had not seen in thirty years. She handed me the telephone and our conversation flowed like it had all those years ago. My next highlight was driving to visit Sylvia Preston at her lovely home in Lukin Drive. "You could've stayed here," Sylvia said when we arrived, continuing, "Hughie will be so disappointed he missed you. He's playing golf in Butterworth. Come in."

We sized each other up before we both concluded that neither of us had changed, despite a lapse of over thirty years. We caught up with family news. Sylvia had fought for her life after a car accident in the Transkei. After a miraculous recovery she was left with a stiff neck. She radiated love and in parting we exchanged email addresses. "Keep in touch," she said waving goodbye.

At the filling-station I recognised my old friend, Rose Blakeway, who had been instrumental in changing my life forever. We fell into each other's arms. She had aged but her Irish accent was the same saying, "My Ronnie passed away," with a tear in her eye added, "and Neil my son is dying. It's so hard to bear all this without Ronnie."

"Rose you poor thing. I'll pray for you and your family," I promised, hugging her again. Rose chatted to George and ended with, "Take good care of Denyse. She's very precious George!" If only we had more time. It was a miracle to meet Rose then before leaving Beacon Bay.

In King William's Town, we stopped at 6 Galloway Road, and from a distance it appeared unchanged; at 9 Stanford Road I wondered if my entry was refused because I was a white woman. It was getting late and driving after dark through the Transkei would be an additional risk so at *The Gables,* I looked from the gate and remembered our happiest years – the children growing up.

Driving on from King William's Town to Grahamstown, we stopped for coffee and admired the Drostdy Arch. I telephoned David Benyon hoping to see him but he explained, "Denyse I'm laid up with a bad back. How are you?"

We chatted and he gave me his grandson's email address requesting a copy of my book. Disappointed not to have seen Dave, I drove to what had been the Training College opened by the Anglican sisterhood in 1894 and which had since merged with Rhodes University. I felt ancient amongst students – some playing tennis and others sitting cross-legged on the lawn. They showed little interest when I said, "I studied here in the 1960's!" Was this my cue to leave?

It would soon be nightfall so we journeyed on to Port Alfred, named after the second son of Queen Victoria. The sun sank over the town. Twinkling lights reflected in the Kowie River as we settled into our accommodation overlooking the Nico Malan Bridge opened in 1972. That evening we enjoyed a delicious meal at the *Ocean Basket* on the river's edge.

Leaving Port Alfred and its past memories behind, we began our long drive to Hoekwil on 19 May. The picturesque resort of Kenton-on-Sea lies between the Boesmans and Kariega rivers. Driving inland to Alexandria we joined the N2 at Colchester. We bypassed Port Elizabeth whereafter the Groot Winterhoekberge and Tsitsikama mountains came into view. We stretched our legs on the pedestrian crossing of the Storms River Bridge, looking into the gorge and river below.

From there we motored on to Knysna. Shacks flanked the motorway on the outskirts. As we descended and came round a sharp bend, a white woman waving her jacket was driving a runaway ox off the road amidst swerving and hooting vehicles travelling in both directions.

"What on earth's she doing?" George asked as we dodged through this chaos unharmed.

We reached the Wilderness where, over a meal, a young waiter gave us directions to Hoekwil. Our wooden chalet was in the *gammadoeloes*. We woke to the sound of birdsong. Peeping through the curtained window, I glimpsed a lake and Macedonian nut plantation beyond, swaddled in morning sunlight.

We were up early to catch the steam train in the town of George once occupied by *Khoi* people, who called this region *Outeniqua* meaning 'man laden with honey'. At the station we were met with bitter disappointment. The Outeniqua Choo-Choo, huffing and puffing between George and Knysna and stopping at quaint stations, no longer operated.

"The new government refused to fix the lines after extensive flooding one year, saying it's a white man's toy!" I had always wanted to ride on this train. Now it was too late.

We wandered through Knysna next. This town is a leading tourist attraction boasting splendid items made from the Outeniqua yellowwood and stinkwood. The Knysna Heads, a pair of huge coloured cliffs which flank a deep and dangerous channel through which the sea pours in to flood the beautiful lagoon at the mouth of the Knysna River, are a unique geological feature on the African coastline.

We stayed at *Busibee B & B* in Oudtshoorn and visited the Cango Caves, a national monument in the Swartberg range covering 3 km. Brilliantly lit-up stalactite and stalagmite formations resemble amongst others, the Pulpit, Madonna and Child and the Organ Pipes. Cleopatra's Needle, a 10 m high pillar, has formed over 150 000 years and Van Zyl's Hall measures 107m x 54m and is 17m high. Before leaving Merilee Martin recognised me. She called, "Denyse from the Lindbergh?"

"Yes. I've not been called that for ages. Hi. Meet George, my husband."

"Pleased to meet you Merilee," George responded. She enjoyed her new career as a tour guide on the Garden Route. Time dictated our respective departures.

Our afternoon on an ostrich farm was informative. George stood on twelve ostrich eggs without breaking them. I sat on a blindfolded ostrich, which kept it stationary. The white wing and tail feathers of the males are sold to fashion houses and the rest of the black and grey plumage is made into feather dusters. Ostrich *biltong* and ostrich steaks are delicacies. Handbags, shoes and belts are made from the leather and bone-meal for chickens from the skeleton. The fertilizer is used on lucerne fields, which is the staple diet of the ostrich. "Nothing's wasted in ostrich farming," I could almost hear my grandmother saying.

"Amazing, ostriches eat stones," George commented "and can run over 50 kph!"

We fell asleep dreaming of ostriches and the Cango Caves before setting off on another long journey to Kleinmond. We drove over awesome mountain passes, stopping in Calitzdorp. The Tradouw pass took us to Swellendam, where we joined the N2 to Caledon. Margy and John welcomed two weary travellers into their lovely home in Kleinmond. Despite the heavy downpour the next day, John and Margy took us for a scenic drive before we enjoyed a delicious stir-fry that evening. We reminisced and exchanged photos on laptops late into the evening.

We visited Eileen Gourley at *Kidbrook* outside Hermanus. "I'm so pleased to meet you George. Denyse has told me all about you," she beamed as we joined her for tea. George listened patiently whilst we shared our golfing days in Gonubie. We left and drove to the Fish Hoek cottages where we had stayed in 2008. Each day we juggled time between seeing my mother at Carlisle Lodge and Chandrè, Anton and the girls at Silverglades. Time raced by.

We celebrated mom's birthday at the Fish Hoek Restaurant overlooking the waves, a memorable day; took Jaime and Adrienne to the V & A Waterfront and up Table Mountain; dined at cosy farm-style restaurants with Chandrè. We listened, laughed and chatted, pouring our love out to each other.

One morning George said, "It's once more time to leave the seaside cottages behind." I found it hard to believe that this was our last day in South Africa. With our luggage in the boot we headed for Carlisle Lodge to say goodbye to my mother. She resides in such a lovely care home, but as usual, we arrived to find her sitting all alone in her bedroom. Neither her television or music centre was switched on for company. My mother is again just sitting in her chair, doing *nothing*. I wondered. What does she think about? Is she remembering her youth? Could she be wishing her life away?

"Hi mom."

"Hi Peggy."

I hugged my mother as she responded with her usual reply, "This is a nice surprise! It's lovely to see you both."

"How are you mom?"

""I'm okay, I suppose. My legs are playing up again." I have heard this every day.

"Shall we go to the lounge where we can sit more comfortably and have a chat?" "

"Yes," my mother replied as she reached for her walking frame.

She was dressed in a pretty blue blouse, beige long pants and wore the beige crocs I gave her in 2009. Following her to the top lounge, which is tastefully decorated, homely and comfortable we were the only occupants. My mother had almost lost her communication skills and her short-term memory had declined since she moved into the care home. I have found it hard to accept that she is content to live this way. The mother I knew had always been so active. When she retired from bowls, she busied herself with sewing, knitting, crocheting, cross-stitch, patchwork, gardening, walking, playing scrabble, Rummikub and canasta, playing the piano, telephoning and writing letters to family and friends, baking, bottling fruit and jams. Year after year, she had spent long hours in her kitchen producing a delicious Christmas cake for her three daughters. Her spare room cupboards were full of baby bootees, bibs and matinee jackets, covered coat-hangers, tea cosies and oven gloves she had made. My mother made nearly all her own clothes and had produced beautiful outfits, jackets and evening-wear for me.

Our once relaxed conversations are now hard going. I hear repeatedly the same phrase, "I'm sorry, but I just can't remember," and am annoyed with myself for talking about current events. However, when I steer the conversation into the past, her face lights up and as she remembers, she recalls in great detail stories I will always treasure.

"I love you mom," I kept telling her and "I've enjoyed playing scrabble, looking at photos on my laptop, sharing an ice-cream at the beach front and just being with you. "

My mother showed no emotion when I told her it was time for us to leave. We hugged and kissed goodbye. As I watched she turned and headed back to her room. "I love you mom," I called out to her for one last time. My tears revealed my pain.

We drove to spend a few hours with Chandrè and her daughters. Anton was at work. Ringing the bell at the gate I realised this was my last visit for a long time. With hugs over we sat and enjoyed a cup of tea in the sunny lounge.

"You're looking lovely today, Chan,"

"Thanks mom. I've had this outfit for over sixteen years."

"Jaime how did you plait your hair? It looks fabulous."

"It's easy to do nana. Like this," as she demonstrated the art of French plaiting.

"It takes Jaime ages to do her hair nana," Adrienne butted in, not to be left out.

"Adrienne, please don't cut your beautiful hair," I urged.

Scotty their scruffy terrier sensed something was amiss and snuggled closer to my feet. Sadness descended over the room even amidst light chatter. Adrienne, using sign language, drew our attention to her sister. Jaime's emotions could no longer be contained. Silent tears flowed. Her body language conveyed excruciating pain. Sharing her chair with my arms around her I struggled to say, "I love you Jaime. Remember all the good times we shared. I'll be back again and we'll have more fun. I promise ..."

I remembered all the tearful goodbyes at Schiphol Airport when she was younger. I did not want to go. When would I see them again? How could I alleviate their pain? What was going on inside Jaime's head?

"Chandrè would you allow the girls to fly to England for a holiday with George and me?" caused Chandrè to succumb to her sorrow and she could not reply. Parting photos were snapped. George and I gave

Jaime and Adrienne cash hoping this would warm their hearts, but by this time Chandrè was sobbing aloud – her body wracked in grief. Goodbyes become more painful with the passing years. I watched my little family waving back to us in the mirror as we drove off until they were out of sight.

Would I ever know the depth of their struggle or the breadth of their courage? I hoped our visit had eased their heartache and given them renewed determination to overcome it. Their story to survive in a desperate world was all down to one thing – faith and the prayer of a humble heart. I thought of my beloved South Africa. Have I become hardened to on-going stories of poverty, crime, the *Aids* epidemic, unemployment and starvation? Listening but the silence is deafening; seeing but the vision is blinding and feeling but emotions are freezing!

There is a story told of two frogs. One sat in cold water to which hot water was added gradually. This frog became so accustomed to the gradual increase of heat that it just sat. Eventually as accustomed as he had grown to the heat of water threatening his life, he never survived. The second frog was taken from cold water and plunged into hotter water and his natural reaction was to jump out as fast as possible and he survived.

Like so many fellow South Africans I have followed the most popularly held choice and jumped out fast to survive. "History repeats itself," Pop had told me when I was thirteen. How true! The majority of whites held the same viewpoint, "If you want to know what's going to happen once these *okes* take over, all you have to do is look at the rest of Africa." Over time the fortunes of Africa have changed dramatically in the more than fifty years since the independence era began. As Whites observed this shift, it was quite common to hear people say, "Look at Zambia, a suitcase of money only buys a loaf of bread! Look at Mozambique. Finished! Look at Uganda, Idi Amin! Best to leave before that day comes!"

33

THERE'S LIFE IN ME YET

In 2012 the police open fire on workers at a Marikana platinum mine, killing 34 people, leaving 78 injured. More than 200 protestors were arrested. In September 2012 the former ANC youth leader Julius Malema is charged with money laundering over a government tender awarded to a company, partly-owned by his family trust. Mr Malema says the case is a politically motivated attempt to silence his campaign against President Zuma in particular, over the Marikana shootings. Mr Zuma is re-elected as president.

AS family survivors we can take ownership of the new South African anthem even though we have, at times, been scattered around the world – New Zealand, United States of America, Holland, Switzerland, Sweden, the Philippines and England.

Nkosi sikelel' iAfrika Lord, bless Africa
Maluphakanyisw' uphondo Iwayo, May her spirit rise high up
Yizwa imithandazo yethu, Hear thou our prayers
Nkosi Sikelela, thina lusapho Iwayo Lord bless us.

Morena boloka setjhaba sa heso, Lord, bless Africa
O fedise dintwa le matshwenyeho Banish wars and strife
O se boloke, O se boloke setjhaba sa heso, Lord bless our nation
Setkjaba sa South Afrika – South Afrika.Of South Africa.

Uit die blou van onse hemel, Ringing out from our blue mountains
Uit die diepte van ons see, From our deep seas breaking round
Oor ons ewige gebergtes, Over everlasting mountains
Waar die kranse antwoord gee, Where the echoing crags resound.

Sounds the call to come together,
And united we shall stand,
Let us live and strive for freedom
In South Africa our land.

No matter where we are, we have this heritage, each with our own story to tell and all sharing the same grandparents, Donald Moses Brown and Eileen Hester Pohl nee Hart. *Yebo.*

My mother Peggy, the sole survivor of her generation will be ninety on 3 June 2013. She has outlived Eric, Phil, Joan and Slabs, Keith and Ruth, Molly and Stewey.

***

What a year 2012 was! On Friday 13 January of the *Costa Concordia* an Italian cruise liner carrying 4,252 people ran aground on a reef when Captain Schettino deviated from the ship's computer-programmed route to salute islanders. Thirty–two lives were lost. On 3 June the *Thames Diamond Jubilee Pageant*, a maritime parade of 1,000 boats, the largest flotilla seen on the river Thames for over 350 years was one of the many celebrations marking Queen Elizabeth II's 60th anniversary accession to the throne. London hosted the 2012 Olympic Games between 27 July and 12 August with 204 nations and 10,820 athletes competing. Great Britain came third, winning 29 gold, 17 silver and 19 bronze medals, a total of 65. The USA won with 104 medals followed by China in second place, with 88 medals.

My early life in South Africa was so different from the lifestyle with my precious husband George, in England. In my 'chocolate box' surroundings, I wake to birdsong; meet dog-walkers and elderly folk keen for a chat on my daily walk round the neighbourhood. Putting the 'clock' on the dashboard of the car I shop, not looking over my shoulder. There is an overwhelming choice of food in every supermarket. Glass bottles are recycled from designated collection points void of vagrants. Re-usable items are donated to charity shops.

So much has changed in South Africa. The childhood memories I held seem like a fairy tale. In Durban the fun-fair and putt-putt course have gone and the rickshaws have been replaced with security guards. Blacks have more access to senior jobs and better pay. Whites are barred from the workforce because of the colour of their skin, called affirmative action.

This enables PDP's (previously disadvantage people) a right to jobs without the necessary qualification. Whites expected less Government corruption after *apartheid,* but just the opposite prevails. The rich grow richer and the poor live below the breadline. Dirty children with distended bellies beg at the traffic lights. Although 1.4 million houses were delivered to the Blacks between 1994 and 2002, millions are still homeless or live in squatter camps.

When the *Whites-only* signs came down, tens of thousands of Blacks descended upon the beaches on Christmas and Boxing Day. Forty to fifty deep, shoulder to shoulder, packed like sardines, they swam in the waves. One year thirteen drowned and life-savers rescued over 1,000 bathers.

Having experienced many hardships I am more appreciative of the good times. My life is no longer threatened on a daily basis. I am free. I can wear jewellery and use my mobile phone. Beggars don't put guilt on me at every street corner nor do I stay locked behind burglar-barred windows and an alarm system day after day. But some things have happened in life and nothing ever takes away the sadness – Nolyn never seeing his grandchildren – is just one that will remain with me until I die. It is sometimes hard to accept the hand of God, but it is a part of life's journey.

My life has been spared more than once. I have seen my children grow up, marry and settle in their own homes. I have shared my grandchildren's growing-up years, their innocence and laughter. I am blessed to have raised such fine people. They have come through life's struggles smiling. My step-children and step-grandchildren are a joy. I love each one and I am blessed to have them in my life. What more can I ask for?

During my life-time there have been many worldwide disasters. Diana, Princess of Wales, killed tragically in a car accident in France on 31 August 1997. Her untimely death touched the world. Millions mourned her death. On 11 September 2001 the Twin Towers disaster killed 2,826 people as it played out like a horror movie on televisions around the world. On 26 December 2004 the Tsunami with waves measuring 30m killed 230,000 people in fourteen countries. This was one of the deadliest natural disasters in recorded history. On 31 May 2011 the Fukushima Daiichi power plant in Japan experienced an oil spill in the sea near reactors 5 and 6 and a blast at reactor 4. Radiation threatened 2,000 workers.

I have learnt that it is better to give than to receive; better to listen than to lecture and better to love, even the unlovely, than to hate. Time slips by so fast. Today is only here once. Being close to my family keeps me from the terror of old age and wanting.

In South Africa once part of the British Commonwealth (1945-1961) we sang *God save the Queen;* during the subsequent *apartheid* era under the Nationalist Government, we sang *'Die Stem'*. From 27 February 1994 with Nelson Mandela as President and FW de Klerk and Thabo Mbeki as vice-presidents, we sang the combined South African anthem under a government of National Unity. I have waved three different flags. I have lived from radio to television, from manual typewriters to laptops and from epidemics to *HIV Aids*. The biggest change occurred when I accepted Jesus into my life.

This allegory is a constant reminder to me of how this happened. When I was working for GELPA, I walked down Oxford Street in my smart grey uniform, high heels with favourite red scarf draped around my neck, swinging my handbag. At the crossroads, the wind whipped off my scarf, twirled it high into the air and floated it above passing cars. It disappeared. "No!" I exclaimed not expecting to find it when I reached the other side. I looked. Just a glimmer of red peeped out from the filthy gutter where the scarf was trapped in mud and grime.

"That's my scarf!"

I wanted the scarf I loved. Putting my pride aside, I picked it up from the gutter. I held it far from me and stuffed it into a plastic bag when I reached the office. At home I dropped my messed-up scarf into sudsy water to soak overnight. When my scarf was washed clean and ironed it was like new. I wore it time and time again.

I was like that filthy scarf lying in the gutter, sinful and worthless. God picked me up, washed me clean and made me His own, a new creation. Today my scarf needs to be washed and ironed periodically as I continue to wear it. In like manner, God continues to wash away my shortcomings (I will never be perfect) whenever I fall short. I am grateful to everybody, too many to name, who have influenced my life and especially those who have forgiven me when I have offended them, knowingly or unknowingly. It is only through God's grace, His mercy and His love that I was rescued, changed and given a purpose for living.

I leave the reader with words from the book of Ecclesiastes:

There is a time for everything, and a season for every activity under heaven:
A time to be born and a time to die, A time to plant and a time to uproot,
A time to kill and a time to heal, A time to tear down and a time to build,
A time to weep and a time to laugh, A time to mourn and a time to dance,
A time to scatter stones and a time to gather them, A time to embrace and a time to refrain,
A time to search and a time to give up, A time to keep and a time to throw away,
A time to tear and a time to mend, A time to be silent and a time to speak,
A time to love and a time to hate, A time for war and a time for peace.

Looking back I acknowledge there have been many times when God's hand has been on me protecting me – the time when John, my black garden boy, suspended me by my ankles down the *long drop* in order for me to retrieve Pandora, our white cat. In the dark and out of reach, Pandora's green eyes stared back at me from the safety of a ledge... if John had let go I would have plunged head first into the cesspit!

– the day I raced wild horses along the shoreline at Coffee Bay with three small children bouncing about in the back of a *Land Rover!*

– when I tried to water-ski in a shark-infested river, falling into the water repeatedly, hoping the sharks would keep their distance before the boat picked me up and I had another go.

It then becomes clearer to me that God sovereignly predetermines all of life's activities. I have messed up many times, but as I mature into my old age, I am at last beginning to acknowledge my limitations and not vex myself with unrealistic expectations. I thank God for everything and for giving me the chance to share some of my experiences with you, the reader. I press on. There's life in me yet and perhaps even another book!

THE FAMILY TREE

John Theodore Pohl Hart 03.02.1862			married 23.08.1893		Ruth Margaret Davoren 25.10.1872
Eileen Hester Pohl	Mary Ruth	Mavis Maude	Paulus Pohl Havelock	Joseph William Adrian	John Theodore Pohl
b:02.10.1894	23.10.1895	22.12.1897	14.09.1899	02.03.1903	09.06.1905

	Donald Moses Brown	m : 17.02.1920	**Eileen Hester Pohl Hart**
b:	13.06.1896		02.10.1894
d:	01.05.1950		23.01,1979

	!	!	!	!
	Eileen Joan Brown	Peggy Estelle Brown	Ruth Gwen Brown	Molly Brown
b:	22.09.1922	03.06.1923	23.10.1924	10.11.1925
d:	29.03.1983		04.04.1986	06.05.1987
m:	06.07.1940	19.07.1943	24.04.1947	20.07.1946
	Samuel **SLABBERT**	**Eric Douglas Killeen LLOYD**	Keith Norman **ROCK**	Stewart **JOHNSTONE**
b:	26.06.1914	29.09.1919	05.03.1923	08.06.1919
d:	27.06.1980	27.08.1974	13.11.1973	19.03.1979
	!	!	!	!
	Vivian Jeanette Neville Diana Eileen **SLABBERT**	Denyse (Neyse) Jennifer (Topsy) Margaret (Margy) **LLOYD**	Myrna Norman June Patricia **ROCK**	David Michael Donnaleen and Ann **JOHNSTONE**

Peggy LLOYD married Philip Hughen LEARY 09.07.1957 !
b: 26.02.1906 !
d: 06.04.1982

Anthony Hughen **LEARY** married Rhoda Nurse
b: 30.11.1936 d: 2008 ! 11.04.1939
Sean, Joanne, Brett, Guy **LEARY**

!
!
Patrick Hughen **LEARY** (11.09.1959)

Chandrè Pegeen Carl Anton de Jager **Brent Lynden Everitt WILD** Alyson Jayne Greenfield **Byron Richard Everitt WILD** Elizabeth Mary Moffet
b: 20.08.1968 27.12.1966 19.06.1970 11.11.1970 18.09.1971 11.09.1973
m: 14.09.1990 10.04.1999 08.07.1995

Jaime Ashley **DE JAGER** (01.07.1994)
Adrienne Kelsey **DE JAGER** (29.12.1998)

Jordyn Courtney **WILD** (12.08.1999)

Peter David **WILD** (24.03.2003)
Matthew Benjamin **WILD** (17.06.2005)

Jennifer Ann LLOYD m: 01.09.1973 **William BOTHA**
b: 11.04.1947 11.02.1941

David Philip BOTHA (06.01.1983)

Margaret Carol LLOYD m: 19.12.1970 **Edwin Karl REICHMUTH**
b: 12.02.1949 17.01.1941 d: 23.07.1998

m: **John Francis LARKAN**
06.07.1940

Jecca Simone REICHMUTH (26.03.1974)

Kirsten Leah REICHMUTH (08.08.1976)

Gary LARKAN !
Jason LARKAN (1998)

GLOSSARY

'Africa', a *Lloyd Triestino* ocean liner
'Out of Africa', title of a movie
ANC, African National Congress
Apartheid, a law separating white and black South Africans
Apfelstrüdel, apple pie
Asseblief, please

Babbelas, hangover
Bakkie, pick-up truck
Basela, payment
Biltong, dried seasoned meat
Blue samango, monkey lives in forest
Blue Waters, townhouses
Bobotie, curried mince, bread and egg
Boeremusiek, Afrikaans music
Boerewors, spicy farmers' sausage
Boetie, *buti*, little brother
Braaivleis, barbecue
Brechanby, our Umtata home
Broekie lace, ornate ironwork
Bushbuck, thickset antelope
Bushveld, grassland

Calabash, shell of a gourd
Cape Doctor, wind of W Cape
Cellphone, mobile phone
Chommie, friend
Circle, roundabout
Ciskei, independent state in 1981:
Coloureds, Brown SA people
Coronation Street, British soap opera
Cozzies, bathing costumes
Crunchies, oatmeal biscuits
Cubbyhole, glove compartment

Dafoo (dam fool) grandpa
Dagga, marijuana
Darl', darling
Dassie, tail-less squirrels
Dickey, outer seat of old-fashioned car
Donner beat
Donsie, little fool
Dop, alcoholic drink
Dopping, tippling
Duikers, buck
Dunhill cigarettes, brand name

Eland, buck
ESKOM, Electricity Supply Company
Fowl run, chicken coop
Frangipani. Sweet scented tree
Frikkadels, meatballs
Fundi, expert
Fynbos, narrow leafed fine bush

Gammadoeloes, very isolated
Gatvol, Fed up, had enough

GELPA, Greater East London Publicity Association
Gilly, bait boy
Gogga, bug in Khoikhoi xo-xon
Gogs, Nolyn's grandmother
Googie, Nolyn's mother

Hadeda Ibis. Large bird
Hairy back, Afrikaans-speaking person
Haw, an expression of disbelief
Highways, motorways
Hoërskool, High school
Holsum, white margarine

Igoli, City of gold
Impala, graceful antelope
Initiation, supposedly an ice-breaker to uphold the hierarchy among students

Ja, yes
Jacaranda, large tree with lilac flowers

Kaffir dogs, derogatory name for black-owned dogs
Käsespatzle, Austrian macaroni cheese
Kindergarten, first two school years
Kist, wooden chest
Knobkerrie, wooden stick
Kombi, microbus
Krantzes, rocky cliffs

Laat lammetjie, afterthought
Laduma, it thunders
Legavaans, Monitor lizard
Lekker, great, tasty
Lion matches, brand name
Location, township
Long drop, outdoor cesspit toilet

Ma, mother
Maas, sour milk made in a calabash
Matriculants, final school year pupils
Mealie bread, bread made from corn
Mealie meal, porridge
Medem, madam
Melktert, milk tart
Microbus. Minibus
Mielie-cob, corn cob
Mielies, corn on the cob
Moegoe, idiot
Monkey's wedding, rain shower and sunshine together

Naartjies, tangerine, mandarin
Nigger-balls, black round sweets
Nolulum, one who never gets angry

Okes, people
Ou Kaapse Weg, Old Cape Road

Padkos, food for the journey
Pangas, sharp knives
Pap en sous, stiff porridge with tomato and onion gravy
Pastis, aniseed flavoured aperitif
Pawpaws, papaya
Piccanninies, young boys
Pondoland, part of the Transkei occupied by the Pondo tribe
Protea repens, sugar bush
Propvol, replete
Prozac, tablet for depression

Qawukeni, the Great Place

Rand, SA currency equals 10p
Remington typewriter, machine with keys for producing print-like characters one at a time on paper inserted around a roller

Rickshaw, a hand drawn cart
Robot, traffic light
Rollers, birds of kingfisher family
Rondavel, round thatched mud house
Rooibos Tea, SA brand of tea
Rooinek, English-speaking S African
Roylat's, Taylor spelt backwards

SA, South Africa
Samp, mixture of maize and beans
Sangomas, witchdoctors
Secretary birds, long-legged snake-eating African birds
Shemozzle, mess
Songololo, millipede
Silverglades, suburb of Fish Hoek
Sisi, little sister
Sjambok, whip made of rhino hide
Skelm, rascal
Skinnering, gossip mongering
Skukuza (he who turned everything upside down) in the Kruger National Park
Slegs vir Blankes, Whites-only
Sosaties, kebab on a stick
Sozzled, drunk
Springbok radio, SA radio station
Springbok, type of SA buck
Standard One, third school year
Stinkwood, deciduous trees
Stoep, verandah
Strelitzia, Bird of Paradise
Sub B, second kindergarten year
Sundowners, alcoholic drinks taken at sunset

Tackies, trainers
Tannie, Aunt
The Gables, 69 King's Road home
Tickey, three pence
Tjierie, girlfriend
Transkei, once independent state in SA
Tsotsi, no-good

Ubuntu, incorporates a people who share, care, trust, respect and help.
UCT, University of Cape Town
Umtiza listerana, Buffalo thorn tree
UNISA, University of South Africa
UPE, University of Port Elizabeth

Veld, bush, grassland
Veldfire, fire in the bush, grass
Vervet, small grey African monkey
Voetsak, go away
Vrot, rotten
Vuvuzulu, Setswana for stadium horn

Weavers, tropical bird of Ploceidae family
Whites-only, use by white S Africans
Wildebeest, gnu native to SA
Xhosa, African tribe

Yebo, yes

Zol, homemade cigarette
Zulu, African tribe

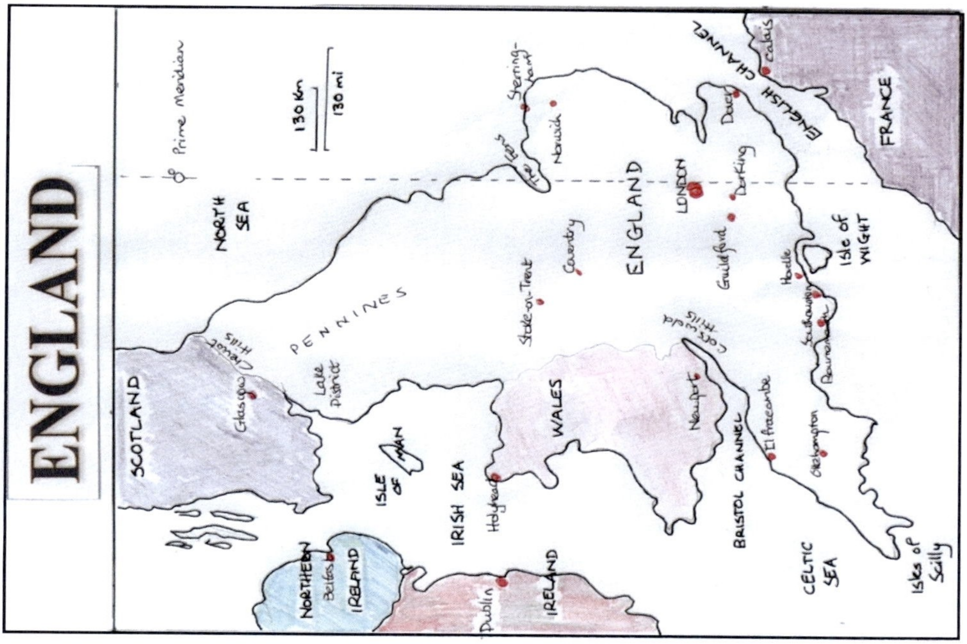
ENGLAND
SCOTLAND
NORTH SEA
Prime Meridian
130 Km
130 mi
NORTHERN IRELAND
Belfast
IRELAND
Dublin
ISLE OF MAN
IRISH SEA
Holyhead
Glasgow
Lake District
PENNINES
WALES
Newport
Cotswold Hills
BRISTOL CHANNEL
CELTIC SEA
Isles of Scilly
Stoke-on-Trent
Coventry
ENGLAND
LONDON
Guildford
Dorking
Norwich
Isle of Wight
Southampton
Bournemouth
FRANCE
ENGLISH CHANNEL
Calais

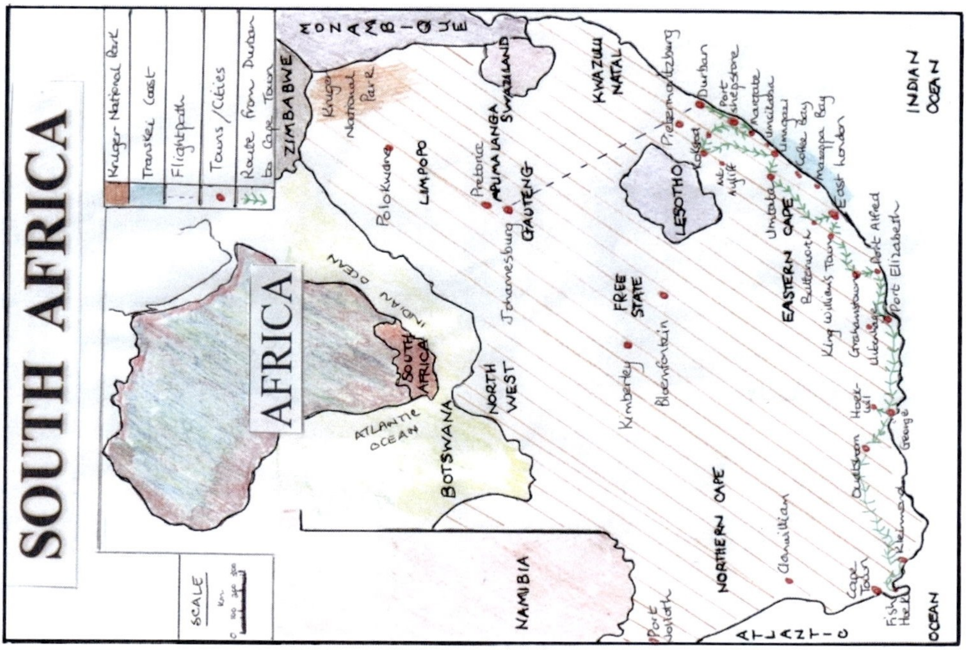
SOUTH AFRICA
AFRICA
SOUTH AFRICA
INDIAN OCEAN
ATLANTIC OCEAN
SCALE
Kruger National Park
Transkei Coast
Flightpath
Towns/Cities
Route from Durban to Cape Town
ZIMBABWE
MOZAMBIQUE
Kruger National Park
SWAZILAND
LIMPOPO
Polokwane
MPUMALANGA
Pretoria
GAUTENG
Johannesburg
KWAZULU NATAL
Pietermaritzburg
Durban
Port Shepstone
LESOTHO
FREE STATE
Kimberley
Bloemfontein
NORTH WEST
BOTSWANA
NAMIBIA
NORTHERN CAPE
EASTERN CAPE
Umtata
East London
King William's Town
Grahamstown
Port Alfred
Port Elizabeth
George
Oudtshoorn
Cape Town
Fish Hoek
INDIAN OCEAN
ATLANTIC OCEAN